OLENA

OATH OF WAR

THE CURSED BONDS
Book Two

For Anna,

The friend I never knew I needed.

The editor who helped my voice be heard.

And the unwavering champion of underdogs everywhere.

Contents

DEAR READER

We appreciate that everyone has a different level of sensitivity and may be triggered by different topics. It is up to your discretion whether you can handle the content in our books.

The book is intended for a mature audience of particular interests. It contains a certain amount of **coarse language, graphic sex scenes** in **MF**, **MFM**, and **MM** pairings, as well as sexual innuendo and **BDSM-related power play**. There are also scenes of death, physical violence, and domestic violence that you may find triggering.

The book is loosely based on **Slavic mythology** and **Eastern European** culture.
If you encounter a new or unfamiliar word and would like more explanation, please check the map or the glossary.

(the definition may be different from what you can find in an external search as I adopted several terms to fit the story)

CHAPTER 1

ANNIKA

I was floating in a stormy sea of darkness. My body rocked back and forth with such force that pain skittered across my awareness in muted colours. The sounds of scratching and whispered hate left fear teasing the edges of my mind.

'Are you sure about this?' I heard someone ask through the haze.

'Yes, the passage through the Rift is too closely guarded to transport her straight to Katrass, and his fae mage showed me how to draw the portal sigil. I have everything prepared; no one will disturb us here. Just make sure there are no witnesses.'

'What if the king asks about her?'

'That damn fool hasn't been lucid for years. Besides, he won't be king for long.'

'We still need her geas.'

'Don't worry about that. Just do your best to ensure the sigil works.'

Danger, whispered my instincts, trying to keep me awake, but another voice lulled me into unconsciousness, and the blackness swallowed me whole.

My awareness resurfaced as my body was buffeted and manhandled, and I felt myself recoil from the distasteful pawing. Rusted hinges screeched, then rough hands grasped my clothes and I had a sudden sense of falling, followed by the painful impact of my head hitting something solid.

1

The unexpected pain that blossomed in my skull overwhelmed me, and the darkness took me once more.

ᛉᚳᚾᚠᛣ

Maybe I was dreaming. Or perhaps I occasionally regained consciousness . . . but I swore someone was pouring something down my throat. The bitter taste was so foul it reminded me of the flavour Katja would make my medicinal concoctions whenever she was particularly upset over something I'd done. I grimaced and choked, trying to tell her I was fine and didn't need any medicine, but nothing stopped the vile liquid as the dream faded into shadows.

A rasping groan woke me, and it dawned on me that it was my own voice protesting the deep ache throbbing through my head and body. Every bruised and battered muscle flared with pain as I tried to lift my head, dragging me back to reality. For a moment, I thought the murkiness around me was caused by the headache, but as my eyes adjusted, it didn't take me long to realise it was my surroundings—a dank cell in gods knew where.

My stomach growled, and I pressed my hand to it. It felt like days had passed since I had last eaten.

'Vahin?' I whispered, testing my magic, but his presence in my mind was missing.

As my memories returned, I recalled Ihrain and his bloody poison and a wave of panic hit me. I slid a hand to my chest, ripping off a few buttons in my haste until my fingers touched the mark of my Anchor bonds over my heart. It was still there. Tracing the sword and the dragon with my fingertip gave me some reassurance. Whatever had happened, the bonds themselves were not broken, only blocked, along with the rest of my power.

I searched around, my probing fingers moving upwards as I pressed against something solid. *It must be a wall*, I thought and shifted over, supporting myself against it. I needed to get up, but my pounding headache made it difficult to concentrate.

It took longer than I wanted to admit, but eventually, my shaking legs pushed me upright as I fought giddiness and nausea. I wondered if I should have stayed on the ground, but I was determined to show I wasn't beaten down and helpless.

'Ihrain! Come out, you coward. Stop hiding in the shadows.'

My voice bounced off the bare walls, its echo giving me the sense that I was in a tall but confined space. *A tower, maybe?* To test the theory, I called out again. 'Hello! Is anyone there? C'mon, you didn't drag me here just to abandon me in this fucking dump.'

I listened, but no one answered. The echoes carried upwards, confirming the emptiness around me. Down here, only a handful of sounds broke the oppressive silence: the steady drip of water, a faint rustling—likely from insects or rodents—and the whistle of the wind above, its icy drafts biting through me. The longer I strained my ears, the clearer it became that I was the only prisoner in this place. The darkness remained unbroken; no flicker of light hinted at the presence of a guard. I was utterly alone, and I couldn't yet decide if that solitude was a curse—or an opportunity.

'Gods, that hurts,' I muttered as I took a few steps forward, feeling the wall with my hands.

The spot under my ribs was particularly painful, as if someone had kicked me there right before they threw me on a pile of rocks, and I cursed each time I took a deep breath. The absence of aether, also, was

3

a strange sensation, almost as if I were missing a limb. It wasn't exactly painful, but it was a very disconcerting and unbalanced feeling.

'Bloody Ihrain and his godsforsaken potions. I will geld him when I get my hands on him, magic missing or not,' I snapped out, followed by a short laugh that ended as a sob.

Who was I kidding? I was locked up, drugged, and injured, likely to be served to the Lich King with a golden bow tied around my neck.

I bit my lip, trying to calm myself, and my fingers slid over my heart, tracing the mark. The image of bright blue eyes, their depths burning with lightning, filled my mind. Vahin, my lovingly hyper-vigilant dragon, would find me. As long as I stayed alive, there was always a chance to escape.

'I'm Annika fucking Diavellar, and I won't give up,' I whispered to myself. 'Ihrain, you will regret messing with me. I swear to the gods, even the Lich King won't be able to resurrect you after I'm done!' I shouted to the darkness above me, smiling at how the promise of vengeance against Ihrain and his accomplices somehow made me feel better.

I knew the potion would wear off eventually. After all, the Lich King wanted a *functioning* conduit mage, not some wreck who couldn't access her abilities. But until that happened, I needed to rely on more mundane means of survival.

Shuffling and feeling my way around slowly, I trailed the edge of my hand along the damp, uneven wall as I groped for any cracks or weaknesses to exploit. The rough texture of sandstone met my fingertips, slick with a fine layer of condensation that made my task all the more difficult. Occasionally, my hand struck cold metal—chains bolted into the stone, their loose manacles rattling with a hollow clang that echoed through the darkness.

'Ewww . . .' I groused when I accidentally slid a finger over two long bones still bound to the wall, but I kept going until I encountered what felt like a door and its lock.

'Great, I'm in a dungeon with a rusted lock,' I mumbled, pondering which slimy establishment they'd chosen as my temporary domicile. I assumed I was in the capital, as that made the most sense. If I was right, there were three places in Truso with dungeons like this.

The first was the seat of the Court of Aether, a structure nestled between the university and the king's court. It housed the Council of Mages, the chamber where geasa were extracted during the Blood Rite, and the geas vault. It also contained a prison designed for magically gifted criminals, fortified with wards and sigils to suppress their powers. However, it lacked a tower, making it an unlikely candidate.

The second possibility was the magistrate's prison in the merchant's quarter. Its dungeon was small, with only a few basement cells where criminals were held before being sentenced. While plausible, it didn't seem to match the depths I found myself in.

That left the royal palace. Though court life now revolved around the sprawling audience chambers, the ancient fort that predated the palace still stood within the edifice. Mostly abandoned due to its crumbling state and lack of light, its dungeons dated back to the Necromancer's War.

I knew of the fort because I'd studied it in detail before using an old, hidden tunnel that spanned the area to slip away without being seen when I faked my death. Its narrow corridors were infamous, with barely-there windows and thick shadows where unruly nobles used to vanish without a trace. If I was right, that was where I was now—a place where uncomfortable secrets disappeared.

'I am one secret that *won't* vanish without a trace,' I said with gritted teeth, picking up one of the discarded chains and jamming it into the gap between the door lock and the wall. I couldn't see much, but I'd felt the rust on the metal, and it gave me hope of forcing open the mechanism.

Escape might be next to impossible, but I had to do *something*. Sitting in the darkness, waiting for my enemies to come, was not an option.

'Gods, I have to find a way out, not just for me but for my men,' I whispered, trying not to think of the turmoil my disappearance had caused those who cared for me.

My one-sided conversation became my refuge against the silence. The true cruelty of dungeons lay in their isolation and the disorienting absence of time, designed to unravel the mind. I understood this all too well, yet knowledge offered no immunity to the slow creep of those tormenting thoughts.

'I would sooner drown this place in blood than give up,' I said out loud. Hatred was a bad advisor, but it was the strongest motivator for staying alive, and I had plenty to go around.

'I'm glad to hear that, my lady,' whispered a voice behind me.

Screaming bloody murder, I spun around, brandishing the battered chain like a weapon. A faint purple glow emanated from the wall, illuminating in eerie detail the skeletal remains of the cell's previous occupant. Before my eyes, the bones began to shift, snapping together with uncanny precision until they formed the twisted shape of a person.

The skeleton rose to its feet, only to lurch backwards as the chain, still locked around its wrist, pulled taut. For a moment, I could have sworn its hollow skull tilted to stare at the shackle in surprise, and I whispered a prayer of thanks to Svarog, god of fire and smithing, for that small protection.

I had no fear of corpses—far from it. I'd faced my share of monsters and studied even more of their victims than I cared to count. But corpses didn't usually *talk* to me. And those that did weren't tied to the intricate glyphs now blazing on the wall. And in the middle of it, as if the situation wasn't horrifying enough, loomed a portal. *A fucking portal.*

I backed away as far as I could. If I hadn't been stripped of my magic, I would have sensed it. Instead, I only noticed it now because the damn thing was glowing like a carnival attraction.

'Who did this?' I wondered out loud, and the corpse must have heard because it turned back towards me.

'You did. Only your touch could activate the sigil,' it said.

I scowled down at my hands, battered with scrapes and bruises from feeling my way along the rough wall. Fresh cuts still trickled blood, evidence of my blind exploration. I must have smeared some on the bones—but had I also touched the glyph?

Someone . . . No, not someone. *Fucking Ihrain.* That bastard had locked me in a cell with a portal glyph and a host, knowing I'd eventually touch it. Now, a shadow from beyond the Veil had crossed into my cell.

'Who were you?' I asked. The skeleton's head slanted slightly, as if pausing to consider its response.

'Were? There is no *"were."* I am, and always will be, immortal and waiting for you. Don't be afraid of the darkness, little mage. You are safe in my presence. My servants brought you here because I wanted to see you with my own eyes.'

The response came from everywhere and nowhere at once, and immediately I suspected I knew exactly who was speaking to me.

'Your eyes rotted away long ago, remnant,' I stated, and the shadowy voice laughed.

'Such fire for someone helpless and imprisoned, but what else should I expect from the mage who tethered a dragon's heart and broke the compulsion on my fae slave?'

'I'm not helpless.'

'Oh yes, you are, at least for the moment. But it won't last forever, and I'm looking forward to seeing what you can do. From what I can detect with my abilities, you are a sight to behold, Annika. I could even forgive you for taking Alaric away from me.'

'I know it's you, Cahyon,' I spat. A hollow laugh echoed within the cell as the skeleton bowed its head.

'At your service . . . Nivale. You know, I have to praise the commander for such an insightful name; a more apt comparison could not be made. Such rare beauty should always be difficult to acquire. Yet here you are, tight in my grasp.'

'What do you want? And don't insult my intelligence by attempting to flatter me. We both know that's never going to work.'

'Today? I simply wanted to meet you and perhaps convince you to join my cause. I may be the Lich King, but I'm bored and tired of being limited to Ozar, my lady.'

'Maybe you shouldn't have fucking murdered and corrupted everyone, then. That way, you'd still have plenty to keep you amused. I've heard it was a beautiful and lively kingdom before you destroyed it.'

'Oh, but destroying them was the most wonderful entertainment. Corrupting the Moroi was quite satisfying, and defying death's hold to create new beings kept me busy for centuries. Now, though, I want a new adventure, and I'm willing to compromise if you'd care to listen.'

'Do I have a choice?' I huffed in annoyance.

'No, sweet Annika, you don't.'

'Well, then, get on with it so I can get back to ignoring your existence,' I said, and the skeleton went rigid, purple light pulsing brightly in its eye sockets.

'Such wit, my lady. I look forward to experiencing it in person when you come to Katrass. My invitation still stands, despite the fact that you killed my poor latawce.[1] Now, take my hand and step through the portal,' he offered, a skeletal hand reaching towards me.

I stepped back, and the skeleton's bones rattled as its hand reached out further. 'Don't you know," he continued with a dark laugh, "that the more you resist me, the sweeter the pleasure will be when you finally submit?'

'Yeah, good luck with that, asshole,' I quipped humourlessly.

'Think about it, Annika,' he said, his voice smooth and persuasive. 'I have no need for war. It was a mistake five hundred years ago, and it would be a mistake now. I've learned from my . . . Well, let's just say I've evolved. I'd like my life to be a different kind of interesting, and having you join me would certainly help with that. I'm no monster, and with you standing by my side, the fertile Lowland Kingdoms would bow before me without the need for violence. Those who would otherwise die in the flames of war will bless your name. You could be their saviour if you join the winning side.'

'No.'

'No?' There was amusement in his voice, but I could sense anger, too. 'Tsk. Keep resisting, and I will take everything from you, starting with your Anchors.'

---

1. **Latawiec(s.)/latawce(pl.)/*pron:Lata-vi-etc/*—shapeshifting demons. They flew in the wind currents. Their physical bodies were similar to large birds, with sharp claws and colourful feathers, but they had human heads.

'Touch them and I will—' I whipped the chain, smacking the effigy of the Lich King in the chest. Several bones cracked, but the skeleton still stood.

'What? Destroy me? I am eternal. As for your men, Alaric is already mine. I can see through his eyes, can whisper to him in his dreams . . . It is just a matter of time until he comes to me.'

'You can't do any of that when he's near me.'

'Poor, delusional Annika. You're not with him now, are you? Your precious ability is of no use to him while you're here.'

'You may see through his eyes, but you don't know the man you're tormenting,' I said, my voice dripping with disdain. 'Go back to whatever shithole you crawled out of and leave me be. I'm bored with your company.' I waved him off dismissively, hoping to provoke him. I needed to distract him; if I couldn't hurt the skeleton, maybe I could disrupt the glyph. To do that, I'd have to get closer to the terrifying creature.

'Annika, your stubbornness is charming, but that, too, has its limits. You will not insult me—'

'Or what? What can you do, trapped in a dead kingdom with your worthless sycophants? You're burning through your stores of aether just to annoy me with your presence, and I'm not even afraid. Look, I'm coming closer, oh mighty Master of Death,' I goaded him, wrapping the chain around my fist as I approached the diagram.

The corpse quietly observed me, its eye sockets filled with flickering purple flames. This time, however, there was no amusement. Harsh, threatening power filled the room. Its suffocating energy, unlike anything I'd ever felt before, enveloped me. The portal widened, as if he'd waited for the best moment to strike, but I didn't let it deter me.

I smiled, twirling around as if taunting him. Then, with all my strength, I hammered my chain-wrapped fist into the glyph, disturbing the first line. The skeleton shuddered, and the depths of the portal gate shimmered with unnatural light. I scraped my hand over the second line, further unravelling the connection. But before I could reach the third, a darkness surged out, its cloying tendrils encircling me and halting my hand.

'Such a savage little mage,' he sneered. 'Have a taste of what awaits you if you insist on resisting, then.'

I struggled against the viscous tendrils as the Lich King's aether spilled relentlessly through the portal. Black strands coiled around me like a venomous vine, contorting my body until my head was forced back. I fought desperately against the suffocating embrace, terror gripping me as the inky tendrils slithered into my nose and pried my mouth open.

'I will burn the aether of a thousand souls until I have you. How does it feel, Annika, to be helpless in my grasp? This is a small fraction of the power you will face, little mage. You have no hope of enduring. I wanted to give you a choice, to join me as my queen, yet you choose to be broken like a slave.'

The sable vines pulled me closer to the portal, and I felt the void dragging me in while I choked and spluttered, fighting to breathe as the vile, corrupted magic pulsed obscenely in my throat.

'Should I show you what I make Alaric suffer through to entertain myself? Why he hurts himself to avoid my nightmares?' he continued.

Laughter echoed through the room, and the pressure in my throat eased as the tendrils pulled out of my mouth, another sliding up my thigh as I inched closer to the portal. I could feel the twisted aether powering the glyph, and the shimmering hatred behind it.

The bastard was going to rape me while pulling me through the portal.

'Go to hell,' I croaked, parting my legs as if inviting him in. I used the brief flicker of distraction to unfurl the chain and smash it onto the glyph, destroying the third line. The Lich King's grip faltered, his power momentarily slackening, and I threw myself to the side of the portal, scratching through whichever line came within reach.

The purple light in the skeleton's eyes dimmed as the portal weakened, then disappeared altogether. I refused to stop, destroying every trace of the foul magic in a desperate frenzy, trying to erase the memory of his sickening laughter.

Soon, the glyph was nothing but stone dust coating my skin, making me shudder with revulsion. My hands were raw and bloodied from the frantic destruction, and only when the last line was obliterated did I collapse to the floor, sobbing uncontrollably. I felt violated. It had only been a shadow, yet it had felt so real . . . as if the Lich King had—

Tears blurred my vision as I dragged myself to the wall and curled into a ball. I sobbed until my throat was raw, the sound echoing in the surrounding emptiness. I felt dirty—tainted in a way no amount of bathing could ever cleanse. But the worst pain came from the knowledge of what he was doing to Ari, and the crushing guilt that I wasn't there to protect my fae.

'I swear I'll kill you,' I whispered. 'Even if it ends me, *I swear* to the gods above and below I will be your death.' With deliberate precision, I pressed my bleeding thumb to my chest and drew the bloody sigil of an unbreakable oath on my skin.

I was the last living conduit mage in the kingdom, and with fury in my heart and vengeance in my soul, I bound myself to an Oath of War.

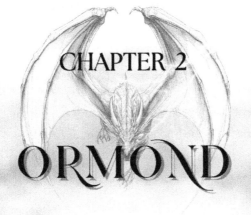

CHAPTER 2

ORMOND

'Ugh . . . What the fuck is . . .? What's that smell?' I groaned, confused and still half-dazed. I lifted my hand to wipe my eyes, but something cold and solid halted my movement.

The metallic clatter of chains shattered the fog clouding my mind, the frighteningly familiar sound jolting me fully awake. A quick glance confirmed where I was—the garrison's smithy.

Why the hell am I here?

I tried to stand, but the sharp bite of iron around my wrists and ankles held me down. Looking closer, I saw the crude iron shackles digging into my skin.

And why the fuck am I chained up like some wild beast?

'Which idiot locked me up in here?' I shouted, yanking at the restraints.

The chains groaned under the force before one gave way, snapping with a loud *crack.*

'Gods, it's starting again. Get the mage!'

Panicked voices erupted around me. One soldier bolted, his footsteps fading rapidly. Another stood frozen, sword half-raised, the blade trembling in his grasp.

'Sir, please—my lord, stop! You need to control yourself!' His voice cracked as he spoke, his throat working visibly. The sword wavered, his fear more palpable than the steel in his hand.

Anger warred with caution as I struggled to piece together what had happened. The last clear memory I had was of finding a barely conscious Alaric in our bedroom and no sign of Annika.

'Fuck!' I roared, swinging my fist, breaking the other chain in the process. Panic surged in my chest, feeding the relentless urgency pounding in my head.

I have to find her. Now.

'Good, you're conscious,' Alaric gasped as he burst into the forge. 'Orm, stay with me. Everybody else . . . Get out, now!' His voice snapped like a whip, scattering the onlookers.

He grabbed my face, his hands firm but grounding, pulling me from the storm raging inside. His touch was steady, and my heart thudded slower as I met his gaze, the swirling gold in his eyes drawing me in.

'That's it,' he murmured, his hand sliding down to rest on my bare chest, just over my heart. 'Stay with me, Orm. Listen to my voice. I can't lose you to the berserker. Not again.'

'Why am I here?' I demanded, my voice rough but calmer.

'You lost . . .' Ari hesitated, his breath catching as he pulled back, but I stopped him, placing my hand on his. He frowned briefly before continuing, 'You lost control of your wild magic after learning about . . .' He paused, his jaw tightening. 'When Tomma told you Ani was gone, you . . . snapped. You destroyed the room trying to rush after her. Gods, Orm, you nearly tore through a solid stone wall. Several men were injured trying to stop you. If it wasn't for Vahin and that half-orc blacksmith stepping in . . .' He shook his head, his voice trailing off.

The memory hit me like a tidal wave. I remembered reaching for Annika's bond, only to find nothing but bleak, suffocating emptiness. The shock had torn my world apart, and everything else was lost in a pure, unbridled rage.

I locked eyes with Alaric, and in that moment, I knew—everything had changed. My life had always been consumed by duty: serving a country teetering on the edge of chaos, protecting a king whose fear had led us here. And for what? To lose the one piece of happiness I had? *No.* This was the end.

I tried to speak, but the words stuck in my throat, scorched away by grief. Still, I forced them out.

'I can't feel her . . . her soul. I can't feel Ani anymore.' My voice was raw, barely a rasp, as the pain cleaved through my chest. Alaric nodded solemnly.

'I know. Vahin said that too, but Orm—'

'Is she dead?' I interrupted, desperation surging. 'Did you find her body? We need to find her. I need to hold her one last time. I can't let her go behind the Veil alone, and without the rites. She hated sleeping alone, Ari! *Fuck*, why—?' My voice broke, the words fracturing under the weight of despair. 'It's my fault. I failed her. And now she's dead.'

The realisation clawed at me, a merciless ache. I would never see that teasing glint in Ani's eyes again. As if it knew, the mindless void opened its maw, beckoning me back into sweet oblivion.

'She's not dead, Orm!' Alaric's voice cut through the darkness. 'Listen to me. She isn't dead. That's what I've been trying to tell you. Ani is alive.'

'What?' I froze, my heart pounding. 'But . . . why can't I feel her Anchor?'

'She's being blocked,' he said firmly, his gaze steady. The truth in his eyes was an anchor of its own, keeping my wild magic at bay.

'During the four days you've been here, chained and half-mad, I searched the castle,' he continued. 'I found evidence in the guest rooms that someone had made lanara poison. Its ingredients were blatantly scattered on a table, as if whoever used them didn't care if they were discovered. It had to be the chancellor; no mage would handle those toxins. That shit would suppress even the strongest magical abilities.'

I felt a strange calm wash over me. 'The chancellor suppressed her magic?'

'Yes, that's why you can't feel her.' Alaric's voice softened, but his gaze sharpened, his tone tinged with unease. 'Orm . . . your eyes.'

'Ari, I don't give a sh—get these damned chains off me! I need to find our woman and kill the bloody toad; and fuck, is he going to *suffer*.'

Alaric moved cautiously, his hands steady as he gripped the chains.

'I understand. We really need to talk about your eyes, though,' he said, his tone calm but pointed. 'That golden halo around your irises? It's otherworldly, Orm. It screams wild magic to anyone who sees it.'

He worked the shackles loose, his cool magic flowing over my raw wrists and bruised skin, soothing away the damage.

'But don't think for a second I'm letting him off lightly. A single death is not enough for the man who dared to touch her. Only you can—' Ari's words faltered as his thumb brushed the old scar on my wrist. His breath hitched, and when his eyes met mine, the deep hatred in his voice clashed with the raw yearning in his gaze.

'I thought I'd lost you,' he said quietly, his voice trembling. 'Some warriors never come back from a berserker's rage. I thought . . . I thought I'd lost you both to his schemes. Orm, I want to kill him so fucking much.'

He pulled his hands back, his touch lingering like an unspoken plea.

I stared at the fae who understood me better than anyone. I would have been halfway to the capital if not for my madness, but he had stayed by my side, ensuring no one slaughtered me like a rabid cur. Despite everything, he had *stayed*.

As the broken chains fell away, I reached for him, pulling him into an embrace he clearly hadn't expected. Alaric gasped, leaning his head on my chest as his arms circled me without hesitation.

'Orm . . .?' he murmured, his voice tinged with shock and hope. I couldn't meet his eyes, overwhelmed by the flood of emotions that threatened to drown me. My hand found his back, stroking gently, but the weight of everything—of Annika still in danger—was too much. I couldn't let myself think about it now.

Still, I needed this. *I needed him.* Just for a moment, I allowed myself the comfort.

'It's time we lived by our own rules,' I said finally, releasing him. 'We'll talk—properly—after we find Annika.'

Ari sighed, his fingers brushing against his temple as he gave me a wry look.

'Just be careful with throwing out the old rules,' he warned. 'Last time, it took Bryna's hammer to stop you from going on a murderous rampage. I'd rather not have to chain you to the garrison forge again.'

As we walked towards the castle, Alaric briefed me on the situation. What he recounted was a blur, fragments slipping through my mind like sand. At least I understood now what had happened when I'd lost control. But going berserk? I hadn't expected that.

As soon as Ari finished updating me, I asked Vahin to fly him to the capital. Alaric had contacts deep in the city's underbelly, and I gave him enough gold to secure the services of the Dark Brotherhood for a year. It wasn't cheap, but the network of spies and assassins was our best chance of infiltrating the palace. My gut told me that unless the chancellor had hidden Annika in the Barren Lands, she was somewhere in Truso—and if anyone could find my lost Nivale, it was the group even the king feared.

I left Tomma and Katja in charge of the fortress. Tomma had proven himself during the latawce attack, and Katja, our new apothe-cary-turned-spokeswoman, had stepped up as a leader. After the chaos I'd caused, the woman had even organised an impromptu town coun-cil, and it was clear why Ani's friend was respected by so many. With her caring for the town and Tomma leading the soldiers, I knew the fortress would be in good hands. It had to be; I wasn't in a fit state to lead.

Once Vahin returned, about a week after Annika's disappearance, I quickly transferred command and climbed onto his back. As we soared towards the capital, Ari's warning before he'd left echoed in my mind: my green irises were now permanently rimmed with golden halos, a mark of my wild magic that unsettled even my most loyal retainers.

I didn't care. I dismissed his concerns—those with me had no reason to fear. As for my enemies, my berserker's eyes would serve as their only warning.

ᛉᚲᚾᚠᛪ

Two days later, I strode through the halls of my ancestral home. As I passed, servants pressed themselves against the walls, heads bowed low. I didn't blame them. News of what had happened at the fortress had spread quickly, and no one wanted to risk drawing my ire.

To my relief, my spies had confirmed that the chancellor had gone straight to Truso and entered the palace, where he had remained ever since. Annika was there—I was sure of it. I planned to attack tomor-row, hopefully giving Alaric's spies time to secure her safety.

'*Can you feel her?*' I asked Vahin for what felt like the hundredth time. I already knew the answer, but it was reassuring to hear his voice in my head. He had become so reticent that it was hard to remember the hours I'd spent arguing with him or listening to his tales of ancient times.

'*No, Orm, I cannot sense or hear her,*' he answered, his worry a constant presence through our bond. '*All I know is that she's still alive.*'

'*We'll find her,*' I promised, anger simmering beneath the surface. '*Even if I have to burn this shithole to the ground.*'

His response carried a rare flicker of amusement. '*Burn it, hmm?*' He projected an image of me at the palace gates, struggling to light a torch while he poured liquid fire from above.

For the first time in days, I almost smiled. His teasing was a welcome reprieve from the grim monotone he'd adopted recently.

Pushing open the war room's heavy doors, I entered with a scowl.

'Reynard!' I barked.

Heads turned in my direction, and I cursed. I'd wanted to speak with my brother alone, but it appeared I'd just interrupted a meeting with his allies.

'Would you join us, Ormond?' Reynard asked, his tone measured. 'It might ease your mind to hear the plans we've set in motion.'

I inclined my head to the gathered nobles. 'My lords, my lady.' Then, turning towards my brother, I continued, 'Your plans need to be accelerated. I've hired the Dark Brotherhood and some mercenaries. I'm going to attack tomorrow and, as I've just promised Vahin, burn that shithole to the ground.' I flicked an imaginary speck of dust from my sleeve, earning an approving rumble from my dragon.

The room erupted in outrage.

'You—you can't!' sputtered one of the nobles. 'You're a dragon rider! You swore to serve—'

I cut him off with a sharp glare. 'I swore to protect this kingdom. If that means protecting it from the king, so be it.'

The room fell silent, their indignation shifting to unease.

'I see the looks in your eyes. If you think I'm just some wild beast, think again. Lady Annika is the only mage capable of fighting the spectrae, the only one who can save your sorry arses when the vampire ghosts swarm this city, and she's now in the hands of a madman. My oath to the king died the moment they took her—but I would never betray my country.'

The gathered nobles avoided my gaze, their expressions a mix of fear and disdain. To them, I was still the younger son—the volatile, rage-filled wild card, tainted from birth and destined to be consumed by the magic in my soul. It was Reynard, the calm and steady heir, who had inherited the duchy of Borovio and the title of Lord Marshal. Yet there I was, overriding their carefully laid plans.

'Reynard, you should muzzle your brother before he destroys everything,' an older man in an opulent kaftan said, the golden embroidery gleaming in the lamplight. The insignia of the Tarvati family confirmed his identity—the duke himself, unless he'd sent an equally vain emissary.

'Yes, Ormond, bite your tongue,' my brother said with a smirk. The bastard looked far too satisfied, as though my outburst against his circle of rebels had somehow played into his hands. Perhaps it had. Judging by the tense silence in the room, they'd been giving him grief until now.

'Oh, I'm calm, Duke. The fact that I'm here, that the palace still stands, is a testament to how calm I am. But have you considered what might happen if the man you wish to depose uses Lady Annika as a weapon?'

The blood drained from everyone's faces, the consequences of the possibility dawning on them. Mutters rippled through the group until I raised my voice again, cutting through their disquiet like a blade.

'Need I remind you that she's destroyed a swarm of spectrae, frozen half a forest in midsummer, and single-handedly brought down an olgoi worm?[1] Do you *really* want her in the hands of our enemy?'

The room fell into a grim silence as they absorbed the implications. Reynard chose that moment to slam his hands on the table, startling everyone.

'As my brother has already decided to take action, we should support him,' he said, his voice steady and commanding. 'We have waited long enough. Each of you will contribute whatever household soldiers you have stationed in the capital. Tomorrow, I will request an audience with the king. That will give us the opportunity to bring your men into the palace as escorts. Once inside, some can slip away and locate strategic positions around the throne room, allowing us to take control of the court with minimal losses. Once the king is detained, it will be far easier to secure the rest of the city.'

It was a sound strategy, but I couldn't bring myself to trust the nobles. Unfortunately, undermining Reynard's authority on this would do more harm than good, so I kept silent.

'Thank you, brother. My lords, lady. I am grateful for your willingness to comply,' I said, carefully keeping any trace of sarcasm out of my voice, before moving to the corner and pouring myself a glass of wine.

I would have killed for the honey cider brewed by Ian at Varta Fortress. This wine was sweet enough but lacked the cinnamon and honey undertones I'd kissed off Annika's lips so many times.

---

1. **Olgoi worm** */pron:ol-g{oi}/* — a giant, blind earthworm with rows of serrated teeth, known for drilling tunnels in the dirt and rocks. They rarely hunt sentient beings, but during starvation periods, can move to the surface to hunt for warm-blooded prey.

They debated for a few more hours, but eventually, Reynard wrapped up the meeting and sent his rebels on their way. After the room had emptied, he joined me at the table, looking more exhausted than I'd ever seen him.

'I need your help as well, Ormond,' he said, leaning back in his chair. 'I need you to speak with the other commanders. Roan and Seren Fortresses will likely join us, but I've had no response from Lonra's commander. I don't want their dragons coming to Truso in a misguided attempt to defend the king.'

I nodded. I knew Lonra's commander well—a paranoid old bastard prone to believing conspiracy theories. Reynard's talk of rebellion had likely sent him into a frenzy. Still, he was a fellow soldier, and I had ways to make him see reason.

'He won't join us, but I can convince him to stay out of it. The dragons may come, but they won't attack the city,' I assured him.

My brother sighed, the lines of tension in his face deepening. 'That's a small mercy, at least. What do you think, Orm? Do we have a chance?'

I hesitated, suddenly noticing how much he'd aged under the load of his responsibilities. Though only two years my senior, he could easily have passed as my twin. His bear-like physique mirrored mine, but while my hair was shoulder-length and often tied up, his was short and perpetually dishevelled from running his hands through it—a gesture of impatience and occasional anger.

'We do,' I said firmly. 'Or I should say, we will—if you give yourself time to rest. What you've managed is nothing short of a miracle. You've taken this herd of hissing cats and gotten them to work together. It's impressive, but you look tired, Rey. I only wish we had more time to prepare for a war. After tomorrow, I'm sure the Lich King will move his army of monsters.'

Reynard nodded, his expression grim. 'I know. Thank you for forcing their hand, even if that wasn't your reason for doing so. I don't want Dagome to rot from within like Ozar until all that's left is the Barren Lands. But they were so reluctant to move.'

I stepped closer, placing a hand on his shoulder. 'Sometimes a lack of choice is the best thing that can happen. You can do it, Rey. If anyone can, it's you. Though keeping those nobles in check? You might have to take the plunge and marry one of their daughters.'

He chuckled, shaking his head. 'I'd rather put my cock on hot coals. No, I've managed this long without bowing to mother's demands to "strengthen" the Erenhart name. Let's keep it that way. But drop the subject, and I'll share a goblet of wine with you and allow you to sing praises of my leadership until we pass out.'

'I can't,' I said, smiling faintly. 'I need to check on Alaric. He's been out working with his spies, and when he's here, he just locks himself in the guest room. Ani means the world to him, and he's been struggling since she's been taken. But this stubborn bastard won't ask for help.'

Reynard's expression softened. 'Just like you. Always taking on the world alone, even when the situation is so dire that it needs an army to fix. I know we couldn't grow up together, but we are brothers, Ormond. Remember that. I'm here when you need me.'

He pulled me into a rib-crushing hug, and I let myself exhale, the weight of it all easing ever so slightly as I patted his back. It had never occurred to me, but being the head of the family was a solitary burden. I should have spent more time with him, even if my own duties made that difficult.

'I'll head off now,' I said when he released me. 'But we'll have that drink, I promise.'

He nodded, his voice quieter now. 'I understand. Take care of your mage, Orm. I hope everything works out for all of you.'

With that I left, heading straight for Ari's room.

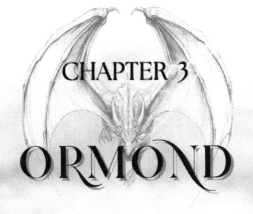

CHAPTER 3

ORMOND

The final blush of sunset faded into shadow as I passed through the long portrait gallery, its light retreating from the works of art lining the walls. I hadn't realised it had grown so late. The war room had no windows and only one entrance, and the entire space was so heavily warded to prevent eavesdropping that the outside world was completely shut out.

Pausing by a crystalline window, I let the moonlight wash over me, time slipping by unnoticed until the deepening darkness pulled me out of my reflections. I straightened and continued to Alaric's quarters.

'Ari?' I called, knocking on the door.

I should have come sooner, but part of me was afraid of what my own emotions might reveal. The embrace we'd shared in the forge earlier lingered in my thoughts, igniting questions I wasn't ready to face.

Have I been blind all these years we've lived at the fortress? I questioned, trying to recall whether I had missed the quiet yearning Alaric's gaze when he'd healed me or soothed my headaches in the past. Standing under the moon's pale light, so reminiscent of Ari's iridescent skin, I realised how much I had ignored the feelings his touch had awakened—curious and confusing as they were.

I heard cursing, and a soft scraping before the door creaked open a sliver. My jaw dropped at the sight of the dishevelled fae, his bloodshot eyes peering myopically through the gap.

'Leave me alone, Orm,' he rasped, his voice so rough I wondered if he'd been screaming all night. 'Hrae.[1] Please. Just go.'

'The fuck I am,' I said, pushing the door open.

His lips quirked in a bitter semblance of humour that worried me as he stepped back. 'Wine?' he asked, shuffling towards the table before he winced, grasping its edge and stumbling mid-step. I'd moved before I knew it, grabbing his shoulders and steadying him as he clutched his chest.

'For gods' sake, talk to me! What's going on? Are you hurt?'

My fear for him had made me snap, and I instantly regretted it, seeing how he flinched at the tone of my voice. From the corner of my eye, I saw the white bed linen covered with bloody glyphs before the hand patting mine distracted me.

'The Lich King is relentless,' Alaric admitted, his voice brittle. 'The bastard keeps trying to worm his way into my mind, promising to keep Annika safe if I deliver her to him.' He laughed sharply, the sound ending with a splatter of blood on my shirt. 'Like I'd ever give him my Domina.'

'You should have told me,' I sighed.

'What would it change?' he asked, his shoulders slumping. 'Only Annika could help, and she's still out there, alone. Just let it go. Come on, have a drink with me. If I numb myself with enough wine, his voice sounds more like the ravings of a drunk mind.'

---

1. Fuck.

Instead of answering, I stepped closer, a memory of Annika's words flickering in my mind. Sliding a hand beneath his shirt, I pressed my palm to his chest, over the faint glow of his marks. Ari froze, his eyes widening.

'What are you doing?' he asked, though he didn't pull away.

'Helping you. Or trying to, at least,' I murmured. 'It's just a hunch, but I can't let you go through this alone. Is it working? The piece of Ani's soul inside me, is it enough?'

'Of course, no . . . erm, yes?' he said after a moment's hesitation. 'I can still hear him, but it doesn't turn my insides into molten agony. Ha! I can ignore his damn voice.' He barked a brief laugh before looking at me. 'What made you think to try that?'

'I remembered something Ani said and, well . . . I carry a shard of her soul. I figured it couldn't hurt to try.'

Alaric stepped back and peeled off his shirt, his movements tentative. Standing before me in only a pair of dark spider-silk trousers, he trembled as he approached again. This time, there was no hesitation as I placed my hand over his heart once more. Relief softened his features, and his eyes drifted closed.

'Thank you,' he whispered, the words laden with an unfamiliar vulnerability. 'I know this isn't something you'd normally do. I—thank you.'

I stepped closer, my voice quiet but firm. 'Ari, stop hiding your pain from me. If I can't help, let me at least be here for you. How many times have you done the same for me? Even before Annika, we were close. Why should it be any different now? If anything, I feel . . .' I trailed off, the words slipping away, unnamed.

I'd always felt at ease with Alaric, even more when Annika was with us. Her presence balanced the bond between us. But here, now, alone with him? It felt different—more intimate in a way that unsettled me.

I couldn't pretend this moment was only about her. Being alone with him made me question everything.

Could what we shared be more than brotherhood?

'Whatever it is, I'll accept it,' Ari said, his voice softer than I'd ever heard it. 'I don't want your pity, Orm. I am who I am. Somewhere along the way, I started feeling . . . something for you. I know you've noticed. You can't hide the questions in your eyes when you look at me.' He offered me a brief smile as he covered my hand with his. 'But I won't let it ruin what we have. Our friendship means too much to me.'

He exhaled sharply, lowering his head. 'And I don't want you to do anything just to please Annika. My feelings for you are for *you* alone, and if you never feel the same, that's alright. Truly. I just needed you to know.'

Ari's words hit me like a blow, raw and unguarded. He looked so lost as he stood before me, stripped of his usual sharp wit and aloofness, exposing a heart I never realised he'd kept hidden. It was a side of him I hadn't seen before, and a strange emotion swelled in my chest—warm, curious, and terrifying all at once. My gaze lingered on him longer than it should have as a thousand questions swirled in my mind.

I'd grown up surrounded by the roughest and crudest soldiers in the kingdom, and even though relations between men were not only common but often encouraged as a way for warriors to bond, I'd felt no desire to join in.

So what is it about Alaric that stirs something within me, something no man has before? And why does this moment feel so different?

A crooked smile tugged at my lips before I could stop it, an instinctive reaction to the flutter of intrigue. But with the intrigue and burgeoning attraction came uncertainty. Could I untangle my feelings for him from those I had for Ani? And if I could, was I ready to face what that might mean for us? For me?

'I don't know . . .' My voice came out hoarse, hesitant. 'All I know is that I need you. Will you let me stay the night?'

He blinked, surprised, before quirking a brow. 'I only have one bed,' he said, a familiar mischievous glint breaking through his sombre expression.

'Then let's hope you don't snore, or I'll go sleep with Vahin,' I shot back, surprised when he laughed.

'I'm a fae of the noblest of houses,' he replied, his grin faint but real. 'We are above such things, unlike a certain brutish rider who snores louder than a forge fire.'

Just like that, the tension cracked—not enough to dissipate entirely, but enough to remind me of who we were. The change between the fae who had opened the door and the one who was now teasing me was astonishing.

This was Ari, the man I'd known and trusted for years. Recognising that made the uncertainty just a little easier to bear. Even more, it seemed as though my touch eased his torment, and there was no way in hell I would leave him alone to deal with that.

'Still better than a drunk fae too stubborn to admit he's suffering,' I countered, gesturing to the bed. 'Grab the wine; I'll get the glasses. Tomorrow's going to be a godsdamned awful day, and I need to discuss our next steps with you.'

I kept my hand pressed to his chest, unwilling to break the fragile connection that seemed to shield him from the Lich King's assault. With Annika, her proximity seemed to be enough, but with only a small shard of her soul inside me, I was certain his pain would return the moment I broke contact.

31

Alaric nodded, and we sat on the bed with a bottle balanced precariously between us. I kicked off my boots and shrugged out of my shirt before stretching to lean against the pillow. Unfortunately, as soon as I stopped touching him, I saw the tension return to his face, the faint lines of pain creeping back in. That wouldn't do.

I patted the pillows beside me while reaching for the wine. 'Come on, come closer. Don't just sit there like you have board shoved up your arse.'

Ari hesitated but eventually settled beside me, rescuing the wine glasses before I could knock them over. I placed my hand back on his chest, but the position felt awkward, and I knew I wouldn't be able to sleep like that. If it were Annika, she'd already have her head on my chest, climbing me like a bloody tree. The thought gave me an idea.

'Oh, for fuck's sake, come here,' I said, laughing nervously as I slid my arm around his shoulders and tugged him closer. Ari gasped but didn't resist, allowing me to shift him until he was half lying on me, his back to my chest. It felt oddly natural.

'Orm, what . . .?'

I shrugged, my voice light. 'It feels right. And I like to have both hands free.'

Ari huffed a laugh. 'If you say so.'

We lay there, sipping wine, and for the first time in what felt like ages, the world seemed to quiet. His hair tickled my skin, and on impulse, I caught a strand, giving it a gentle tug. Alaric chuckled, pulling it from my fingers. I felt like a thief caught red-handed but seeing him smile again was worth it.

'We're going to commit treason tomorrow,' I said to cover my embarrassment. 'I thought we'd only be slipping in with the Dark Brotherhood, but Reynard wants to use this to start his rebellion.'

Ari's head shot up, his golden eyes sharp with alarm. 'So, what's the plan? Because if we attack openly, won't they just slit Ani's throat? If we're going to rebel, let me go in before dawn. I'll take a few assassins with me and find her before you and your brother storm the front gates.'

He sat up straighter, hands curling into fists. 'Hrae! The pain made me forget—Valaram is planning something. I found out he's requested an audience with the king, and tomorrow morning the Crown Office is issuing an edict calling for the heads of all noble families to attend.'

'Valaram?' I repeated, leaning forward. 'As in the dark fae ambassador Valaram?'

Alaric had managed to surprise me. I knew he had access to Truso's underground, but getting information from the dark fae embassy was the achievement of a spymaster, especially since their mages closely monitored the place.

'Yes, and I don't like it. Making a move now could end badly—' He paused, muttering under his breath, before nodding and looking me in the eye. 'No, you're right. We don't have a choice. Even the common folk whisper that the king is no longer capable of ruling. We need to control the situation before fear makes people grab their pitchforks and torches. You wouldn't believe the gossip I've heard—some have even mentioned seeing the Moroi.'

'The Moroi?' My brows furrowed. 'Here? That can't be right.'

'Maybe,' Ari murmured, placing my hand on his chest. 'But the Lich King's magic is becoming more intrusive, almost like a compulsion, like he's running out of time. After tomorrow . . .' He exhaled heavily. 'Orm, I have a bad feeling. War is coming, and we don't even know who will stand with us.'

I rubbed my temples, the weight of it all pressing down. 'Then we take control before it spirals. Send some of your assassins to join Reynard's guards. We've requested an audience with the king, so gaining entry won't be an issue. I'll leave it to you to disperse them throughout the palace, but I want someone at the gates ready to open them for the rest of our men when the fighting starts. Find Ani, lead her to the courtyard, and don't look back. Vahin will be overhead, ready to extract you both.'

Alaric frowned. 'You expect me to convince Annika to leave you behind? She'll never—'

'Lie if you must. Drag her if you have to. Do whatever it takes, but I want her far away from Ihrain and the chancellor.' My voice cracked despite my effort to keep it steady. 'If she refuses, guard her with your life. We can't risk her getting caught in the chaos.'

'You know I will.' He reached for my shoulder, his grip firm. 'But be reasonable, Orm. Even without her magic, Ani's a fighter. She can hold her own.'

'She shouldn't have to!' The words tore out of me before I could stop them. Shame and anger swirled as I admitted the truth I'd buried deep. 'If she had her magic, whoever took her would be ash by now. I failed her, Ari. I failed as her mate, as a commander. And it won't happen again.'

The silence that followed was heavy, my confession hanging in the air like a storm cloud. Alaric squeezed my shoulder, his voice steady and unyielding. 'No more of that, Orm. Guilt won't bring her back. Tomorrow, we'll fix this. Tonight, you need rest. Both of us do.'

He shifted, laying his head on my chest, his breath warm against my skin. I stared at him, this man who, despite the darkness tormenting him, always found the words to dispel mine. When I didn't respond, his body tensed, and he started to pull away.

Instinct overruled reason. I caught his chin, tilting his face towards mine. His golden eyes widened, filled with a hesitant understanding that made my chest ache. Slowly, I bent down and pressed my lips to his. The kiss was soft, tentative—a question I hadn't meant to ask but couldn't stop myself from voicing. Ari gasped, his mouth parting in surprise, and I deepened it, savouring the warmth, the trust, the tender fragility of the moment.

I expected confusion. Maybe regret. Certainly guilt. But instead, something new and unexpected bloomed inside me—a connection as delicate as it was undeniable. My tongue grazed over his small fangs, and I recalled the blood bond he had performed with Annika. *Maybe one day we would be ready to have our own*, I thought.

When I finally broke the kiss, I let my hand linger on his cheek, my thumb brushing against his skin. 'Good night, my friend,' I whispered, the words laced with more meaning than I intended.

'Good night, my lord,' he murmured, his voice thick with raw emotion.

I closed my eyes, willing the flood of desire away, knowing if I didn't, I would use his beautiful mouth in an entirely different way.

And I feared he wouldn't object.

CHAPTER 4

ALARIC

Creeping consciousness slowly stole away my dreams until I opened my eyes to a new dawn, perhaps even a new world. Orm's arm rested on my hip, and my mind struggled to comprehend the changes it brought.

He had been different since Ani went missing, as though the loss had carved something vital out of him. I remembered how, after the fire at the boarding house, he'd come to my room, soot-streaked and exhausted, coaxing me to drink the honey-milk concoction for my damaged throat he'd sworn could heal anything. Then Tomma rushed in with the news, and everything fell apart.

Disbelief had struck Orm like a thunderclap, and I could do nothing but watch as shock and sorrow tore through him. His clothes were still scorched and smoke-stained from the fire, a testament to the fact he hadn't spared a thought for himself that day. Yet when the realisation hit, the sound that escaped him was inhuman—a keening cry that still echoed in my mind.

'I can't feel her . . .' he'd whispered, his voice broken. Golden flames engulfed his eyes, and the man I called my brother had roared like a beast.

The world seemed to pause, frozen in the wake of his anguish. Horror squeezed my heart as I understood the gravity of his words.

Then Orm had stormed out, scattering those who tried to stop him. But the berserker couldn't be tamed by men alone.

I'd known he loved Ani. I just hadn't realised how deeply. Now, the man who loved as fiercely as dragon fire burned had *kissed* me.

The Orm of that night bore no resemblance to the peaceful giant sleeping beside me. His steady breaths brushed against my skin, his snoring a soothing rhythm that seemed to tether me to the moment. I let my hand trail over his chest, a part of me wishing he'd asked for more last night. I was ready to give him everything, but I knew it had to be his choice. For now, I was content—grateful—that his touch shielded me from the Lich King's constant intrusion.

The room around us was serene, with its minimalist décor and tall window framing the night sky. But the scent of spilled plum wine and blood lingered, silent witnesses to my failed attempts to drown out the voices in my head. A cold autumn breeze slipped through the open window, raising goosebumps along my skin. Before I could reach for the blanket, Orm shifted, pulling me closer and pressing my back to his warmth.

'No. Mine,' he muttered, still lost in sleep. His arms tightened around me as he nuzzled my neck.

A small smile tugged at my lips. His breath tickled me, and I let myself sink into the comfort of his embrace. Just as sleep began to reclaim me, the silver runes etched into my chest flared to life, burning through my mind like fire.

ᛞᛒᚾᚠᛒ

Something pulled at my awareness, a viscous net wrapping around me, paralysing me and pulling me under.

Hrae! Dreamwalkers! My heart pounded as I fought the compulsion. *Why now?*

I tried to resist, pouring every ounce of willpower into strengthening my mental defences. Casting a counterspell was impossible, but I refused to yield. The net tightened, dragging me further into the dreamwalker's construct. Just as despair began to set in, a voice rang out, and time ground to a halt.

'Ari. Alaric. Please stop fighting me. Please, Ari ...'

The voice was older, more mature, but unmistakable. My breath hitched.

'Ro? How—? You aren't ... are you?'

Rowena'va Shen'ra, my sister. A powerful mage and necromancer, she was a strong summoner capable of returning life to the dead and imbuing decayed flesh with aether to create the semblance of life. Dreamwalking was secondary for her—a skill she'd never mastered. Her reaching me like this shouldn't have been possible.

'Alaric, I finally did it. No, don't speak—he may sense you. Just watch, please. Just watch.'

Ro's words, strange and urgent, echoed in my mind, but they made little sense. Why reach out to me if she didn't want to talk? Before I could process her meaning, a blinding light enveloped me.

Orm's hand remained on my hip, grounding me in reality, but when my vision cleared, I found myself walking through a corridor. Intricate tapestries adorned the stone walls, their vibrant embroidery dimmed by age. My sister's presence lingered, urging me forward.

Whatever this was, I had to trust her. Wary of dreamwalkers, I forced myself to relax, opening my mind to what she wanted me to witness.

Through her eyes, I saw what might have once been the grand castle she had described in her letters, its magnificence now ravaged by time.

The tapestries were paper-thin, frayed at the edges, and everywhere I looked, decay spread like a sickness.

It's falling apart, I thought, feeling my sister's agreement ripple through our link.

The corridor ended in a vast chamber with towering ceilings. Ornamental carvings of climbing vines and roses adorned the walls, their elegance muted beneath a heavy layer of dust. In its prime, I imagined the room had been illuminated by a thousand candles; now, it was a graveyard of forgotten splendour.

'Rowena, where have you been? Have you made progress with the trolls I sent you last week?'

The voice was smooth, commanding—a pleasant baritone that belied the rot beneath its surface. My gaze snapped towards the speaker, and rage surged through me as I recognised him.

My father.

The bastard who had destroyed my life.

He stood beside another man, his face drawn into the same sour expression I'd never forget. Thin lines etched his features, but my resemblance to him was uncanny. And while Roan'va Shen'ra had aged well, looking at him was like staring into a mirror that reflected a possible future I wanted no part of. His stern gaze bore down on my sister, unrelenting, heavy-handed—exactly as he'd always been. A despot who demanded perfection and crushed anything less.

Once, I had yearned for his approval. Now, I despised him.

'I was preparing the army for our lord,' Rowena replied coldly, her tone as sharp as a blade. 'Not tinkering with those defective trolls. Your spell scrambled their minds so badly that all I could create were more mindless beasts we'll have to release near the border.'

Her voice was icy, unrecognisable compared to the sister I knew.

'Let her be, Shen'ra,' another man said, his tone casual, almost bored. 'As soon as we have your boy, none of this will matter. He will lead them all.'

My sister's gaze moved to the figure sitting on the throne. The man was striking in a conventional way—dark hair dusted with silver, fine lines framing his eyes. He was well-built, perhaps too much so for his apparent age. Yet as he rose from the throne, I caught a shimmer of magic rippling across his form.

An illusion.

Beneath the glamour I saw what must have been the mummified husk of Cahyon, the Lich King. His desiccated body betrayed his immortality, but the illusion persisted. *Why?* I wondered.

Vanity. He wants to be an emperor of men, not a king of the undead.

My sister's thought came through unexpectedly, but it made sense. Why would he think I would ever lead his abominations, though? Even if he dragged me to Katrass, his plans were doomed.

'My lord,' Rowena said carefully, her words laced with scepticism. 'Alaric can be wilful. Are you sure he has enough power to control so many creatures?'

The Lich King's expression darkened, displeased by her doubt.

'Once the bond is complete, and our connection is forged, he will have my power as I will have his mind and obedience. Alaric's necromancy already exceeds your father's, and with the conduit mage he loves . . .' Cahyon's lips curled into a smug grin. 'Tell me, my dear, who will be more powerful than my puppet and I?'

He turned, grasping my father's chin as though handling a pet. 'Look at your father. He knows Alaric will be more than enough. Such jealousy from a doting parent,' he sneered, patting Roan's cheek mockingly. 'It amuses me.'

Rowena gasped, but I felt immense pleasure at the insult. My father's thunderous expression soured further, yet he didn't pull away from the king's grasp. He endured it silently, as though such humiliation was routine.

'You see, my sweet Ro,' the Lich King continued, his tome almost conspiratorial. 'Your father hates competition. He couldn't bear other men looking at his wife, and he disliked it even more if someone's magic was stronger than his. He might pretend to care about legacy, but even your mother was chosen because her psychic skills and dreamwalking were no threat to him.'

Cahyon's smile widened as he stroked my father's cheek, his words dripping with venom. 'Imagine his shock when she bore a son whose mastery over the dead impressed even the empress. And then there's you, Rowena—a shining star who received both parents' powers and has outdone him entirely. Such delicious irony.'

I could feel my sister struggling to not react, but she remained still, unflinching.

'Isn't that why you hate your son so much, Roan?' The Lich King's voice dropped, cruel amusement flickering in his eyes. 'And what about letting me use your wife to renew myself? Was it to punish her for trying to leave you? For not being the meek little mouse you wanted her to be? Such a shame you didn't tell me your little spell would turn me into a fucking monster.'

The last word was punctuated by a savage backhand that snapped my father's head to the side.

'You wanted to live forever, and that was the price,' my father spat, cradling his cheek. 'Did you really expect to do that as a human? As for my wife, she was the most compatible for the ritual, though it didn't hurt that she'd also outlived her usefulness.'

Rowena didn't react. There was no pain, no sorrow, as though she'd heard this all before.

So Cahyon didn't intend to become a lich? I thought, the realisation sinking in. Ro's silent agreement confirmed it.

There was a grim poetry to it. To exist as a lich, unable to savour food, drink, or love—it wasn't power. It was torment. At least I still had the chance to be with someone I loved, while the Lich King's body was a dry husk filled only with aether.

Rowena cleared her throat, drawing both men's attention.

'My lord, those in stasis in the keystone cave won't be easy to control. Even if my brother agrees, no mage has the power to sustain them indefinitely. The only reason the spell holds is because of the keystone's stored aether, and you saw what happened to the artefact.'

Another secret unravelled in front of me. Now I knew why the Barrier was fading and why the monsters hadn't attacked Ani and Orm while they explored the caves. I was betting that was also the reason Annika felt something wrong with the keystone. It was all beginning to make sense.

'The keystone will hold as long as it has to,' the Lich King declared, his tone sharp. 'I could send your father to lead them, but his magic is nothing more than a mindless hammer. Unchecked, he'd reduced Dagome to yet another desolate wasteland.'

'Alaric's psychic skills are insufficient,' my father interjected, his voice laced with indignation. 'And unless you complete the curse, you cannot fully establish the connection.'

'Still unwilling to admit he bested you in all that's important?' Cahyon's laugh was a low, mocking rumble. 'Don't fret, Roan—you'll have your moment. If our plan fails, I'll allow you to destroy Dagome and the dark fae empire as you've always dreamed. But have faith in your son. The curse is nearly complete, and he'll manage. I've sharpened his abilities with my little games—each moment of pain, each whisper in his mind, has expanded his power. Soon, he won't be able to resist my commands. Every god needs an avatar, and he is just perfect for the role.'

The Lich King's chuckle darkened as he turned to Rowena, who instinctively stepped back when he reached for her. 'You'll see your brother soon, my dear,' he murmured. 'Just as you are building my army, he will lead it.'

'Even if you manage to control Alaric,' my father cut in bitterly, 'the conduit mage remains out of your reach—'

Gods, I wanted to laugh so hard, hearing his surly tone. The old spider was caught in a net of his own making, and now he had to wait hand and foot on a man who couldn't wait to have his son to unseat him. If not for Annika being dragged into this, I might have savoured the sight.

'I nearly had her last night, Roan.' Cahyon's voice took on a predatory edge. 'Such a beautiful creature, though obstinate and a little unruly. I'll enjoy breaking her to my will, just as I did with our sweet Ro. In the end, they all submit.'

'How— Did your spies—?'

'Where there's a will, there's a way. Your idea of allowing some humans and Moroi to survive and breed was inspired. I wish I'd spared more of them, but hindsight is a luxury.' The Lich King frowned, his eyes gleaming as they focused on Rowena. 'Just in case, find me a body. One that's functional enough for the Anchoring process. We can't let my future Anchor suffer unnecessarily. And find a handsome one—maintaining the illusion is tiresome.'

Rowena's shock radiated through me like a palpable wave. 'My lord, we've already tried that. I don't think it is possible—' she began, only to falter as his hand closed around her throat.

'Did you think I was asking?' His voice was a venomous hiss. 'That was an order, and you will obey.'

I felt the pressure on her throat as if it were my own. Her struggle for breath sent a surge of rage through me, and before I could think, I willed her hand to strike back. I felt her pushing me away, trying to break the link. The sensation of dry flesh and bone beneath my fingers was disorienting, but I held firm, forcing her to grip his throat.

The Lich King's face twisted into a grin as he stared directly into my—Rowena's—eyes. 'Ah, Alaric,' he purred. 'So nice of you to join us. You've found a way into your sister's mind. How unfortunate that you overheard my plans.'

His grip tightened around Ro's throat, and his manic smile grew. 'But perhaps it's for the best. I'll give you a choice: come to Katrass willingly, serve as my general, and Annika will remain yours, unharmed. Refuse, and I'll drag you here as my slave. Consider it carefully, boy. Now, leave your sister's mind alone.'

His final words shoved me from Rowena's consciousness with the force of a hammer blow. I woke with a gasp, bolting upright as my heart beat out of my chest.

'What's going on?' Orm, awakened by my sudden movement, was already reaching for his dagger. His curse when he realised it wasn't there was colourful and filled with fury.

'Give me a moment,' I rasped, nausea twisting my stomach. I bent over the edge of the bed and retched, the sound harsh in the still room.

Orm's hand was suddenly on my back, his touch firm but soothing. I forced myself to breathe, to gather the chaos in my mind, and finally turned to him with a grim expression. His hand shifted to my shoulder, his grip steadying me.

'Talk to me, Ari. Whatever it is, we'll deal with it.'

'My sister pulled me into a dream,' I began, my voice heavy. 'I saw the Lich King . . . and my father. I know now why they want me—and Annika. The curse . . . it was meant to awaken my psychic potential and tie me to the lich. Hrae! I've been their puppet the entire time, groomed to command that monster's army.'

I shook my head but couldn't dispel the feeling of hopelessness that settled over me.

Orm's grip tightened as his golden eyes burned with fierce determination. 'Forget him. His curse lay dormant when Annika was around, and I'll never let him have you.'

'We need to find her,' I said, recalling Cahyon's words. 'He claimed he almost had her yesterday, but he didn't say how.'

Orm nodded, his gaze shifting to the window, where dawn painted the sky. 'The day is breaking anyway. Come, let's warm up before the fight, and you can tell me everything.'

'Why not here?'

'Because I'd rather not face armed guards with stiff muscles,' he replied with a smirk. 'And you look like you need to stab something.'

I watched as he dressed and then rose from the bed myself. 'Me? Warm up? Unlike some decrepit, overgrown rider, I'm always ready,' I teased.

Orm's smile turned predatory. 'Fine. Come because I want to beat the living daylights out of someone who won't faint at the sight of my fury. So, are you up to the task, or should I wake my brother? He won't be happy, but he'll understand.'

'Oh no,' I said, matching his grin. 'The privilege of drawing your blood is all mine.'

The golden light in Orm's eyes flared. 'Don't tease the beast, reckless fae,' he said with a vicious grin.

I let my own dark aura swirl around me. 'Tease? I thought I was taming it.'

He laughed, the sound rich and unrestrained—a spark of life I hadn't seen in him since Annika vanished. Thrusting his hand towards me, he grinned again.

'Yes, maybe you are, in a way. More than I ever thought possible. Let's go, we have a fight to win and not much time to prepare.'

I was already out of bed, tugging on a shirt, when an idea struck me. 'How about a wager? The winner gets the first night with Ani once we get her back,' I said with a smirk.

Orm shook his head, his response so nonchalant it nearly made me drop my daggers. 'No need. This bed is big enough for the three of us, and I don't think I ever want to sleep alone again.'

For a moment, I just stared at him. 'Hrae, why wait for your brother? Let's go and get her now. For that, I'd die happy.'

Orm rolled his eyes, already moving towards the door. 'Trust the necromancer to find joy in flirting with death,' he muttered, and we set off towards the training grounds.

CHAPTER 5

ANNIKA

A bone-deep chill woke me, followed by a shiver that shook my entire body, chasing sleep from my mind. I didn't know how long I'd been lying there after the Lich King's assault, but the next item on my newly formed escape plan was a weapon.

I spent what felt like hours crawling in the dark, running my hands over the filthy floor. But besides the skeletal remains of my predecessor, its hollow sockets glaring at me in silent accusation, the place was empty.

Determined to avoid more magical surprises and paranoid Cahyon might return, I had checked every inch of the cell for hidden sigils. It took far too long, but when I finally came up empty, a sliver of relief steadied my nerves. As for a weapon, the best I could do was the femur of my unfortunate cellmate.

Whispering an apology to their restless soul, I got to work, grinding the bone against the rough stone wall until it formed a crude spike. When it was done, I raised it to the faint, grimy light filtering through the window. Primitive, yes, but I prayed it would be enough to find its way to Ihrain's black heart.

I allowed myself a brief, savage grin, shaking the weapon in defiance, feeling like a barbarian ready to destroy my enemies. The moment shattered as the sound of shuffling feet echoed from the hallway. My muscles tensed as I spun to face the latest threat, the bone spike steady in my grip.

'Annika Diavellar?' a voice asked quietly. The hooded and masked speaker stepped into view, their features obscured and their tone neutral.

'Who's asking?' I countered, not confirming my identity. 'If Ihrain sent you, why ask? Afraid you chose the wrong cell?'

'Oh, ye'r be 'er. Th' dark fae said that ye'r be shrewish when angry.'

After deciphering the mangled words, I lowered the bone slightly and asked, 'Alaric is here?'

The figure shook their head. 'No, but 'e sent me to lead y'er out of th' palace when th' fighting' starts.'

'Fight? What? Now? Open the cell—I need to join them.'

'Th' only key is with tha' mage twat who waves 'is nose in th' air n' walks like 'e shits gold,' they replied, peeling off their mask. The rodent-like face beneath matched the sneering voice, complete with scraggly beard and beady, amused eyes.

I wondered whether he was testing my patience or just had a death wish, but I was on the wrong side of a locked door, and he was the one sent to free me.

'What kind of rogue doesn't have a lockpick? Never mind—how long will it take you to steal the key from Ihrain?' I asked calmly.

He grinned, chuckling in response. 'Did I say I didn' ha' one? Ye'r talking to th' best thief in th' Lowland Kingdoms, lady. But I was warned ye'r might be . . . unpredictable. So what'll it be? Ye'r be calm and follow my orders?'

I nodded, trying to place his accent. It sounded southern with how he maimed his aitches, probably from the coastal area near the light fae kingdom, a no-man's-land filled with ghosts and ship-wrecks.

'I'm the epitome of calm. Now, would you kindly open this fucking door because I don't have all day to waste—'

'Alright, alright. I'll just tell 'em I *tried* to keep ye'r safe,' he muttered, pulling out his tools. The lock groaned in protest before giving way with a loud *click*, the door creaking open.

Stretching, I stepped into the hallway and fixed him with a sharp look. 'Which way to Alaric?'

'No, I told ya, ye'r t' come with me t' th' kitchen gardens. Yer man said th' dragon will take ya.'

I raised an eyebrow in disbelief. 'Alaric told you to do that?'

'Aye, kind of. He'll only pay if ye'r alive . . .'

'Splendid, then let's make sure I stay alive. Do you have any extra weapons, or will I have to swing this bone around like a lunatic?'

'I don't 'ave weapons, and we 'ave no time for this. Come, I know all th' secret passages in this castle. Ye'll be free in no time.'

'Right, let's make this clear, my friend. I'm going where my men are, and you're showing me the way,' I said firmly, daring him to argue.

He sighed heavily. 'Fine, at least change ye'r clothes. Th' guards are swarming like fuckin' ants, and if ye'r gonna start a fight, I'm out. I'm only paid for freeing ya, not to die for ya.'

He threw a servant's dress at my feet. Without hesitation or a shred of modesty, I swapped out my old battle mage robe, still singed from the fortress fire, for the simple attire. Then, we moved.

The narrow stairway reeked of mud and decay, the air damp as we wound through the maze of musty corridors. Light filtered weakly through cracks in the stone, barely cutting the gloom.

'Gods, was the bottom of the prison recently flooded?' I mused, wiping slime off my hand after touching the wet wall.

The palace was built on a steep incline with many beautiful terraces, but the old castle was cut from the granite bedrock of the hill rising from the river that meandered past its walls. I'd bet the lowest part of the dungeon was frequently flooded during the spring.

'River takes care o' th' bodies. Just open th' door, and off floats th' poor sod,' the thief said, and I realised that could have been my fate.
Lovely.

We were nearing the end of the corridor when he suddenly stopped, grabbing my arm. 'Someone's comin'. Hide!' He dragged me into a curtained alcove just as heavy footsteps approached.

'Check if she's still there,' snapped Ihrain's unmistakable voice. 'If the portal sigil failed, take her to the trapdoor—there's a boat waiting below to take you to the island. The boatman will take care of the rest. The poison should last, but just to be sure, make her swallow this.'

Rage flared in my chest, and I reached for the aether. But all I managed was a faint glow at the tip of my bone weapon.

'Fuck, no. No fightin',' the thief hissed, pressing us against the wall and covering me with his body.

Ihrain's voice receded as he gave more orders.

'If she is not there, report to the throne room. I need to set up an ambush by the servant's entrance, then I'll meet you there. Reynard thinks he can sneak his soldiers in under my nose, damn fool . . .'

When the corridor fell silent, I shoved the thief away.

'Let's go. I need to warn Reynard.'

He shook his head. 'I told ya I won't fight for ya. Ye' can go wherever you want, lady. I'm outta 'ere. If that mage prick knows of th' attack, I ain't gonna get paid. I don' wanna become one of th' bodies left t' rot.'

'Coward,' I muttered.

'Better than a dead fool,' he retorted, disappearing into the shadows.

I let him go without protest as he slipped away towards the kitchens. Partially because he was right, but also because I realised who he was.

The tattoo on his temple, faintly visible beneath his hairline when he pinned me to the wall, marked him as a member of the Dark Brotherhood. Their loyalty extended only as far as the gold in one's pockets. Even if I could use his skills, I had no means to compel him to fight for me.

I came to the gallery bridge connecting the old castle with the luxurious palace and crossed it quickly, trying to look like I belonged. As soon as I reached the nobles' quarters, I slowed and lowered my head, hiding the bone spike in the folds of my skirt. With a tray I'd picked up and the servant's dress I'd donned, I blended in seamlessly. An overwhelming nervousness permeated the palace, and several nobles hurriedly packed as I walked past their rooms.

Despite my earlier bravado and the rush of energy that came with escaping my cell, I was muddled from hunger, and when I found myself in an unfamiliar corridor, I realised I was lost. As I looked around to find the exit, I caught part of a conversation as two guards passed me by.

'You know what's going on?' one asked, his voice low. 'I heard the lord marshal's taken his men to the throne room, and now we're being called to protect the king.'

'Bad luck for us,' the other muttered. 'And here comes more of it.' He straightened abruptly, saluting as an officer approached.

I held my breath, trying to disappear into the shadows, straining to hear more about Ihrain's plans.

'You two—go by the servants' entrance and grab any guards you meet on the way. Hold up the duke's men as long as you can. I don't want any of them in the throne room. We need to contain the marshal and his brother before reinforcements arrive.'

The officer's words were a splash of ice-cold water down my spine. I observed as they gathered a few extra men and headed downstairs. Only then did I dare to move.

Slipping through a discreet servant's door, I found myself in a narrow passage leading to the throne room. My pulse quickened as I recognised it—every crown mage had been brought here once, shown the alcove where they could eavesdrop on foreign dignitaries and political dealings. The hidden vantage point offered me a view of the throne room's unfolding chaos.

The grand chamber was just as I remembered it, with its high, frescoed ceiling and gleaming marble floors. Carvings of legendary heroes and beautifully woven tapestries covered the walls. But today, blood marred the polished surface, and soldiers herded nobles into a corner like cattle. Opposite them stood the king's guards, swords drawn, ready to fight.

Two imposing figures commanded attention at the centre of the room. My heart leapt at the sight of Orm, and for a moment, I forgot everything else. Beside him stood a man so strikingly similar in stature and bearing that I knew it must be his brother, Reynard. Together, they looked like mythical warriors come to life—a stark contrast to the frail, cringing form of the king, who shrank back from the tension radiating through the hall.

I scanned the scene, my stomach knotting with anxiety as I searched for Alaric. He was nowhere in sight, and I didn't dare reveal myself—not yet. Instead, I focused on assessing the situation, determined to find a way to help.

Orm's voice cut through the air like a blade, deep and commanding. 'Sire, why have you done this? We came to beg for your aid in defending the kingdom from the army gathered under the Lost Ridge. Yet you align yourself with those who would see this kingdom fall and allow a conduit mage—our only conduit mage—to be taken under your orders.'

The king blinked, his weak gaze shifting to the chancellor, who stepped forward with a sneer. 'You keep insisting on saying that, Commander, but what proof do you have? You revolt against the king, kill his guards to force yourselves in here, and for what? For the return of a woman? A mage who, by law, belongs to the Crown.'

'Lady Annika belongs to no one, and I address the king, not you, vermin!' Orm's fury was palpable until Reynard placed a calming hand on his shoulder. 'Even as a crown mage, you have no right to hold her imprisoned.'

Ihrain emerged from behind the throne, his expression smug as ever. 'A bold claim, Commander. But if reports are accurate, you yourself forced Lady Annika into a bondage contract.'

Orm's glare could have burned through stone, his hand tightening on the hilt of his sword. But it was Reynard who stepped forward, his voice measured but no less dangerous. 'Those same reports say she entered the fortress voluntarily. Now, everyone knows you should not separate a conduit mage from their Anchors. Therefore, we insist you bring Lady Annika here. Then we can put this matter to rest once and for all.'

'Lady Annika is enjoying the king's hospitality and is currently unavailable. I'm sure she'd condemn the violence you've wrought in her name,' Ihrain said with such superiority that I thought Orm would lose control of his temper. 'If you refuse to kneel to your king and beg forgiveness, she would be the first to call for you to be punished. Now, if you ever want to see the lady again, surrender to His Majesty.'

Ihrain was working on getting himself killed, but what worried me more was the increasing yellow glow of Ormond's eyes. They were using me to destroy his image, and I couldn't let Ihrain's lies stand. I need to act, and fast.

'Stop with this nonsense now!' Reynard's voice caused everyone to freeze. 'What law justifies the imprisonment of a lady of the Erenhart family?'

'Law? She is a crown mage. You, Lord Marshal, and your brother are traitors. I hereby remove you both from your posts and will strike your family name from the kingdom's heraldry. Stop this madness and lay down your weapons *now*,' the chancellor said, and the eyes of everyone present turned to the man on the throne.

'Do you consider yourself king, Chancellor? The ruler I pledged my sword to is the man sitting beside you, not you. Why are you dismantling this country brick by brick?' Reynard queried calmly, and I caught the subtle gesture he made as he spoke, after which several nobles left the room. 'Or is this by the order of your true master? The monster who wants us helpless and on our knees, ready to be taken like low-hanging fruit?'

The two men stared each other down, taking the measure of their opponent before a slow, cruel smile spread across the chancellor's lips.

'What ridiculous conjecture, Reynard.'

I stepped forward from my hiding spot, intending to wipe the smirk from the chancellor's face, only for someone to grab my arm with such strength that it made me stagger. The tray I was carrying fell to the floor, startling everyone into silence as they turned to look.

'I've got her, sir!' the guard holding me announced. I recognised the voice of the person who went to check the cell. Before I could react, all hell broke loose.

'Get your hands off my woman!' Ormond roared, rushing in my direction. Two guards stepped in front of him, but he was unstoppable, punching one man in the chest and simultaneously sinking his dagger in the other's throat. I felt my jaw drop at the speed with which he killed them, but more stepped in front of him after Ihrain shouted.

'Guards! Now! Take His Majesty to safety. Attack the rebels!'

This is an ambush, I thought, as I grabbed a metal pitcher and smashed it over the head of my captor. Despite the blood that gushed from the cut on his forehead, his grasp on my shoulder didn't falter.

Suddenly, every door to the throne room burst open. Countless armed men poured into the room and sprang into action while Reynard's soldiers created a wall of steel around him. Most of the attackers headed for Orm, thinking an unprotected man an easy target, but, like a bear, he ripped through the crowd, fighting them off as if they were a pack of dogs.

'Fuck it,' I said, throwing my head backwards with all the force I could muster. The sickening crunch of my skull connecting with my attacker's face was eclipsed by his bellow as he grasped his broken nose. I reached to grab his dagger but stopped when the sharp touch of cold metal cut into my neck.

'You're coming with me, Annika,' Ihrain said, so close to my ear that his breath gave me goosebumps. 'It's time for a little visit to Katrass.'

'Veles' pit will freeze over before I give in to you,' I answered, ignoring the blade that cut my skin as I turned around. Bloody droplets ran down my neck, but it didn't stop me from reaching for my makeshift weapon and thrusting it at his face. Before the splintered end could spike him, devastating pressure crushed my mind, and I staggered, dropping the bone.

Tears poured from my eyes as the world swam in and out of focus, but I managed to catch a glimpse of someone grinning and swaying to some unknown tune.

Fuck, it's a broken mage, I thought. It was worse than I expected. Broken mages were magical executioners whose minds had been destroyed when having their geasa extracted. Their psychic power then served to distort the aether, causing immeasurable pain.

Ihrain smiled, wiping his knife as I clutched my ears, trying to drown out the terrifying sound.

'Hurry, secure her before that beast gets here. I don't think the guards can hold him for long,' Ihrain directed as I stepped back, barely able to stand.

'Either he will rip your head off, or I will. If you take me, I will turn you, and anyone around you, into a pile of ash before we ever reach the Rift,' I growled.

'Why do you have to be so fucking stubborn?' Ihrain replied, reaching into his pocket, and I muttered a curse. The pain was blinding me, but even so, I knew he intended to use lanara poison on me again.

'Hold her. I need to inject the poison while they are busy with the guards. Then we can get out of here,' Ihrain muttered.

I ducked his outstretched hands, barrelling into the broken mage's side and ripping the dagger from his belt, thrusting it into his unprotected flank. Warm blood splashed over my hands right before another psionic wave hit me square between the eyes, and I fell to my knees, retching on the floor.

So far, the broken mage had been gentle with me. Now, his expression filled with strain and hatred as he continued his assault. The whites of his eyes were filled with darkness, and I understood one simple truth: I had to kill him before they could take me away.

I felt another pair of hands pulling at the collar of my dress, likely to inject me with another dose of poison—or worse, Ihrain getting ready to use his magic on me. He mumbled some incoherent words, ripping my dress in his fervour, but as my body flailed, my hand landed on the rough surface of the bone spike.

'Annika!' Orm yelled.

Something hit Ihrain, and the impact jerked my body out of his grasp. I dodged to the side, only to catch a glimpse of his horrified grimace as he held Ormond's dagger embedded in his stomach.

I had one chance. In my weakened state, starved, and fighting a psychic assault, I did the only thing I could. As the broken mage drew their sword to finish me, I lunged at the hand holding it. I was unable to lessen the impact, but I diverted it to the side. The pain when it sliced through my flank fused with Ormond's roar, but I had my enemy where I wanted him because as I pulled him closer, the bone of a long-dead man impaled his stomach, the sharp tip forced upwards until it pierced his heart.

The song stopped, and the agony with it. The world swam back into focus, and I looked around, worried that there might be more attackers.

With the last of my strength, I struggled free of the dead weight and searched for Ihrain, but he was nowhere to be seen. Only a trail of blood leading away from where I last saw him remained. I pressed my hand to my bleeding side, gasping when a loud voice thundered across the room.

'Lay down your weapons, or your master dies!'

Reynard was standing by the throne, holding a blade to the chancellor's neck.

CHAPTER 6

ANNIKA

Despite Reynard's threat, soldiers still fought. However, that changed when the throne room's doors crashed open, and the deafening blare of trumpets brought everything to a halt.

The male that strode in, resplendent in imperial dark fae armour, made jaws drop, but the woman who followed provoked a wave of astonished gasps. Magnificent in a long, flowing robe, tall and silver-skinned, she dominated the room with her mere presence and looked down her nose at the carnage with no attempt to hide her disgust.

My amazement at the spectacle turned to confusion. I recognised the male in the armour. Valaram'sa Dern'ra was the dark fae ambassador in Truso, but the woman? Several moments passed before I realised who she was. Valaram, a conceited male who never bowed to anyone, had kneeled to lay his cloak before the beautiful female.

Is she? What the—? Could she be the dark fae empress?

The ambassador stood up, his arrogant smirk back in place as he turned to face Reynard and the helpless chancellor. Unfortunately for him, no one noticed, as all eyes were riveted on the empress as she stepped forward onto her subordinate's cloak.

'You were right to bring my attention to the events in Dagome, dear brother. Still, I didn't expect such ... barbarity in the court of our allies,' she said, casually drawing a complex sigil. As soon as she finished, immense power flashed out, and all the dead soldiers rose up, surrounding each fighting group in the room.

'Since I now have everyone's undivided attention, shall we talk? Who is in charge of this charnel house?' she asked. I couldn't stop staring. She shouldn't be able to cast in here, yet she had torn through the powerful wards without a second thought.

Silence reigned until, with a clatter and a curse, Alaric burst into the room. Covered in blood and sporting a wild, unhinged look, my fae cast around, ignoring his empress and the gathered nobles until his eyes fell upon me, and he let out a short cry.

'Domina, I thought I was too late!'

The relief in his tone dulled the pain of my injuries. When he took a step towards me, two fae guards blocked his way, and I heard coldness replace the disdain in the dark fae woman's voice when she spoke again.

'Well, well . . . Alaric'va Shen'ra, it has been too long. Won't you greet an old friend?'

Alaric turned, looking as if he'd only just noticed her presence.

'Oante'terec evako, Domina Tenebris,'[1] he intoned, dropping to one knee. I was beginning to think everyone had turned to statues. Not one person dared to move as the situation unfolded.

'So, you haven't forgotten how to be a noble of my dark court,' the empress crooned, approaching him with a soft, gentle smile before gesturing toward Valaram. 'Val, darling. Kill him. But make it quick.'

'As you command,' the fae male answered, and I felt the aether gathering around him.

---

1. I kneel before you, Dark Lady. (*Domina Tenebris* is an official title of the dark fae empress.)

Rage—pure, unbridled fury—blinded me. I didn't care why Alaric was so casually sentenced to death, or that Valaram was kin to the dark fae empress and a legendary primaeval high mage. He would not kill my man. Ari belonged to me, and even if Veles, god of the Underworld, came to claim his soul himself, I would fight him.

'No!' I shouted, staggering forward, but I was too slow. Still, my actions seemed to break whatever spell held everyone silent, and chaos erupted.

The dark fae ambassador cast a spell over Alaric, its silver threads covering my lover and ensnaring him. I recognised the net from my duel with Ari at the fortress. However, this one seemed more substantial, more dangerous, and I felt a shiver of fear run down my spine at seeing him held in its deadly embrace.

I threw myself forward, skidding across the bloody floor. The breath knocked out of my lungs as Orm picked me up before I hit the marble tiles. He turned, pointing his sword at my attackers, shielding me with his body from the two dark fae guards.

'Nivale, you're bleeding. You've got a godsdamned hole in your side!' he muttered frantically as I pressed my hand to the still-seeping wound. 'You need a fucking healer!'

'I'm fine—stop worrying about me. We need to protect Ari!' I answered, and he supported me as we moved to face the empress. She looked at me with such smug superiority, clearly enjoying the moment.

'Tell your mage to release my fae,' I demanded, not even bothering with pleasantries.

'*Your fae?* The Shen'ra family belongs to me. His life is mine, and I've already decided his fate.'

'I won't let you do this,' I said, reaching for the aether. I had little time. Soon, blood loss would render me unconscious, but with Orm holding me, I felt able to access the aether long enough for a single attack.

As I opened myself up to the power, Reynard pushed the chancellor into someone's arms and jumped in front of us, arms outstretched.

'No, Lady Annika, Valaram will kill him and you if you fight.'

The incantation died on my lips, but I held onto the aether with uncertain control. Suddenly, a mournful keening interrupted our standoff as the king's groom staggered through a small back door, wailing like a vjesci.[2]

'The king... the king is dead. The mages killed the king! The blood ... Oh gods, the blood ...'

The world I knew crashed and burned before my eyes. I didn't know what to do. The old fool may not have been a good king, but his presence kept the nobles from tearing each other apart to replace him. Orm had told me that when they'd discussed the rebellion, most of the nobles had agreed on Reynard becoming king. Still, they'd planned on deposing the king, not *killing* him. Now we had to deal with the dark fae empress witnessing not just a rebellion but the regicide.

I had to salvage this situation in our favour, and if I couldn't fight, I needed a king to fight for me.

I detangled myself from Orm's grasp and hobbled to the centre of the room, feeling all eyes on me as I concentrated on not falling. I stopped next to the groom, and Ormond moved to my side. Locking eyes with Reynard, I sank to one knee with as much flourish as I could muster.

---

2. **Vjesci (s./pl.) /pron: vi-yes-chi/** — an undead demon that preserved the thoughts, personality, and body of a person. Their cry is a premonition of upcoming death.

'Long live the king! All hail King Reynard Erenhart!' I exclaimed. Then, surging unsteadily to my feet, I pressed a fist to my chest, saluting as a crown mage. 'I, Annika Diavellar, conduit and loyal battle mage, hereby acknowledge Reynard Erenhart as king of Dagome on behalf of the Council of Mages and Court of Aether.'

Reynard's eyes widened before I saw the hint of a smile. We both knew I didn't have the authority to make such a proclamation, but once he took over the kingdom, whoever had a problem with my unwarranted statement could take it up with the new king.

'I, Ormond Erenhart, Lord Commander of Varta Fortress and the dragon riders, acknowledge Reynard Erenhart as king of Dagome on behalf of the Conclave of Dragons.'

A few nobles dropped to their knees, followed by a few more, until, after several moments, all the nobles of Dagome had kneeled and pledged their loyalty to the new king. I turned to look at the dark fae empress, who, in turn, stared back. The broken mage's blood still dripped from my hand, staining the polished floors as we measured each other's resolve.

'Thank you, little mage. Now I know who to discuss matters of state with,' she said with a smirk. I didn't smile back.

'If you are grateful, then release Alaric,' I responded without sparing a glance at the man I'd just proclaimed king.

'No, I don't think I will. But I have to say, I enjoyed the show. I'd heard so much about Dagome's conduit mages, and you didn't fail to impress. I hadn't thought you aspired to be a kingmaker. So refreshingly bold and unlike others of your kind who follow their male guardians.'

'Really? Maybe you should meet my friend Bryna,' I quipped. Both the pain and her attitude had grated on me. 'I can show you just how bold I can be if you don't relinquish my fae. So I ask again, politely. Please, Your Majesty, as one woman to another, release my mate.'

'And if I don't?'

'Then I will request the presence of Vahin and use conduit power laced with dragon fire to change your mind,' I said, surprised by the satisfied smile that transformed her face into a breathtaking work of art.

From the corner of my eye, I saw Ormond shift his stance, his jaw clenching, and I hoped he wouldn't throw himself at the fae ambassador just when the empress' smile hinted that we were getting somewhere.

'What is your name and affiliation, mage?' she asked, snapping her fingers and gesturing at a woman wearing a veil. 'Heal her. I don't want her bleeding out before we finish our conversation.'

'Annika Diavellar. I'm of the Primal Order, and my element is fire,' I said, nodding to the healer when she approached me.

I didn't trust the empress, but I wasn't going to look a gift horse in the mouth if this could keep me conscious a few moments longer. When the healer's fingers dug into my wound, it took all of my strength to stay upright and hold back an agonised sob. *Another fucking test*, I thought when the empress's eyebrow lifted as I refrained from screaming.

'Alaric'va Shen'ra is a fugitive of the dark fae court who killed his compatriots, including a member of the royal family, to escape. He also released a malevolent spirit in the palace catacombs, a former dreamwalker that drove several warriors to madness. Some even took their own lives to escape the nightmares. That doesn't even include the charges that put him there in the first place. Alaric was to be tried for his part in Roan'va Shen'ra's betrayal and the subsequent war,' the empress stated before nodding toward her captive. 'You want to save your mate, but I want justice for mine.'

'His part? What part could an unfledged youth have had in creating an undead monster and starting a war? If we're apportioning blame, then who was it that sent Roan'va Shen'ra to appease that insane mage in the first place? Alaric is a victim of this insanity as much as anyone, and you, instead of blaming the person who betrayed his people, tormented a son still grieving his dead mother. You disappoint me.'

The sound of a dozen swords being drawn drowned out the murmuring of the surrounding crowd as the dark fae soldiers reacted to my words. Only Valaram nodded approvingly before turning his head to the side, trying to hide a smirk.

'You would risk starting a war for this criminal?' she asked, waving a hand toward Alaric.

'Would you risk one to kill him?'

Footsteps sounded behind me. I didn't turn, assuming Orm was joining me, but to my surprise, it was Reynard who stood by my side.

'Why fight a war with each other when a common enemy threatens us both?' he asked.

'So you will not object if I deal with my subject as I see fit? Despite the objection of your kingmaker?'

'Give me an army to fight the Lich King, and I won't.'

I sucked in a hard breath as Reynard's words punched me in the gut. I looked up at the man who was actively betraying my trust and met his apologetic eyes.

'I'm sorry. One life for the lives of the kingdom? If it was mine she demanded, I would still agree.'

The empress thought for a moment before speaking. 'That is wise. I will consider abiding by the terms of our two nations' treaty. Could we discuss the details in more pleasant surroundings?' she said, extending a hand and dismissing my presence as she waited on the new king's response.

Reynard stepped forward, a confident statesman's smile on his face, but stuttered to a halt as Orm burst into action.

'Enough!' Orm bellowed, pushing towards Alaric, but my attention was firmly on Valaram, who'd been staring at me since I'd started arguing with the empress.

'There is always the Dark Mother's mercy. If Lady Annika is willing to face the trial,' he mentioned nonchalantly, but something in his posture felt odd—as if he was testing me. The empress' head snapped in his direction.

'That is for blood-bonded dark fae only. Humans can't appeal for the trial.'

Noticing her angry expression, I realised how much it irked her and eagerly leapt at the opportunity.

'I agree to this trial. I call on the Dark Mother's mercy,' I proclaimed loudly enough that Reynard flinched, Alaric gasped, and Valaram looked at me with a small half-smile and an expression I couldn't decipher.

'Do you even know what you are requesting?' the ambassador asked.

'I have no fucking idea, but if it saves Ari, then I'm all for it,' I responded in kind. As soon as I spoke the words, the net around Alaric's body loosened, and Valaram bowed to his empress as he spoke.

'Domina Tenebris, even you cannot go against Dark Mother's will.'

'Annika, it's a trial by combat. You have to fight for the privilege of begging for the Dark Mother's mercy. It's just a way for the empress to look merciful while still executing those that defy her,' Alaric said, straining to be heard, but I huffed, ignoring the desperation in his eyes, before I turned to the empress.

'So, Your Majesty, if this trial is such a hopeless task, can you trust in the judgement of your goddess? Alaric submitted to me. I can go through any test you desire in order to prove I'm blood-bound to him,' I said, using the strategy Valaram had moments before. 'I have one request, however, if you're willing? If I survive, will you still fight with us against the Lich King?'

The empress frowned, no longer amused by my resistance, before she grumbled with annoyance, shaking her head.

'You arrogant . . . Are you trying to goad me into allowing this? I should just kill you both and leave Dagome to its fate,' she said before looking at my broken fae.

'Annika, no, it's too dangerous. I won't accept the trial.'

'It is decided, then. Alaric has refused. Valaram, put an end to this farce,' the empress snapped.

'Decided, is it?' Looking Ari in the eyes, I lifted my bloody weapon, lighting it with aethereal fire. 'Then watch me die fighting for you, knowing it is your decision. I won't let them touch you, Alaric'va Shen'ra. You belong to *me*.'

'Annika, no! Stop! I agree!' Alaric's voice cut through the mayhem of Orm grasping my arm and immobilising me completely. I nearly cried when the big bear of a man kissed the top of my head and spoke up.

'I will fight as Annika's champion, but after this idiocy is over, Alaric will be free from your machinations and be allowed to live freely wherever he chooses.'

'The trial is the duty of the accused couple. No other can bear the burden. It is between the goddess and her daughter whether his redemption will be granted,' Valaram said, and I felt Orm's arms tighten around me.

'Are you challenging me, Lord Commander?' The empress' voice dripped venom, her measured poise fracturing as her power erupted, rippling through the chamber. Her beautiful face twisted with a hatred born of centuries of grief. 'For five hundred years, I have endured the knowledge that the murderer of the man I loved walks free, unpunished, and you think I will let him escape so easily? That I would allow you to fight in place of the woman who offered such insult to my face? No, Commander. I will not be taken for a fool a moment longer.'

The empress' mask of disdain shattered, revealing the raw agony beneath. Her grief resonated with my own pain, and I spoke softly, hoping to pierce through her fury. 'I'm sorry. I know the pain never truly fades but punishing him won't bring you peace. Let me put an end to this. Let your goddess decide. I'll go through the trial—for your mate and mine.'

For a moment, her rage abated. I glimpsed the bitterness etched into her soul before she hid it once more behind an indifferent façade. 'Very well, little mage,' she said, her voice cold but composed. 'Let the goddess judge you both. But understand this—if you fail, whatever treaty exists between our kingdoms is null. You are not just fighting for him; you're fighting for *all* of them. I have no wish to ally with a nation of regicide and traitors.'

Reynard's face darkened with disbelief. 'You can't lay our future on the results of this trial.'

'I can, and I will. Your court is riddled with the Lich King's spies, and my informants report that you have no army to fight him off. I would be better off seeking an alliance with other nations while that monster wastes his time destroying yours. However, if our Dark Mother lets her live, then I'll consider aiding you.'

Nodding to the ambassador, she turned to me and said, 'I'll grant you two days to say your goodbyes.'

The spell holding Alaric dissolved, freeing him, and the older fae looked at Ari with a strange combination of pity and envy. 'You chose your domina well. May the Dark Mother have mercy on you,' Valaram said, pulling out a golden vial from beneath his breastplate. Whispering a few words, he drew a glyph with his sharp nail, and the contents of the vial blackened in front of my eyes.

'Drink,' the ambassador said, passing the vial to Alaric. 'If she fails, death won't be swift.'

With a bow, my broken fae accepted the ominous liquid. 'As long as I follow my domina, nothing else matters,' he said, tipping the thick, oily liquid into his mouth.

'What is it?' I asked, dread curling in my stomach.

'Icta poison, to ensure Alaric won't flee once he's free of his bonds,' Valaram stated.

I scoffed, masking my fear. 'Alaric isn't someone who backs down from a challenge.'

'No. Neither are you, it seems.' The fae mage bowed, taking my bloodied hand and kissing my knuckles. 'It's a shame you aren't dark fae. I would fight for the privilege of serving you. Perhaps I still will. Your resistance was . . . enlightening.'

I stood there, stunned, as he rejoined the empress, who spoke with bored disdain.

'It looks like we have two days to discuss how involved our empire will be in your fight if the mage succeeds. My courtiers will call on you presently. I will leave you to sort out your . . . succession, King Reynard.' Her gaze swept the room with disgust. 'Hopefully, when I come tomorrow, you will still be sovereign.'

Without another word, she departed, the undead she'd raised collapsing lifelessly to the floor. As the last of the dark fae vanished, I turned to Orm. His worried expression deepened my exhaustion.

'Can we go home, please? Wherever it is, can we just go?'

Instead of my man, Reynard spoke up. 'My home is yours, my lady. Especially since I have to stay here now. Use it as you please . . . and I'm sorry Orm, but we need her to even stand a chance.'

He looked genuinely remorseful, but I'd just been dragged through a pit of pain, and I wasn't even sure if we'd won or lost. Even if the man I had declared king deserved compassion or understanding, I couldn't forget that he had chosen to sacrifice Alaric, so all I had to offer was civility.

'I will . . . Your Majesty,' I replied dryly.

Reynard sighed but nodded, turning away as more nobles poured into the throne room in response to whatever gossip had undoubtedly swept through the palace halls like wildfire.

'Ormond—before you leave, call for my officers. I need to secure the palace,' the king ordered. 'Someone clean up the bodies and mop the floor—it looks like a slaughterhouse in here.' Finally, he turned his gaze to the chancellor and the men restraining him. 'Lock that traitor in the darkest cell you can find, then hunt down that bastard, Ihrain.'

'You can use the one I was in. It's rather cosy,' I muttered.

'Yes, sire.' The guards saluted before dragging the bound and gagged chancellor away. Reynard smirked, turning to the gathered nobles.

'Go home. Prepare for war. Any household with their own guards must return with them in two days. Those who don't comply will forfeit their wealth. As for your grievances, I will open petitions tomorrow morning. You are welcome to bring them up then. For now, I grant you leave to put your affairs in order. Go!'

Gasps rang out, and several nobles left quickly. Others lingered, protesting, but Reynard silenced them with a sharp gesture. As the throne room doors closed behind the last of them, my strength finally gave out, and I crumpled to the floor.

CHAPTER 7

ANNIKA

I frowned, looking up at two sets of glowing eyes: one swirling with crimson light, the other blazing gold like the midday sun.

'Godsdamn it! I thought the healer did her job,' Orm muttered, his voice sharp with agitation.

It took me a moment to piece things together. I recalled Reynard dismissing everyone before a wave of dizziness washed over me, then nothing. The realisation that I had fainted like some delicate damsel in distress sent a flush of heat to my cheeks.

Orm and Ari seemed oblivious to my stirring as they continued worrying. I closed my eyes again, letting them fuss to their heart's content.

'She did, but Ani spent several days in prison, and gods know what they did to her. Give me a moment to check her injuries.' Alaric's voice lost its soft timbre once he opened the collar of my dress. 'Hrae! Those bastards strangled her. These bruises . . . I am going to flay the skin from their bodies for this.'

'Get in line. How serious is it? Is her life in danger?'

Orm was frantic, and I tried to speak, but the raw emotion on their faces stole my voice. I took a slow, deep breath to centre myself, the scent of their closeness soothing my senses.

'No, but she's exhausted and malnourished. There's a cut on her neck, but it's superficial, as well as her other bruises and cuts. The healer repaired her biggest wound well enough, though it'll leave an ugly scar,' Ari responded as he ran his hands over me, whispering an incantation. Warmth spread through my body, dulling the ache and pulling me into a haze of comforting magic.

ᛉᚲᚾᚠᛉ

The feeling of weightlessly swaying welcomed me as I slowly awoke. I smiled, enjoying the sensation, too sleepy to pay attention. When a deep yawn interrupted the moment, I pouted, then cracked an eye open to look at my surroundings. I was cradled in Orm's arms, bundled in a cloak, riding on a horse through the city.

After days in a cell, I wanted to enjoy the fresh air, so I wriggled free, taking in the cool breeze, decadent architecture, and intricate gardens of the noble mansions lining the street. It wasn't long before the luxurious area gave way to lively and colourful shops with loud street merchants advertising their goods, but it was the smells—oh gods, the scent of food being cooked—that made my mouth water.

The aroma of freshly baked bread and exotic spices overpowered everything else. My stomach rumbled, encouraging me to leave Orm's protective embrace. He tensed instantly, and when I looked up, the ring of gold in his eyes grew bigger. A woman carrying meat pies came closer, and I could feel a tremor running through his body as he moved his horse away.

'Please, let them come,' I whined. I would have killed for a meat-filled pasty or a sweet roll so sticky with sugar I'd want to lick my fingers raw. But each time I caught the eye of a seller and waved them to approach, Orm glared at the unfortunate soul and whatever money they thought they'd make quickly lost its appeal under the commander's hostile stare.

'They're just merchants,' I murmured, noticing the way Orm clenched his sword.

'Or assassins,' Orm countered darkly. 'Ihrain is still at large, and the empress has made it clear she wants you dead. Reynard may have claimed the throne, but his enemies—and yours, especially since your proclamation of support for him—are everywhere. No one is safe until the lords of Dagome officially name him their king.'

'I know, but—'

'No buts, Nivale. I just lived through the worst days of my life, thinking you were lost to me. When I couldn't feel your Anchor, and Vahin told me he couldn't reach you . . . it *broke* me. Even now, holding you, I can't help wondering if I'd paid closer attention, those bastards wouldn't have taken you, wouldn't have brutalised you. The marks on your body . . . Gods, I can't—' His voice cracked as he held me tighter.

'Orm, stop,' I interrupted gently. 'They didn't . . . I was unconscious for most of it. Like a sleeping beauty, only with rats.'

It was a poor attempt at levity. He clenched his jaw, and his horse snorted in agitation, mirroring his fury.

'You don't remember, but I do. And it haunts me. I failed you, Nivale.' His golden eyes burned with guilt.

'You didn't fail me. You found me. And now Reynard is king. The rebellion succeeded. I'll face the empress' trial, and it'll work out.'

'Worked out?' He barked out a laugh. 'I barely have you back, and you have to do that damn trial. I can't even fight for or with you.' Orm signed, the tension in his shoulders easing slightly. 'It's difficult. I just . . . I love you so fucking much, Ani. It terrifies me.'

I smiled, brushing a hand against his cheek. 'Then trust me to fight my battles. I'll make it right. Even a dragon rider in shining armour needs to have a little faith.'

He barked a laugh. 'My armour isn't shining these days. Maybe Bryna can fix that—she was practically drooling over it before . . . everything.'

I chuckled before sighing. 'You know I'm not reckless—mostly—but they had Ari . . . and when I'm done with whatever they throw at me, even the empress will have to agree to my terms.'

I glanced to the side and noticed Alaric looking at us longingly from the corner of my eye. He made no move to come closer, however, as if he sensed Orm needed time with me alone.

'You will be the death of me, woman. You declared my brother king. Now you want to take on the empress? I'm having doubts about whether even three of us are enough to keep you out of trouble,' Orm teased, finally relaxing his grip before pulling my hair to the side and kissing the crook of my neck.

'What are you doing? We're in the middle of the street!' I laughed.

'And? In a city where you can find a brothel on every corner, you think anyone would be shocked to see me kiss my woman?' he said before pressing me to his chest and laying his chin on my shoulder. I could only shake my head and sigh, trying to hide my smile.

'Where is your decorum, Lord Commander? Onlookers may think you are harbouring strong affections for m—' I jested when he suddenly tilted my head back, sealing my lips with a long kiss.

'If they want to watch, they can. I'm not harbouring affection—I'm *obsessed* with you to the very core of my being,' he said, pausing for a moment, and I saw the muscles in his jaw tick rhythmically. 'Unless . . . you want me to hide it?'

'Well, no. I don't mind showing affection, but judging by the strength of your . . . enthusiasm, I'm worried your beast will take over and publicly stake your claim.' I chuckled, stroking his face, and he turned, kissing the soft skin of my palm.

'No, I'm not quite that beastly,' His eyebrows drew together in hesitation until the dam he was building in his mind broke loose. 'I want to marry you. I want to stand before the gods and pledge our love in a handfasting ceremony. I want to make it so fucking grand that not only Dagome but all the fae and human kingdoms know you've chosen to be mine. I won't allow any twat on the throne to ever question that you are my family.'

'You know that the current twat on the throne is your brother?' I teased, trying to lighten the mood that had suddenly grown too serious. I didn't realise he felt so strongly about formally announcing our bond. Anchoring someone was a lifelong commitment, so having a handfasting ceremony had never occurred to me.

'Any *other* twat,' he said with a smirk. 'If this world needs proof you chose me, I'll ensure every living soul knows that you are, and always will be, the one who holds my heart. Please, will you—'

'We've arrived,' Alaric called out and I turned to see a sprawling mansion on the riverbank, but Orm tightened his grip on my waist.

'Annika?'

'After the war. And if you try to put me in a white dress, I'll run away. Also, that was the most awkward way ever to propose to a woman.'

He shrugged. 'You agreed, so it worked,' he said with a content smirk. 'You can come naked for all I care. It may even make it easier later—'

I smacked his shoulder. 'Ormond Erenhart! What would your mother say if she heard you right now?'

'Knowing her, probably *"fucking finally."* Shame she is not here at the estate. You could have asked her yourself,' he replied, pointing towards the main building. 'See that balcony, that's your bedroom.'

The building stood like a vision from a storybook—majestic and timeless but imbued with the lightness and charm of light-fae architecture.

A sprawling courtyard brimming with vibrant wildflowers welcomed us, their untamed beauty blending seamlessly with the structure's elegance. Ivy draped the pristine white walls and sunlight danced off the exterior, making it shimmer like polished gemstones, lending the place an ethereal air. Yet beneath its beauty lay subtle defences: turrets manned by sentinels, servants with military precision in their movements, and a nearby guard post that could have passed for a fortress. Its position beside a landing field hinted at the presence of a dragon.

Just then, a deafening roar split the sky, and a black shadow plummeted to the earth.

'Vahin!' I cried, my voice trembling with emotion as I tore myself from Orm's protective hold. Tumbling off the horse, I gathered my dress and sprinted towards the dragon.

Vahin landed hard, sending a tremor through the ground, before rushing to meet me. His enormous body coiled around mine in a wall of warm scales and muscles, his deep rumbling purr resonating through my chest as I clung to him, wrapping my arms around whatever part of him I could reach. His forked tongue flicked across my cheek and neck, a tender greeting akin to a flurry of kisses.

'Little Flame, you're back at last, but still can't I hear your thoughts,' he hissed, his voice rougher than usual.

'My magic isn't working properly yet, but it's coming back. Vahin, gods, I missed you so much.' I laughed as his tongue tickled my neck. 'Don't—I'm filthy!'

'There's blood on your face,' he growled, licking it clean before pulling back to study me with a sharp, probing gaze. 'But some of it is yours. Who did this, Little Flame? Who made you bleed?'

'It's nothing a proper bath and bit of salve can't fix. My cell wasn't exactly luxurious, and the battle was a little messy, but Ari took care of me. I'm nearly good as new—just starving. Ormond scared off all the merchants—'

'Little Flame. Who. Did. This?'

'If you want revenge, you'll have to ask Alaric to resurrect him so you can kill him again. I dealt with it, and I'm safe.' I pressed my hands against his warm scales, soothing him with my touch.

His anger and fear weighed on me, evident in every hissing syllable. I rubbed the delicate skin of his eyelid, and his tail thudded against the ground before he curled around me tighter, a fortress of flesh and scale.

'When we learned you were being held in the palace, I wanted to go there,' Vahin confessed, his voice low and raw. 'I wanted to burn, smash, and tear it apart to reach you, but I was afraid you'd be hurt. I have never felt so powerless.'

'Oh, Vahin,' I whispered, my heart breaking for him. 'I'm here now. I'll stay with you until you can hear my thoughts again.'

'No, Little Flame. You need to rest. Go back to Orm before I steal you away, my precious treasure.'

I kissed his cheek, and Vahin uncurled, revealing Orm patiently waiting. The dragon lifted his massive head and locked eyes with the commander. Their silent telepathic exchange left me feeling conspicuously excluded, stirring a vague unease. I braced myself for an argument, anticipating overprotective measures after my kidnapping.

But just as I was becoming agitated over my own assumptions, Orm nodded, and Vahin nudged me gently towards him.

'I sent Ari to prepare a bathing chamber,' Orm said, his hand cupping my cheek. His thumb ghosted over my bruises, his scowl deepening as he surveyed the marks. 'Once you've rested, food will be brought to your room. You must be exhausted, Nivale.'

'Orm, I appreciate the idea of a bath and sleep, but I'm starving. Feed me, or I'll whine about it until you plug my gob with a bun or I get so desperate I hide in the stables and steal the horses' oats. *Please*, show me the way to the kitchen before I start gnawing on Vahin's tail,' I begged, causing both man and dragon to laugh.

'I see Orm is being neglectful. I will hunt something for you. What game would you like, Little Flame?'

'For fuck's sake, I'm not being neglectful. I will order food to be brought to the bathing chamber. Every single bun the servants can find in this damned city.'

The promise of food was all the motivation I needed. Since Orm mentioned a bath, I couldn't stop fantasizing about scrubbing away the grime that clung to me. My time in a cell felt like a stain that soap alone couldn't erase. Combined with the sweat and blood from the fight, I was ready to scour my skin raw.

'Lead the way,' I said, already anticipating the relief of hot water. 'I have so much to tell you. The Lich King—'

My words turned into a startled squeal as Orm pulled me into a fierce kiss, lifting me off my feet. Without breaking his stride, he carried me towards the mansion.

'Not today, Nivale,' he murmured against my lips before quickening his pace.

'Orm!' I laughed, clinging to him. 'What are you doing?'

'I'm making sure you end up naked in a steaming bath, a bun in your mouth, and too blissfully sated to complain when I fuck you so hard you see the stars you pray upon,' he said, his voice a low growl. 'I want to see you smile again, Nivale, and I will.'

His grim determination was so at odds with his words that I burst into laughter.

'Wipe that stern scowl off your face,' I teased, 'and you can do whatever you want to me.'

Servants scattered like startled birds as Orm barrelled through the hallways, shouting for them to clear the way. I could hardly breathe from laughing as he carried me, his strength and stubbornness leaving no room for protest.

'Orm, please, I can walk!' I protested, squealing as he finally stopped before a set of massive, ornately carved doors. Steam seeped through the gaps, curling in the air like a promise of paradise.

'I don't care,' he said, his tone rough and resolute. 'I want to carry you, pamper you, touch you. I'm not above begging to have what I want.' With a kick, he opened the doors, the heat of the bathing chamber rushing out to greet us.

I could feel the raw power coiled in his body, the need in his every move. With a contended sigh, I tilted my head to look at him.

'After such a promise, how could I ever ask you to beg?'

CHAPTER 8

ANNIKA

Verbena-scented steam billowed into my face, the warmth instantly misting my lashes. I blinked the droplets away, my breath catching when my eyes landed on Alaric lounging in the crystalline water of the deep pool. He was completely naked, his lean, muscled body on full display, and his smirk turned wicked as he caught where my gaze lingered.

'You could've opened the door normally instead of flexing,' Ari quipped, his tone light. 'Annike already knows how strong you are.'

Orm's deep laugh rumbled through me. 'Maybe I just felt like it,' he replied, setting me gently on my feet before turning to a lingering servant. 'Fetch food from the kitchen. Tell the cook Lady Annika will be dining here and bring a bottle of sweet wine as well.'

I tried to ignore the loud grumble of my stomach, focusing instead on the two men before me. Ari stepped out of the water, his movements so fluid and graceful he barely created a ripple. Water cascaded down his toned frame as he approached, and my throat suddenly felt too dry to speak.

'Will you let me stay?' he asked, his voice low and inviting.

'I . . . Yes, but Orm . . .' I hesitated, feeling completely at a loss. I wanted to be with them both, but I didn't want to impose anything on Orm, who, surprisingly, seemed quite comfortable seeing Alaric in all his naked glory.

'As if I'd let you leave. There's no need for false modesty, so help me undress her,' Orm answered before I could form a sentence.

I blinked at him, stunned, as a wave of heat spiralled down my spine. Ari's smirk widened, and as he passed his discarded clothes, he picked up a small dagger. The sinful gleam in his eyes made my breath hitch.

'This dress,' he murmured, his voice dark and velvety, 'offends your beauty. Fortunately, I have a solution.'

The blade's tip slid beneath the delicate lace of my bodice, and I froze, caught in the intensity of his gaze. His hand moved in a blur, and with a soft hiss of fabric, the laces fluttered to the floor. Cool air brushed my skin as goosebumps rose in the wake of the dress falling away.

'Hrae, you are perfection,' Alaric murmured, his voice reverent. He stepped closer, guiding me until my back pressed against Orm's broad, firm chest.

The dagger's edge traced featherlike paths over my skin, cutting away the remnants of the dress. My knees buckled, but four strong arms caught me, holding me upright.

'Steady, Nivale,' Orm whispered into my ear, his tone both teasing and protective. 'A single drop of your blood could send our fae into a frenzy. You know how serious dark fae are about bloodletting. Look—he's already hard for you.'

A whimper escaped me as molten heat replaced my shivers. Ari's eyes turned into a crimson maelstrom at my reaction. He moved with liquid grace, his lips trailing heated kisses along my neck.

'If I wanted to draw blood,' he murmured against my skin, 'I wouldn't need something as crude as this.' He discarded the dagger, taking my hand. 'Come, my lady. Let me care for you while this oaf undresses. Let's see how well his famous control holds with my hands on your body.'

He led me towards the water, Orm's deep chuckle rumbling behind us.

'Teasing me, fae? Aren't you supposed to respect and admire your lord commander?' Orm called out, his voice laced with amusement as he shrugged off his shirt.

Ari glanced back, his lips curving in a playful smirk. 'I've always been a rebel. That's how we ended up in this mess.' His hand covered my breast as he added with a wicked gleam in his eyes, 'The question remains, can you control your beast, Ormond?'

Fuck, these two will be the death of me.

My heart thundered in my chest, and I squeezed my thighs together, trying to quell the heat pooling low in my belly. 'What is going on with you two?' I demanded, my voice breathless. 'I was gone for a week. What happened?'

'Having you taken from us was ... enlightening,' Alaric admitted, his tone softening. 'We realised our connection had maybe grown more than we understood. I hope that doesn't bother you?'

'You thought I'd be upset?' I asked, baffled by his doubts. I turned to Orm. 'And you're okay with this?'

Orm's expression relaxed. 'These emotions ... they feel right. As for what they mean or where they'll go? I'm taking it as it comes.'

Ari smiled and drew me into the pool, the warm water enveloping us as it rose to my chest. He lifted my hand to his lips, gifting me soft kisses along my fingertips and up the inside of my arm. My pulse fluttered as he nibbled lightly at the sensitive skin of my neck before claiming my lips in a searing kiss.

'I live for you, my Domina,' he muttered against my mouth. 'For your courage, for the taste of your lips. You are the light to my darkness. Of course I was worried.'

The intensity of his words left me reeling, but a sudden draft sent a shiver down my spine. Orm joined us moments later, carrying an enormous tray laden with food and wine. Setting it beside the pool, he slipped into the water, his hands finding me almost immediately.

The slow, deliberate caresses of his fingers trailed water down my back, and I arched into the touch, my body responding to the double onslaught of their attentions. Whatever had changed between them in my absence, I knew one thing: I would never feel this cherished, this utterly adored, by anyone else.

'Share, Alaric. I missed her too, and my control has its limits,' Orm said, taking my chin in his hand and slowly turning me towards him. I was drowning in their sensuous heat, and when he kissed me, his tongue slipped into my mouth, teasing me mercilessly.

Yet even in this wonderful fantasy, a distant need gnawed at my awareness. My fae's hand roamed down my body, leaving sparks in its wake, just as the warm, intoxicating aroma of fresh bread and melted butter invaded my senses.

A loud, insistent growl erupted from my stomach, breaking the spell. Alaric froze, his hand pausing mid-descent as a bubble of laughter escaped me. The absurdity of the moment—the visceral need for food clashing with the electric heat between us—made me grin.

'Why now?' I sighed theatrically, placing a hand on each of their chests. 'This is perfect, but please, a woman has to eat.' I dove for the tray of food, earning twin chuckles from my lovers.

Before I could claim the golden, sugar-crusted bun that had captured my attention, Orm's strong arms caught me mid-lunge. 'Oh no, you don't,' he teased, holding me effortlessly in place as I squirmed.

'You're digging your own grave, dragon rider,' I growled playfully, glaring up at him. 'You can't just deny a hungry woman her bun. Ari, do something, I'm starving here.'

My theatrics earned more laughter as Orm settled us onto a sub-merged seat, his grip firm yet gentle. 'Patience, my heart,' he murmured, his voice a soothing balm. Alaric, grinning mischievously, slid the tray closer, finally allowing me to grab the bun and take a triumphant bite.

'Gods, you're delicious,' Orm said, one hand holding me against his chest while his other picked up a ripe, juicy piece of fruit. 'Be a good little mage and open your mouth for me.'

His irises filled with gold when I licked the sweet juices off his fingers. 'Just like that, Nivale,' he purred as his cock jerked under my arse. 'You want me to take control, yes?'

The growl in his voice was an unmistakable sign that the inner beast was holding the reins, but he still asked for my consent.

'Please,' I whispered, and he inhaled deeply as if my words had released some pent-up energy.

Alaric, ever the tender contrast, knelt in front of me with a soft cloth and scented soaps. His hands moved with reverence, creating a fragrant lather that he swept over my arms as he healed my cuts and bruises and washed away the grime of captivity. Every touch was a silent promise, every glance a reflection of his devotion. His lips curled into a silent snarl until his spells left only unblemished skin.

'You don't have to do this,' I protested half-heartedly, enjoying his attention.

'I don't have to do what?' he asked, and the low timbre of his voice sent another shiver down my spine while his dextrous hands eased my legs apart. He raised his head to look at me, and he looked so breathtakingly beautiful that I forgot what I was going to say.

'T-This,' I stuttered, gesturing at him.

'What if I want to? What if this makes me happy?' he said, leaning to kiss the soft skin of my inner thigh. 'You still don't understand, my love. While Orm is happiest by your side, I am happiest kneeling at your feet.'

What have I done to deserve you? I thought.

I studied the beautiful male kneeling before me, and I saw a strength that humbled me. I couldn't resist reaching out and trailing my fingers over his soft lips, a radiant smile transforming his features as he nipped my fingertip.

'Why?' I asked, trying to understand.

'Ani, what you did for me—' He paused. 'Why do you think Valaram mentioned the trial? He was testing you because deep down, despite all his magic and power, he envied me.' Ari placed his hands on my thighs. 'It is a privilege and the highest honour bestowed by the Dark Mother to have a domina willing to fight for you, and you proved in front of the most powerful of the dark fae court that I'm worthy . . . Ani, you gave me back my pride. How can I not kneel for you? How can I not worship you?'

Gods, I want him. I want him so much it hurts, I thought as Orm growled a curt command.

'Show her, my fae. Worship her as she deserves.'

Alaric's lips quirked into a roguish smile as he glanced at Orm. 'As you command, my lord, but I cannot breathe underwater.'

With a shared understanding, Orm lifted me to the edge of the pool. Alaric's hands slid to my knees, parting them with deliberate care as he placed kisses along my skin. I sighed, relaxing under his touch, and turned my head to the side to nestle it in the crook of Orm's neck. Orm's hands, rough and commanding, cupped my breasts while his lips teased my shoulder.

The world dissolved into sensation—their touch, their warmth, the quiet reverence and unspoken promises woven into every movement.

I was theirs, wholly and willingly, and in their arms, I found something I'd thought lost forever: a sanctuary.

Orm's lips brushed my ear, a soft caress that sent shivers racing down my spine. 'Do you like it?' he murmured, his voice low and heavy with desire. 'Fuck, I've dreamt of this—watching as he touched you, my powerful Nivale, surrendering to your men.' His calloused fingers traced fire along my skin. 'Gods, your skin is burning hot . . . You love it, don't you, sweetheart?'

'Yes,' I moaned, letting him guide me, my body ablaze with a sensation so intense it left me trembling. Helpless, yet so right. Alaric's lips pressed a languid path downwards, his mouth brushing ever closer to my aching sex. I reached for Orm's hardness, my fingers encircling him. He groaned, his fingers pinching my nipples, his teeth grazing my shoulders and neck in a flurry of sharp, biting kisses.

'What are you doing to me?' I whimpered as anticipation coiled tighter in my belly. My Ursus lifted me effortlessly onto his lap, spreading my legs wider.

'Whatever I want,' he growled, his commanding tone resonating with molten heat. 'Let Ari make you ready because I'm going to fuck you so hard you forget your name. Now, are you done protesting, or should I take you right now and tell our fae to quiet you with his cock?'

Orm's words burned through my defences, leaving only raw desire. 'I'd prefer to have my fill first,' the dark fae remarked with a smirk.

'Ari, please . . .' I gasped, trembling as his tongue found me. Pleasure spiralled out of control, my body arching, but Orm held me firm, spread open for Alaric's wicked attentions.

'It's too much. Please . . .'

I didn't know what I was asking for—too lost in the feeling, breathless and needy. Even Orm's breath against my neck was another maddening caress. The aether swirled around us, awakening and growing stronger, reacting to my pleasure and tugging on my connection to Ormond.

'Gods, Nivale,' Orm groaned, his voice thick with longing as magic filled our bond. 'I'd fight a thousand battles for this. For you.'

Alaric chuckled darkly, the sound vibrating through me. His fingers traced an electric path across my stomach, teasing sparks of aether with every movement. 'Wait until I make her come undone. I want to see what it does to you, Orm.' He pressed a finger into me, and my body instinctively tightened in response.

'Shh, my love,' Ari crooned as I cried out, the feeling as he added another finger overwhelming. 'Relax. Let me take care of you before this brute sticks his big cock inside you.' The damned scholar was studying my reactions for his own deliciously perverse pleasure, all while teasing and testing me.

My nails dug into Orm's thighs, drawing blood, as I fought to ground myself in the storm of pleasure. But Alaric's relentless teasing pushed me higher, closer to the edge, only for him to pull back again and again.

'Please, Ari,' I begged, desperation colouring my voice. 'Stop fucking around—let me finish!'

He finally relented, his thumb finding my clit and unleashing a tiny spark of aether that left me gasping. 'She's ready for you,' he declared, and Orm wasted no time, positioning me above him. His thick length pressed against me, and I groaned as he filled me, inch by excruciating inch.

Orm kissed me deeply, claiming my lips as completely as he claimed my body. His thrusts were deliberate and unyielding, each one igniting every nerve. Through our bond, his emotions poured into me—desire, pride, and an overwhelming love that suffused my being.

But it was more than that. Ormond Erenhart was a commander, not just because he was a leader, but because that was who he was. The man dominated everyone he encountered, and that force of nature now revelled in controlling Alaric and me. Deep down, my loving and respectful Anchor was bound to a beast that was no longer caged and, now that he accepted that part of himself, never would be again.

Orm's chuckle as he broke the kiss was filled with dark desire, leaving me wanting more. 'Open your mouth, Annika. Ari has served you well. Now it is time to reward him.'

Alaric stood, his arousal heavy in my line of sight. I obeyed, taking him in my hand and guiding him to my lips. His groan was music to my ears as my tongue traced his length, savouring his taste.

'That's my girl. Feed her, Alaric, and ensure she swallows all of it,' Orm commanded before quickening his pace, his growls reverberating through me as Alaric's hand tangled in my hair, urging me to take him deeper.

They worked in tandem, their movements pushing me beyond reason and beyond control. Orm's growled encouragement spurred me on, and I surrendered utterly to their demands.

My instinct took over, reaching for the fae, the binding words forming in my mind, trying to force the Anchor bond. Alaric must have sensed my magic because he shook his head, pulling my hair to distract me as he pushed deeper into my mouth while Orm took me from behind, pounding my flesh with sweet abandon.

'Hrae! Domina, can you—' Ari grunted. His body shuddered, and I grabbed his thighs, sinking my nails into his silvery skin. He tensed, crying out words in his native tongue, so melodic that they sounded like a prayer.

'Do it again, Ani,' Orm instructed, his hips bucking when my core tightened, reacting to Ari's ecstasy. 'Again, Nivale. Make it good for him,' he growled, slapping my arse and ramming his hard cock to the hilt. Stars exploded across my vision, and I scored Alaric's flesh with my nails.

I felt the swell of Ari's cock, his hand tightening on my hair when he unleashed himself in my mouth. My throat instinctively constricted when a salty taste hit the back of it.

'Swallow, Ani,' Orm grunted, his hips bucking in reaction to my fae's ecstasy. Pleasure blinded me with its intensity. My body spasmed in a powerful catharsis that wiped my mind blank. Orm came with a roar, his cock pulsing as he filled me while I sucked Alaric dry.

My warrior crushed me in his embrace, his hands soothing me as my body quaked in the aftermath. 'I think I died a little,' I murmured, barely able to keep my eyes open. Gentle hands wiped away the evidence of our lovemaking, but exhaustion pulled me under. They had worn me out, and I was falling asleep in Orm's arms as Ari finished washing my body.

'Dark Mother, she's perfect,' Alaric whispered reverently. '. . . And she's asleep.'

'She is,' Orm replied, his voice thick with emotion. 'And I'll destroy anyone who tries to take her from us again. Look at those bruises . . . Damn it, Ari, they starved her. I am going to *destroy* them for this, I . . . Double the patrols and ensure one of us is always with her. Ihrain is still dangerous, and several disgruntled nobles will be trying to oust Reynard. They will use anything and anyone to their advantage.'

'I will enlist the Brotherhood to watch over her. So far, they've delivered on their promises.'

'It would be better to set them on Ihrain's trail. I won't be calm until I see his dead body at my feet. That man is *fucking vermin*,' Orm whispered angrily, and I fought my exhaustion to keep listening.

'Wouldn't it be better to ask the mages?'

'The mages? If anything, they've caused more trouble than anyone. For now, concentrate on preparing for the trial. What is it exactly, and why was the empress so sour about it?'

'I'll tell you more later, but it's a political tool that can give your brother not only the army but also the support of the entire dark fae empire.'

'No discussing things without me,' I mumbled, trying to argue, but a big yawn interrupted my tirade. Orm bent down and kissed my forehead.

'Let us take you to bed, sweet flower. We can talk tomorrow. It will be a difficult day, but for now, you must rest,' he murmured into my ear as he lifted me out of the water. 'Ari, tell the kitchen to send snacks and bring some mead to the room. I'll be returning to the palace to see Reynard, but I want to make sure Annika is comfortable.'

I grumbled under my breath, and Orm chuckled before shaking his head.

'Try to relax, Nivale. Thanks to our brief interlude, I have a little too much energy and I intend to use it while Ari cuddles you in bed.'

'But I want you to join us.'

'And I will, but later. After you regain your strength, you can come with me anytime you want, but only if you can keep your eyes open.'

Unfortunately, he was right; my eyelids kept closing no matter how hard I tried to fight them. 'Fine, but you have to tell me everything . . .' I muttered.

'I will. Every single detail,' he promised with a smile as I slipped into the land of dreams.

CHAPTER 9

ANNIKA

Warmth surrounded me, comforting and familiar, laced with the rich scent of clove and musk underpinned by sharp, exotic spices. Silken fabric rustled as I stretched, and I couldn't help my sigh of pleasure when I realised the source of my serenity: both my men, wrapped protectively around me.

I turned to cuddle into Orm's muscular torso, enjoying the tickle of his coarse hair against my skin. A firm hand tightened on my thigh as I shifted, and I glanced down, savouring the sight of our intertwined legs and the possessive grey hand gripping my thigh.

The memory of their coordinated efforts to drive me wild ignited a blush that warmed me from the inside out. I still couldn't believe it. After all my worries, Orm not only accepted sharing me with Alaric, but if the relaxed intimacy between them was any indication, he'd also accepted Ari's company.

Makosh, Goddess of Life, bless my family, I prayed silently, overwhelmed with gratitude. *I can't live without them.*

The bed's high canopy, made of deep blue gauze, diffused the morning sun into a soft glow, turning dust motes into tiny dancing faeries. The room's décor—a mix of pastel walls, colourful drapes, and dainty furniture—was so incongruous against the rugged warrior and brooding fae beside me that a laugh bubbled up unbidden. Only their serene expressions held it at bay.

Careful not to disturb them, I slowly untangled myself, hissing as my bare feet met the cold stone floor. For a moment, I considered crawling back into their warm embrace, but a different urge took hold.

'*Vahin?*' I called out for my dragon, testing our mind's connection before reaching for the aether. Strands of magic flew to me unrestrained, wrapping themselves around my body, the power caressing me like a long-lost lover.

'Thank the gods.' I breathed a sigh of relief when aethereal fire blossomed on my palm, unfurling as I shaped it into a peony. Whether it was because of the passage of time or our vigorous lovemaking, the lanara poison had finally been purged from my body, and I felt a need to use my magic.

If I knew my way around, I could have gone to the training grounds to light up my sword with fire and dance, practising the battle mage kata until exhaustion took over. But my circumstances dictated patience. I had no sword, no clothes, and besides, my men deserved their rest after everything we'd been through.

I snorted at the absurdity of it all. *From hedge witch to kingmaker in three easy steps.* What a ridiculous story my life had become. The mental image of me dictating my scandalous exploits to a frazzled scribe almost drew a chuckle.

The sound of a deep sigh behind me caught my attention. I turned to see Alaric nuzzling into Orm's chest, the fae's body instinctively seeking warmth. Orm's strong arms encircled him without waking, their peaceful intimacy tugging at my heartstrings.

This is perfect, I thought. Everything I had wished for had somehow come together; just when I thought I couldn't be happier, Vahin's voice filled my mind.

'*Little Flame, you're awake at last. I thought they'd worn you out yesterday—or at least that was the worry I sensed in Orm's mind.*' Relief and joy radiated from him, and I couldn't help but smile. I could finally hear my dragon, and there was nothing that could compare with feeling his consciousness merging with mine.

'*I was tired,*' I admitted, '*but far from worn out. Where are you?*' I asked, moving to the window where a bowl of fruit and a carafe of wine waited. My stomach growled as I picked up a piece of exotic fruit, its velvety sweetness bursting on my tongue.

'*I'm enjoying the morning currents. Would you like me to return?*'

'*No, but talk to me, please. I missed you,*' I said, leaning on the windowsill. The sight of him gliding effortlessly above the mansion stole my breath. '*Your voice . . . I was alone in the darkness, powerless without my magic, but that didn't scare me as much as not being able to hear you.*'

'*And I missed you, Little Flame. Your absence . . .*' His voice faltered, emotions bleeding through our bond as he executed a dramatic loop in the sky.

'*Vahin!*' I scolded, heart racing.

'*You are mine to protect,*' he declared, his tone firm but tinged with vulnerability. '*I will never let the world take you from me. If the bond between us must break, it will not be my doing. I'm yours until the time stops and even the oceans turn to dust.*'

His words struck a tender chord, though beneath them, I sensed a lingering darkness—a scar left by our separation.

'*Whatever happens, even if I pass behind the Veil, you will always have a shard of my soul,*' I answered, trying to soothe him, but Vahin's thoughts became more depressive, and I felt my dragon trying to shield them from me as our happy interlude came to an end.

'*Do you know anything about this trial?*' I waited, the silence on the other side of the bond speaking louder than words. '*Vahin, tell me. Whatever it is, I want to be prepared.*'

'*Only that it forces you to face your deepest fears alone. I can lend you strength, bolster your magic with dragon fire, but beyond that . . .*' He hesitated, pain echoing in his words. '*Letting you endure this is agony for me. My kind do not take loss lightly.*'

'*You can give me strength? Are you telling me Orm is built like a brick outhouse because of you?*' I asked teasingly, trying to hide my fear from the dragon. '*Should I be worried about becoming a big, burly, hairy bear?*'

'*No, Orm's bond is different. I'm not responsible in any way for his natural attributes,*' he answered, mirth sneaking into his words before he paused. '*Annika, with you . . . Your grief called to me all those years ago. The moment I first saw you, filthy, your heart torn asunder, and determined to die and join your loved ones, I wanted you to live. I wanted it so much that my soul reached out, giving you the strength to survive, hoping one day you would find me again.*'

His memory of me—broken, caked in dirt, and determined to die with my Anchors in that avalanche—flashed through my mind. I saw myself as he had: stubborn and wild, yet alight with potential. If not for him, I'd have perished then and there, never to meet Orm or Ari.

'*Thank you,*' I whispered, tears falling from my eyes.

'*It was an honour, Little Flame. You burn so brightly, and I won't let anyone steal your light. Just remember how strong and loved you are. Whatever you face, you are no longer alone. Promise me you'll believe in yourself.*'

The determination of his thoughts made me sigh. '*Do you think it will be that bad?*'

'*I don't know,*' Vahin admitted. '*But those who survive this trial are few, and whatever they face seals their lips. Dragons know little about it, as none of them were bonded to my kind. I don't like not knowing, and it worries me not having an answer for you.*'

'*Me too,*' I replied softly, catching a glimpse of Orm stirring in bed. '*But as long as I can save Alaric, I can handle anything.*' I tore my gaze from Orm and added, '*I need to dress and meet Reynard, but I'll come to the landing field later. I have to tell him what I learned about the chancellor and the Barren Lands. My mind wasn't working yesterday, and I had . . . other things to do, but I have to tell the new king that the kingdom is riddled with enemies.*'

Vahin chuckled, the sound warm in my mind. '*Those "other things" are burned into my memory. Orm was projecting so strongly I had a front-row seat. No need to explain, Little Flame—it would only make me jealous.*'

I choked on a piece of fruit, coughing out a laugh. 'Vahin!'

The noise woke Orm, who blinked before understanding flashed in his sleepy eyes.

'You can talk to the dragon in bed, Nivale.' He smiled, stretching in a long, deliciously shameless motion. 'I wouldn't mind cuddling for a while.'

I pointed at the now nearly empty bowl of fruit. 'I can talk to him, yes, but I was famished, and the only thing I ate yesterday was a sweet roll and . . . erm, Alaric.'

Orm burst into laughter, sliding off the bed. 'We can't have you going hungry. Shall I wake Ari to feed you again, or would you prefer a normal, boring breakfast?'

Alaric's eyes cracked open, narrowing into a glare.

'Boring breakfast, please, and we need to talk to your brother. Besides, Ari doesn't look particularly edible, all scrunched up and frow—' I yelped as a pillow suddenly flew towards my head.

Orm leapt forward, grabbing me and capturing my lips in a kiss. 'No berating your man's looks after he worked so hard to ensure your good night's rest,' he teased.

I huffed, punching his chest. 'Stop it! If you're trying to punish me, shouldn't we head to the training grounds? I'm more than happy to beat you up and kiss it all better later,' I replied with a wink.

Golden flames lit in his eyes, and I knew I'd said exactly the right thing to spark his interest. Still, despite the flare of his nostrils and the way he lowered his head to nip at my neck, he shook his head.

'I wish we had time,' he murmured against my skin. 'You make me so bloody happy. I love your laugh, your teasing, even the little crease between your brows when you tell me off.' He kissed my shoulder and pulled back reluctantly. 'Come, let's dress and face the world's woes. We need to find out more about this trial. The way the dark fae reacted . . . There isn't much time to prepare, but how about we invite Valaram over and see what we can learn?'

'If you think it's a good idea,' I answered.

Orm clearly hadn't heard the last of Valaram's statement in the throne room, where he suggested courtship. Still, he must have sensed my reluctance because he tilted my chin up.

'Yes, I think it is, but I'll promise you something. Tonight, we'll lock ourselves away from the world and see just how edible Alaric truly is. They say the dark fae are at their most appetising in the moonlight,' he teased, his hand sliding suggestively over my hip.

Ari watched us from the bed with a confused expression. 'What in Veles's pit are you two talking about?'

ᛉᚳᚾᚠᛉ

The morning passed quickly. After devouring a breakfast so rich and plentiful that both men watched me in astonishment, I dressed in some of Ari's spare clothes before heading to the chambers prepared for me. Inside, Agnes was already excitedly bossing around two servants, her petite frame radiating authority as she orchestrated preparations.

'And what are you doing here?' I asked, amused at how my fresh-faced maid had taken charge of someone else's servants.

Agnes whirled around, her face lighting up. 'Lord Ormond sent a dragon to fetch me. He said you'd need a friendly face to help you recover. Your friends are too busy running the fortress to come—Miss Katja is leading the new council, and Miss Bryna has the blacksmiths crafting armour and weapons for the townsfolk, women included. I packed your sword, your verbena soap, and your clothes, but I thought you'd need something finer for city living. The servants here brought this dress . . .'

I crossed the room, pulling her into a tight hug as she continued to babble. 'Thank you, Agnes. You're the best lady's maid a battle mage could ask for.'

She patted me awkwardly on the shoulders. 'No, my lady. You shouldn't . . .' Then she whispered in a secretive tone, 'At least, not in front of them.'

'Right, so what is this?' I asked, releasing her and picking up the delicate green fabric skilfully draped over the hanger. The servants assigned to me blushed heavily under my scrutiny.

'A dress, my lady? You're Lord Ormond's mage, and your maid said it had to be good enough for a highborn noble . . . We can't have you wearing anything but the best . . . my lady,' one said, and I sighed deeply.

'Alright, but *this*? Where do I hide my daggers? Does it even have a slit so I can reach my thigh holsters?' I asked, inspecting the opalescent dress shining in the sunlight.

'You heard my lady—bring her something more practical,' Agnes snapped and attempted to snatch the dress out of my hand while the door behind her opened and my men walked in.

Alaric snorted, but Orm, ever the diplomat, came to the poor maid's rescue. He leaned in, brushing his fingers lightly against my cheek as he whispered, 'Humour me and wear it for today. On the way back, we'll buy you something more suitable with slits and extra space for weapons.'

'Off you go, I will help my lady. You don't want to be here when the masters are in the room,' Agnes urged the surprised maids out while Orm helped me out of Alaric's clothes. 'Trust me, you really don't.'

I couldn't refuse Orm's request. Even if the dress was ridiculous and left me feeling half-naked, the way both men looked at me when Agnes finally finished lacing the bodice made it worth it.

'You look divine, Domina. The entire court will envy us. What do you think, Agnes?' Ari teased my maid, who stood with arms crossed, watching him like a hawk as he pinned a flower into the updo she'd created from my messy hair.

'I think you'd better not ruin her hair, my lord,' she snapped.

I looked at my reflection in the mirror and sighed. 'We need to talk about the trial.'

Alaric's hands stilled on my shoulders. 'I don't know much, only that those asking for the Dark Mother's mercy must fight their way to the portal leading to her original temple. Ani, few reach the portal, and those who do almost never return. No one knows what horrors await beyond it.'

'So, I'll need to kill virtuous warriors and face some eldritch horror in a temple. Bloody wonderful,' I muttered, glaring at my reflection. 'And what will you be doing?'

Ari's smile was bitter. 'I'll go with you. Only the Dark Mother's touch can purge icta poison. If you fail to reach the portal, I die with you. That's all I know. Everything else is just an old legend.'

Orm pulled up a chair, his posture radiating the sharp focus he reserved for planning his military campaigns. 'What legend?'

Alaric leaned back, his gaze distant. 'About the origin of the trial. In the infancy of our race, a selfish male committed an unforgivable sin against his kin. It was so appalling that the gods sentenced him to an eternity of pain and nightmares, forcing him to drink poison. Once ingested, the poison weakened his body while his soul experienced the pain of those he killed—but stretched in time and amplified a thousandfold. His soul was torn apart in perpetuity, never letting him pass beyond the Veil.'

I frowned. 'So he suffered. But what does that have to do with the blood bond?'

Alaric's lips curled into a faint smile. 'The man had a mate. A woman who fought her way through her people's warriors to reach the Dark Mother's Temple, where he was imprisoned. They say the ground was soaked with blood before she knelt and begged the goddess for mercy. Moved by her strength and determination, the Dark Mother defied the other gods, allowing the female to attempt his salvation.

'When they emerged from the temple, they spoke nothing of what transpired, but the man was forever bonded to her, enthralled in her service. That's how our customs came to be, why women will always be above men—to guarantee we never stray again.'

I couldn't help a dry laugh. 'Only the dark fae could think of such a trial—and such an elaborate excuse to ensure women rule.' I turned to Ari, my voice softening. 'But I can fight. I'll fight the world for you. For all of us. And I'll live, if only to spite that silver bitch. Let's see how she reacts when I return, blessed by her goddess.'

I faced the mirror again, taking in my reflection. The woman staring back at me wasn't just a battle mage. She was a dignified domina, wearing her courtly armour, ready to face kings, empresses, and gods for her men. And cause bloody mayhem to save them, if necessary.

'I think I'm ready to see our new king now,' I said, a determined smile curving my lips.

CHAPTER 10

ANNIKA

We were expected—or at least that's the impression I got as we breezed past deferential guards and officials, not one asking us to wait or offer a reason for our presence.

We arrived at a small, ornate door, and Orm pushed it open without knocking. I didn't know if he knew we had permission or assumed that no one would dare to stop him.

The sight that greeted us drew a gasp from my lips as I gazed at row upon row of books and scrolls. It was the palace library. At its centre stood Reynard, bent over a map of the Lowland Kingdoms. Several tomes lay scattered around him, their titles hinting at being about the Necromancer's War or magical defences.

Up close, Reynard Erenhart was even more formidable than the bloodstained warrior I'd seen before. Even dressed for comfort, he radiated authority and control, a wild bear of a man so similar to Orm. But his eyes lacked the warmth of Ormond's and seemed as if they were assessing one's worth even when focused elsewhere.

I found myself squirming uncomfortably, but then the new king looked up and smiled. The transformation was startling. It was as if I stood before an entirely different person.

'Lady Annika,' he said warmly, gesturing to a chair. 'Please, sit down, little sister, and tell me how you tamed my cold-hearted brother.

Orm's lack of romantic success had me thinking he was saving himself for his dragon.'

'We're here to discuss plans, not my past love life,' Orm barked, his cheeks reddening under his brother's teasing.

'I didn't tame him. I just love the wild beast as much as I love the man,' I said, smiling at Alaric, who'd found some wine and was offering me a goblet. He stood behind me with a hand resting on my shoulder, and I promptly covered it with mine just in case he needed my touch to silence the Lich King's voice.

Reynard chuckled before his tone shifted. 'Well, then. If you've come to plan, then let's plan. But first, I need to know everything about your kidnapping. Annika, what happened the night you were taken?'

As we settled into nearby chairs, I recounted the events in detail: the lanara poisoned dart, Ihrain's involvement, and finally, the revelation I had saved for last.

'What do you think about the chancellor and his lapdog Ihrain, Your Majesty?' I asked, noticing his wince at the title.

'They're power-hungry fools that think arranging a deal with the Lich King gives them an advantage,' he said with vehemence. 'The chancellor thought acting as king would secure his hold, and I'd wager your abduction was his final move to usurp the crown. Damned idiot—his ambition nearly destroyed the kingdom.'

'You're wrong. He didn't want to be king.' My voice cut through the tension. 'Both the chancellor and Ihrain are agents of the Lich King. They came to Dagome from the Barren Lands, and they aren't the only ones. His people are everywhere.'

'What?' Reynard jerked from his chair and started pacing the room. 'How? The Barrier—'

'The Barrier is fading,' I said, my voice steady. 'And even at full strength, it only stops those with foul magic. It was made that way to allow dragon riders to pass, but it means that any human, or even a mage of the High and Primal Orders, can pass.'

He slammed his hands on the table, the sound reverberating through the library. 'Damn it! I was supposed to be defending this kingdom—the Lord fucking Marshall, and I've been following the orders of the enemy's dog this entire time.'

Orm approached his brother, his voice low but firm. 'We all were. It doesn't make you less of a leader. What matters now is that this kingdom needs you more than ever, my king.'

Reynard's shoulders sagged. 'Our rebellion wasn't supposed to end with me as king. I'm a general. I will see this country through the war to come, but that's all. There isn't a drop of royal blood in our family tree. The crown isn't mine to take, and judging by the unrest, the court and town agree.'

'Royal blood? What difference does your parentage make when you're the best person for the job?' Orm insisted. 'If you don't accept the title, there will be civil war as the nobles scramble for power. And while we're busy tearing ourselves apart, the Lich King will laugh himself hoarse all the way to enslaving us all. You *will* be king because *you're* the only one who can drag this kingdom out from the hole it's fallen into and stop that undead bastard from destroying our home.'

Reynard shook his head, a bitter smile tugging at his lips. 'Fuck, Orm. Not holding your punches, huh?'

'Someone has to make you see sense,' Orm replied with a shrug. 'I know it's a thankless task, but I know of no better man to do it. I'm sorry, Rey.'

The brothers exchanged a look of weary understanding. Acting on instinct, I stepped forward, placing a hand on each of their shoulders.

'We'll stand with you,' I said softly. 'Against all enemies. We are—'

My words cut off as a wave of magic surged through me, stealing my breath. I dropped to my knees, instinctively reaching for my Anchors, trying to ground myself with their strength, but nothing helped.

When I caught sight of my arm, it took a moment to realise my skin was glowing, a crimson hue surrounded by a strange haziness. However, the fear I felt from seeing it disappeared as an immense wave of aether poured into my body.

'Annika!' Orm groaned, his hand pressed to his chest. I heard the pain-ravaged roar of a dragon, then an echoing crash which focused my mind through the torment.

'*Vahin!*' I screamed in my mind, only calming slightly when re-assuring thoughts—albeit tinged with Vahin's own struggles with the torrent of power—flowed through our bond.

My Anchors couldn't withstand the aether filling my body, and I didn't know how to stop it.

'What's going on?! Someone call the royal mage!' Reynard barked to the guards, trying to make himself heard over the sudden tolling of every bell in the capital.

'No one touches her!' Alaric commanded, dropping to my side. 'Annika, look at me.'

'Don't,' I choked out, my body spasming. 'Don't touch me.'

'Trust me, Domina,' he urged. 'Let the aether flow.'

'It'll kill you,' I stammered, tears streaking my face. 'You're not my Anchor.'

The tidal wave of power that had started this was gone yet my body still blazed with the energy left behind. I didn't know why. But I was a conduit, not made to contain the aether, and my attempts to dissipate the magic were killing my Anchors.

'Domina, I'm used to pain, and I can burn off this power using a spell I would normally reserve for the battlefield. Please, Ani, let me help,' he begged, gently stroking my sweat-streaked cheek.

I nodded, biting my lip as Alaric opened his vein, using a quill from Reynard's desk to draw a complex sigil on the floor. 'Now, give me your hand,' he instructed.

I grimaced, reaching out to him without hesitation. We both winced as lightning jumped between us when our hands touched, yet I refused to let go, trusting Alaric with all our lives.

As soon as he placed his free hand in the centre of the sigil, the aether roared through me, the vortex of power pouring into Alaric. He muttered an incantation, and green light erupted, bathing the room and beyond. As the magic subsided, I collapsed against him, trembling but alive.

Reynard stumbled backwards, at the same time seeming to grow taller and stronger, until he looked at my fae with a giddy smile and asked, 'Gods, what was that?'

Voices in the corridor grew louder, followed by laughter and joyful shouts as the spell spread outwards.

'The Last Breath,' Alaric said, his tone weary but relieved. 'During battle or as a last resort, a fae healer can sacrifice their life force to create a curative spell that spreads out like a wave, healing those around them. The more powerful the healer, the further it reaches before it burns through the life of the fae. I simply used Annika's excess power to fuel it. Judging by its effects, everyone in the palace—and probably a few streets beyond—just had their ailments healed.'

Ormond came to sit beside me, and I took advantage of his closeness to lean on him, painfully aware that although I had two Anchors, neither was a mage who could help in moments like this.

'What just happened, love? Why are the bells tolling?' Orm asked, brushing strands of hair from my forehead.

Since taking from the keystone to collapse the mountain so long ago, my magic was attuned to it. In the last burst of power, I felt a pulse—a shattering wave I knew could only mean one thing. 'The Barrier has fallen,' I replied, my voice heavy with grim certainty.

The silence that followed was suffocating, almost tangible. All three men stared at me, their expressions a mix of disbelief and desperation, as if silently hoping I'd tell them it was some cruel joke. But I couldn't.

'Are you certain?' Reynard finally asked.

He looked defeated. We had run out of time, and the man now bore the unbearable weight of leading us into the Second Necromancer's War against the Lich King. I could see in his eyes how much he hated it.

'Ormond, you and Vahin will fly to the border to confirm this,' Reynard ordered.

Orm's jaw tightened, his eyes narrowing. 'Annika's trial is tomorrow. I can't—'

'Orm, I'm not asking. If you go now, you can be back before the trial. All I need is confirmation of the Barrier's status,' Reynard asserted before turning to me. 'Ani, tell me what else you know. Anything you can remember, anything you overheard while captive, may be of value.'

I licked my dry lips, and Reynard passed me a pitcher of water. After taking a sip, I answered, 'Not much. I know there are some human and Moroi settlements in the Barren Lands beyond the reach of the dragons. That's where both the chancellor's family and Ihrain are from, though I don't know exactly where. The Barren Lands aren't as barren as we thought, and the monsters we've encountered are meant to prevent riders from venturing too far.'

Orm frowned. 'How far away are these settlements?'

'I don't know.' I shrugged. 'But they're likely too distant for a dragon to reach without a conduit mage.'

Reynard tapped his finger against the table, deep in thought. 'Anything else?' he prompted, pacing the room.

'The portal . . .' The three of them looked at me expectantly, and I sighed. 'Ihrain—or another of Cahyon's servants—discovered how to create a portal to the Barren Lands. The bastard nearly dragged me through one.'

'Fuck!' Reynard cursed, his frustration boiling over. 'What can I do to stop those?'

I could only shake my head. 'If the university mages agree, we could sweep the palace and city for sigils. Ihrain must have used one to evade capture. I don't have time to search myself with the trial tomorrow, so we'll need help.'

'Yes . . . the trial.' Reynard sighed, rubbing his neck. 'I wish that situation could have been quietly swept under the rug, but we need the dark fae army. Their ambassador visited me earlier to request the use of our arena. He, too, said something about portals, but his explanation only seemed to concern your trial, not Ihrain. His eagerness to showcase your ordeal seemed, well, unhealthy, but I couldn't refuse him.'

'Did he say anything else?' Orm asked, but Reynard shook his head.

'Only that the empress and her court will attend to bear witness. I didn't argue it as more witnesses make it harder for her to back out of our deal.'

'You *what*? What kind of plan requires Annika to become a spectacle?' Ormond's voice was so frigid that even Reynard flinched.

'The kind that wins a war, brother. We need allies, and the Lowland Kingdom's banner is no longer enough to call them to arms. With the Barrier gone, I don't have time for white-glove diplomacy to convince the fae and dwarves to accept my lead. I need this to pull them to our side. I needed to show them what our conduit mage can do.'

'The threat of slavery isn't enough for them? What else do they want?' Orm was fuming, but Reynard shook his head.

'Clearly not, since my letters went unanswered. Only the dark fae showed interest, and I suspect that was likely due to Valaram's influence. If they didn't listen to an out-of-favour Lord Marshal, maybe they'll listen to the king who's just enlisted the dark fae army.'

Orm still didn't look convinced, but I placed a hand on his cheek, forcing him to meet my gaze. 'Take Vahin and check the border. I'll be fine. You can't be selfish, not right now. If you return in time for the trial, I'll be grateful. If not, I'll see you after I win.'

'I'm not leaving you,' he said hoarsely. 'I can't.'

'Yes, you can, and you will,' I insisted gently. 'Because the man I love would never abandon his people.'

Orm's hands gripped my neck as he pulled me close, searching my face for something—anything—that would let him resist. Finally, he surrendered, wrapping me in his arms.

'Why, Nivale?' he whispered into my hair. 'Why is it always us who face these trials, who sacrifice the most?'

'Because someone has to,' I murmured. 'If life were fair, my Anchors wouldn't have died, Ari wouldn't be suffering, and you wouldn't have spent your childhood beaten and broken like a rabid dog. Fate is a cruel mistress, but perhaps it's those sacrifices that brought us together. Just like us, steel is also folded and hammered to become stronger; we *have* to endure because if the strongest refuse, the weakest will break. We have so much, Ormond. Even if life is hard now, we have been given the power, skill, and opportunity to make it better for others.'

Orm exhaled deeply, his resolve hardening.

'Fine, but just to scout,' he conceded, turning towards Reynard. 'And I'll be your commander after the trial, but tomorrow, I will be with Annika. They're risking their lives, Rey. Don't ask me to stay away.'

'Thank you,' I said, kissing his cheek as Reynard uttered a silent thank you as well.

'I'll help, too,' Alaric said suddenly, drawing our attention. 'If we survive, I'll be cleared of the empress' charges and, by the Dark Mother's will, bound only to Annika.' I smiled, as that was precisely the outcome I wanted.

'When you march to battle,' he continued, 'I will come with you. The Lich King wants me because I can control his monsters, and though I'm not Anchored, I have power enough to make a difference.'

'Are you certain?' I asked, my voice catching. 'You can come as a healer—you just showed us what you could do. Why use the magic that's caused you so much pain?'

'Because my necromancy surpasses even my father's,' Alaric said firmly. 'If you insist on saving my life, I'll be embracing it as the Dark Mother intended.'

'She didn't intend for you to be a weapon.' I turned to Ormond to seek his help but was surprised to find him nodding with a knowing smile.

'Thank you. I'm sure my brother will accept your generous offer. Our lady will understand that some choices are yours and yours alone,' he said, avoiding my eyes, and I huffed my frustration.

'I understand. I just . . . Is this how you both feel when I decide to do something stupid and refuse to listen to reason?'

Despite the grim situation, all three men burst out laughing before Reynard approached Ari and extended his hand. 'Orm is right. I gratefully accept it, and I promise not to abuse your offer, even if I have to use it . . . Welcome to the family.'

Reynard's calm acceptance lit up Alaric's eyes as he shook his hand. 'Thank you, Rey.'

'Rey?' the king asked, a genuine smile gracing his face. 'Only Orm calls me that, but I like it coming from you.' He chuckled, the weight of his responsibilities briefly lifting. 'Now, you'll have to forgive me. I need to send my brother off and, for a change, be a king. Those bells tolling means the palace will likely soon be overrun with people demanding answers.' Turning, he said, 'Come, Ormond. We have much to discuss before you leave for the border.'

I stepped closer to Orm, placing my hands gently on his shoulders. 'Be careful, and don't worry about us. Just scout the area and return as soon as you can.'

He buried his face in my hair, inhaling deeply, as though trying to memorize the scent. 'Wait for me, troublemaker,' he murmured, kissing my forehead. 'I'll be back by noon. Don't fight without me, or I swear I'll lock you in Vahin's lair.'

I couldn't help but smile. 'I may even allow it, Lord Commander. Now, the sooner you fly, the sooner you'll come back to me.'

CHAPTER 11

ANNIKA

O nce Orm left, the meeting wrapped up with me volunteering to talk with the mages, though the idea of seeing my old colleagues left me feeling tense.

'Ani, someone else can deal with the council. It doesn't have to be you,' Alaric said as soon as we left the throne room. I sighed heavily, realising I hadn't hidden my feelings as well as I'd hoped.

'No, we need their help with the portals and . . . I know those assholes. With the bells tolling, they'll lock the gates and sit behind the walls like frightened sheep bleating about how to avoid fighting. I'm going to knock some heads together before they can talk themselves out of joining us. I just wish I was better dressed for the occasion.'

He chuckled slightly. 'Do I sense some lingering resentment?'

'No, I just . . . I wanted to return to university dressed like a battle mage, wearing my pin with pride. To show them I had survived against all the scheming. Instead, I'm arriving like some married noble who's forgotten they even have magic,' I said, gesturing to my courtly dress. Much to my dismay, Alaric was now openly laughing.

'You look powerful, Domina, but if you want to show them who's in charge, ride in on Orm's stallion. With a dark fae who is ready to serve you at the snap of your fingers and a mount ready to bite off the hand of anyone that dares touch you, no one will question your authority.'

'Ha! I'd prefer making an entrance like the empress. That woman turned my blood to *ice* with her stare.'

Alaric only smiled, leading us to the stables, and I couldn't help but stare at him as we walked. My beautiful, wicked fae looked so dangerous that I was sure no one would pay attention to me, even in my hideous dress.

He'd dressed in a black kaftan and matching trousers with long daggers attached to his belt. His hair, braided on the temple, not only revealed but enhanced his dark fae traits. I smiled when he reached out, smoothing a few unruly strands of my own hair that curled around my neck.

As he effortlessly lifted me onto my horse's back, I said, 'You know what? I've changed my mind. I don't want to be an empress. Being your domina is all I'll ever need.'

ᚢᚲᚾᚠᚼ

Our ride through the city was uneventful, bringing us quickly to the university grounds. The place was isolated, built on a large island created by the meandering river centuries ago. The single bridge was heavily guarded by wards and charms, and if that wasn't enough, the illusion of its never-ending path was bracketed by tall walls and heavy stone gates guarded by mages.

I looked up, exhaling slowly as I listened to the shrieks of river birds while I gathered the courage to enter. All the memories of my happy years spent in training with Tal and Arno were locked behind those gates, along with the betrayal of the events after their deaths. Though I'd finally accepted their passing, it was still a dull ache in my soul.

'Wait here, be a good boy, and I promise to bring you some tasty oats from the kitchens even if I have to steal them,' I whispered to my mount, sliding off his back. When I patted the soft mane on his neck, the stallion snorted and pawed at the ground. I swear he understood me, but when I raised an eyebrow at Ari's amused expression, he just smirked and shrugged his shoulders.

I walked towards the guard post with a confidence I didn't feel, and the men instantly straightened, sigils of ward spells lighting up at my presence—a warning and a precaution, ready to be discharged as we approached.

'You heard the bells, my lady. The grounds are locked to visitors. Please step away.'

I raised an eyebrow. 'I'm not a visitor. I'm our kingdom's single conduit mage and I demand to see the provost.'

The men shuffled uncomfortably, eyeing my dress. 'Our orders are explicit. We're in a state of emergency. Unless you are a student or faculty, you shall not pass, my lady.'

I felt sorry for them, but I didn't have the time nor patience to deal with overly zealous guards.

'I know about the emergency. I felt the Barrier fall; its power still fills my veins. So, I ask you kindly—please go to the provost and tell him that Annika Diavellar is waiting. I will enter one way or another. It is his choice whether he gets to keep these gates in one piece.'

Alaric snorted, trying to cover it with a cough. I had to resist the urge to smack him, imagining how hard he must have been rolling his eyes. We both knew the problem with my threat: both of my Anchors were slightly too far away for my comfort, and I didn't want to cause too much damage.

'Go, send the message,' the older guard said to his younger colleague, observing me warily.

'Wise choice,' I said, adjusting my dress when the damned thing billowed around my knees from a gust of wind. As I was fighting with my unruly outfit, the second guard returned to whisper something in the other's ear. Both men bowed deeply before the younger rushed to open the gate.

'Lady Annika, we meant no offence,' the older one called as we passed, and I turned towards him with a smile.

'I know, and thanks to your understanding, we avoided any unpleasantness, so no offence taken. Is the provost's office still in the main building?' I asked, and the man nodded.

We walked away undisturbed. As soon as we were out of their line of sight, Alaric came closer, whispering, 'I love this imperious look on your face.'

I chuckled, feeling the tightness in my chest ease a bit.

'It didn't put you off?' I asked, still troubled about Alaric resorting to playing my guard.

Pointing to his trousers and raising an eyebrow, he responded, 'Darling, I enjoyed it *immensely*.' And I wanted to smack the impossible rogue, but we had an image to maintain.

Alaric fell back a step as we marched towards the provost's office while I pondered my options. I wasn't sure what I was going to say, but I had to ensure the mages' cooperation.

The groups of students stared at us, whispering as their eyes tracked our movements, while expressions of hostility mixed with awe on their faces. One young mage traced the sigil for protection as I passed and I stopped, looking him straight in the eyes as I opened myself to the aether just enough for my power to be felt. As the poor boy's knees buckled, I smirked and turned away, forcing the connection closed.

At the sound of a familiar voice, my smirk dropped, and I turned.

'Lady Annika, it is a pleasure to see you again.'

The elderly artefact master approached slowly, the ornate crutch he used to compensate for the leg lost during an artefact hunt clicking steadily as he drew close. I felt myself relaxing, and the sincere smile that tugged at his lips reminded me of the fantastical stories the professor had spun about the loss of his leg.

The last story he'd regaled us with mentioned an attempt to tame a striga. Unfortunately, the sausage he'd used as bait had contained garlic, and the demon decided to take his leg instead. I suspected the old man just enjoyed fabricating more and more impossible tales.

'Master Nurad, it is a pleasure to see you,' I said with a polite bow.

'Are you surprised I'm still alive? Admit it, girl. And who might this young man by your side be? Hmm?' he asked, patting my shoulder. From the corner of my eye, I saw Alaric shift closer, but I shook my head.

I liked the old teacher. He was a powerful mage, yet so cheerful and straightforward that he'd almost convinced me to try my luck at being an artificer.

'This is Alaric'va Shen'ra. He is my . . . ehh . . . kind of husband,' I answered, wishing I could just call him my Anchor. Much to my surprise, Nurad reached out and grasped Ari's chin, tilting it to the light before stepping back.

'Shen'ra? It seems the apple fell far from the rotten tree if our Ani chose you. We all carry our own sins, boy, so don't let your father's infamy weigh on you.'

I bit my lip at the irony of calling a five-hundred-year-old fae a 'boy,' but Alaric didn't seem to mind. In fact, he placed his palm above his heart, bowing slightly, pure mischief flashing in his eyes.

'Thank you for your wise words, Master Nurad. My "kind of wife" and I will remember them, and your kindness.'

'We're going to the provost,' I cut in. 'Master, you must have felt the wave of magic. I need to find the royal mage. If you knew where he was, you would tell me, wouldn't you?'

He looked at me with gentle pity in his eyes. 'The royal mage has good reason for being difficult to find—but go to the provost as you planned. You will find your answers there.'

'Thank you, Master Nurad. I'll go there immediately.'

Pivoting to Ari, the old teacher issued him a warning. 'Guard her, boy. Even here, you will find rotten seeds.'

Alaric nodded, saying his goodbyes, before heading towards the provost's office, leaving me no choice but to follow him.

'How do you know where to go?' I asked, and he rolled his eyes.

'I spent hundreds of years searching for a way to remove the curse, remember? It's safe to say I know every university, library, and bookstore in the Lowland Kingdoms.'

'And now, my wise old man, you are bound to a fledgling,' I teased.

Ari stopped abruptly, turning to face me. The sudden movement caught me off guard, and I slipped on the fallen leaves of an old cherry tree. Before I could hit the ground, he was there, his arms steady around me, his crimson eyes meeting mine. I hadn't even realised he'd moved. The vibrant tree branches framed his face like a living portrait, but it was his gaze that held me captive.

I swallowed hard, glancing away as warmth crept up my neck, desperate to compose myself. His nearness made it impossible.

'Now,' he said softly, 'I'm bound to a woman who cradles my heart in her hands, my "kind of wife." I would give up all my years, all my knowledge, for one day with you, even if that was all the time I'd get.'

Before I could say a single word, his lips brushed mine, silencing my racing thoughts.

'You're irresistible when you blush,' he murmured as he pulled back, his breath warm against my cheek.

'Sweet talker,' I muttered, trying and failing to sound indifferent. 'And stop calling me your "kind of wife." I panicked, okay? I didn't know what to say, so I made something up.'

'Oh, but I like the sound of it,' he replied, a playful glint in his eyes.

The moment sharply ended as I caught the words being said behind us.

'Look, the necromancer and his whore,' someone sneered, their tone dripping with malice. 'He dragged the dark fae empress here to slaughter the rightful king.'

I turned slowly, my gaze locking on a group of young mages loitering beneath the tree. They seemed oblivious to the precarious situation their slander had just led them to, secure in the supposed safety of a mob.

I memorised each face, and my mind was already planning a fitting retribution, but Alaric had other ideas.

The temperature dropped, the air tinged with the unmistakable chill of necromancy. The metallic scrape of daggers leaving their scabbards cut through the tense silence.

'Care to repeat that?' he asked politely, though his quiet tone didn't mask the menace beneath his words.

'You wouldn't dare!' one of the mages stammered, trying to project confidence. 'We're on university grounds. Duels are forbidden.'

In a blur, Alaric closed the distance between them, the sharp edge of his dagger shaving a layer of skin off the man's throat. I shook my head in disappointment at the mage's lack of defence. *Did he forget he could cast? He didn't even try to set up a shield.* The rest of his cohort scattered, hastily drawing protection sigils.

'Duel?' Ari's voice was soft, almost conversational. 'I don't duel—I kill. But for someone who insults my domina, I might make an exception. Perhaps I'll grant you a long, agonising existence instead. And if I get carried away, don't worry—I can always bring you back. I am dark fae, after all. We find blood to be an excellent cleanser of disrespect.'

The dagger pressed deeper, drawing a bead of blood. The mage whimpered, shaking like a leaf as his skin turned ashen grey. When purple tendrils of necromantic magic coiled around him, the acrid scent of urine filled the air, and he crumpled to the ground, unconscious before he hit the dirt.

The remaining mages hesitated, then rallied, casting hastily drawn sigils towards Alaric. He flicked his wrist, and their spells fizzled into harmless sparks, dissipating in the air. He smirked as they scrambled to try again.

'Stop.' I sighed. 'I'm not so offended that you need to kill this many mages. Leave the fools alone.'

Alaric paused, his shoulders relaxing. Without a word, he crouched by the unconscious mage and carved a small sigil into his cheek. The act was precise, almost delicate, and I shivered at its implication. Then, as swiftly as he'd moved before, he was back at my side, his crimson gaze steady on mine.

'As you wish, Domina.'

The man screamed as magic burned deep into his skin, cauterising the wound and scarring the sigil into his flesh. I placed my hand on Alaric's forearm as we continued on our way to the library, quietly watching as the mage's friends picked him up and stumbled away.

'That was unnecessary. He was just a stupid child. You realise everyone will have heard about this by tonight?' I asked when we were a safe distance away, noticing everyone dispersing from our path the moment they spotted us.

'There is no excuse when it comes to defamation like that. Once someone makes such claims, they make the rounds, and soon, no one will remember that Ihrain killed the king. They will blame Reynard, or the empress, or even you. Now, the idiot will think twice before opening his mouth. And anyway, I enjoyed making him suffer. He called you a whore, and for that alone, I should have cut out his tongue.'

'So you made him piss himself for political expedience?' I sighed, trying to hide my irritated smile. Alaric just shrugged before entwining his fingers with mine.

'Yes, that sounds like a valid reason. Besides, as I said, no one insults my domina.'

'Alaric'va Shen'ra, you are an incorrigible bastard,' I said, choking on laughter, and he sighed dramatically.

'My mother would respectfully disagree, although my father would be happy to know if that were true. Family does seem to always make life complicated . . . or cursed, in my case.'

I couldn't help laughing at his self-deprecating joke. If we survived the trial, I vowed to make this delightfully impish male as happy as I was right then with him.

ᛉᚳᚾᚠᛉ

The provost's office was just as I remembered it.

The room held a massive table entirely covered with manuscripts, a large bay window, and a strange candelabra with fae lights floating above it, all vying for space amidst rows and rows of shelves overflowing with even more old volumes and manuscripts. Then there were the precious artefacts radiating strange power yet sitting haphazardly on piles of books or loose vellum. Among others were sigils whose magic made the room one of the most secure in the entire academy.

There were also uncomfortable chairs where students awaited the provost's mercy or punishment. I remembered those monstrosities far too well, and I was sure they were bespelled to make your rear end ache in the most unexpected ways.

Talmund and Arno's faces flashed in my mind's eye, Tal insisting I sit on his lap when I complained of my backside hurting while Arno counteroffered with a healing massage. I smiled at my reminiscence. What was once a painful dagger to my heart was now a bittersweet memory; I could look back and fondly remember the men who had been my entire world.

I turned towards Alaric, who watched me with an eyebrow raised in an unspoken question.

'Just a fond memory,' I answered, stepping closer to embrace him, laying my head on his shoulder. I wondered if Ari, too, would offer his healing services.

We were alone, which was an incredible show of trust from the provost's aide—leaving us unattended in a room filled with precious artefacts. It made me wonder if we were being observed.

'I advise you to wrap up this observation period, or we're going to make out on your desk, and trust me, you don't want a dark fae messing with your precious manuscripts,' I said loudly, pressing my lips together to prevent my manic laughter from escaping at seeing Ari's shocked expression.

'Annika, what—?' he asked, shaking his head.

'*Three . . . two . . . one . . .*' I mouthed before a hidden door opened and an old man with a lion's mane of grey hair stormed in.

'Annika Diavellar, don't you bloody dare!'

'Pleased to see you again, provost. I was hoping to see the royal mage as well. After what happened with the king, and now the Barrier, his death is the only acceptable excuse for not showing up,' I said, placing my hand over the symbol of my Anchor bonds in a battle mage salute.

Suddenly, Alaric pulled me away, positioning himself in front of me, a dagger and shield sigil appearing under his hand.

'What—' I began, just a noise alerted me that something wasn't right.

'I knew the dark fae were sensitive to magic, but I didn't realise how much. I'm glad you survived, child. Now, can you tell your fae to lower his weapon? I don't want to get skewered before he realises I'm not a threat,' said the man who emerged from behind the provost.

'Ari, that's the royal mage,' I said, placing my hand on his until he lowered the blade. 'My lord, I'm happy to see you. It is about time we talked.'

'I know who he is, but what I don't know is what Ambassador Valaram is doing here,' Alaric responded, staring straight into the darkness of the passage.

A rich, melodic laugh flowed out and Valaram emerged.

'Is that everyone, or should I expect a party? I don't know if I should call for reinforcements, not that a dragon would fit in here anyway, but we could try,' I deadpanned, hoping they wouldn't see through my bluff.

'Your dragon is flying to the borderlands as we speak. Stop posturing, child. We are all here because we're concerned about the same things,' the provost said, gesturing towards the chairs and transforming them into a comfortable sofa. 'Let's sit.'

'I bloody knew it,' I muttered under my breath before addressing the royal mage. 'If you all knew that Vahin was flying to the border, you know the Barrier has fallen. I can't be the only one who felt that wave of aether.'

'Yes, we know,' the provost admitted. 'Is that why you came? To deliver the news?'

I looked each of the three men in the eyes. How were they so calm? There were *people* in the borderlands, most with no idea that the Barrier had collapsed. Yet here we were, sitting around like it was high tea.

'No, I came to tell you it's time the Council of Mages pulled their heads out of their arses and help. You have trained battle mages, healers, and artificers, and I want to send them where they are needed most. I get it—the old king was a puppet controlled by our enemy, but now? Why are you just sitting here when there is so much to do?' I turned towards the royal mage. 'And why aren't *you* in the palace helping Reynard? Where were you when Ihrain drew the portal to drag me to Katrass?'

'I can't help because Ihrain has my geas,' he finally confessed. 'When I first noticed something was wrong, I confronted him, only for the scum to pull my geas from his pocket. The only thing I was able to do was give Ormond yours to protect you.' Seeing my shocked expression, he continued, 'I'm not in court because I still have a key and spells that unlock the geas vault. Would you like me to give it to him when he orders me to?'

'What—? Fuck. *How?* Only the king holds royal mages' geasa—' I started.

'And we both know how lucid the king was,' he interrupted.

'But you can help now. With Reynard as king . . . You know about the Barrier, but did you catch the part about Ihrain creating portals to the Barren Lands? You need to send a team to the city to ensure all those who serve the Lich King are brought to justice. You should also send battle mages and healers to the borders and, for the gods' sakes, have them train with dragons—*really* train, as in, fighting in the air on dragon back.'

The royal mage looked at me for a long while. The silence stretched on, and the provost shifted uncomfortably in his seat.

'She may be right, Riordan.'

'I never said she was wrong. Alright, Lady Annika. Here is my compromise: the council will support your king, and we will follow your demands . . . under one condition.'

'Which is?' I asked.

Judging by the smirk that ghosted his lips, I knew I wouldn't like the answer.

'If you survive tomorrow's trial, you will find and kill Ihrain and become my apprentice, just like I had planned for after you killed the wlok.'

'What?' I gasped, and only Alaric's quick reflexes saved the wine glass I'd grabbed when I cocked back my arm to launch it at Riordan's head.

'That has to be the—I don't have the patience or desire to deal with the politics of that position. Besides, I'm needed in the army. The riders need me to fight the spectrae,' I said when I regained the ability to speak.

He simply shrugged. 'I can't live at the university until Ihrain is dead, and I need someone who can speak to the king on the council's behalf—someone the king will trust.'

'Fine,' I conceded. 'If you don't find a better candidate, I guess I can do it.'

The ambassador chose that moment to begin slow clapping, startling me.

'Bravo, my lady,' Valaram declared with an inscrutable smile. 'I look forward to working with you and your king.'

'And what about *your* people?' I snapped. 'Will you fight with Reynard?'

'That's not my decision to make, pretty mage. The empress is the only one that can make that choice.'

'Okay, then what can I do to convince her to join? Our two nations won't stand a chance apart; together, we might defeat him,' I urged, desperate to get something from him.

'Survive the trial, lara'mei.[1] My empress cherishes strength, and I've given you the opportunity not only to save Shen'ra's line but make her believe humans can be worthy allies.'

'So that's why you helped me?' I asked, confused. 'What if I fail? You're wagering the fate of two kingdoms on a supposedly impossible task.'

Something in Valaram's stance softened at my words, though his expression remained unreadable. I thought I may have even detected a flicker of sincerity, a wish for my success.

'I helped you to see how far you'd go to defend your man,' he replied. 'But even if I hadn't, there is no other way, lara'mei. Your court is not the only one affected by the Lich King's corruption. When your king faded into insanity, messages promising peace and prosperity to the fae and dwarven kingdoms arrived from the Barren Lands. *If* we sacrificed Dagome. Even my empress is swaying, believing she may have to choose the lesser evil for the survival of our people.'

---

1. **Lara mei /pron:Lara-may/** — My chosen. Endearment used by dark fae males for the women they consider suitable mates—a signal of intention used in courting rituals.

The world slowly began to tilt beneath me. I placed a hand on my chest, breathing hard as my heart raced, fighting a wave of panic.

'Breathe, Domina. There is still hope . . .' Alaric's voice echoed through a fog.

Now I understood. No one else had answered Reynard's call for aid because they sought to purchase peace at the expense of Dagome's future.

Valaram's voice broke through my thoughts. 'But the empress cannot refuse the goddess. Those who survive the trial earn the right to speak for the Dark Mother. All you have to do is ask for what you want.'

A question surfaced in my mind then, insistent and unshakable. 'How did you know to bring the empress at the exact time of the attack?'

'I have my spies,' Valaram admitted with a faint smile. 'I knew Alaric was in the city. What I didn't know was whether the rumours of you being blood-bonded with him were true.'

This male—this scheming politician—had orchestrated events to force the empress into a corner, gambling my life on the slim chance I could accomplish the impossible.

I stepped forward, extending my hand to him. 'Thank you.'

Valaram hesitated before taking my hand, his eyes searching mine for any sign of unease at touching a dark fae. His magic tingled on my fingertips as he bowed and lightly brushed his lips along my knuckles.

'You're welcome, lara'mei. What an intriguing creature you are. It's a shame you are already mated—' Valaram's voice was velvet smooth, but it cut off as I felt Alaric's hand settle firmly on my waist, pulling me closer to him.

'She is,' Alaric said, his voice laced with menace. 'So please remember she is not your lara'mei.'

Valaram's lips curved into a smirk, his head tilting slightly, unfazed by the warning. 'My apologies, Shen'ra. But if your domina has any objections to me, I'm sure she's capable of speaking for herself.'

I glanced between the two men, unsure of what had just happened. Valaram's smug composure contrasted sharply with Ari's coiled fury. Unwilling to be caught in the middle of their posturing, I turned towards the royal mage.

'Are we done?'

'Yes, we are done,' he answered.

I exhaled slowly. 'Good. Then I'll see you tomorrow. Let's hope the Dark Mother truly proves merciful.' Not waiting for a response, I turned on my heel and left without a backward glance.

ᛟᛈᚻᚨᚼ

We slowly made our way to the gates, my mind racing over what we'd learned. Even though we'd gained more than I expected, I couldn't escape the feeling that I was a puppet on someone else's strings.

When we finally reached the horses, Alaric placed a hand on my shoulder, turning me before grasping the nape of my neck and kissing me, roughly staking his claim for the entire world to see.

'Ari?' I asked, my voice tinged with uncertainly as I pulled back slightly. This wasn't like him—not my calm, steady fae. I'd have expected such an outburst from Orm, not Alaric.

'Don't let him get into your head,' he said. 'Valaram may have helped us, but don't let him court you. You might think it's harmless wordplay, but he knows exactly what he's doing.'

Crimson swirled in his eyes, and his fingers pressed painfully into my flesh.

'Are you jealous?' I asked softly, the realisation dawning on me. My question seemed to strike a chord, and his grip softened as a shadow of guilt crossed his face.

'Yes,' he admitted after a long pause, his voice quieter. 'I thought I was above such things, but I'm not. You are *mine*, Annika, mine and Orm's. And I can't—'

'You don't have to,' I interrupted gently, placing a hand on his chest. 'But please . . . take me home. I'm tired, and if I'm meant to face the fates tomorrow, I need to rest. You do, too.'

His second kiss stopped me before I could say anything more.

CHAPTER 12

ANNIKA

I sank neck-deep in the verbena-scented bath Agnes had ordered me to take. I was beginning to think that sweet, innocent girl had been possessed by the soul of some ancient warrior queen. One unflinching look from her, and I'd meekly undressed and climbed in without argument.

I couldn't deny it was exactly what I needed. The tension of the day slowly melted into the steaming water, but just as my muscles began to unwind, a glowing portal shimmered into existence above me. A letter materialised and floated before my eyes, demanding my attention.

The moment I read it an icy chill settled over me. I tossed the letter and it landed on the floor, pristine despite my rough handling—yet another silent testament to the empress' power. As if creating a portal to send it through wasn't enough.

The message contained my instructions for the trial. No weapons. No armour. Only the 'clothes of the penitent,' which would be delivered later. I snorted at the absurdity. *Someone clearly enjoys dressing up her playthings.*

Ever since I'd agreed to the trial, I'd kept myself busy, trying to avoid thinking about it. But now, alone in the bath, intrusive thoughts threatened to choke me.

I should be preparing. But preparing for *what*?

I knew how to fight the dark fae, and entering a portal didn't take much unless I somehow forgot how to walk, but Alaric didn't know what awaited me in the Dark Mother's Temple, and I didn't trust Valaram enough to ask.

'*Vahin?*' I tried to reach out to my dragon, desperate to feel his reassuring presence. But he was still too far away. While Orm had promised they would be back by tomorrow, flying day and night without rest would be arduous.

I had very little hope they would return in time. The journey to the borderlands took a full day under perfect conditions—clear skies, steady winds, and a direct path—and I doubted Orm and Vahin would be so fortunate. So, I tried to mentally prepare myself to face the trial alone.

If I could create a portal and bring them back ... I thought. But that was fae magic, instinctual to them and maddeningly complex for human mages.

My mind began to drift, thinking about it and mulling over the distinctive magical traits of the various races. Conduits were born almost exclusively to humans, and every dark fae seemed to be born with some form of necromancy, while mentalism was the domain of the light fae. All races had developed some form of combat magic, but humans excelled in it, and we had several bloodlines that produced primal-order paladins of legendary power. Then there was wild magic, which no one seemed to understand, except maybe the dragons and monsters, but none of them were sharing anything about the ferocious power.

My distraction lasted for a few minutes, but I'd never been interested in the academic side of magic and soon gave up. I left the bath before Agnes came back, knowing she would be displeased by my show of independence. My *personal* maid took her responsibility seriously. I indulged her because, for some inexplicable reason, it gave her so much pride and joy to wait on me that I didn't have the heart to tell her I was perfectly capable of looking after myself.

Water dripped onto the stone floor as I stood before the mirror. I looked at my body, the muscles and scars from years of fighting monsters a reminder that I'd never shied away from a challenge. Despite that, when I looked at the emblem of my Anchor bonds, I felt my heart beat harder.

Come on, Ani. You've survived so much. You'll survive this, too. You have *to.*

I repeated the words like a prayer, but the doubts I'd pushed away returned with a vengeance. How could *one* person stand against a power that predated humanity? Against politics that turned allies into foes, that stripped Dagome of all support, and threatened to kill my fae?

The room darkened as a draft from the open window snuffed out most of the candles. Wrapping a towel around myself, I abandoned the idea of finding a nightdress and crawled into bed, curling around the pillow that still smelled of musk and cloves.

'My Ursus,' I whispered, burying my face in the softness. 'I need you so much.'

The tears came then, silent and bitter. For the world, for Alaric, even for Vahin, I was strong. But with Orm, I could just ... be. His love was an unyielding fortress, and as the fear of not being good enough—strong enough—choked me, I wished he was there to hold me.

A soft knock broke through my quiet sobs, and I hurriedly sat up, wiping my face. With a flick of my fingers, I coaxed the aether to extinguish the remaining candles, cloaking the room in shadow. I didn't need Agnes to see me like this.

'Enter.'

The door opened, and Alaric walked in carrying a tray that smelled of fish stew and freshly baked bread. It was my favourite comfort food. But tonight, the smell turned my stomach. Moonlight spilled through the window, highlighting the furrow in his brow as he scanned the room.

'Why are you sitting in the dark?'

'I'm tired and wanted to rest early. After all, I'll need to be in top form tomorrow,' I answered, injecting as much cheer into my voice as I could muster.

Alaric placed the tray on the nightstand, his expression unreadable as he stepped closer. Conjuring a soft light above us, he tilted my face to look up at him.

'You lied to me,' he said, his fingers brushing over the streaks my tears had left.

'It's nothing,' I muttered, turning my head.

He sat next to me, pulling me close. 'And now you're lying to me again. What is it, Ani? Don't hide from me, my love. If you're trying to protect me, don't. It will only make me worry more.'

'I'm afraid. That's it, I promise. I'm just afraid of tomorrow.'

'I'm afraid, too. I can feel the icta poison coursing through my body, and I wish there was something I could say or do to stop you from going through the trial.' I looked at him sharply. 'But there's nothing that would change your mind. I know you, Domina. I know that tomorrow, you will do whatever it takes to win. I don't have faith in the Dark Mother's mercy, but I have faith in *you*.'

His smile carried a hint of sadness as he bent to kiss the tip of my nose, and the tenderness in his eyes made my breath catch.

'We can't control what tomorrow brings,' he said, his voice steady, 'but let me hold you tonight. Rest will make it easier to face our fears.'

I nodded, shifting to make space for him on the bed. The silken sheets rustled as he slid in behind me, wrapping me in his warmth.

'Sleep, my love,' he murmured. 'Whether or not I survive tomorrow, holding you brings me peace.'

I had no answer to that. Instead, I let his heartbeat lull me to sleep.

ᛟᚲᚾᚠᛉ

'My lady, wake up! Please wake up! The fae came to take Master Alaric, and swords have been drawn.'

'What?!' I bolted upright, looking at the bed beside me only to find it empty. After Alaric cuddled me, he had stroked my back until I'd fallen into a deep, dreamless sleep, and I was still confused after being unceremoniously woken up.

Agnes threw a simple blouse and kirtle over my head, ignoring my curses as she helped me fight the unruly garment. A moment later, I rushed down the stairs towards the raised voices and unmistakable crackle of magic.

'You are not taking me until my domina is aware of the situation.' Alaric's angry tone could be heard on the stairway. 'I can't disappear on her.'

'What the fuck is going on?' I shouted, charging down, ready to rip some heads off.

I pushed my way to stand between Alaric and the soldiers with their swords drawn. My magic flared to life, and the fool who had almost stabbed me in the stomach was about to learn that pissing off a mage before she'd had her breakfast was a bad idea.

'Annika, no!' Alaric caught my arm, but my anger needed an outlet.

'Sheath your toothpick or I'll melt it down and feed it to you,' I growled at the soldier, grasping the sword and sending a wave of fire up the blade. The guard paled under his helmet but held the warping metal as he stumbled back.

'I'm under orders from my empress,' he stammered. 'The accused must be delivered to the mages to prepare for the trial.'

'And what preparation would that be?' I snapped, though dread coiled in my stomach.

'I'm not privy to the details, my lady,' he said, his voice faltering. 'But the empress foresaw your reluctance and instructed me to remind you that icta poison can only be neutralised once you reach the goddess.'

The stench of burnt flesh permeated the space before I realised my anger had infused my spell with too much power. I released the blade and turned towards Ari, finally allowing him to pull me to his side.

'I have to go, Domina. I just didn't want to leave without saying goodbye.'

'She should have warned me about this instead of sending a useless letter,' I said, swallowing hard.

I hadn't expected this. I thought we would go to the arena together, and even if Alaric wouldn't be fighting, at least he'd be there with me. Without Orm or Vahin, I needed him to keep me grounded, but the empress had apparently decided to strip me of any support.

'No, this isn't goodbye. Just . . . wait for me and don't let them hurt you, will you?' I said, fighting back tears.

Alaric embraced me, his lips brushing over my forehead in a chaste kiss. Looking up into his eyes, I knew what he thought our chances were.

'Always, my Domina,' he whispered. 'If death comes to take my soul, she will have to fight a very determined necromancer.'

He was cracking a joke for my sake. I nodded and forced a smile, pretending to play the game as he turned and left me standing on the stairs while the guards escorted him away.

I still had three more hours to go, three more hours to stew in my thoughts.

ᛉᚴᚾᚠᛦ

'There, now you look every bit the veteran battle mage. Not a strand will dare slip loose,' Anges said, tying off the intricate dragon braid she'd woven. 'You could even hide a stiletto blade in here, disguised as a hairpin,' she mused, looking at the many daggers Alaric had left behind that morning.

'Your Ladyship isn't allowed to take any weapons,' a voice drawled from the doorway behind us, causing Agnes to jump and yelp.

I threw a bolt of energy towards the voice, only to see it stall near Valaram's outstretched hand. The dark fae ambassador simply stood there, studying my impromptu creation with unbridled curiosity.

'How interesting; you plucked the aether out of thin air. Impressive trick, my dear. You will certainly need it,' he commented.

I rose to face him. 'What the fuck are you doing here?' I asked, fighting to calm my racing heart. I hadn't heard him arrive or sensed a powerful mage, and that didn't bode well for the upcoming trial.

'I came to deliver your penitent's robe,' he said, dropping a package onto the table. 'A ridiculous tradition, by my lady insists.'

He shifted his attention to Agnes. 'Take it, child. Make it ready for your mistress. I need some time alone with her.'

Agnes stiffened. 'No. You've already taken Master Alaric. Some-one has to look after my lady, and I won't leave her. You'll have to kill me first.'

'Should I grant your wish? I could kill you, then revive your corpse after I finish my conversation,' he threatened, the corner of his lips tilting up when a pale Agnes turned towards me with a haunted expression.

'Can he do that?' she whispered, and I huffed, shaking my head.

'No,' I said firmly. 'He's just a man who thinks he has power here. However, I'd like you to do as he asked. I'll be fine, I promise. Just make whatever's in the package presentable.'

Agnes nodded before casually strolling to the table and taking the package, but as soon as the door closed behind her, I could hear the pounding of her feet as she ran down the stairs.

'Curious little creature you have there,' Valaram murmured as he approached me. 'Curious and loyal.'

I took a step back, then another, but the further I retreated, the sharper his expression grew. Finally, there was nothing but the wall behind me and the looming fae in front of me. Time seemed to stretch as he leaned forward, bracing a hand against the wall beside me.

'Are you afraid of me, Lady Annika?' he murmured, his voice a silken trap.

'Of course I am,' I replied, lifting my chin. 'I've fought Alaric. It's given me a healthy respect for dark fae magic.' My voice re-mained steady, though I frowned as he slowly wrapped my braid around his other hand.

'Clever answer,' he said, his tone laced with intrigue. 'Would you give me another? Why do I keep seeing you? That scene in the throne room . . . I can't forget it.'

'How should I know?' My patience snapped. 'And I have a question, too; I want to know what the fuck you think you're doing. Get out of my face before I punch—'

Before I could finish, he dared to press a finger to my lips, silencing me.

My knee shot up and Valaram crumpled, a gasping laugh escaping his lips as he fell back several steps.

'Just *what* is so funny?' I was utterly baffled by his behaviour. Why was an elegant and experienced diplomat acting like some horny teenager?

'You are, Annika,' he said. 'Humans don't live long enough to become interesting, yet you fascinate me like no other.'

I blinked at him, wary as his expression shifted from one of mischief to seriousness once he'd recovered from my assault. 'I am here to remind you of the trial's rules. You're forbidden from carrying weapons into the arena. To seek the Dark Mother's mercy, you must demonstrate absolute faith—hence the penitent's robe and annoying rituals. But heed my advice: though you can't *enter* with a weapon, you can *leave* with one. What you gain in honest combat is yours to keep. And you'll need every advantage when you pass through the portal.'

That nugget of information was worth its weight in gold, and I understood why he had insisted on making Agnes leave. If his empress learned he was telling me this, I didn't think even the Dark Mother's mercy would save him from that vicious woman.

'Why are you risking helping me?' I asked quietly, narrowing my eyes as he took a step closer.

'Because I believe the Lich King must be destroyed, not appeased. The only way my sister will change her mind is if the goddess blesses those willing to fight him.' A shadow of doubt crossed his face before he added, 'And because I want you to win, lara'mei. A woman like you deserves more than two mates, and those chosen by the goddess have the pick of any male in our empire.'

Well, that escalated quickly.

'You mean I can choose you?' I asked, rolling my eyes when he inclined his head in agreement. 'No, thank you. I already have one dark fae in my bed; I've no room for another,' I said, but Valaram only smiled.

'I'm a patient and persuasive man. I can wait until you change your mind.'

'Maybe you can, but I'll be long dead by then,' I answered with a shrug, ignoring the twitch of his jaw. 'Now tell me what other surprises your empress has in store for me.'

'No surprises, lara'mei,' he replied. 'All you have to do is to open the portal. Once you cross over with Alaric, the rest will just happen.'

'Can Alaric open the portal? Is he coming with me or are you sending me all alone like a lamb to slaughter?'

He shook his head. 'You are no lamb, and yes, Alaric can, but not without you. He was taken to learn the spell, but the portal requires blood. You must be willing to fight for your mate, to bleed for him,' he said, pausing for a moment. 'Once you're through, you'll be in another plane with its own rules. If you succeed in entering the Dark Mother's domain, nothing will be as it seems—even time passes differently.'

'Wonderful, so I'll arrive on the divine plane wounded and bleeding?' I asked, incredulous. 'And I'm supposed to take Alaric with me, but won't he be sick from the icta poison? Am I supposed to find a magical herb to heal him or something?' I bit my lip before asking, 'Do you really think I'll encounter her, or is it just another fable?'

'The goddess' mercy will purge him,' Valaram said simply. 'That is the legend.'

'And what of the goddess herself? Does the legend say how to charm her? Is there a specific offering or prayer that might win her favour?' His only answer was a slightly raised eyebrow. 'You know what, never mind, I'll think of something when I get there.'

Just then, the door burst open, and Agnes stormed in, shaking a white scrap of fabric in her fist.

'They are trying to humiliate you, Ani. This rag will barely cover your tits!' she fumed, blushing when she noticed Valaram still there, standing in the shadows.

'Yes, I'm still here,' he said, unbothered. 'Now, dress your lady so I can escort her to the arena.'

He settled into a chair uninvited, and I stepped behind the privacy screen. Fighting him would have been pointless. The look he gave me told me that no matter how nicely I asked, the dark fae wouldn't be leaving.

CHAPTER 13

ANNIKA

I pulled on the long, flowing skirt, thinking that maybe Agnes had been exaggerating. The slit ran relatively high but covered everything quite well. However, when my maid helped me into the linen shirt, it soon became a battle for us both to close the buttons over my breasts. After several minutes of yanking, cursing, and praying to the gods, my dignity and my breath had long since left my body—but I was finally ready. I exchanged a knowing glance with Agnes, and she quickly found me a shawl.

'I look like a sacrificial virgin—or a prostitute on her debut,' I muttered, covering the straining fabric.

I was going to fight a bloody battle in a negligee that would likely prompt cheers for all the wrong reasons. It didn't help that Valaram's smirk transformed into a broad, shameless grin the moment I stepped out from behind the privacy screen. If looks could kill, he'd have been a pile of ash on the carpet, but nothing seemed to faze him, so I simply ignored him.

The journey to the arena was thankfully short and silent. Soon, we were in front of the gates to the pit, the entrance for performers and combatants. The heavy iron grate seemed more fitting for a prison, speaking volumes about how the kings of old loved to watch their offenders fight monsters. The arena itself was a towering three-story structure, complete with a special seating area for nobles and a royal balcony, all surrounded by the muffled roar of an eager crowd.

They were here to see me die—spectators with wine-stained lips and greasy fingers clutching roasted meats, ready to enjoy a night of carnage at my expense. I felt utterly alone.

'Vahin, I'm afraid and angry. I miss you so much. Wherever you are, if any shred of this reaches you, remember that I love you, my beautiful soul.'

My thoughts drifted to Orm, my other Anchor, and how much I wished he were here. Not to fight my battle, but to hug me before I faced it. *I bet he'd love my outfit*, I thought, chuckling and imagining how hard he'd roll his eyes at seeing it.

Interrupting my reverie, the sound of trumpets startled me from my thoughts. With a screech of its unoiled hinges, the iron grate slowly open, and an officer gestured me forward. I walked alone, gripping the hem of my dress when the wind whipped the fabric up around my knees. Not that it mattered.

The hum of the crowd quieted to an eerie silence as I entered the fighting pit. To my left, a massive portal sigil loomed on the wall, etched in a dark red substance that I refused to believe was blood. Several dark fae mages stood near it, nodding in greeting as I passed. The simple gesture halted my steps, and I stood, glancing at the size of the portal until the fae guard touched my shoulder.

'You are expected to address the empress first, my lady,' he said, motioning to the royal balcony at the far end of the arena.

I turned towards the balcony, my attention snapping to the figure seated in the centre. The empress. Talena'va Daren'ra. She was beautiful, her silvery skin glowing faintly, her mature but timeless eyes set in a heart-shaped face and framed by a cascade of jet-black hair. Her cold, unyielding gaze could have frozen fire, but I refused to flinch. Next to her sat an uncomfortable-looking Reynard.

My focus shifted, and my stomach churned. Alaric. *That bitch chained my fae,* I thought. My mate stood shackled on a dais below the empress, dressed only in black leather pants, his wrists bound in iron. Two veiled priestesses flanked him, their presence a sinister omen.

'What a shit show,' I muttered under my breath, 'but at least we have equally ridiculous outfits.'

The guard behind me snorted, his laughter almost friendly. 'It will be a shame to kill you, mage,' he said as we walked towards the balcony. The sincerity in his voice surprised me.

'I don't intend to die,' I replied evenly, 'so don't get in my way.'

'I serve the empress, my lady, and I will do what I'm ordered,' he countered. 'Still, it is a shame.'

Before I could respond, a spell-enhanced voice cut through the arena.

'Bring the penitent closer,' the empress commanded.

Her words carried weight, and I felt it like a shove. Sand crunched beneath my boots as I walked towards her. I understood her need for revenge after her mate was killed, but it didn't mean I would let her kill mine.

The chanting of mages filled the air, their melodic tones weaving an invocation I couldn't understand. The thumping of heavy boots was almost deafening as soldier after soldier entered the arena—but I refused to look away from the empress until her mouth twisted in disdain.

'Behold the one who, in her arrogance, challenges my judgement. She demanded the right to appeal to the Dark Mother's mercy for this callous murderer chained before you.' Her disdainful glare bore into me. 'Did you know that only two couples have survived this trial in its entire history?'

'Well,' I replied, my tone casual and defiant, 'at least that means someone survived, and facing certain death isn't exactly new for me. I keep trying to die, but it appears Morana[1] doesn't want me yet. Ask my necromancer. He's healed me enough times to know that near-death experiences are my favourite pastime.' I rolled my shoulders with a smirk, as if warming up for a fight.

'I almost admire your arrogance. Fine, prove me wrong. See if you have what it takes to draw enough blood for the portal's magic.' She gestured towards Alaric. 'My brother told me you strive to protect others. Let's see if you can strive equally well to kill.'

'Care to elaborate? I must have skipped a few classes on dark fae customs—I'm not sure I grasp the rules. Who do you want me to kill?'

Talena's wording, especially the mention of drawing 'enough' blood, gave me chills. *Did she really expect me to kill people?*

'To open the portal, you must saturate it with the blood of the fallen. A sacrifice is required to enter the Dark Mother's domain.'

'I'm assuming we aren't sacrificing a goat?' I asked, and both Reynard and Valaram had sudden coughing fits, trying to cover their laughter.

'No, but you can withdraw, and Alaric will face the consequences of his actions. Enough of this, Lady Annika. End this charade and let me call the executioner!' The empress' voice surged with authority, a menacing wave of purple energy radiating from her.

'If you want me to kill your warriors, I'll do it, but why not let us go? Let bygones be bygones. No matter how painful the past is, his death

---

1. **Morana** — goddess of death and winter.

won't bring your mate back,' I told her, but her expression remained stone-cold. She wasn't backing down.

'We are not barbarians, my lady,' Valaram interjected. 'No one needs to die except the guilty. All you have to do is shed enough blood to activate the portal. Our healers are ready to take care of the wounded.'

I inhaled sharply. He was risking his empress' wrath to reassure me.

'Brother, until the trial is complete, you are not to speak another word, or I will charge you with treason,' Talena snapped. The ambassador bowed slightly, placing a hand on his chest before sending me a radiant smile. I wasn't sure why, but his unrepentant help made the ordeal feel slightly less dreadful.

My attention shifted to Alaric as he was dragged towards the portal sigil. Two priestesses chained him in place, their ritualistic movements slow and deliberate. When they cut into his forearms, crimson streaks darkened his pale skin, and I gasped, instinctively stepping forward. Valaram shook his head, halting me. Fury burned in my chest as I watched the priestesses trace the finishing runes in his blood.

'Alright, Your Majesty. Now that you've set the board, what's next?' My tone dripped with disdain, and Talena's lips spread into a cruel smile, her cold eyes gleaming as she studied my outrage.

'Attack!' she commanded, her voice reverberating across the arena.

Her order hung in the air for a breathless moment before chaos erupted. The thunder of boots made me turn just in time to see a unit of fae warriors charging towards me. I'd expected more tedious rituals, more theatrics. This outright assault caught me completely unprepared.

Spinning to face the oncoming soldiers, I stumbled on the hem of my torn dress, and the fragile fabric ripped, sending me to the ground.

'Look out!' Reynard shouted. I cursed up a storm, but my fall saved my life as a spear flew past, embedding itself in the wall being me.

'You *motherfucker*,' I gritted through clenched teeth, eyeing the soldier who threw it. I tore away the remaining fabric binding my legs, ignoring how it left my thighs exposed. The arena seemed to shrink as the warriors closed in, armed and relentless.

The situation appeared hopeless. There were at least thirty of them, if not more—all trained warriors, armed to the teeth. Meanwhile, I stood there unarmed and holding the white hem of my dress like a flag of surrender.

Make them bleed, I repeated in my mind, the words becoming a mantra. That was all I had to do—draw blood. My breathing slowed as I entered a hyper-focused state, detaching from fear, anger, and pain. The world around me dulled, narrowing to the singular task ahead.

I noticed that some of my enemies weren't rushing forward. I felt the telltale shift in the aether; they were casting spells while the others prepared to overwhelm me physically. Their precision, their unity—it was intimidating, but I wouldn't let it break me.

I looked at the faces of the men rushing towards me, remembering the guard that had accompanied me earlier. None of us had a choice, but it was for Alaric and the future of Dagome. So I would break through the metal and leather armour, smash apart the magical shields protecting them, and make them bleed.

I was no hero. I was simply a woman struggling against the odds to find a sliver of happiness. I didn't want to leave behind a sea of tears, but I wasn't afraid of getting my hands dirty.

I slid my foot back, bracing myself as one soldier swung at my chest. Time slowed. I sidestepped, looping a scrap of fabric around his wrist and twisting sharply. His momentum sent him sprawling. Planting my feet, I yanked hard, and a sickening crunch signalled his defeat as he dropped his weapon.

Another soldier lunged at me, but I was quicker, ducking under his blade to seize the hilt. Pain seared my arm as someone else's blade sliced through my flesh, but I ignored it, not noticing the way the sand hissed when my blood fell onto it, too focused on securing my weapon. When my fingers closed around the handle, a familiar blue fire erupted down its length. Satisfaction flickered as fear lit my opponent's eyes.

'That's right, pretty boy, now run,' I muttered, slashing his arm and sending a spray of blood into the air. The crowd roared, their cheers drowning out the strange hiss of the sand beneath me.

Surrounded, I released a surge of raw power. It cost me, but it scattered my enemies, giving me precious space to move. I launched into the *Dance of the Dead*, a deadly kata of fluid movements and precise strikes created for battle mages and designed to allow for the most effective use of blade and magic. It'd been Talmund's specialty and watching him perform his dance always took my breath away.

My former lover had taught me the basics, and after much trial and error, we had choreographed something that suited my unique talents. Speed and agility were my strengths, and I used them to deliver a flurry of shallow cuts, wearing down my opponents.

The stolen sword sang in my hands as I ducked, spun, and struck with relentless precision. My monster-hunting experience paid off as I moved like a shadow, avoiding fatal blows while I defended myself. When the soldiers pressed too close, I unleashed bursts of magic, though each one drained my strength.

The sand continued to hiss like a viper's pit, and the sigil on the wall shimmered ominously, its chalk lines bleeding into a dark, wet red.

'You're fighting for a murderer!' a soldier snarled as he fell to the ground, clutching his side.

'I'm fighting for the whole damn realm,' I panted, my voice rough. A wave of nausea hit me as magic from the royal balcony lashed at my reserves, sapping my energy.

So much for a fair fight.

I smirked, gripping my sword with trembling fingers. I must have looked like an upiór[2] —a night creature that fed on blood. My smile, now more of a grimace, was likely as appalling as the carnage surrounding me.

With Talena joining the fight, avoiding injury became nearly impossible. Each strike and parry demanded more effort than I could spare, and the relentless bloodletting took a toll on me. Sweat mingled with blood, blurring my vision until my enemies' faces blurred into one. My knees buckled as I stumbled a few steps closer to the portal, its sinister hum vibrating through the air.

But even as exhaustion weighed on me, I refused to collapse. 'I will not die here,' I hissed, dropping to my knees and digging a hand into the sand. It was a risky move, but nobody said I had to play fair.

'*Išātum exu affla!*'[3]

Fire erupted from my fingertips, surrounding me as the sand bubbled up and solidified into jagged spears of glass. In desperation, I flung my hand out, the spikes impaling my enemies. Blood poured from their bodies as they screamed, trying to escape, and that was finally enough. Alaric's iron collar snapped open, falling to the ground. With a distressed cry, he pointed at the portal.

---

2. **Upiór /pron:u-pi-oor/** — an undead being that arises from one cursed upon their death, appearing as a freshly deceased corpse. An upiór drives their strength from drinking and bathing in the blood of the living and can kill with their shrieks.

3. *Burn into a shape!*

'Run to me!' he called out, casting a spell. '*Avri're wrot a Mater Tenebri!*'[4]

The portal shimmered, its surface bleeding crimson before darkening into an abyss so black it seemed to devour the light.

Summoning every ounce of strength I had, I stumbled to my feet, carving a wind sigil into the air. I poured my dwindling aether reserves into the spell, and as the wind pushed against my back, I ran towards the gleaming portal as fast as my legs would carry me.

Just as I neared its threshold, so close that I almost felt the bitter touch of the void, a bolt of energy slammed into my back, sending me sprawling into the sand. Pain erupted as I rolled over, only to feel the sharp sting of an arrow embedding itself in my sword arm.

A scream tore from my throat as I grabbed the wooden stake, yanking it free with shaking hands. The pain blurred my focus, but the distant roar of a dragon jolted me back to the moment. Vahin must have been close, but as another arrow landed close to my head, I didn't have time to think.

'*Little Flame,*' his thoughts thundered through my mind, furious as he sensed my pain. '*Stay where you are. I will* burn *the bastard that attacked you. I'll turn this place into a funeral pyre for what they've done to you!*'

'Please no, just wait for me, promise me you'll wait . . .' I cried, grunting when Alaric wrapped his arm around my waist to drag me through the portal. As we crossed the threshold, the icy fingers of the void enveloped my mind, breaking our connection.

---

4. *Open Dark Mother's gate.*

For one long, weightless moment, it was just me, the bitter regret of all I hadn't said, and my fear that there would be nothing to come back to after my dragon unleashed his wrath on the city.

I wish I'd had time to say goodbye . . . Why didn't I tell him I loved him?

Something had changed in Vahin's heart. His thoughts, usually calm and steady, were filled with grief and violence—and the primal fear that he would lose me, too.

And when dragons fear, death dances on the bones of the living.

CHAPTER 14

ANNIKA

I stood surrounded by swirling fog, its cold tendrils caressing my skin and sending shivers down my spine. As a whispering breeze parted the grey curtain, I caught glimpses of a weathered path, its paving cracked and overgrown. I swayed, unsteady, and nearly collapsed before Alaric caught me. His arm circled my waist, steadying me as my strength faded.

'Ani, lean on me,' he murmured, lowering me to the ground when my knees gave way.

The stone beneath us was ancient, its worn surface cloaked in a thick layer of moss, and when I looked up, the mists withdrew completely, exposing a structure in the distance.

It wasn't what I'd expected. I had assumed there would be a magnificent temple worthy of a goddess. Instead, what stood in front of me was a monolithic black wall, its edges disappearing into the fog, glowing blue inscriptions scribbled over the surface.

I raised my hand to wipe the condensation beading on my forehead, wincing as pain flared in my shoulder. At least the bleeding had slowed.

'Gods, Annika,' Ari said, kneeling beside me, his gaze flicking over my wounds. 'You fought like a demon—let me try to heal some of it. I've never been so proud . . . and so terrified, helplessly watching you as you tore through those fae warriors and made them bleed.'

'They weren't the only ones bleeding,' I muttered, gritting my teeth as I tried to ignore the aches and stinging cuts scattered across my body. But my shoulder refused to be ignored. I could barely lift my arm. 'If you insist on using your magic, can you fix this? I'll manage better with both arms working.'

'Of course, Domina.' There was a concerning rasp in Alaric's voice, but his adoring tone made me smile.

I sighed when he placed his hands on my shoulder, warmth spreading from his fingertips. Within moments, I could breathe easier and even move my arm, but as soon as he drew the sigil, he hissed, turning away to hide his expression.

'What's wrong?' I asked.

'The damn icta—it's affecting my magic. I'm so sorry, Ani. That's all I can do.'

'No matter.' Rising to my feet, I gestured towards the structure. 'I think that's where we're meant to go.'

ᛉᚲᚾᚠᛣ

We walked for a while before stopping in front of a smooth, dark door made of a heavy metal I didn't recognise. It looked out of place, gleaming from the condensation covering its surface, distorting our reflections.

'Should we knock?' I asked quietly, but Alaric shook his head. 'Well, then. Here's hoping she doesn't keep guard dogs,' I muttered, pushing the door open.

To my surprise, it yielded easily, swinging silently inwards to reveal a corridor veiled in darkness. Only the faint glow from outside lit the entrance, fading quickly as the door shut behind us.

'Any advice?' I asked, summoning a soft orb of light in my palm. 'Or . . . restrictions? I don't want to offend the Dark Mother.'

Alaric shook his head, his lips pressed into the thin line that usually meant he was in pain. 'I don't know,' he said. 'Those who returned never spoke of it.'

'Of course not, because why make it easier for the empress' next unlucky victim?' I snapped, not bothering to hide my sarcasm.

The temple felt like a place meant to draw out people's fears. The darkness pressed in, almost tangible, swallowing everything beyond a few feet ahead of us. The light I'd created offered little comfort. It gave us no advantage, instead making us a target, but I kept it going because its faint glow made me feel less alone.

Then the voices began.

A chorus of whispers echoed through the darkness, rising and falling like a haunting tide. They pleaded for release, promised power and glory, offered me the world if I would only leave the door open long enough for them to escape.

I froze, clutching Ari's hand. 'I don't like this,' I whispered. 'The whispers . . .'

'Don't listen to the dead, Domina.' Alaric turned me to face him, his hands cradling my face. 'Don't let them in. The dead will linger if you allow them.'

'Is there a way to silence them?'

He shook his head, and I shuddered. 'Fine. I can handle this. I—oh, fuck!'

Something small and furry ran over my foot, sending a jolt of panic through me. I leapt onto Ari, wrapping my legs around his waist.

'It was a rat, my love,' he said, his chuckle rumbling against my chest.

I shuddered again, gesturing for him to put me down. 'Whatever it was, you won't say a word about it to Orm or Vahin. It never happened.'

His grin softened the harsh lines of his exhaustion, though the dark circles under his eyes betrayed how much the icta was draining him, and as much as I wanted to enjoy the fleeting moment of levity, I couldn't ignore the weight of our task pressing down on us. If the Dark Mother had sent a creature to hurry us along, I wasn't about to wait for her to send something worse.

I took the lead, trailing my fingers over the wall while we made our way into the gloom. After what felt like hours, we encountered the first fork in our path. I felt something niggle at the back of my mind and let the feeling draw me to the right.

At the second fork, I hesitated, realising the feeling from earlier had been the voices, their whispers now louder and telling me to turn left this time. But when I glanced at Alaric to ask his opinion, I gasped. My companion was swaying, sweat pouring from his skin. I didn't know what to do, so I took a chance, listening to the whispered advice and turned into a small chamber.

'I think we're lost,' I said as Ari placed his hand on my shoulder with much more weight than I would expect from a casual touch.

'Just keep going, Domina. We don't have a choice,' he replied, leaning heavily on me.

'Ari . . .' I whispered, touching his face. Even if I couldn't see well in the darkness, I could feel the heat of his fever. 'How long do we have? Can I do anything? Tell me how I can help!'

'You can't, my love. My time was up the moment I took the poison. It's simply coming to an end now we've entered the temple,' he said, pressing his back to the wall before sliding down to sit. I sat next to him, shivering, my penitential clothes providing little warmth.

The echo of dripping water lent the place an oddly soothing atmosphere. Fatigue from the day's struggles flooded through me, and even though I knew we had to continue, I closed my eyes. I just needed to catch my breath before we resumed our search.

'*Wake up! You'll die if you fall asleep . . . Don't sleep . . .*' The whispers battered at my mind so insistently that they jolted me awake and something crunched under my foot. I released my light, directing it upwards, and what it revealed carved itself into my mind.

Skeletons littered the floor, their flesh turned to dust long ago—though some golden and silver jewellery remained sadly draped over the bones. From the shape of the skulls, I could tell they had been fae; likely dark fae, given where we were. I blinked once, twice, before the realisation hit me.

The voices. They were their spirits. *Why am I hearing ghosts?*

I jumped to my feet, tugging Alaric up with me. His head lolled, and for a moment, he looked at me with glossy, unfocused eyes, but I kept jerking his arm until he stood up.

'We need to go,' I hissed, throwing his arm over my shoulder. 'Come on, don't make me drag you.' Nodding towards the strange crypt, I said, 'Thank you for the warning. May you find peace,' before bowing as best as I could in respect to those whose warning saved us from their fate.

We left the chamber, and the voices fell silent for a few seconds, almost as if in surprise. The silence was a relief, but the cacophony quickly returned as we carried on.

Dizzy from the ghastly incident, I walked further along the corridor, avoiding turns where the voices grew more substantial. They may have helped me once, but I knew that if I followed them, I'd just find another dead grotto where I could not resist eternal slumber.

161

I didn't know how long we'd walked for, but as time passed, it wasn't only Ari whose feet dragged as we moved forward. We couldn't keep going like that, so I finally stopped, letting a short sob escape my lips.

'It's hopeless, it's so fucking hopeless,' I muttered, fighting my panic. What sense was there in continuing if there was no way out? My muscles were spasming from exhaustion, my thoughts were muddled, and my fae was dying. The only feelings I had left were hopelessness and rage.

So, in desperation, I chose rage.

'Are you enjoying this?' I screamed, uncaring of if I angered the Dark Mother. 'Stripping us of hope before we end up like those dusty bones? Do you honestly think I'll let him die while I do *nothing*? You foolish, *hateful* goddess—I'll destroy everything here to save him! I'll fucking burn the *world* for him, so come out and face me. Face me or see just what I'm capable of!'

My voice echoed, multiplying as it spread. I was beyond caring. I would welcome the chance to fight, would welcome *anything* to break out of the endless, exhausting corridors. If I had to die, I would take this dismal prison down with me. Yet, as I stood there, panting hard, nothing emerged from the darkness.

'Annika, don't temp fate,' Alaric whispered, but I only huffed, turning back to him and cradling his cheek.

'Fate can kiss my bruised arse. I don't care what she thinks. I can fight my enemies, but if I have to take one more step in this endless maze while you're fading, I will burn it down, even if it's the last thing I do.'

I exhaled slowly, letting my anger fuel me, even as weariness threatened to pull me under. Then I felt it—a tug on my spirit . . . then another. Whether it was from my outburst or just my desperate imagination, I didn't care. It was something to hold onto. Clinging to the lifeline like a drowning sailor, I closed my eyes and let the feeling guide me forward.

The corridor soon felt different, and my worries subsided with each step. At some point, the floor became soft, even springy, as if I were walking on moss or a plush carpet. The surrounding air grew colder, and I even felt a breeze on my cheek. But I didn't allow my hopes to grow.

Is this an illusion? Was the whole journey just a massive hallucination? I asked myself, huffing in annoyance at my limited knowledge of order magic. If it was a trick, I'd walked into it like a cheerful toddler, unaware of the danger.

The breeze grew stronger, the chill seeping into my bones. I squeezed my eyes shut against the unnerving sensation of walking on a giant sponge, refusing to give in to the mounting unease. Then, with a rush of air and an ominous *snap*, something lunged at us.

'Fuck!' I shouted, grabbing Alaric and dragging us to the ground just in time to dodge a massive set of snapping mandibles. My heart thundered as I realised the ground wasn't ground at all—we were standing on a spiderweb.

The silken strands, thick as my thighs, stretched in all directions, intertwined with finer threads to form a dense, silvery carpet.

And there, in the centre, was our host.

I still had my sword, but I needed more than that if I hoped to kill the monstrosity. However, after from its initial attack, it simply stood there, motionless. I didn't sense any corrupted magic, and once I recovered from my shock, I noticed it looked like an overgrown huntsman spider. My instincts were screaming at me that it was the guardian of the temple.

The spider's eight eyes followed my every move, the eerie sense of being studied making me shiver. It was the size of a carriage, its pale white body covered in strange markings that looked like ancient runes, with two sets of jaws and clawed front legs.

I'm undoubtedly excelling as a battle mage—casually strolling over a spiderweb while its creator eyes me like a plump snack that has delivered itself to its open mouth, I thought.

The beast clattered its fangs as a small sigh of exasperation escaped my lips.

Alaric groaned beside me, his face ashen and his golden eyes dull and unseeing of the horror that lay before us as he fought to stay upright. I couldn't decide which was worse: being devoured by an overgrown arachnid or watching my love fade away while we hopelessly wandered.

I was about to surrender, to spend what little time we had left holding Ari close, when a glimmer of light caught my eye.

A doorway.

Beyond the spider, the dark entrance gleamed, its edges outlined in warm, inviting light.

That had to be it.

My back straightened. I didn't care what price I had to pay. I was going to drag Alaric to safety.

'Look,' I said to the spider, 'if you can understand me, I want you to know I *need* to see your mistress. I didn't come here to cause problems, and I don't want to hurt you. But if you try to stop me, I will burn you, your web, and this entire maze. I'm tired, scared, and at the end of my patience. I've hurt enough people today to make my guilt ride my conscience to my last breath, so if we can resolve this without fighting, I'll be forever grateful. So *please*, oh big and spindly one, let me pass.'

I executed a lopsided bow, worrying when Alaric shifted slightly, but his words were marked by his usual mischief when he spoke.

'Are you trying to charm the spider out of its dinner?' he asked, and I felt a hint of a smile where his cheek pressed against my neck.

'If it works, I swear I'll never kill any of its smaller cousins ever again. Let's go now, one last effort.'

We stumbled forward, each step cautious on the taut webbing. We were trying to be careful, but Ari and I were spent. The spider's fangs clicked, the vibrations of our movements no doubt registering on its sensitive strands. But it didn't attack.

Whether it was my speech or something else, I didn't know. I kept talking, babbling on about my life, how grateful I was it let us pass, and how magnificent it appeared. It didn't react, simply tracked us, more interested in observing us than sinking its fangs into our bodies.

Finally, we reached the webbed bridge that led to the doorway. 'Good boy . . . or girl,' I murmured, balancing on the final strand. 'Give me a moment, and I'll be out of your web.' As if it only then noticed we were going to leave, the spider hissed, but we were already beyond its reach.

With one last step, the light engulfed us, blinding and overwhelming.

We were safe. Or as safe as one could be in the Dark Mother's Temple.

CHAPTER 15

ANNIKA

I thought we were safe, but as tears of relief streamed from my eyes, I was knocked to the floor.

My eyes finally adjusted, and I realised Ari had bowled me over and was covering me with his body. Still struggling to see beyond his concerned face, I gave him my trust, letting him protect me from whatever threat his heightened senses had detected.

The air had turned colder, thick with the scent of night-blooming flowers and an exotic incense I couldn't place. A soft rustle echoed in the stillness, like silk brushing restlessly against itself. Magic hummed in the air, the aether prickling my skin, raising goosebumps like the moment before lightning strikes.

'Ari? Can you see?' I asked, placing my hand on his back, startled when I felt it tremble.

'Not much, but there is a power in this room. Don't move, Domina. Let me gauge the threat.'

'You can barely stand,' I protested, but my words died in my throat as the strange rustling sound intensified.

Then, a voice, soft and melodic, resonated from all directions, carried on waves of palpable power. It stole my breath, each word like a strike against my chest.

'You succeeded, child,' the voice said. 'I was curious about how you'd react to the Grotto of Dreamers. Many perish there, but I would have been disappointed had you done so. I didn't want to miss out on sampling your memories. Thankfully, you were perceptive enough to survive, and you didn't attack my guardian—that makes you a rarity among your peers.'

Alaric dropped to his knees, bowing as the voice faded into silence. 'I, Alaric'va Shen'ra, and Annika Diavellar greet your magnificence, Dark Mother, Goddess of Fate and all dark fae.'

The reverence in his voice sent a chill down my spine, but I forced myself to stand tall, swallowing my fear.

'And you, Annika Diavellar?' she purred, curious. 'Do you greet me with reverence and awe? What can I do for the woman who, instead of brandishing a blade, talked to the monster?'

'You are power beyond time, Dark Mother,' I replied, my voice steady. 'I acknowledge this, but I do not come before you in fear. I passed your trial. Please honour it and grant your mercy to my mate. I beg you—purge the poison from Alaric's body.'

The voice chuckled, rich and unsettling. 'Oh, child, you believe the trial is over?' Shadows coalesced in front of me, and she emerged.

I gasped. The Dark Mother towered above me, terrifying and beautiful. Her youthful face radiated a cold, alien perfection, and her eight eyes held all of time in their faceted depths. Long, dark hair cascaded down over her body, but I could still see her slender shoulders; feminine, petite breasts; and delicate glowing skin. Below the waist, however, she had the abdomen of a spider, six spindly legs that carried her, and two smaller appendages that endlessly weaved thread.

The sheer weight of her presence pressed on my chest. Aether poured from her in a swirling vortex, pulling at the magic within me as though trying to forge a connection. I clenched my fists, digging my nails into my palms. The sharp pain grounded me, restoring my focus.

'Only you can extract the icta poison from his body,' I said, stepping closer. 'If it's not over, then please, tell me what more I must do.'

The Dark Mother tilted her head, a motion uncannily reminiscent of the spider we'd encountered outside. Her lips curled into a smile that revealed needle-sharp teeth.

'You are brave, proud mage. That pleases me.' Her voice softened, almost a croon. 'You intrigue me. For his kind, the dark fae, I am the Dark Mother. Others have known me as Przadka, Uttu, Neith . . . but you may call me Arachne. Speak my name, and I will listen. Icta, you see, is derived from my venom. It can bend time, a gift reserved for the royal fae line—though their priestesses haven't come here for centuries. So, what did your man do to earn their ire?'

Her clawed fingers reached for my hand, but I instinctively flinched. She frowned. 'Are you afraid of my touch, child? Then tell me, what are you willing to sacrifice for him?'

'Anything,' I said without hesitation, then added, 'except my Anchors.' I stepped forward, closing the distance between us, and reached for her hand, wanting to erase the mistake I'd made. 'Please. Help him. He doesn't have much time left.'

Her eyes narrowed, their glimmer hypnotic. Then her smile widened, her voice laced with cruel amusement. 'Anything but your Anchors? Very well.' She paused, turning away from me. 'Come, child. Your man is safe here. I command the passage of time within these walls. He will not die until I permit it . . . Let us see if your love is strong enough to save him.'

As she led me deeper into the temple, the blinding brightness that had initially overwhelmed me began to take shape. It radiated from countless tiny lights swaying gently on delicate threads near the ceiling.

Long-forgotten knowledge stirred at the edges of my mind . . . a goddess weaving threads, a web, the Weaver of Fate bound forever to the mortal realm, guarding the lives of all creation. A shuddering breath escaped me as I looked up at the ceiling—so full, so alive with blinking lights, pulsing with energy.

Could it be . . . ?

'Yes, mage, those are the lives of those on this side of the Veil. I weave their threads, and I cut them when the time is right,' she said, even though I hadn't asked my question aloud. We stopped before a stone altar, and Arachne raised her hand, summoning one of the lights to her.

'Alaric'va Shen'ra . . . What an interesting specimen he is. Hated from birth, tainted by a curse, yet his light is so bright. I could give him the peace of a painless death, or let him go back to the world where his suffering will continue . . . for the right price. Time for your decision, mage.'

Dread rose in my core. 'What is it that you ask of me?'

'You have earned him a peaceful death by making it to my sanctum. He will drift away, his light fading as he relives the happiest moments of his life,' she said, pausing to observe my reaction before a smirk lifted the corner of her mouth. 'But for his life, I want a place in your soul.'

'What?' I gaped at her as she approached, shuffling backwards until my body hit the edge of the altar.

'I see their threads,' she said, raising a clawed finger to stroke my face. 'The man and the dragon bound to you, entwined in your soul, so different and yet so much a part of you. I can see where they end, and you begin. I've never seen such a rich tapestry.'

Where is she going with this?

'I could cut those threads,' she mused, 'take them for myself, but no . . . I want something more. I will make you my avatar. Through you, I will walk your world.'

Her focus bore into me with such hunger that I couldn't stop trembling. My breath hitched and sweat slicked my palms as I gripped the cold stone altar behind me. Her power was suffocating, pressing down like the oppressive heat before a summer storm, growing heavier with every passing second as black threads seeped from her body to wrap around mine.

I knew it was no idle threat. She could force the spirit out of my body and take possession of my form. There was nothing I could do against a goddess, yet as quickly as it arose, her power receded, and Arachne smiled.

'That is your decision to make,' she said smoothly. 'Let him die peacefully, or accept my darkness. Allow me to live through you so you both may survive.'

I couldn't stop shaking, even less so when she raised a single claw and tore through the thin strap that bound my breasts. 'I see your scars . . . but I want more. You will Anchor the fae. I want to feel his life, too. You came seeking a bargain with a goddess—that is my price.'

A cold shiver ran down my spine, Arachne's beautiful, cruel smile sending chills through me as she watched me, waiting for my decision. I couldn't bear the weight of her gaze any longer.

'I can Anchor Alaric, yes, but I can't fuck a corpse. I need him alive and . . . erm . . . ready to perform?' I stumbled over the words, heat rushing to my face.

She threw her head back and laughed, the sound echoing around us like the chime of a death knell. 'Oh, I will have so much fun with you,' she purred. 'So, you accept my bargain?'

I swallowed hard and nodded. The moment my assent was given, she snapped her fingers, and Alaric rose from his knees. His movements were stiff but purposeful, walking towards her like a puppet on invisible strings. He stopped before her, his posture rigid.

'Alaric'va Shen'ra, give yourself to me,' she commanded, and with a gentleness that surprised me, she wrapped her hand around his neck, tilting his head to the side before sinking her fangs into his throat.

The soft, sickening sounds of her feeding tore at my nerves, and I had to fight the overwhelming urge to drag her away from him. But as my eyes locked with Ari's, I could see the tension easing from his face, the pain dissipating with each pull of her lips. Colour returned to his cheeks, and my heart clenched with relief. Whatever consequences awaited me, it was worth it.

When she finally withdrew, her lips slick with his blood, Arachne turned her gaze towards me, and I nodded in silent agreement. It was my turn now.

'Kneel and wait for us to finish,' Arachne ordered, but Alaric looked at me, his jaw bunching in defiance.

'Please.'

It was one word, but the moment I spoke it, he knelt, his eyes refusing to look away from mine.

'Delightfully obstinate. He was able to resist me because of you,' Arachne remarked, licking her lips. 'Are you ready, child?'

'No,' I replied honestly. 'But what difference does it make?'

'No difference at all, but I let you keep your life. Does that not warm your heart?'

Inhuman appendages grabbed me by the waist, drawing me closer to the ever-weaving arms of the goddess. I gasped as the silk strands twisted into darkness, and before I could flinch, a single thread was thrust into my chest, briefly eclipsing the sigils of my Anchors.

'Yes . . .' Arachne's voice dropped to a low murmur. 'You feel so right, so beautiful with my web weaved around your heart.' The darkness spread through me, the pulse of her power sending my heartbeat into a frantic race. I felt her presence nestle within me, like a shadow.

She placed me gently on the altar, her movements graceful as she dangled above me on a silver thread. 'Calm, child. Let it settle,' she whispered, her voice a caress as I lay there trembling, exposed and cold.

I forced a breath, summoning every ounce of my will to meet her eyes, pushing my fear aside.

'Will you possess me now, or imprison my soul?' I demanded, my voice stronger than I felt.

'Neither.' Arachne laughed, her voice dark and sweet. 'You are already mine.'

Her laughter reverberated in my soul as the pressure around my essence tightened. She clenched her fist in front of my face, and I felt the connection between us solidify. 'Only death can remove our bond. Now, Anchor your fae, child. I want to feel it, to experience it as it forms.'

I turned to Alaric, his body straining against some invisible force, but his eyes locked onto mine with unwavering intensity.

'Ari,' I said, my voice gentle. 'It will be alright. We can do this.'

'No, Annika.' His voice cracked with pain. 'I won't force myself on you. Even the gods couldn't make me.'

His eyes blazed with fury as he glared at his goddess. 'I prayed to you, *worshipped* you, and you enslave the woman I love?' Alaric was ready to fight his deity to protect me, but all our struggles would be in vain if he died angering her.

'Alaric'va Shen'ra,' I said, my voice sharp, commanding his attention. 'Look at me.'

His eyes met mine, and I released the breath I'd been holding. 'There are worse things in life than having sex on an altar with a voyeuristic goddess watching, but I'll understand if this isn't something you can do—'

'What? No! Never. But Annika, not like this, not when this is precisely what the Lich King wants. Not when she is forcing you . . . I won't be your weakness. I won't be the cause of your misery.'

'She is not forcing me, and I don't care what Cahyon wants. I don't even care if Arachne drools all over us making love. I want *you* as my Anchor.'

I didn't know how else to convince him, so I reached out to my fae. 'Ari, I love you. In every shade of time, with everything I am, *I love you*. It is not her decision, it's mine. I've wanted you as my Anchor since our duel in the fortress. Please, all I ask is that you love me back.'

Unguarded emotions flickered across his face—love, anger, wonder, and resentment—until his shoulders sagged, and he exhaled, shaking his head.

'This feels wrong, Domina,' he murmured, his voice hoarse. 'I should worship you on the finest silk, not take you on hard stone.'

Still, he stepped closer, the tension in his movements betraying his inner conflict. I moved to sit at the edge of the altar, spreading my knees as he stood between them, his hands grasping my thighs. When his forehead rested against mine, I felt his pulse thrum in tandem with my own. A vein stood out in his neck, and my chest ached with the urge to assure him that this was what I wanted. That I had wanted his Anchor for so long, I could do the deed in front of an army, not just one curious spider.

'The circumstances and timing may be wrong but Anchoring you will always be right. What we feel is *right*. Touch me, Ari. We can pretend it is just us in a cosy candlelit cavern. Make us feel good before I speak the Anchoring Oath.'

I kissed him and eventually felt his resistance melt as my tongue parted his lips.

'Annika,' he groaned as I raked my nails over his skin. 'That is an unreasonable, dangerous thing to do . . . yet I want it so much,' he finished with a moan that only encouraged me to keep exploring. He grasped my arse, pulling me closer, and I placed a hand on his chest, feeling uneven skin where the curse marked his body. Alaric grunted, pressing his hips to my thigh, and I felt his length hardening in his trousers.

I noticed Arachne had withdrawn into the shadows but felt her presence when she reacted to Ari cupping my breast and stroking my sensitive nipple. As his hand continued its questing journey upwards, his thumb brushed across my lips, and I couldn't resist biting it, making him jerk in surprise.

'Fuck, Domina. What are you doing to me?' he whispered, his husky voice sending shivers down my spine.

'Whatever I want. You will give in to me and take me like the world depends on it because maybe, just this time, it does. Show me how much you want me, Alaric, and fuck me like you've never fucked anyone.'

I cried out, feeling his hand on my sex, fingers rubbing the sensitive spot, touching it with such mastery that my world swam out of focus. My back arched, legs falling open, inviting him in.

Passion flared in Alaric's eyes, crimson fire eclipsing his pupils. The purple strands of his necromantic power appeared, pulsing as they wrapped around my wrist, pulling my arms above my head.

'As you command, Domina.'

Alaric's fingers slid inside me, curving gently as he moved them in and out while his thumb continued to press on just the right place, and its circular movements sent me into a frenzy. 'Fuck me, Alaric!' I commanded, and he laughed.

The deep, throaty timbre of his voice reverberated in my core, and nothing could have made me look away from my lover. He opened his trousers, and my hips involuntarily jerked forward to meet him, but again, he denied me. I was trembling with anticipation, whimpering quietly as he aligned himself to my entrance. He paused, his eyes locking with mine as his unspoken question lingered between us.

'Please, don't stop now,' I pleaded, and a mischievous smile tugged at his lips. We were both dirty and tired, but Alaric was hard as a rock, and as a tremor ran through his body, he pushed forward.

'I will never make you regret this, Annika. You are the light to my darkness, and I *will* be worthy of you.'

He sounded so sincere, my tormented fae whose spirit burned so bright it had surprised a goddess, but I didn't need any reassurance. I was at peace. Darkness slowly seeped from my chest, a ring surrounding the sigils over my heart. The presence of a being so ancient and powerful merged with my soul as the goddess echoed my moans of pleasure at each thrust of Alaric's hips.

I was drowning in ecstasy when her presence returned to my mind. I could feel her loneliness, her need to feel again. To remember how it felt to be a woman, and not simply enduring an eternity of guarding the fates of those who begged for help in their darkest hours.

I pitied her.

'*I don't want your pity, little mage,*' whispered a voice in my head.

'*But you want to feel the love of someone who would burn the world for a hint of your smile, don't you?*'

My question was met with silence. I opened myself to her, welcoming not just the power of the goddess who ruled over the living but of the woman who deserved to experience life herself. I felt her surprise at my acceptance, her pleasure that mirrored mine, and the awe when we came close to cresting.

'*Let me feel you both*,' came the pleading whisper. Feeling my body tighten in anticipation, I grasped Ari's arms and gazed into his beautiful, crimson eyes.

'*Su aetheram, vede aligname faleter.*
Me tuor, la'coren datro, sa fallorn.'[1]

The Anchoring Oath slipped eagerly from my lips, and its magic tore away a shard of our souls, the pain triggering Alaric's climax. My body jerked, and euphoria overwhelmed me as the darkness of Arachne's magic and Ari's spirit fused with my own.

I could feel them both: Alaric's love filling my soul, and Arachne's awe and burning desire to feel more, to be more, to *live* more. My fragile, mortal body had humbled the goddess, and for a moment, I sensed her fear of losing me and her access to the world she'd left behind.

'*You will live and live well. I give you my blessing and will shelter your thread. Remember my name, child. You'll need it.*'

The goddess shuddered, her spindly legs contracting, pulling her away. The wave of power subsided, but my soul was still struggling to accept the new bonds, and I slumped into Ari's comforting embrace. As I sighed in contentment, the gentle caress of a hard claw on my cheek nearly made me scream, but as I turned, I saw Arachne's tender expression and took a shuddering breath in relief.

'Thank you, sweet child. You have found yourself a good man.' Her syllabic voice was surprisingly comforting now that I could feel the

---

1. *With aether aligned in this world and beyond.*
Forever united with our Anchoring bond.

emotion behind it. 'And I certainly approve of our combined symbol on my avatar's body.'

I pulled back slowly, looking down to see my Anchor mark enriched by a dark ring with thorny vines wrapping around the sword and the dragon. It was done, and I was exhausted.

I wrapped my arms around my chest, feeling vulnerable, and as if sensing my discomfort, Arachne laid a soft, grey robe over my shoulders. The fabric was warm and cosy, weighing almost nothing despite its thickness, and I quickly pulled it closed, revelling in the feel of it.

'What now?' I asked, studying the content expression of the goddess.

'Now . . . I will look over you, Annika. You've given me more than I expected. I will visit every now and again, but you are free to live your life, even if that life belongs to me.' She shifted her gaze to Alaric, and his magic responded, reaching towards her. 'As you are mine.'

Her gaze flickered to his chest, and I gasped, seeing the curse transform to mimic the markings that covered her back.

'What . . .?'

She smirked. 'I can't allow anyone to mark what is mine,' she responded before turning to Ari, who patted his chest in awe. 'You are free from your curse.'

I gaped at her in disbelief, grasping my throat when a string of darkness flew from the goddess to wrap itself around my and Alaric's necks.

'You will not speak of this day's events. Some secrets must stay shrouded in mystery. Enjoy your life, little mage. I can't wait to see what you do with your Anchors and my blessing.'

The world dimmed and faded away. The soft skitter of countless legs the last sound we heard as we fell back into our own world.

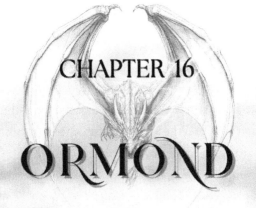

CHAPTER 16

ORMOND

A day before the trial

The wind lashed my face as Vahin leapt into the air, his formidable wings slicing through the sky. I raised a hand to shield my eyes, bracing myself for the punishing ride ahead. My anger simmered. I'd had two bloody days to enjoy being with Annika before duty dragged me back to the borderlands.

'*I don't want to part with her, either,*' Vahin grumbled, his voice a growl in my mind. '*But Reynard's concerns have merit. If the sleeping army has stirred, we need to know—and warn the fortresses. You know I'm the only one who can get us there and back in time for the trial.*'

His logic only sharpened my frustration. I should have sent a warning the moment we had uncovered the monsters beneath the keystone, but Annika's capture and my inability to think straight had delayed everything.

'*I know my duty,*' I snapped, the words bitter. '*But the trial is* tomorrow. *The love of my life isn't just fighting for the kingdom—she's fighting for her life. And there's a chance I won't be there.*'

Vahin rumbled uneasily, exhaling a stream of fire that shimmered in the icy air. '*No, Orm, we'll be there. We will be there even if I have to break my wings to get us back.*'

I knew his barracks humour was a misguided attempt to soothe my worries, and I smacked his scaled neck, the gesture more fond than reprimanding. *'Just pray the winds favour us,'* I muttered, leaning into the saddle as he climbed higher, where the air thinned and froze. It was hard to breathe at this altitude, but Vahin needed speed, and I trusted him with my life.

'I don't need to pray, Ormond,' he replied with draconic pride. *'I've been flying this world since before your kind learned to crawl.'*

The hours blurred in the bitter cold, each gust of wind cutting deeper than the last. By the time Vahin descended back through the clouds, exhaustion radiated from his body. He'd pushed harder than ever, and I felt a pang of guilt for asking so much of him.

'Where do you want to go first?' he asked, his voice laced with fatigue.

'The Rift,' I said, my answer ready. *'We need to see what's emerged after the fall of the Barrier. If the Lich King has lost control of the monsters, the land will be swarming with them. Then we should fly to Roan Fortress, where you can rest and eat. Roan's commander can send word to the other fortresses while we return to the capital.'*

Vahin grunted in agreement and adjusted his course. It took us another hour to arrive at the Rift, and I instructed him to stay high in case Cahyon had released any spectrae. Surprisingly, both the sky around us and the ground below were calm. The semi-transparent barrier that had guarded our kingdom for centuries was gone, and below us stretched a wasteland—gnarled, rotting trees and barren earth.

I sheltered my eyes against the sun as we circled lower until Vahin's wings almost scraped the top of the dead trees.

'I don't like it,' I muttered. I'd expected chaos, not complete silence. It was as if the shattering of the crystal had erased the army beneath it. *'Take us to Roan.'*

'Varta is closer,' Vahin countered.

'*Yes, but my men know how to fight and keep watch. Besides, they already know what to look for. The other posts are blind and deaf to the danger thanks to Ihrain and the chancellor's interference.*'

Vahin was quiet for a long time, but I could feel an undercurrent of restlessness in his thoughts.

'*What is it, my friend?*' I asked. '*Your feelings are seeping into my consciousness; I know you're unsettled.*'

He hesitated. '*I fear for Annika, as you do,*' he admitted. But there was more—something he wasn't saying.

'*I know you love her, but she's human,*' I said cautiously, '*and you'll eventually lose her, just like you'll lose me. If not to the war, then to the passing of time.*'

'*Ani's connection with me has increased her lifespan and likely yours, but even if you both only live a short while, I've already decided. When her light fades, I'll return to the mists,*' he said, his voice heavy with finality. '*I'm tired of being alone, Ormond. I've existed for millennia, and bonding with you and meeting my Little Flame has brought me joy I never thought possible. I cannot go on without it, without her. Just . . . I'm not ready for this yet.*'

The raw emotion in his words and the darkness I glimpsed in his mind was worrying, but I couldn't coax another word from my dragon. We rode in silence until Roan Fortress appeared on the horizon, and he prepared to land.

I straightened in the saddle, my gaze fixed on the fortress ahead. Its black turrets reflected the fiery hues of the setting sun, a stark yet mesmerising contrast. All fortresses except Varta were named after their first commanders, and I often marvelled at what kind of person the original builder was to raise the walls from polished black stone.

From a distance, it was a striking sight—a tranquil stronghold with closed gates, clear skies, and flags dancing in the breeze. Yet, apprehension prickled at the edges of my thoughts. As I stared at the crimson-streaked horizon, the realisation struck me like a blade.

There were no dragons.

'*Vahin, gain altitude,*' I commanded, my gut churning with apprehension.

'*Why?*' he asked, tilting his head to look at me.

'*There are no dragons.*'

Vahin's vertical pupils narrowed. '*Spectrae?*'

'*Most likely.*' I nodded, knowing there was not much—besides the vampiric ghosts—that could empty a fortress of their dragons. '*Circle from above. We need to scout from a distance before landing.*'

Vahin's powerful wings carried us higher, his agility allowing for a near-vertical ascent. Hidden in the clouds, we circled the fortress. The silence was unnerving—there were no birds, no life. When my dragon dipped below the cloud line, the truth became painfully clear.

Roan Fortress was a tomb.

Spectrae could not feed on the dead, and the outpost I'd known so well was now a desolation of broken bodies and shattered wings. Dragons lay strewn across roofs and courtyards, their scales dull and wings torn. Soldiers' remains were barely recognisable, their swords and scraps of chain mail the only signs of who they'd been.

Vahin's roar of anguish split the air, a long, keening cry that pierced my heart. His grief was overwhelming, eclipsing even my own.

Maybe if I had been lucid enough to send them a message, Roan's commander would have been able to avoid this carnage.

'*This is a graveyard of my kin,*' he said, his voice thick with sorrow.

I tightened my grip on the pommel, my throat dry. 'I'm so sorry.'

He descended slowly, his massive body trembling with emotion. I'd seen death before, but the sheer scale of destruction here was paralysing.

We landed in an open space within the courtyard, and only then did I realise why it was empty. A lone, charred red boot lay abandoned, its flamboyant leather scorched black, the ashes of its wearer still clinging to the remnants of a foot. It had belonged to the fortress mage—a young orc whose talent lay in manipulating fire. The scorched earth we now stood on had clearly been where he'd taken his last stand.

I dismounted, standing motionless as my ragged breaths filled the stillness. Wild magic raged within me, clawing for release, demanding I let my pain erupt in a berserker's rampage. As my hands shook and my muscles tensed, a pair of eyes filled with crimson fire and understanding flashed through my mind.

It surprised me that it wasn't Annika's presence I reached for in that moment, as I might have expected, but Alaric's. Ani would have told me it wasn't my fault; I knew that well enough. But Ari . . . Ari would have held me through the grief and the rage and just let it burn until I felt under control.

Vahin's mind brushed against mine, searching for the words that would ease my conscience, just like Annika would. He was my dragon, but he was Annika's Anchor, through and through.

'Don't,' I rasped. 'I need this. I need this . . . hatred. Maybe when I've drowned Katrass in the blood of my enemies, I'll be able to live with this guilt.'

Vahim rumbled softly, a sound more sorrow than reproach. 'No one could have stopped this, Ormond,' he offered, but he withdrew from my mind, giving me the privacy I needed.

'Search for survivors,' I ordered, my voice rough. 'Burn the dead. They don't deserve to lie here and rot. Turn this whole place into a funeral pyre if you want but give them peace.' I couldn't help them, but I could give their memory the dignity that death had failed to provide.

He nodded and took to the air, his flames igniting the broken structures from above. The acrid scent of smoke and charred wood mingled with the sickly stench of death as I moved from body to body, turning them over, hoping for a sign of life, and finding only the faces of the dead—twisted with terror and pain.

The burning fortress cast flickering shadows as Vahin's grief poured into the flames. Each burst of fire was a lament for his kin, and it mirrored the anger roiling inside me. The very walls of Roan Fortress seemed to cry out in mourning.

If not for Ihrain's treachery and betrayal, Annika could have been here fighting the spectrae while the soldiers dealt with the other monsters. The very thought was painful. *One* person, *one* conduit mage connected to a dragon, could have saved them. Instead, she was stuck in the capital fighting a senseless trial to amuse the dark fae empress.

'Fuck! Fuck! *Fuck!*'

I smashed my fist into the black stone wall until the skin of my knuckles split and blood stained the surface. Not that it made me feel any better. My mind was spiralling into a mindless rage when Vahin's voice cut through the destructive thoughts.

'Ormond. Enough. We have no time for this if you want to make it back before the trial.'

I focused on my dragon's words. Taking control of my rage and wrestling it into submission was hard, but eventually, I pushed it to the dark recesses of my mind, ready to unleash it on my enemies when I encountered them.

'I'm calm now,' I muttered. I brushed my hand over the ridges of his eyelid, drawing strength from the contact. 'Just give me a moment to check the commander's log. Maybe he left behind something that'll let us know what happened here.'

I could still hear the hissing of the flames behind me as I climbed the steep steps to the office. I paused, watching the raw anguish of my dragon as he burned the bodies of his kin. The fire was growing, spreading to engulf the fortress.

With a deep cleansing breath, I hurried onwards, ripping away the broken door to search for clues until I found the logbook, miraculously intact.

'Who are you? How did you get here?'

The voice startled me, and I spun, my sword already drawn. A young rider stood at the doorway, his leather armour tattered and streaked with grime. He clutched an iron key, his eyes wide with terror.

'My name is Ormond Erenhart,' I said, lowering my blade as the boy's knees buckled, sending him crumpling to the floor.

'Are you . . . are you really him?' His voice trembled. 'The Lord Commander? Does that mean the Varta riders are here with a mage? Please, gods, tell me you brought a mage. We need one—badly. The spectrae come whenever the sun sets, as if they know we are still here . . .'

The desperation in his voice was a knife to the gut, and I hated that I had to crush his hopes. 'No. I came alone. Tell me what happened. Are there other survivors?'

'Just me and my dragon. He's injured—his wing membrane was torn during the attack, and the commander . . . he told me to stay hidden in the caves. Gods, you have no mage. Quick, you must hide before the spectrae come.'

Though the young rider was shaking, he managed to grab my sleeve with a firm grip. 'The sun is almost set. We must go *now*.'

'*Vahin, there is an injured dragon in the caves. Please check on him.*' I sent the thought out before assessing the soldier in front of me. He was maybe sixteen years old and a skinny little thing, far too young to face the horrors of war.

'What's your name?' I asked gently.

'Adam, junior rider, second unit, sir. Come with me if you want to survive. What those creatures did to the dragons . . .' His voice faltered, and a tremor ran through his body as I helped him stand.

'I need to fly to the capital, but as soon as your dragon has recovered, I want you to go to the other fortress commanders. Start with Seren, then go to the next in line. Tell them what you saw and deliver this log,' I said, handing him my discovery. 'Now, let's go see your dragon before I set off.'

'No, you can't go now. The spectrae—they'll be circling the fortress until the morning,' he sobbed, looking at me as if I were insisting on suicide. '*Please.* Come with me. I'll show you where we can wait out the night.'

Adam led the way down to the dragon caves and brought me to one of the smaller nooks where a dragon rested on a flat rock. He wasn't moving, but he and Vahin had their foreheads pressed together, a blue glow pulsing where they touched.

'Your dragon will recover,' Vahin said aloud, his voice weary yet steady. 'If he could feed, he'd be healed by now, but I've helped him enough to mend his wing.' To me, he said, 'It was carnage, Orm. The riders couldn't even manage a formation when the spectrae first attacked. Apart from those of us at Varta, no one else believed the Barrier could fall, and these fools paid the price.'

Adam stood gaping. 'Gods, he can *talk.*'

'Yes. I can,' Vahin replied before turning his head towards me and gesturing to the injured dragon. 'I saw what happened in Meleki's memories. This was no random attack, Ormond. They came in calculated waves, the spectrae testing the defences before the army launched their full assault. This was planned.'

'Yes, that's how Meleki was injured,' Adam confirmed. 'We were dealing with a group of ghouls when two strigae came out of nowhere, and one dragged their claws through his wing.'

I sighed, rubbing my neck as I addressed Vahin. 'How long until Meleki can fly?' The injured dragon's wing was knitting together at a glacial pace.

'Bring him meat, and it'll go faster. He's been starved for the last couple of days, and I'm still drained after our flight.'

I could sense how concerned he was for the much younger dragon. 'Adam, is there anything left?' I asked. Much to my relief, he nodded.

'Yes . . . well, I think so. I was searching for the key to the pantry when I found you. I don't starve my dragon, sir, I *swear*. The other monsters . . . they only left this morning, and I was waiting to see if they would return. I should have gone earlier, but—'

'It's alright, Adam,' I said, patting him on the shoulder. The kid had seen things that would break even the toughest warriors. I couldn't blame him for wanting to wait until the danger had passed.

ᛉᚳᚾᚠᛞ

After a quick run to the kitchens, we'd returned to the cave with two pig carcasses. I sat inside, watching Vahin feed himself and the younger dragon, Meleki, while I shared my rations with Adam. Luckily, Meleki could now move his wing and was stretching it out slowly, testing the membrane.

As we ate, I passed Adam my Commander's ring. 'This will open every door for you—do not lose it. When your task is done, go to my family's house in the capital. You'll be safe there.'

He clutched the ring tightly, nodding. 'Yes, sir. Meleki and I will do our best.'

I sighed, hoping I wasn't sending the kid to his death—but we had to warn the other dragon riders, and I had a promise to keep.

'Go. Your dragon is fed and rested. I have to leave for the capital now.'

Adam shook his head, pointing to runes over the entrance to the caves. A ring of old protection spells carved into the stone shone dimly with a blue aether.

'You can't go now, my lord. The spectrae are already here, and those glyphs are the only thing stopping them from feeding on us. If you go now, they'll tear you and your dragon apart. You'll have to wait until morning, sir.'

'What? I don't have time for this,' I said, rushing towards the entrance with Vahin on my heels.

My dragon stretched his wings, ready to leap into the sky as soon as I climbed into the saddle, but as I looked up, all hope died, leaving only pure, blinding rage.

The sky was a seething mass of spectrae, their ghostly forms swirling like an endless plague. Breaking through them would be impossible. I would not be returning to Truso in time to support Annika.

Frustration boiled over, and I paced the cave like a caged beast. The reasonable part of me, the part trained for battle, knew all too well that we couldn't escape their piercing tendrils, even if Vahin took us high above the clouds. But the man forcibly separated from his love was *raging*.

Adam curled into Meleki, and from the worried looks he gave me, I knew he must have been terrified by my lack of restraint.

Vahin, however, was silent. Ever since we'd seen the spectral horde overhead, he'd been sitting at the cave's entrance—as motionless as a marble statue—looking at the sky. His mental barriers were raised, cutting me off from his thoughts. The absence of our connection was a cold void in my mind, amplifying my sense of helplessness.

'Vahin?' I approached him, placing a hand on his long neck to draw him back from wherever his mind had wandered.

Otherworldly light blazed in his blue eyes, and I felt it then—not the comfortable touch of a dragon soul I was familiar with, but an infinite, weary spirit filled with grief and fear I now intimately knew. I stepped back in shock at the power radiating from him, and he turned his head back towards the sky.

'Leave me be, Ormond. I'm trying to protect you. You wouldn't be able to bear it,' he said with such heavy emotion that I couldn't turn away. Instead of abiding by his wish, I stepped between his front paws, drew my sword, and knelt with the naked blade across my knees.

'I don't need your protection, Vahin. I need you. And you need me. Don't lock me out. I know you are mourning, and I know we both love her—'

'No, Ormond. You do not know.' He paused, his pain spilling over. He shifted closer, lowering his head until I felt his warm breath on my neck. 'My kin are dead, senselessly slaughtered by that human mage's creations. Yet here I am, bonded to not one, but two humans. My fury at— no, my *hatred* for your kind wars with the love I bear for you and my Little Flame. It is tearing me apart, and, for once, I don't know what I should do. I almost wish I'd never met her . . . never awakened.'

The thought was a tortured whisper, and I clenched my jaw and opened my soul to his pain. 'You are the best of us, Vahin,' I said, forcing our bond wide to help my oldest friend share the burden. 'Now let me help you.'

He released a plume of smoke, the emotions he could no longer suppress flooding out like a torrent.

'Pray to your gods, Ormond. Pray that Annika survives tomorrow. Because if she doesn't, I will unleash destruction on this world until there is nothing left but dust.'

With that declaration, Vahin turned back to stare at the sky, and I prayed to the All-Father for my dragon and his broken heart while his mourning song filled my soul.

CHAPTER 17

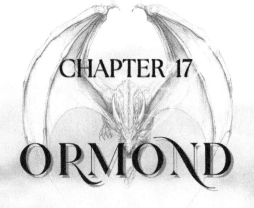

ORMOND

We left the moment the skies emptied, Vahin exploding from the cave with an urgency that bordered on desperation. He flew with breathtaking speed, his wings slicing through the cold air, and I didn't dare waste breath on words. Every ounce of strength, every precious second, was focused on returning to Ani's side.

The flight was torturous, the freezing wind leaving my hands and face burning from the cold, but we didn't let that keep us from returning to our family. I couldn't see the ground beneath us, but I didn't have to—Vahin knew exactly where he was going.

In the end, however, it didn't matter how fast we flew. The sun was already reaching its zenith, and the trial had been set for the dawn. We were late, and the implications of that froze my heart even more than the icy winds.

As the walls of the capital shimmered on the horizon, I broke the silence. '*Can you sense her?*'

'*Yes,*' Vahin replied, his voice strained.

I felt his fatigue as keenly as my own. The oldest and most powerful bonded dragon on the continent was nearing the limits of his endurance, but he didn't falter. He didn't slow. We hurtled over the city walls, heading straight for the arena.

When the sound of cheering reached us, Vahin roared in fury, a primal sound that sent shivers through me. *Those fuckers are cheering while she fights for her life?* His outrage became my own, fuelling a fire that burned hotter than the freezing air.

Vahin tucked his wings and dived, plummeting towards the arena floor like a thunderbolt. I braced myself, ready to leap from his back and cut down anyone who dared threaten Ani—or anyone who dared revel in her suffering. My disgust at my own people churned in my empty stomach.

We smashed into the arena floor, sand exploding upwards and filling the air with choking dust, but even as the grit stung my eyes, I saw her. Ani. She moved in a deadly dance, weaving between her attackers with lethal grace, staining the sand red with blood.

I cried out when a blade sliced across her chest, but she twisted just enough to avoid a killing blow. Pressing my knees into Vahin's sides, I urged him to attack her enemies, but before we could move, a wave of power surged through the arena, turning the sand before us to glass, and Vahin froze.

Ani's name left my lips as I bellowed, seeing just how outnumbered she was. This wasn't the political charade I'd expected, a face-saving show to give the empress an excuse to join the war. No, that damn woman wanted them dead, no matter the cost. She truly intended to kill the only conduit mage we had left.

And like a fool, I'd let it happen.

I'd examined the situation and calculated the odds like a commander but had underestimated Talena's hatred. Alaric had killed the empress' mate. For that, she'd thought he had to die, and she didn't care who died with him.

Another explosion shook the ground as we tried to move forward. The fire and smoke blinded me, and I cursed the fates for my helplessness until I saw Annika through the clearing haze. I punched the air in triumph, only for the feeling to be short-lived as Ani and Ari fell into a swirling black void. The portal vanished, and they were gone.

Vahin roared, his wings snapping open with a thunderclap. The lightning that penned us in stuttered and disappeared, but it didn't matter. The Black Dragon of Dagome was enraged. He lunged forward, smashing through glass spikes and fae warriors alike, tearing towards where the portal had been.

Panic spread like wildfire. Warriors and spectators scrambled to escape as Vahin's fury turned the arena into chaos. His scales blazed with blue light, raw primordial magic radiating from him. The air thickened, heavy with power, and cold sweat pooled under my collar. I'd never seen him like this, and I knew there was no controlling him now.

Vahin's mind was locked onto one thought. Ani.

'Open the portal!' he roared, his voice a thunderclap that shook the ground. The mages that had surrounded the portal collapsed to their knees, shaking in terror.

'Vahin, no,' I begged, acutely aware that he was preparing to unleash an inferno. 'Please. Annika wouldn't want this.'

'*She was bleeding!*' His voice trembled with anguish. '*My Little Flame was injured, and they sent her beyond my reach! She made me promise, Orm. Even now, the promise I made—*' His roar shook the arena as he dropped to all fours, releasing short bursts of fire. '*I'll honour it, but pray your gods have mercy on your kin because if my light is gone from this world, I will turn it into dust.*'

I thought the wild magic burning inside me was relentless, but as I felt Vahin's rage, I knew nothing could withstand the dragon's fury. But if he lost control and destroyed the city before Ani returned, he would never forgive himself.

Just like I'd done at Roan, I opened myself to Vahin's fury, allowing it to flood through our bond. I accepted his rage, his hate, his anguish, and gave him my love and unwavering support in return. Together, we sank into the storm of his emotions, the world beyond our connection fading into insignificance. Slowly, the tempest began to subside. Vahin's control returned, and I allowed myself a moment of relief—until an arrogant voice shattered the fragile peace.

'Welcome back, Commander,' Talena drawled, her tone laced with mockery. 'Unfortunately, you missed the most entertaining part of the trial. The conduit mage fought well—far better than I expected. Imagine my surprise when she managed to open the portal.' Her voice turned cold, and she gestured dismissively towards the arena floor. 'But since we don't anticipate her return, we can end this farce and consider the matter concluded.'

My head snapped towards the balcony where she stood. Even as she held herself with pride, wrapped in her magic like a shield, I caught the tremor in her hands. 'What do you mean, *concluded*?' My voice dropped, each word a warning. 'Choose your next words wisely, my lady. My dragon is on edge, and so am I.'

Her smirk widened, a venomous expression that ignited my rage anew. 'Only twice in the history of this trial has the Dark Mother granted her mercy to the penitents. I wouldn't hold your breath for their return.' She turned to her attendants, her tone flippant. 'I think a mourning feast is in order. Shall we?'

Every fibre of my being screamed for vengeance. I wanted to kill her, to rip her into pieces and watch her bleed on the same sand stained with my Nivale's blood. But Vahin's rising heat beneath me reminded me of the fine line we walked. If I gave in to my fury, so would he.

'*No,*' I told him. '*We can't kill her yet. Maybe one day, but not now. We need her, and Annika* will *return. Trust your Little Flame to find her way back to us.*'

As if summoned by my plea, a new voice broke through the tension.

'My lady, trial laws demand we wait for at least two hours before concluding the matter,' Valaram declared with perfect indifference, though his body radiated tension. I frowned, puzzled by the ambassador. He was clearly acting against the empress. *Why?*

Talena's head whipped towards him, her eyes narrowing dangerously. 'I don't appreciate your insubordination, brother dearest,' she hissed in an attempt to keep her voice low. 'Ever since you met this woman, you've questioned me far too often. You've never taken such an interest in females before, yet now you're arguing with me over a *human*? Do you wish to end up like my Erestis, slaughtered by the very one he sought to protect?'

Valaram's expression didn't waver, but his reply carried a subtle edge. 'Alaric's hand may have held the dagger, but the Lich King's had guided it—and you know it. It's unreasonable to kill our strongest weapon. As for my fascination with the human,' he added with a faint smile, 'I find Annika most entertaining.'

Despite his casual tone, something in his voice felt off. I focused on our unexpected ally as he leaned towards the empress, placing a hand on her shoulder. 'C'mon, sister, let's make a wager. I'll even put up that artefact you've always wanted, the necromancer's ruby, that she'll return. Annika is quite the resourceful little fox.'

'Your infatuation with this girl is blinding you,' Talena snapped, suspicion flashing across her face before she conceded. 'Fine, get your ruby ready to be delivered to my throne room. And what will you demand if your precious mage does indeed return?'

The ambassador's smile didn't falter. 'I want command of the army for a year.'

Her gasp echoed across the arena. 'You planned this!'

'Perhaps.' Valaram shrugged, and I tightened my grip on my pommel, fighting the urge to intervene.

'I will add to the wager,' Reynard said suddenly. 'The Zielands—those fertile lands your empire has long coveted. I wager them on Annika's return. Unless, of course, you are afraid to lose, my lady?'

The empress' face darkened, a sneer twisting her lips. 'I will take that bet. And what do *you* want in return, King of Dagome?'

'Not much,' Reynard replied smoothly. 'Just to offer your brother the position of my advisor, if he wouldn't mind accepting it.'

If the wager were not on my Nivale's life, I would have admired my brother's genius, but Annika was lost in a different realm, and they were using her life as a bargaining chip. Before I could speak, Vahin's roar silenced the arena.

'Fae Empress,' he thundered, levelling his massive head with the royal balcony, 'despite the passing of many years, you remain as reckless and impulsive as when you were a child.' His voice rumbled like an oncoming storm, and Talena stiffened under his glare.

The tension between them crackled, raw power radiating from both sides as they held a staring contest. The empress stepped back, her nostrils flaring as she summoned her magic, until Vahin's furious growl shook the arena.

'Sit. *Down*,' he commanded, his voice filled with ancient authority. Talena fell back into her chair, the weight of his words pressing her into submission. 'We will wait, and you should pray that your recklessness doesn't bring destruction to your people. Pray to your Dark Mother and hope that she returns my light to me. Hope that she shows you mercy. Because I will not.'

The conviction in his voice sent ripples of fear through the crowd. Many dropped to their knees, whispering desperate prayers.

The Vahin who had once laughed at Annika's antics and snorted at her requests to rub his belly was gone. Before us now was a creature of raw power and fury, his scales sparking with lightning as the sand beneath his claws melted into glass. The very air hummed with electricity, and I knew that no force in this world or the next would stop him if Ani was truly lost.

Talena trembled, her wide eyes fixed on Vahin in utter disbelief. 'My father spoke of your kind—the eldritch dragons, the Elementals. You're one of them,' she whispered, gripping the armrests.

'Yes,' he replied, his voice like distant thunder. 'I am Vahin of the Firstborn—the Aether of Storm. Don't think to test me, stripling, unless you are willing to face the fury of the tempest.' With that, he stepped back and turned to wait in the centre of the arena, his scales dimming as they returned to their usual hue.

'*Aether of Storm?*' I asked, still grappling with what I'd just heard. In response, Vahin showed me a vision: raging thunderstorms setting fire to the land with every strike, consuming everything in their path. And in the midst of the inferno, clashing dragons fought for dominance.

'*I'm sorry, Ormond,*' his voice echoed in my mind, heavy with weariness. '*I am much older than you could imagine. The Primes—my kin—nearly destroyed this world in our reign of fire. We who survived swore an oath to the skies, vowing never to meet again, lest our power shatter the world anew. With Annika carrying a shard of my soul, if she were to die, it would break me. I would be lost, and the world would experience a thunderstorm that would horrify even the gods.*'

There was no reply I could make to that, not when the beast in my heart roared, clawing its way out at the thought of losing my Nivale.

And so, we waited—our fates resting in the hands of an unknown goddess and a stubborn mage.

An hour passed. At some point, I'd slid from Vahin's back, leaning against his paw and absentmindedly stroking his eyelid as we stared at where the portal had been. I would have missed it if Vahin hadn't startled me, his sudden shift nearly planting my face in the sand—a strange pressure that made you grind your teeth to relieve it.

'*She's coming. I can feel her again!*' He roared, silencing the murmuring crowd surrounding us.

I jumped to my feet, sprinting towards the shimmering light that materialised, but Vahin was faster. How such a gigantic creature could move so quickly was baffling. In one fluid motion, he moved from his resting position to coil protectively around the woman who appeared in midair, cushioning her fall.

The joy Vahin was projecting overwhelmed my senses, and I stumbled, but I fought to stay upright. This moment was too important to falter now, so I closed our bond and rushed forward, looking around in distress. Annika was here, but where was my other mate?

My question was answered moments later. As Annika disappeared within the coils of Vahin's body, Alaric appeared, only to fall to the ground, hitting it so hard that the glass cracked beneath his body.

'Hrae! You overgrown, slow worm. There are *two* of us, you know,' he cursed, wincing as he tried to sit up.

I reached him first, pulling him into a crushing embrace. Relief flooded me, leaving me breathless and grinning like an idiot. 'You survive a goddess and still have time to whine about not getting a cuddle from a dragon?' I teased, pressing him so hard to my chest that his bones creaked.

He muttered something unintelligible, but all I could think of was that I had my fae back in one piece. 'No,' I growled quietly when he tried to push me away. 'I need to hold you, just for a moment.'

'Fine, but you're choking me,' he answered with a laugh.

After a moment, I reluctantly let him go to focus on my dragon and the treasure he held close.

'Vahin, give Ani a chance to breathe, please,' I said, my throat tightening with emotion.

'So you can crush her next?' he retorted with a glee. Vahin slowly unfurled his wing, allowing me to see my Nivale. She was battered and bruised, dressed in a strange grey robe that seemed opalescent in the sunlight, but she was alive. I could see a fresh scar where something had pierced her shoulder and various half-healed cuts across her body, but none of that mattered.

She smiled at me, and suddenly, all I knew was her radiance and the love warming our bond. Every rational thought left my mind, and I couldn't move, shaking at the realisation of how close I had been to losing them.

'You made it back in time. I heard Vahin when . . . I thought I'd never see you again,' she said, reaching for me, and *still*, I stood there like a dumb rock, afraid that if I moved, if I tried to touch her, she would disappear. Annika frowned as her outstretched hand hung in the air. 'Orm, I'm here. Aren't you happy—?'

I didn't let her finish. In seconds, I was by her side, sweeping her into my arms.

'Happy?' I growled, my voice shaking. 'I'm fucking furious. I'm *never* letting you leave my side again. I'm gone for one day, and you and this rogue vanish to gods know where. I watched you *disappear*—both of you! Do you have any idea—' My voice broke, the weight of my fear choking me. 'Vahin was ready to destroy the world, Ani. And I

199

would've helped him. You're my everything,' I said, forcing myself to take a breath. 'And you need a fucking healer.'

Alaric cleared his throat beside me, resting a hand on my shoulder. 'If you think I'll let another healer touch my domina, you're mistaken,' he said, his tone light. 'I'm her healer, and I recommend Ani be waited on by both her Anchors in a tension-melting bath.'

'Don't be ridiculous. Vahin wouldn't fi—' I began, but the words caught in my throat as realisation struck. My eyes darted to Alaric's chest, where his curse marks had been. 'Ari?'

He grinned and Annika jumped up to kiss my neck. 'What the *fuck* happened on your little detour?' I demanded.

'It was bound to happen,' Annika replied, though her expression was tinged with confusion. 'When we . . . when we . . .' She trailed off, glancing at Ari, who shrugged.

'Don't even try, sweetheart. You know how the trial's details are kept secret,' he said. 'I'm sorry, Orm. I don't think we're allowed to talk about it.'

I frowned but relented. 'Fine, but your curse—'

'Is gone,' he confirmed.

I let out a disbelieving laugh, overwhelmed by a rush of emotions. 'We need to celebrate,' I said, closing my eyes against the onslaught of relief and joy. 'Fuck, I can't believe it.'

'Warn me before you start anything amorous so I can fly high enough that your celebrations can't reach me,' Vahin grumbled. 'One experience of your bathing antics was more than enough for this old dragon's mind.'

We burst into laughter before a sharp voice shattered our moment of happiness.

'Annika Diavellar, how long will you make me wait?' Talena sounded furious, and I realised we'd been ignoring everyone in our happy little bubble.

Annika stiffened, a dangerous glint in her eye. 'I am going to knock her teeth out. Let me go, Orm. I have some issues to put to bed.' She pushed away from my chest, her body trembling with restrained energy that left no doubt she meant to do exactly what she said she would.

'I'm sorry, love,' I said with a wry grin, wrapping my arm around her waist. 'We still need her, so please try to be satisfied with watching her eat her humble pie. Reynard and Valaram have already handled it.'

'Oh?' she asked, but I didn't want to spoil the surprise.

'You'll see, sweetheart. You'll see.'

Annika narrowed her eyes but allowed me to guide her towards the royal dais. She met Talena's venomous glare with a smirk, unbothered by the hatred radiating from the dark fae empress.

'Congratulations, human,' the empress sneered. 'Alaric'va Shen'ra is cleared of his crimes and may live freely in the Care'etavos Empire.' Her expression was so sour I wondered if she was chewing on a pickle.

'And?' Valaram prompted softly.

Her lips curled in distaste, but she continued. '*And* my brother is free to command the dark fae army for a year. If he wishes, he may also serve as your king's advisor.'

Annika's eyes lit up, and she turned to the older fae with a triumphant smile. 'You got the army,' she said.

Valaram stepped forward and kissed her hand reverently. 'I knew you could do it, lara'mei. You were incredible.'

Before she could respond, Ari's voice cut through the air, cold and razor-sharp. 'She is not your *lara'mei*. Are you challenging me, my lord?'

The ambassador raised an eyebrow, unfazed. 'I already told you, Shen'ra. It is not your decision to make. But you are welcome to issue a challenge. I haven't fought a duel in years, but I'm sure I still remember how to wield a dagger.'

'This is absurd,' Talena snapped. 'She is not your lara'mei, and there will be no challenges.'

Annika let out an exasperated sigh and stepped forward, hands on her hips as she glared at the gathered nobles.

'I've had enough of this nonsense. I'm not sure what you're all playing at, but you will *all* calm down, or I swear I'll make you regret it. I'm tired, dirty, and my body still aches from all the beatings I've been put through. I have no interest in two men measuring the size of their . . . daggers, and I've *really* had enough of you, Empress.' Her voice sharpened as she addressed Talena directly. 'You've hated me from the moment you set eyes on me, and you know what? I'm a gnat's nose hair from sorting this out right now and putting you out of the misery of your existence.'

I pressed my lips together to suppress the laughter that threatened to escape my control. Annika was magnificent, even if she looked like a furious cat hissing at her enemies.

'My lady—' Valaram began, but Annika cut him off with a raised hand.

'Enough! You're old enough to know better. And you—' She whirled on Alaric, who suddenly looked sheepish. 'If you want to play soldier with Valaram, be my guest. I'm going home, and I'm sleeping with the dragon tonight. He's the only one with any sense left.'

I lost control of my laughter, my sides fit to burst as I looked at Talena's horrified expression. Annika gave me an accusatory glare before storming down the stairs, Alaric hot on her heels, his face bright red.

My expression sobered once they'd left, my gaze hardening as I turned to the empress. 'Will you keep your word and fight with Dagome?'

She hesitated, then sighed. 'Yes. I didn't expect her to return, so it must be the Dark Mother's wish that I ally with you. Dagome will have the support of the Care'etavos Empire, though I'll leave the fighting to my brother,' she said before gesturing to her guards and nodding to the king as she left. 'Send a message to Valaram when you're ready for the war council.'

'Good,' I said grimly. 'Roan Fortress has been obliterated. Dragons, soldiers, civilians—everyone. The place is swarming with spectrae. That's why I was late. The war has already begun, and we must confront them before more lives are lost.' I turned to Reynard, gritting my teeth at the still-raw grief. 'Shall I meet you at the palace to plan?'

He shook his head, his expression sombre. 'No. Go home, Orm. Be with your family. We'll need you rested and clearheaded when the council convenes. Just be ready to come when I call for you.'

I nodded, relief washing over me at the reprieve. Ari had anchored Annika, and I was curious to find out what that meant for us. I needed time with my family. After nearly losing them both, I realised my fear was not only for her but also for a roguish fae who'd stealthily stolen my heart.

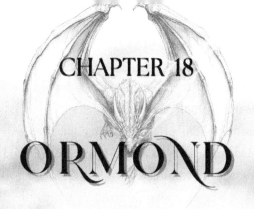

CHAPTER 18

ORMOND

I sent someone to fetch us some horses and hurried after Anika. When I saw her cuddling Vahin's neck and stroking his scales, I couldn't hold back my smile. Gone was the threat of death and destruction, the fury melting away like last year's snow under her touch.

Alaric rested against the dragon's paw, his eyes closed and a peaceful expression on his face. The scene was so idyllic that even as Vahin noticed me, I urged him to stay quiet as I crept up behind Ani and swept her off her feet.

She squealed, fire sparking in her palm before vanishing when she realised who it was.

'How are your injuries, sweetheart?' I murmured, needing to hold her close.

'I'll be fine, Orm,' she grumbled, though I caught the note of pleasure in her voice. 'You can put me down. I'm not made of glass.'

Alaric opened his eyes, his crooked smile as familiar as it was devastating. 'No, you are certainly not made of glass,' he agreed smoothly. 'Glass would've shattered under such duress. You are a pure diamond—precious and unyielding—meant only for those strong enough to hold you.'

Ani blushed, suddenly preoccupied with combing my hair with her fingers. 'Sweet talker. You think buttering me up will earn my forgiveness after challenging Valaram?' she asked, but the gentle rebuke did nothing to hide the soft smile she gave him.

'A hint of jealousy is the spice of life,' Ari replied, his grin entirely unrepentant. 'Does it make me a wicked man if I can't stand how he looks at you? You are mine, Annika.'

'Oh, she is?' I quipped, raising an eyebrow, and the devilish man rolled his eyes.

'Fine—ours. But I'm the only dark fae she'll ever love.'

'*Really?*' Ani teased. 'Maybe I've acquired a taste for older men. Valaram *is* a silver fox. All that scheming and charm . . .'

'No, listen to your Anchor,' I interjected with mock gravity. 'Alaric is right. And if you want someone older, then look no further than Grandpa Dragon here. His scales are a much better colour than any silver fox.'

Vahin's tail thumped the ground, startling Annika into clinging to my neck in alarm. 'I'm not *that* old, puny human,' he rumbled.

With exaggerated solemnity, I bowed. 'Of course, you aren't, O eldritch terror born at the dawn of time.'

Vahin's roar filled the air, his lips pulling back to expose the rows of sharp teeth while unbridled amusement radiated through our bond.

'You're a menace, Ormond. A pimple on my arse I tolerate only because you make my Little Flame happy.'

I smiled. 'And yet you chose me when I needed you most,' I said, meeting his brilliant blue gaze as he lowered his snout to touch my cheek.

'And I've never regretted it.'

We were still waiting for the horses, and I briefly thought of using Vahin, but my dragon was exhausted. His muscles ached, his hunger gnawed, and I knew the moment he took to the skies, he'd need to hunt. Hoping to distract him, I turned to my mates and asked, 'Do you think you'll ever be able to share what happened on the other side of the portal?'

They shared a glance before Annika sighed. 'I don't know. It's not that I don't *want* to tell you, but every time I try, my thoughts get muddled. I can't find the words.'

'It feels like some kind of geas,' Alaric added. 'All I can say is that Ani made a bargain that ended my curse and earned my freedom. I'll spend the rest of my life trying to be worthy of her.'

Ani reached out and gently stroked his face, her expression softening. 'You were already worthy. I love you. So, stop thinking that way. There's no tallying gains or losses here—I've already won. I have a second chance at love, and I'll fight for it because life without you three wouldn't be worth living. I hope, one day, you'll stop believing you're not enough.'

Alaric was right—she was a diamond. I felt it deep in my soul, the purity of Annika's feelings, the impressive strength that made her bargain with a goddess for our mate. She had a sharp tongue and refused to bow to anyone, but under the sass, brass, and wicked temper was a spirit that entranced us all.

Through our link, Vahin's voice interrupted my thoughts. *'She is all that and more. That's why the goddess let her leave. But I can feel a tether, a touch of darkness. It isn't harming her, but it clings to her soul. It is so strong that my Little Flame will never be free of it.'*

The bitterness in his tone revealed his unhappiness, and I understood. Annika had sacrificed more than she'd ever admit to save us.

'How are you feeling?' I asked him. *'Today was ... difficult.'*

'Hungry. Tired. Nothing you wouldn't expect after a strenuous journey,' he responded after a moment of hesitation. *'But I don't want to leave her. After seeing what happened to my brethren, I was ... afraid, and that fear brought out a part of me I thought long buried.'*

The uncertainty in his thoughts indicated that the admission surprised him.

'*You mean when you threatened to unleash destruction on that petulant bitch?*' I joked, trying to lighten the mood. '*You just said what we all were thinking, so maybe we're a bad influence on you.*' I gestured towards the sky. '*Go hunt. You need to look after yourself. Annika already said she's spending the night with you, and as much as it pains me, I won't be an arse about it.*'

The wave of gratitude flowing through our connection made me smile. Sometimes, Vahin felt like just another man, hopelessly in love with the force of nature who had ensnared us all.

'*Oh, but I do love her, Orm,*' he thought, unfolding his wings. '*Just because I can't be with her in the way you are, it doesn't make those feelings any less valid.*'

Annika looked up at Vahin, surprised by the sudden movement, and he backed away as he prepared to take off. 'I need to feed, Little Flame,' he said, and she nodded, sheltering her eyes from the gusts of wind as he disappeared into the sky.

'Let's get you home, Nivale,' I said, noticing a soldier by the gate gesturing to catch my attention. We left the arena, and I looked around the crowded street, trying to find our mounts, frowning at the carriage with the royal insignia blocking my view as we approached him.

'His Majesty thought a carriage would be better for Lady Annika after her ordeal,' the soldier said.

Embarrassed that I hadn't thought of it myself, I silently blessed my brother for the thoughtful gesture. But as we walked towards it, I snorted at the gold-covered monstrosity—Reynard had clearly gifted it to us to avoid using it himself.

Inside, however, the plush red cushions and delicate fabrics were surprisingly inviting. The carriage smelled of flowers, their fragrance soft and calming. Ani let out a tranquil sigh as she nearly disappeared into the cushions, placing her feet on my lap, and I gently massaged her muscles.

She drifted off to sleep quickly, her breathing steady, while Alaric rested beside me, his hand on my thigh. The soothing weight lulled me into a sense of contentment, but just as I began to relax, his grip tightened painfully, jolting me awake.

We'd left the heart of the city and were moving through the noble district when I realised that Ari was deathly quiet beside me, the tension in his body disturbing me more with every passing moment.

'What is it?' I asked.

'We're going in the wrong direction,' he said, his voice low. 'I initially thought it was just to avoid the merchant quarter, but the sun is to the west, and we are heading towards the river port.' He paused, then added, 'And . . . I feel sleepy. I don't want to fight or care . . . it's not natural.'

He was hesitant, but seeing the deep frown on his face, I rose from my seat and grasped the carriage door, waking Annika as I moved. She shook her head, disoriented, while I yanked at the handle. The door was locked. I tried again, and familiar, taunting laughter rang out from outside, triggering the berserker in me.

'Don't bother, Commander. The carriage is sealed and bespelled, and by the time we reach our destination, my concoction will have done its job. You'll be as docile as a little lamb.'

'Ihrain,' Annika whispered, her pupils dilating with fury. Her hand shot forward.

'*Quanre.*'[1]

---

1. *Open.*

Nothing happened.

She turned to Alaric, whose grim expression mirrored her own. 'I can't cast either,' he said, holding onto the ornate frame when the carriage jolted, picking up speed. 'That venomous viper! He must have sprayed lanara and masked it with a floral scent.' His hand slipped, and he stared at his palm in surprise. 'Hrae! He used nivale oil. That explains why we're so drowsy.'

My stomach dropped. Nivale root, often used to ease the dying into a peaceful transition, was readily available. But nivale oil, distilled from its fiery petals, was far more potent and extraordinarily rare. It was typically reserved for the gravest of agonies, applied to a cloth and held gently over a loved one's face, granting them a fleeting moment of tranquillity before death. To coat the entire interior of the carriage with it was an act of grotesque extravagance—one that must have required months, if not years, to gather such a quantity.

'Your stupidity blinds you if you think I'll allow you to take me again.' Annika was seething, and I felt a pull in my chest as she drew on the aether. For a moment, I worried she might blow the carriage to pieces, but the sensation faded, and she slumped back, shaking her head.

Ihrain's voice oozed satisfaction. 'Predictable as always, my dear. Your conduit abilities mean nothing when you can't cast. How does it feel to be helpless? Delivered to our master in a royal carriage, no less—a beautifully wrapped little package.' He laughed. 'I made it ready for you when I first saw you at Varta Fortress, and just look at how perfectly it fits the occasion. You'll eat from the Lich King's hand and grovel at my feet when I'm done with you.'

I braced to smash through the doors, but Ani's hand on my sleeve stopped me. 'And how do you intend to do it? Vahin will burn you to a cinder the moment he knows. You'll never get to the Rift,' she said, tapping a finger to her lips, signalling for me to stay quiet.

'The Rift? Gods, how naïve you are,' Ihrain sneered. 'It took years to find a surviving Moroi mage, and even longer for them to pass the Lost Ridge. But once they did, all they had to do was find the ruins of Netaré and activate the old fae portal there.'

He laughed, dark and menacing. 'You all forgot that Dagome had a trading agreement with Ozar to exchange diplomats and knowledge. The old portals still stand. All we had to do was bring them back to life. Such a shame only the living can pass through, though; otherwise, Truso would have been overrun by monsters long ago.'

I glanced at Alaric, who nodded bleakly, confirming the truth in Ihrain's words. I remained quiet, but was already planning ways to destroy the ruins we were being taken to. If there really was an active portal in Netaré, did the Council of Mages know? Or had they failed to uncover this critical threat? Twice now, mages had taken Annika. I couldn't afford to dismiss the possibility of betrayal or incompetence.

'If that's true, why did you bother using the Rift for so long?' Annika asked scornfully, using Ihrain's arrogance to keep him talking. 'Do you take me for a fool, Ihrain?'

'It was a distraction, keeping the dragons occupied so we could take over without interference.' His voice turned bitter. 'You've always been a fool and a whore, Annika. I can't believe I wanted you. If you weren't a conduit, I'd have killed you years ago.'

I shook from the rage his words provoked, and it took all my self-control to not rip the carriage—and him—to pieces. I felt the wild magic negating the effects of the nivale oil, its power utterly unaffected by the lanara poison.

To my surprise, Annika smiled—a sharp, feral grin, holding my hand and pointing to the door.

'Ihrain, you are so smart.' Her voice dripped with mock admiration. 'You thought of everything, and I commend you for expertly mixing the poisons, but I think you missed one tiny, little detail,' she crowed, still grinning like a madwoman. 'Tell me, Ihrain. Do you know what happens when you lock an enraged bear in a cage?'

Ani let go of my hand, and I roared, the sound ripping through the night. Letting go of my restraint, I jabbed my fist into the carriage wall—all the frustration, grief, and pain focused on the robust wood. Wood splintered and flew as my hand smashed through the frame.

On the other side, a man let out a startled cry before I dragged him back through the broken wall. He didn't even have time to scream as Alaric punched him in the face and stole his dagger, thrusting the blade deep into the flailing man's chest.

The horses panicked, bolting forward in a blind frenzy. I grabbed Annika, pulling her close to shield her from the chaos. I widened the hole in the carriage, desperate to get us out. Alaric jumped through the opening, and I heard the familiar sound of dying men, the stench of blood and urine filling the air, accompanied by the rising pressure of gathering magic.

'Orm, get her out of here! It's heading for the river!' he shouted. Before I could respond, a bolt of magic crashed into his back, sending him flying.

I grasped the doors, ripping them off their hinges, but the terrified neighs of the horses told me there was no chance of stopping them before it was too late. 'Hold tight, my love,' I whispered, clutching Ani tightly before jumping from the moving carriage.

The ground rushed up to meet us. The impact knocked the breath from my lungs, and as we rolled across the grass, my back slammed into something hard, momentarily blacking out my vision. But even then,

I didn't release Annika. I could die breaking my fucking neck, but I wouldn't add another bruise to my Nivale's body.

'Orm, are you insane? Let me go!' she shouted.

Shaking off the fog in my mind, I staggered to my feet, looking for Alaric. He was battling a small group of horsemen with nothing but the stolen dagger, his movements fluid and lethal. I laughed as the outmatched fae, his back still smoking from the previous magical attack, leapt up, embedding his blade into the armpit of one man while he kicked another off his horse.

'Ari, look out!' Annika's shout brought me back to reality as a bolt of energy flew over Alaric's head. It looked like Ihrain had finally regained control of his horse long enough to cast another spell.

Ani tensed beside me, reaching for the aether. I placed a hand on her shoulder, shaking my head. 'You've fought enough today. Don't engage unless we actually get into trouble. We'll handle this.'

She opened her mouth to protest, but I bent down and kissed her forehead. 'Just once, let your men look after you.'

With that, I charged into the fray. My fist connected with one man's kidney, sending him sprawling from his horse. Another rider barrelled towards me, hoping to use his mount as a battering ram. I sidestepped, seizing his stirrup, and yanked him to the ground.

In my current state, the men were no problem, but Ihrain was an issue. He had finally given up trying to control his horse and had dismounted, the murderous look in his eyes not boding well for us.

He muttered something, his hands tracing out a spell. I watched as a flurry of semitransparent blades headed straight for me, but Ari pushed me aside, his free hand moving rapidly in the air. Most of the aethereal blades disappeared, absorbed by a miraculously appearing shield. All except one that slipped past, scoring a long cut along his ribcage.

'How?' Ihrain gasped.

'Lanara works through continuous exposure. That's why it's so effective when ingested or injected. Your little trick stopped working the moment I wiped the damn stuff off onto the grass,' Alaric answered, throwing his blade into the back of a fleeing soldier.

I brought my boot down on the neck of the man I'd dragged from his horse, though Alaric didn't seem to notice. His focus was singular, his movements predatory as he stalked his prey, a snarl curling his lips. There were no more thugs to fight. We were alone on the road, and I doubted anyone would be coming this way now.

'Are you done? Can I come out now?' Ani shouted, rising from the grass, juggling a small fireball in her hand. It seemed her casting ability had also returned after her exposure to the lanara.

I revelled in the panic on Ihrain's face. He knew he'd lost, and even better, he knew nothing could save him now. Desperation flickered in his eyes as he turned to run. With a single word, Alaric's magic lashed out—purple ropes of aether shooting out to coil around Ihrain's legs, pulling him to the ground.

'You filthy fae bastard,' Ihrain sneered. Ari calmly walked towards him, stopping only to retrieve his dagger from the dead soldier's back.

'I promised you retribution the first time you offended my domina, but I intended to make your death swift,' Alaric said, viciousness burning with crimson fire in his eyes. 'Now I will delight in your suffering.'

Gone was the flirty rogue that brightened my day with his throaty laughter, replaced by a dark fae—cruel, vengeful, and deadly.

'You can't kill me! Your sister—' Ihrain's words turned into an agonised scream when Ari drove the dagger into his thigh.

'Whatever happens to my sister, you will have no part in it,' Alaric hissed, twisting the blade. 'You *will* die, Ihrain, and it will be slow.

Painful. Beautiful.' His grin was savage. 'Do you know what's most interesting about those who enjoy pain? We know *exactly* how to inflict it without killing.'

'Ari, we need to question him,' Annika said, approaching us tentatively.

Alaric smirked, his shadowy tendrils pulling her gently towards him. 'I don't need him alive to question him, my Domina,' he told her. 'He's a lying rat who'll say whatever you want to hear to save his own skin, but the dead can't lie to a necromancer, and he'll soon happily answer all of my questions.'

Ihrain howled as Ari twisted the dagger again, the sound tapering into a pathetic whimper. When his eyes began to roll back, he was rewarded with a hard slap across the face, and the former royal apprentice cursed and spat. Tears flowed down his cheek as he tried to crawl away, but Alaric's magic held him in place.

'Just kill him,' Annika said softly, her lips tight. 'I don't want . . . I know he deserves to die, but don't play with him. Please.' Her voice was quiet but resolute, and I noticed her wince as Ihrain's cries hit a higher note.

'Why don't you gather the horses for us, sweetheart?' I said, giving her an excuse to escape the bloodshed. She hesitated but nodded, walking away.

When she was gone, I turned to Alaric. 'What are you going to do with him?'

'Kill him, of course,' he replied, his voice a mix of venom and dark amusement. 'But not before I've had my fun.'

I frowned. 'Not when Ani's watching—'

He placed a hand on my shoulder, his expression softening. 'Of course not. Scum like him doesn't deserve to see her face in his final moments. Besides, I need more time than it'll take for Ani to return to

215

satisfy this need. Once I grasp his soul, he'll tell me the location of all the portals and traps he set for Annika.'

I nodded. He was right, and I wouldn't deny him his vengeance. 'Gag him and make sure he's secure. We have cells at the mansion. Do it after Annika's asleep. That will be easiest for everyone.'

Ari smiled, placing a hand on my cheek. 'I will. I knew you'd understand.'

Ihrain thrashed and screamed as Alaric bound him, gagging him before Annika returned with three horses in tow.

'Is he alive?' she asked, frowning at his immobilised body on the grass.

'Yes, Domina. I apologise for upsetting you. I will take him to the mansion for questioning,' he said, bowing his head when she approached to pass him one of the horses' reins.

'Ari, I know you're going to kill him. Just be quick about it,' she said, biting her lip.

I lifted her onto the nearest horse, distracting her. 'Come, Nivale. Our fae will do what he has to in order to find out what the bastard's been up to. We have our own tasks—like tending to that gash on Ari's side. And later, we'll talk about what I think of him jumping out to shield me with his body.'

Alaric grinned as he mounted his horse. 'As always, I am at your command, my lord. But—if I may be so bold—I will always shield you from danger. I have claimed it as my right.' He glanced ahead. 'Now, should we go home? I'm afraid the longer we're here, the more likely we'll have to face an enraged and anxious dragon if he doesn't find us at the mansion when he arrives.'

I shook my head with a chuckle. 'Dark fae—all sass and blades.'

Annika's laughter broke through the tension, and for a moment, the weight of the night lifted.

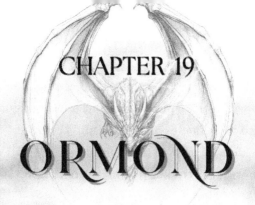

CHAPTER 19

ORMOND

'Lord Commander, you've received a message from your brother.'

We'd barely stepped through the door to the mansion when the seneschal made his announcement. He extended a sealed missive, and I fought the growl rising in my throat as I glanced at it.

'Get the baths ready, call Agnes to attend to Lady Annika, and bring us food. Has Vahin returned?' I asked, the pounding headache in my temples preventing me from asking the dragon myself.

Is Reynard summoning me? I didn't want to leave the mansion, not with Ihrain bound like festive sausage and Annika falling asleep in my arms. If I read that letter, I wouldn't have a choice in whether or not I reported to him, so I ignored it for the moment.

'Yes, my lord,' the seneschal replied. 'Your dragon has returned and is resting in his lair. I'll make the arrangements—'

A shrill shriek interrupted him, making us both wince.

'My lady! Oh, my poor lady! What have they done to you?' Agnes was running down the stairs, wailing like a vjesci.

'I'm fine.' Annika jerked awake in my hold, sending me a pleading look, but I knew better than to get between my woman and her maid. From the moment I had chosen Agnes to serve Ani, the girl had surprised me with how protective she was of my Nivale.

217

'Agnes is right, my love,' I said softly. 'You're exhausted. Let her look after you while Ari and I deal with our unwanted guest.'

Alaric looked at me questioningly. 'Ihrain,' I clarified. 'We need to secure him, and I'll need to read this bloody letter.' I exhaled sharply. 'Then we'll all get some rest. Please, both of you, listen to me for a change.'

Annika moved closer, concern etched on her beautiful face, but I stepped back. Something about coming home had loosened the emotions I'd wrapped into a tight knot deep in my core. My family was safe, but for how long?

The memory of the massacre at Roan Fortress surged unbidden, and it took every ounce of restraint not to let it show when I looked at her. To me, she was a woman burdened with too many scars. To the rest of the world, she was a weapon—a tool to win not just battles, but wars. Few cared how that role weighed on her.

'Something's wrong, isn't it?' she asked, her hand resting gently on my cheek. 'Don't lie to me. I know that look. Something's bothering you.' Her concern bled into our bond, filling the cracks I was desperate to keep sealed.

'Roan Fortress was attacked. It was a massacre,' I admitted, pressing a kiss to her palm before pulling away. The pain of losing so many souls was finally catching up with me. I needed space—distance—to keep from unravelling in front of her. 'Please, let me take care of things, then I will join you. It's better that way.'

My throat was too tight to say more, but I knew she could feel the maelstrom of emotions burning inside me. Sadness filled Annika's eyes; my rejection must have hurt her, but she straightened her back and forced a tight smile. 'I understand. Take your time, but promise me you won't be alone. Maybe you can spend some time with Ari?'

'I will, sweetheart,' I said, managing a faint smile. 'And I'll make sure he rests, too. Don't worry about me—I'm just an old soldier who has seen too much. I'll be fine. Go find that grumpy dragon. He misses you. He flew faster than the northern winds to reach you.'

She hesitated, her worry lingering, so I teased her, 'I expect to see you on the training grounds tomorrow. You were injured, and I suspect my battle mage has gotten a little sloppy lately.'

Annika huffed, feigning annoyance. 'Don't worry, I'll show you I can still beat your arse.'

As she walked away with Agnes, Vahin's voice rumbled through my weary mind. *'Thank you, Ormond. I need her more than I could ever explain.'*

Gesturing for the guards to take Ihrain, Alaric turned to follow them.

'Not yet,' I said, stopping him. 'Take the piece of trash to the cells, then bathe and wait for me in our bedroom.' He turned back, raising his eyebrow as if my commanding tone were the last thing he expected. 'Please, just do it.'

I turned away, unwilling to face having to make another decision, yet heading straight to the war room to do so anyway. That damned letter was burning a hole in my psyche, and the sooner I knew what my brother wanted, the sooner I could report on my findings at Roan Fortress. Once that was done, I could take the time to face my own emotions.

ᛉᚳᚾᚠᚼ

An hour later, I was done. The missive was nothing urgent—simply Reynard sending his regards and informing me of the war council the

219

next day. I quickly wrote a response, attaching the report on Roan, the details of our latest misadventure, and the location of Ihrain's portal. It was crucial Rey had this information before facing the other leaders—better to prepare him than let him be blindsided later by my revelations.

With the task complete, I made my way to the bath, eager to wash away the grime and tension of the day. Afterwards, I headed to the bedroom, hoping Alaric was already there.

By the time I opened the door, my mind was a mess of tangled emotions, all held together by uncertainty about our future. There was so much I needed to get off my chest, but could our newly blossoming relationship survive me sharing it all?

Inside, the unflappable bastard stood by the table, pouring a glass of wine. The sight of him stopped me in my tracks. He looked so much better. A bath and a change of clothes seemed to have restored the silver glow of his skin, but the most significant change was his eyes, gleaming with a golden light. There wasn't a single hint of the pain that so often hid there. I stopped to study him, dressed only in spider silk, his shirt unbuttoned, openly showing the curse's silver marks he'd been ashamed of for years, but even those had changed.

'Wine?' he asked. 'Have a drink and tell me why I had to postpone the interrogation. You know my hands are itching to show Ihrain what "filth" can really do.' He smirked, but his expression faltered when I crossed the room in two strides, slamming him against the wall.

My hand locked onto his throat, but he didn't flinch, just calmly placed the goblet back on the table. 'You spilt the wine,' he whispered, the tease in his voice almost maddening. His body relaxed in my grasp—a show of trust that stole my breath. I needed him, and as his throat bobbed beneath my hand, I crushed my lips to his in a punishing kiss.

'Next time you jump in to shield me, I'll kill you myself,' I growled, pulling back just enough to meet his gaze as my thumb traced the bruise on his cheek. 'How dare you endanger yourself? I can't fucking lose you, you stubborn bastard.'

Ari inhaled sharply, crimson light beginning to swirl in the depths of his eyes as he slowly licked his lips. 'Dare?' he asked. 'You're asking me how I dare to love you? How I dare protect the man who sees me for what I truly am and still accepts me? For all these years, you've meant more to me than anyone ever before. I'd die a thousand times for you, Ormond Erenhart. I *dare* you to question that.'

Alaric's voice was hoarse with emotion as he swallowed. When he turned his head to catch my thumb between his teeth, I groaned, forgetting my dark thoughts. *Gods, I want him so fucking much.* I pressed myself against him, pinning his body to the wall.

'I thought I'd lost you. I thought we'd returned too late, and in a way, it brought clarity to my mind. I can't deny us, so if you have any doubts, stop me,' I murmured, breathing in his crisp, masculine scent. 'Stop me, because if you don't, I will make you mine, Ari, and when I take you, your body and soul will never be free of me.'

'No,' he whispered, his body trembling under my touch. 'I know what I want, Ormond; I was just waiting for you to want this, too. Do your worst. I can take it. I can take . . . you.'

'Fuck,' I muttered as the last barrier between us crumbled. I leaned in for a kiss, and its searing heat reforged years of friendship into something more. Something so profound that it changed who I was. I didn't have the words to describe it.

My hands shook with uncharacteristic vulnerability as I pulled back. 'I don't know what to do,' I confessed, a quiet laugh escaping me. 'I've never been with a man.'

Alaric's eyes brightened with joy. 'And you never will be with another,' he said softly. 'Do what you feel is right, and I will tell you if it becomes too much.'

My possessive fae had staked his claim and gave me the freedom to explore, but this wasn't the teenage fumbling I'd witnessed in the barracks. I wanted something better for the both of us, and a sudden thought crossed my mind.

'I know we're both Anchored to Ani, but I . . . I want a bond shared between the two of us, too, not just . . . Is the . . . Is it possible for us to share the blood bond, too?'

I was tripping through this like a nervous colt, my lack of knowledge failing me. I didn't know if the blood bond was practised between dark fae males or whether it was only for a male and his domina, but I wanted it, and when he nodded, I acted on my craving.

My hand slid into his long, white hair, and I wrapped the strands around my fingers, twisting cruelly, never once looking away from his crimson eyes. With his lithe body pressed against mine, I kissed him again, licking across his lips until they parted, and I pushed inside. Ari moaned as I took control, and when my tongue slid over his fang, the soft flesh parted on its sharp edge, making him whimper.

'Ormond,' he gasped, breaking the kiss, his eyes searching mine. 'Remember that for me, this is . . . forever.' His expression was so open and full of yearning that I wanted to pull him back to me, but he had to choose this.

'I fucking hope so,' I said, the words spilling out like a vow. 'You're the only one, Alaric'va Shen'ra. The only man I could ever love. You're more than a friend, closer than a brother. I want you to know I want this—I want *you*.'

'No regrets?'

'Only that I waited so long,' I admitted, cupping his face. 'I was blind, Ari, just a man set in my ways, unable to see love when it smacked me in the face, but that changes now. I want the entire world to know you are mine, and if anyone ever questions this, we can just unleash Annika on them.'

Alaric laughed, the sound like a balm to my soul. 'I wouldn't wish her wrath on my worst enemy,' he said, pressing his leg against my hard cock. 'I want this so much, but Ani will always come first. You understand that, don't you?'

'Understand? She made all of this possible. You, me, Vahin. For all of us, she will always come first, but loving you differently doesn't mean I love you less. So, are you going to let me in, my roguish necromancer, or will you continue stalling for time?' I asked, and his breath came in shuddering pants.

Alaric reached up and gripped my shoulders, tilting his head as he answered. 'I accept. Dark Mother, is this real?' he asked right before leaning forward for a kiss.

He was shaking like a leaf, looking so overwhelmed that I let him set the pace. The caress, when it happened, shattered my world. Roughly sensual and masculine, his fingers stroked through my beard, surprising me with how different it felt from the passionate softness of Annika's touch.

'Make me bleed, Ormond,' he whispered, his voice low and throaty. The words struck something primal within me. 'Make me bleed for you.'

I didn't hesitate. My teeth found his lips, biting down until the tang of blood filled my mouth, sharp and metallic. The coppery taste mingled with his essence, intoxicating me as I sliced my tongue over his fang, deepening the connection between us.

'Making demands, are we, my fae?' I growled, barely holding myself back. His eagerness had me questioning why I hadn't seen it before. Looking back at all those moments when his touch had soothed my pain, when he had healed my injuries and lingered just a little bit longer . . . It made me realise how much I had missed—how much *we* had missed.

Desire surged through me, and I bent him back as he yielded. Alaric's submission wasn't weakness—it was trust, freely given, and it set me aflame. His fingers moved to my chest, unbuttoning my shirt and sliding it off my shoulders, stripping me of my clothing as a dark aura flared around us.

I don't think Ari even noticed his magic slipping loose as he kissed my skin, nails scratching over my chest, my abdominal muscles tightening in response to his touch. I was hard as a rock, my cock throbbing painfully in my breeches, but I wasn't rushing this. I savoured the moment.

'The blood bond is sealed,' he said. 'I'm yours. Hrae, I'm finally yours.' Alaric's laughter was pure and unrestrained, a sound I hadn't realised I'd been waiting to hear.

'So you are,' I teased, a grin tugging at my lips. 'And what are you going to do about it?'

His gaze dropped to my chest, and his lips followed, trailing kisses along my skin. I gripped the table for support, my breath hitching as his mouth moved lower.

'*Fuck*,' I snarled. I didn't know why seeing him kiss his way down my body aroused me so much, but I had to close my eyes because the view in front of me threatened my senses. I was close to finishing without him ever reaching my cock.

'Should I continue, my Domine?' Alaric asked, looking up. Mischief flickered in his eyes, a long-forgotten spark that sent a shiver down my spine. This was more than acceptance. I had been gifted the position of prime male in our household.

'Are you trying to make me beg?' I breathed, unable to calm my racing heart, groaning when he toyed with my belt buckle before freeing me from my constraints.

'Beg?' he teased, his lips so close to my shaft that I felt his breath waft over the sensitive head. 'Could anyone make my commander beg? But . . . if you're so impatient, show me what you want.'

'Stop taunting me, fae,' I rasped, the intensity of the moment almost unbearable. His hand wrapped around me, stroking, and my knees threatened to buckle. I reached for his hair, fingers tangling in the silky strands as I watched him. His tongue darted out, tracing over the sensitive head, and I hissed, overwhelmed by the sensation.

'What do you want me to do?' I murmured, tightening my grip on his hair and twisting just enough to draw a moan from him. He looked back up at me, his pupils blown wide, and when I pushed forward, he hungrily took me into his mouth.

I groaned as his fangs scraped against me, the hint of danger adding to the thrill. His mouth was hot and relentless, and I couldn't stop myself from rocking into him, chasing the pleasure he offered so willingly.

'Is this what you want, my love?' I asked, my voice strained as I fought to maintain control. Alaric didn't answer—he couldn't. The deadly warrior was greedily sucking the very soul out of me. His hands gripped my thighs as he tried to hold himself back, but I didn't relent until he swallowed every last inch, gagging on my cock until his throat relaxed around it.

'Fuck, you're perfect,' I muttered. I knew his tastes leaned toward the darker, his love of pain a part of him both he and Annika had hinted at. *Can he take the beast?* The thought burned through me, but I held back, unwilling to assume.

Pulling him off me, I revelled in the disappointed pout that crossed his lips. I tilted his head back, forcing him to meet my gaze.

'Do you like being helpless?' I asked, pulling his head further back until he whimpered. 'If you want me to hurt you, you have to ask. Beg me for it, Alaric. Beg me to give you what you need.'

My voice was low and rough. This had to be his choice, freely given. But gods, I hoped he would beg.

Alaric's hooded gaze burned into me, his fangs flashing as his whimper transformed into a moan. I held him firm. I needed to hear it—needed his words, unvarnished and free of hesitation. I would rather gut myself with a dull blade than be violent against his will.

'How do you . . .' His voice cracked. 'Hrae, Annika?'

Yes,' I murmured. 'She told me, but I already knew.' My grip on his hair tightened just enough to elicit another moan. 'Now answer me. Do you want me to make it hurt?'

Ari gasped, his reaction giving me a clue but not the clarity I demanded. 'Alaric,' I said, my voice breaking into a plea, 'please . . . beg me.'

'Yes, Domine,' he finally whispered. 'I like it. Please, make it hurt,' he moaned, reaching for my cock. His voice came out so breathy that I instinctively tightened my grasp, hurting him more, watching as his cock stirred in response.

'*Fuck,*' I groaned, overwhelmed by the force of his admission. 'Just promise you'll tell me if it's too much.' I wanted to ravage him until his throat became raw from my cock and fuck him until his voice became hoarse from screaming my name; I wanted to see the bruises from my fingertips on his silver skin. I wanted all of him and more.

He nodded, his lips parting in surrender, and I couldn't hold back any longer. 'Pleasure me, Alaric,' I commanded, thrusting into his mouth. His throat tightened as he gagged, and I nearly lost myself in the sight of him—beautiful and undone.

'Just like that. Fuck, you feel so good,' I almost purred, watching tears streak down his flushed cheeks. I loosened my grip just enough for him to catch his breath before I fucked his throat, setting a brutal rhythm. He welcomed me with every thrust, his obedience only spurring me further until I felt the blissful oblivion darkening my thoughts.

But it wasn't enough. My pleasure alone wasn't enough.

I pulled away so suddenly Alaric fell forward, his wide eyes meeting mine as he gasped for air. I didn't let him recover, dragging him to the bed with a feral urgency.

'I am going to fuck you until you beg me to stop,' I growled, yanking down his trousers in one rough motion. Gripping his hips, I pulled him flush against me. 'You'll plead for my mercy like you begged your goddess. This is your last chance to say no.'

His needy groan nearly made me climax on the sheets. 'Do it!' he breathed, his words defiant yet yearning. 'How many times must I tell you I crave you? Or do you just love hearing me beg that much?'

He turned his head, capturing my lips in a kiss that was both challenge and submission as he pushed his rear back against my hard length. But when I smacked his ass, the sharp crack of the impact echoed, and his defiance crumbled into a whimper. My palm left a vivid red imprint on his silver skin, and I couldn't hold back any longer.

Sliding my cock between his cheeks, I took a deep breath. My mind was a chaotic mess, but locking onto a shred of sanity, I entered him slowly, giving his body time to adjust, trying to control my urges. His trembling didn't stop him from pressing back, impaling himself further, his tightness making me ache with the effort to hold back.

My hips came flush with him, my hard cock entirely inside, and I nearly lost control. His translucent, sweat-slicked skin gleamed under the light, and his moans turned ragged as he rocked against me. My own breath shuddered as I battled to control myself and resist the urge to explode at the intensity of the feeling.

'Next time,' I whispered against his ear, my teeth grazing his neck, 'I want Ani to hear your sweet little moans. I want her to kiss them away, to hold you while I take you.' The image burned through my mind, my cock throbbing as I claimed him.

His answering whimper was pure longing. 'Hrae, yes,' he choked out.

I gripped his cock, stroking in time with my thrusts as I buried myself in him, relishing every shudder and cry. The thought of Annika's soft hands on him, silencing his cries while I took him raw, sent me over the edge. My pace turned brutal, my control unravelling.

I must have projected my pleasure because I felt Vahin's presence in my mind, his surprise shifting to approval before fading, leaving me alone with my fae. Alaric's voice, hoarse with pleasure, grounded me.

'Yes . . . gods, yes . . . I'm so close.'

His husky voice, filled with desire, tied my heart to his in the most primal way. I was blessed to be with a man who took pleasure in my violence, and I gave him everything, my thrusts becoming erratic as I felt his release nearing.

His cock jerked in my hand, and his cries filled the room as he came, his body clenching around me. My own climax followed, violent and blinding. My world splintered as my wild magic surged, my cock thickening with one final thrust before I poured myself into him, our bodies trembling in shared ecstasy.

My Ari, my dark fae, beautiful in his submission, had taken my soul, owning it completely. We collapsed onto the bed, sweat-soaked and spent. I pulled him into my arms, unwilling to let go, my lips brushing his hair.

Alaric's laugh startled me, a low, contented sound that resonated through my chest.

'What's so funny?' I murmured, still catching my breath.

He turned, resting his head on my chest. 'You. Me. The way you brutalised me in the most delicious way. I'm just . . . happy. Happier than I've ever been in my long life.'

I kissed his head, smiling despite myself. 'Brutalised? I thought I was considerate, giving you exactly what you asked for.' My smile faded, concern creeping into my voice. 'Do you need a healer?'

'What?'

'I wasn't gentle and . . .' Uncertainty crept into my voice. 'I will get you a healer. Besides, once Ani hears about this, you can bet gold against apples, she'll insist on a repeat performance, so we better have you properly looked after.'

Alaric's laugh was so free and unrestrained that it made my heart soar. He turned to face me, his eyes gleaming with mischief.

'Anytime, anyplace,' he said, his grin wide. 'And no, I don't need a healer. I'm ready to give our woman a show she'll never forget.'

For a moment, his happiness made me forget about the horrors of Roan Fortress, and I found myself lost in it. But even now, I knew it wouldn't last, at least not for me.

'One day,' I murmured, my voice softening, 'once it's all over, we'll return to Varta. You're nearly immortal, Vahin definitely is, and Ani wields the power of creation. But I'm just a human, Alaric. My time is limited. I don't want to waste a second of it—not a single minute without you all. So we'll live the time I have left enjoying every single day as if it's the last.' I tightened my arms around him, as if holding him closer could slow the ticking of the clock.

Alaric's expression softened, his silver skin luminous in the faint light. 'I can promise you this, Ormond,' he said with calm certainty. 'We'll cross the Veil together. Without you and Ani, there is no life for me.'

A shiver coursed through me at the conviction in his voice, goosebumps prickling my skin. Before I could respond, his lips quirked into a smirk. 'Or,' he added lightly, 'I could just use necromancy to bring you back. I'm sure you'd make a very handsome lich.'

I smacked his thigh. 'Sleep pilchard. Maybe a good night's rest will strip you of this morose humour.'

'You started it,' he muttered, his voice full of mock petulance.

I didn't have the energy to argue. The exhaustion of the day finally caught up to me, dragging my eyelids down like lead. I wrapped myself around the man who meant more to me than I could ever express, my thoughts drifting to the woman who held the other half of my heart.

CHAPTER 20

ALARIC

O rm had finally fallen asleep. He lay beside me, his slow, steady breathing brushing against the hair covering my sensitive ear. I felt the guilt for placing Annika in danger slowly wash away, admitting to myself that when Valaram had captured me in the palace, I'd felt relieved, knowing my suffering was ending on the edge of his blade.

But Ani had refused to allow it. She had defied not only an empress but a goddess—for me. If I thought I couldn't love her more, she had proven me wrong. *Who would do that? And for the cursed fae who had schemed to deliver her to the Lich King.*

I huffed softly, still unable to believe my luck. Here I was, an Anchor for my domina and blood-bonded to the only man who had ever offered me friendship in a world that had abandoned me. Annika could have chosen anyone. The Dark Mother's mercy had granted her freedom to select any dark fae in the empire—even bloody Valaram, who practically wagged his proverbial tail to get into her bed. But she chose *me*, freeing me in ways I hadn't known I needed.

My fingers absently traced the powerless marks on my chest. I would spend the rest of my life striving to repay the goddess' trust, to protect Ani and give her all the love she deserved. Still, I was old enough to know that happiness was fleeting, but I was determined to guard mine with everything I had, starting with Ihrain.

Carefully, I slipped from Orm's embrace. He muttered some-thing unintelligible, his hand reaching out instinctively, and I quickly tucked a pillow into his grasp. The room was dark, but my fae eyes needed no light to navigate. I dressed swiftly, pulling on a dark shirt and trousers—practical for my plans, particularly given the blood that would be spilt. Selecting two daggers from the table, I checked their edges before tucking them into my belt.

Protecting my family was my priority. But they didn't need to know the lengths I'd go to for them. Ihrain's death was neces-sary—not just for retribution, but to extract the secrets he carried. His suffering wouldn't be senseless. I intended to use it to contact my sister, Rowena, deep within the Lich King's court. I needed to know Cahyon's strategy, and I needed to give her hope—hope that we could finally help her escape.

The mansion was silent as I moved through its empty corridors. A few scattered guards nodded as I passed, none questioning my purpose. I stopped at the door next to the wine cellar, the innocu-ous entrance hiding the cell where Ihrain lay swaddled in the la-nara-soaked drapes from the carriage. The space was underground but dry and surprisingly spacious. It was a comfortable place for a prisoner, and I almost regretted having to spoil it with the blood of its current resident.

I stepped inside, my gaze settling on the bundle of fabric on the floor. With a sharp kick, Ihrain jolted awake, his eyes darting toward me, wide with panic.

'Ihrain,' I said, my voice dripping with mock cordiality. 'How nice to see you. I trust your accommodations have been adequate?'

He spat in my direction, jerking violently against his restraints. I tutted softly, shaking my head. 'Now, now, don't be like that, old friend. I only want to have a little chat before you leave us to meet the Dark Mother.'

'You'll get nothing from me,' he sneered, his voice laced with venom. 'You think you'll achieve anything from this? You're going to die, and that whore of yours will die, too.'

I smiled coldly as I used the tip of a dagger to slice through the rope binding him. Ihrain scrambled to free himself from the drapes, retreating to a corner as he crouched, his gaze fixed on the blade twirling between my fingers.

He hastily sketched a protection sigil in the air, attempting to pour his magic into it. When nothing happened, I watched in amusement as his expression shifted from fury to confusion, then to despair as he tried again, cursing under his breath.

'That's how my domina felt when you stole her power,' I said, my tone icy. 'I wanted you to experience that despair when you realised you were entirely at my mercy.' I paused, letting the words sink in before adding, 'Not that I have any.'

With deliberate precision, I began weaving a sigil in the air, ensuring Ihrain saw every intricate detail. As the aether began to take form, I had to rein myself in, holding back my magic when I realised that my bond with Annika, enhanced by our perfect synergy, allowed me to draw energy from my surroundings.

'How are you doing that?' Ihrain stammered, his voice trembling. 'The master said the bond couldn't—'

I released the spell before he could finish, its glowing strands sinking into the stone and latching onto his wrists. They solidified, binding him in place. I debated securing his legs but decided against it. I wanted him to struggle, to feel the false hope that he might escape—even as his blood fuelled my magic.

I approached him slowly, enjoying the panic that radiated from his trembling form. Drool and snot mingled on his face as he whimpered, repeating the same phrase over and over.

'This isn't what he promised . . . this isn't what he promised . . .'

Gripping his hair, I yanked his head back until his tear-streaked face tilted up towards me. Annika had once thought me broken, a man defeated by his curse. But thanks to her, I had survived. My sweet domina had seen whatever light was hidden within my darkness and bound it to a shard of her soul.

Her love had not just saved my life but made me want to be a better man. Now, it was my turn to ensure that no one least of all Ihrain—ever threatened her. I would die for her, kill for her, and protect her even if I had to dirty my hands with the dark arts. It was time her enemies learned that whoever threatened her light would die in my shadows.

'You believed the lies that desiccated corpse fed you? You belong with each other, you arrogant, malicious piece of *shit*,' I spat, my voice sharp with anger as memories surfaced. I forced myself to calm down. 'It doesn't matter now.'

I raised my dagger, and Ihrain started thrashing so hard I was left with clumps of his hair in my fist.

'No! I'll talk! About the portals, the Moroi . . . I'll tell you who works for us. Don't do it! Don't!' His screams broke into desperate sobs as I dragged the blade across his neck, just enough to let dark, opalescent blood drip steadily to the floor.

'No, please! I'll tell you about the chancellor,' he blurted. "I saw corrupted Moroi heading to the palace before the trial. They're going to free him! He knows where the wraith army is, where the Moroi generals are stationed. If you go now, you can catch them. Just—please, stop! I'll tell you everything! Just please don't kill me.'

'You'll tell me anyway, my friend,' I said coldly, my voice steady as I surveyed the growing pool of blood at my feet. 'The dead don't lie to a necromancer.'

Wielding my dagger like a quill, I began inscribing symbols on the floor. Each line, each mark, had to be perfect—one mistake, and my mind would shatter under the spell's strain. The weight of what lay ahead pressed heavily on my shoulders. Ever since Ormond had told us about Roan Fortress, I knew I had to contact my sister. If she could stall the Lich King until Reynard could gather an army, the Lowland Kingdoms would have a chance of surviving.

It took several minutes for Ihrain's cries to quieten until only defeated whimpers fell from his lips. It wouldn't be long now. I knew it. I had taken pleasure from taunting him, but now I almost cursed as the thought of Annika's disappointment flashed through my mind. My hand slowed, moving to carve the last symbol, one that would set Ihrain on his final path.

I called forth the power of my necromancy. Purple strands of energy wrapped around my hands before drifting to the marks on my victim's body and infusing them with primal power. I had to be quick. The spell would only work while the sacrifice was on the brink of death, still tethered to dying flesh but already drifting towards the Veil.

'Rowena'va Shen'ra, I call upon you,' I whispered, binding the spell to my sister's mind.

The world darkened. My body felt weightless, as though I was falling into a deep well. The sensation intensified as I felt the familiar touch of her mind, and my perspective shifted. Before I could adjust, I heard my father's voice.

'This is the last time you will hide things from me, daughter,' my father snarled. 'He punished me for your insolence—me! When it is all your fault. Why didn't you tell me your research was successful?'

The crack of a whip followed, and pain lanced through our connection. I shared her suffering, but I couldn't reach her. She was staring straight ahead, eyes fixed on the wall. There but not there. I realised that my deranged father had whipped her into a semiconscious state, where the mind seemed to detach itself from the body.

Rowena wasn't aware of my presence, shielding herself so strongly that I barely felt her. I still tried to get her attention, but just then, another voice interrupted my efforts.

'What is going on in here?' The dry snap of the Lich King's criticism made my father bristle. 'You were supposed to extract the information on her discovery, not kill her.'

'She is stubborn, my lord, and she isn't dead,' my father replied, his tone obsequious. 'She's not even unconscious. She just drifted away, but I'll find a way to reach her. We will start again once her mind returns from the void.'

I'd always known my father was a sadist with no respect for life, but hearing him speak so emotionlessly, as if torturing his own flesh and blood was nothing, made my blood boil.

'No, you will not. You've destroyed every tool you control, Roan. It's almost as if you don't want us to succeed. I sent a Moroi mage to free the chancellor and recall Ihrain to Katrass; he has become a hindrance and will be more useful as a subject for one of Rowena's experiments.'

'The Moroi can't be trusted, their hunger—'

'They are good at spying, especially those whose illusory powers were enhanced by the blood hunger, and they *can* be trusted. They simply hate you.'

'So, what happened to turn you against your pet, Ihrain?' My father's niggling tone made me smile. It was petty, but I loved to see him not getting his way.

'He endangered my conduit mage and disappeared to gods know where for days,' Cahyon growled. 'But this afternoon, I received his drivel through the portal. Apparently, Annika survived the trial. So did your boy. Ihrain claims he found a way to bring them here.'

The room fell silent for a moment. When the Lich King finally spoke again, his voice cut like steel. 'But I don't trust that incompetent fool. Prepare to advance our plans. We need to make a move before the empress brings her army to help Dagome.'

My father muttered a curse under his breath. 'We should wait . . . my lord.'

'Wait?' The Lich King's voice rose, brimming with disdain. 'For what? I'm sure they're building portals even as we speak. Why was I cursed with such fools? Your schemes handed Reynard a kingdom. Talena stands with him. Annika bears the Dark Mother's blessing, and now the entire empire rallies behind their goddess-chosen.'

He began pacing furiously before halting to glare at my father. 'It was supposed to be a simple takeover. We nearly had Dagome on a silver platter! If Ihrain hadn't killed that senile bastard, I'd already be king. Now, we'll be lucky if I don't end up ruling over another desolate kingdom.'

'Will it be desolate once we defeat their army? Is it inevitable?' My father's smirk was brazen, though he tempered his tone with mock humility.

'If I didn't need you . . .' The Lich King's knuckles whitened as he clenched his fists. 'Get the chancellor and the Moroi to mobilise my army. We just need to hit them before they're ready. A single, decisive strike should wipe out their forces. If only I could increase the distance of my influence over the monsters . . .' He trailed off, then pointed to Rowena.

'Call for a healer to tend to her.' As my father reluctantly complied, he added, 'Tell me what you've discovered so far. Is it true that she can do it?'

The question, tinged with excitement, unsettled my stomach. Cahyon's skeletal fingers brushed my sister's tear-streaked face with grotesque tenderness.

'The notes I found in her study suggest so,' my father admitted. 'What I found interesting is that she was trying to hide it. There were only a few details, but from her scattered notes, it's clear she's discovered a way to transfer your spirit into a living body. I even found references to preserving your original body. I gather it means you could live forever if it is kept safe, but her notes were incomplete.'

My blood ran cold. I knew Cahyon wanted to be free of his torturous existence as a lich, but if he could leave Katrass without relying on the constant influx of its magic, Dagome was in more danger than anyone thought possible.

'Do you know how to perform the spell?' The Lich King's voice betrayed his eagerness.

'No, not yet at least. Only my daughter knows, but it's just a matter of time before she tells me.'

'You are a fool, Roan, and you always will be. You lost Alaric to your petty jealousy, and now you are making the same mistake with your daughter. I need Rowena to work with us, not plot against us. How can I trust her with my spirit if she hates being here?'

'And you think she loves being here . . . my lord?' my father sneered, correcting his tone only as he added the honorific.

'Love? No, but she has a comfortable life under my protection. As long as she produces results, I will keep her safe. Now wake her up!'

A splash of cold water hit Rowena's face, followed by a wave of healing magic, pulling her psyche out of its hiding place. I felt her shock when she noticed my presence.

'There you are, my dear Ro. Your father seems to have purposefully misunderstood my orders . . . again. I only sent him to ask how far you were with your research, not hurt you. But that is done with now. I will look after you.' He turned to my father, a sneer twisting his lips. 'You will never touch her again.'

A dry finger trailed over my sister's cheek, wiping away her tears as he held her to his chest. I knew he was good at manipulating people—that's how he'd taken over the Kingdom of Ozar. I didn't suspect his manipulation would work on my sister. She must have known him well enough to see through his pretence, yet I saw her wrap her arms around his neck.

'I've let him hurt you for too long, but no more. It will just be us, my queen, and if you can give me back my body, the years of misery in this desolate place will soon be a distant memory.'

'I haven't finished . . . I've only outlined the basics. Even if I perfect the spell, there's no fae powerful enough to hold your spirit without losing most of your power. The host would also need to be of a similar age to you, or your mind might reject it. It's so complex that I don't think it will ever be possible.'

Her voice faltered, giving way to quiet sobs as her frail body shook in his arms. Cahyon sighed softly, a mask of benevolence settling over his decayed features. Yet, as soon as her gaze dropped, his lips curled into a cruel smile, sharp and predatory.

'A powerful fae of similar age to my old self?' he mused, looking at my father. Roan instinctively took a step back, as if sensing danger.

'Guards,' the Lich King commanded, his voice cold and final. 'Take this old fool to the dungeons.'

Two massive clay golems stomped into the chamber, their eyeless faces betraying no emotion. Soulless constructs—perfect tools for subduing a necromancer. My father's eyes widened in disbelief as the realisation hit him.

'You can't! You wouldn't dare!' he sputtered, retreating until his back pressed against the cold stone wall. 'Use Alaric! He's stronger, more suited for this!'

'True,' Cahyon replied, his tone eerily calm. 'But he's too young. Besides, I have other plans for him. He'll make an excellent advisor once he's tethered to me.'

Roan snarled, summoning a glowing shield glyph that flickered before him as he attempted to hold off the advancing constructs. Magic crackled in the air, but clay was resistant to spells, a lesson the Moroi had learned when the Lich King conquered their kingdom. Now it was my father's turn.

I had to give it to him. He fought well, but death spells couldn't harm something that had never lived, and eventually his energy dwindled. At last, he collapsed, his magic spent. The golems seized him, their grip unyielding as they hoisted him off the ground while he spat curses at the lich.

'You swore to serve me,' Cahyon said, his false smile unwavering. 'Your final act will be a noble sacrifice, my friend. I'll make sure to raise a statue in your honour.'

'Fuck your statue!' Roan shouted, foaming at the mouth. 'You will never win. They have a conduit, and you have nothing. You think my useless daughter is *helping* you? She has her own agenda!'

The Lich King merely shrugged, his indifference cutting deeper than words. 'I have the chancellor and the Moroi. I have an army centuries in the making. I'll offer Dagome a chance to surrender, but even with a conduit mage, they won't be able to stop me in my new body. What can one woman do against thousands of deathless soldiers?'

My father's laughter was bitter defiance. 'You arrogant prick. I built that army! She'll grind you to dust. I hope Reynard comes to Katrass and scatters your bones so your soul will never know peace. You'll die a pathetic, meaningless death, Cahyon Abrasan.'

The Lich King waved dismissively, and the golems carried him from the chamber, his curses echoing in the hall.

Turning back to Rowena, Cahyon's expression softened as he crouched beside her battered form. 'Now we can begin anew,' he murmured, his tone dripping with mock tenderness. 'Your tormentor is gone. He'll never hurt you again. Will you help me now?'

'You want me to use my father?' she asked, sagging into his arms when he scooped her up. 'I'll help you . . . but on one condition.'

'Name it.'

'You leave Alaric alone,' she said, her words barely more than a plea. 'I want my brother to live free.'

'That's not . . .' The Lich King hesitated, then nodded with an indulgent smile. 'Alright, if that is what you wish.'

Fury burned in my chest as I watched him manipulate her, his skeletal fingers brushing her hair with mock affection. My sister rested her head on his shoulder, defeated. He had broken her.

'*Rowena, don't!*' I shouted into her mind. '*He's lying to you. Deep down, you know it! Ro, talk to me! I'm already free. You don't have to do this!*'

All I felt was deep, abiding sadness. She didn't care anymore, and I didn't know how to reach her.

'*I'm tired, Ari. Tired of the pain, of making monsters, of always looking over my shoulder. Maybe . . . Maybe if he finally gets his kingdom, this will end. Maybe no one else will suffer. You won't have to suffer.*'

'*No!*' I cried. '*I told you—I'm free. The Dark Mother granted me mercy. Listen to me, Ro. Give me a few days. I'll open the portal. Just be ready to leave—*'

The blood spell faded, cutting me off mid-sentence. I was wrenched from her mind, my connection severed. Ihrain must have died, the bastard's meddling ending at the worst possible moment.

A scream escaped my lips as I opened my eyes and struck his lifeless body. I couldn't let this happen. I had to reach Rowena before it was too late. Annika would never agree to me going alone or, worse, she'd insist on going with me. But Ro was my sister. Only a coward would turn his back on his family.

Hrae! She will be furious, but if Orm can be persuaded . . .

A plan formed in my head while I gathered the surrounding aether, tinted with my signature necromantic power. I let it seep into Ihrain's corpse. His dead eyes filled with otherworldly light, and his body straightened in its restraints, following my movements as I approached.

'Good,' I said, stepping closer. 'Now we can talk.'

CHAPTER 21

ANNIKA

Nothing came close to being surrounded by Vahin's massive frame, his warmth radiating through me as a soft purr reverberated from his chest. It was like being cradled by love, knowing nothing in the world could hurt you.

I smiled, running my hand over his smooth scales. Yesterday, servants had brought a mattress and the softest of pillows for me to sleep on, but I'd simply grabbed a sheet and snuggled up against Vahin's chest, giggling when he curled himself around me, locking me away from the outside world.

I'd fallen asleep in moments, and as the first rays of the sun teased my senses, I tugged his conveniently placed wing up over my eyes, determined to ignore life a little longer.

I was glad I'd come here. Vahin's cavern, though not as deep as the one at Varta Fortress, was spacious and full of quiet charm. Vines and roots crept down the walls, softening the stone with touches of green, while moss thrived near shallow pools of water, lending the space a gentle cosiness.

The moment I'd seen it, I'd praised his grotto, seeing how happy it made him when I added a few floating firelights, bathing it in a warm, golden glow. Vahin had preened at the compliment, but it was him that made it truly feel like home.

'Vahin? Did I ever tell you how much I love you?' I asked, inhaling his metallic scent and basking in the heat radiating from his scales.

A wave of affection flowed through our bond, enveloping me like a comforting blanket. *'What use are words when I can feel your heart in mine, Little Flame?'*

I had once tried to describe to Orm how I felt about Vahin, but I couldn't find the words to express how transcendent it was. All I knew was that even if the wheel of time rolled over us, grinding millennia into dust, my dragon wouldn't forget me.

'I just wanted you to know. Yesterday, my biggest regret was not saying goodbye. I wasn't afraid of death, but I feared it would hurt you,' I said, stretching in my snug, cosy dragon nook. *'Today I can tell you and . . . I just want you to know that even if I have to fight the gods themselves, as long as I live, I'll return to you.'*

A deep, rumbling laugh vibrated through his chest, and he shifted his wing just enough for one vivid blue eye to meet mine.

'Only you would wake up with a challenge to the gods for the sake of a scaly old dragon,' he teased, pulling his wing away.

I grabbed at its hard edge, fighting against his strength. *'Don't you dare! I don't care who I need to fight, but if you pull this wing away, I swear I'll bite your membrane. It's way too early and way too bright.'*

'We can't have that. My wings are far too precious. You win, I bow to your wishes.' He paused, his tone shifting. *'But I woke you because I can sense Orm's unhappiness. Something's happened, and he is conflicted but keeping me away from his thoughts.'*

'If it's because I slept here, he'll survive,' I said, though I realised I had to talk to both men.

I had *three* Anchors—only one other conduit in history had more. My potential to process aether was unparalleled now, amplified by my perfect synergy with Alaric's calm strength and sharpened by Orm's ironclad control over the wild power of Vahin's fire. Together, they were the reason I could wield so much power.

'*He may survive,*' Vahin teased dramatically, '*but will I? Have mercy on me and spare me his complaints about hogging your attention.*' A flick of his tongue against my calf made me laugh, the ticklish sensation breaking through my thoughts. '*And quit overthinking. You have us to help you manage the aether.*'

I was still giggling when the sound of approaching footsteps echoed through the cavern. Vahin stretched languidly, easing me gently to my feet. Nudging his head against my hand until I laughed again, he purred contentedly as I stroked his eyelid.

'To hear your laughter, I would summon thunder to a summer sky, or light it up with a meteor shower,' he said, his voice brimming with sincerity. 'All those aeons of waiting in the darkness was worth it for the joy you've brought me, my beautiful flame. You've made me a very happy dragon.'

Before I could respond, Orm and Alaric appeared on the final step of the cave's entrance, smiling smugly as they took in the sight of us.

'See, that's how beasts lure pretty maidens into their lairs. You should take notes, Ari. You're fae, after all—poetry should come naturally to you,' Ormond teased, but his tense posture contradicted the cheerful words.

Alaric arched a brow, his smile sharpening into something impish. 'I'm *dark* fae. Our "poetry" is the screams of the victims we torture to fulfil our perverse needs, or so I'm told. But if it'll please you, I'm willing to serenade Annika with sweet words of love, provided you learn to purr half as well as Vahin.'

Only then did I notice the clothes draped over Alaric's arm and the boots Orm carried.

'I really don't know why you two think you can do better than a dragon,' I huffed with an exaggerated eye roll. Leaning on Vahin, I gestured to the clothes. 'Are we going somewhere?'

'Reynard has called a war council at noon,' Orm said, his voice turning serious. 'I need to check on the garrison first, but . . . we need to talk.'

The teasing melted away and I realised I was speaking to the commander of the dragon riders—and he was as tense as if he was about to walk into battle.

'Ani . . . Domina, you won't like what I need to do,' Alaric said, coming closer and reaching for me with a remorseful expression, 'but I hope you will hear me out.'

'Hold on, what do you need to do? What's going on? Are we under attack?' My gaze darted to Orm. 'Is that why you're going to the garrison?'

Snatching the clothes draped over Alaric's arm, I started dressing in haste, using Vahin's forearm to steady myself. 'Did you interrogate Ihrain?'

'Yes, he did,' Orm answered. 'And no, Rey sent a letter summoning me to the garrison to show me something. Calm down, love. We're not under attack, but Ihrain's corpse gave us the names of those allied with the Lich King. I want them rounded up and put under lock and key before the war council meeting begins. The last thing Reynard needs is a rebellion in the capital while we march towards the border.'

'That's good news . . .' I said, 'so why are you frowning? Did he give the location of the portals? I can help destroy them—'

Dropping my nightdress without a second thought, I was interrupted by twin gasps. I glanced up to see both men staring at me, wide-eyed. 'What?' I demanded. 'It's not like you've never seen me naked.'

'Oh, we know,' Orm said, a rare grin lifting his lips, 'but have mercy on your poor men. We can't go out in public sporting raging hard-ons.'

'Stop looking at my tits, and it won't be a problem,' I retorted, smirking as Alaric moved to help button my bodice.

'It's my fault, Domina.' He sighed, tenderly kissing my neck. 'I'm trying to delay telling you, knowing we're about to argue.'

A prickle of fear slid down my spine. I stilled, stepping away slowly, my eyes narrowing as I studied my men.

Orm's face had shifted to the blank mask he wore whenever darker emotions threatened to break free, while Ari's expression was one of icy determination. I inhaled slowly, arching a brow and letting the silence hang in the air.

'Alaric is going to Katrass to save his sister.' Orm's words hit me square in the chest. Whatever else he said was drowned out by the blood roaring in my ears. I barely heard his explanation of Cahyon's planned invasion and Rowena's ability to free him from the magic keeping him in Katrass.

'Domina . . . Ani, I have to do this,' Alaric said, his voice snapping me out of my stupor. 'I promised my sister I would come for her. If the Lich King is allowed to possess my father's body, nothing will stop him.' He took my hand, squeezing it tight. 'I know how dangerous it is . . . but I don't have a choice. Rowena is breaking under his relentless assault. She lets him hold her, and she believes the only way to free me is to fulfil his wishes.' He held me even as I tried to pull away. 'It is not a whim or a reckless decision, sweetheart. I need to do this. For her. For Dagome. For you.'

I stood there, stunned, silent as they spoke. It had taken less than a day for my happiness to crumble like a house of cards. *It's not real. It can't be real. He can't go.*

'No,' I snapped, my voice rising as anger exploded out of me. 'Over my dead body!' I shouted, pulling away and stumbling back towards Vahin. 'You are not leaving. You're going to get yourself killed! We will rescue your sister, but it isn't as simple as walking into Katrass.' I was panting as the aether curled around me, rising in turbulent waves.

Alaric followed me, his tone resolute. 'Domina. I'm not asking for permission, but I am hoping for your understanding. Orm and I have discussed it. I'm going to use the portal before you destroy it. Once I have secured my sister, I'll wait for you at Varta Fortress. It may take some time, but I *will* come back to you. I won't fail you.'

I whirled on Orm, realising that he'd known about this idiocy, hence his tense posture. 'And you agreed to this?'

'It's not my decision to make, my love. Alaric is his own man. If I can't stop him, then I want to support him in whichever way I can.'

I shook my head in disbelief at his indifference. 'Support him? This is madness!'

Orm's voice was calm, the commander bleeding through. 'Ani, if we set emotions aside, this plan *has* merit. I would prefer someone else execute it, but what happened in Roan Fortress must never happen again. If Alaric can steal Rowena away, Cahyon would still be trapped in Katrass. We could fight in the Barren Lands instead of having to defend our towns and villages. Strategically, it's the best move.'

'*Strategically?*' I spat. 'This isn't a battle plan—it's Ari! And you're ready to *sacrifice* him for a fucking war? What is wrong with you?'

I shouldn't have shouted, but I was seeing red. I'd barely gotten them back, and now Alaric was planning a suicide mission while Ormond had regressed to being the stone-cold commander who thought of us as weapons of war.

'It's my decision, Ani,' Alaric tried again, reaching for me. 'I *will* return to you. I was a spy and an assassin before I became your "Ari," remember? If not for the curse and the Barrier, I would've taken my sister back years ago.'

I shook my head, trying to hold back angry tears.

'Domina, please . . . the Lich King has *broken* my sister. I saw it when I connected to her mind. He's broken Ro's body and will, and once she begins trusting him, he'll have access to everything. Every monster she's created, her research, her magic. I can't let that happen. If he grows even more powerful, imagine the danger that would put you in.'

'Then let me go with you. You brought me to Varta to be your weapon, so let me be that weapon.' My vision blurred as tears fell from my eyes. 'I *can't* let you go alone—'

'You cannot go, Annika,' Orm cut in. 'Your presence would endanger him, and worse, if you were captured, Cahyon would torture you both until you'd do whatever he wanted.' He said it so evenly, and I wanted to *rip* the emotionless mask off his face. 'He could even force the Anchor bond on you. It's . . . That's what I'd do.'

'And how exactly do you intend to stop me?' I asked, seeing his jaw tighten in response.

'Domina, only the fae can manipulate portal magic,' Alaric murmured, 'and I will ensure you cannot pass.' He lowered his gaze, his hands balled into fists as if he were in an ocean of pain.

'Domina? Alaric'va Shen'ra, if I'm your domina, then . . . you have to do as I desire.' I hid my face in my hands, sobbing uncontrollably while Vahin hissed, his tail thumping the floor in distress.

'Ani . . . I have to go,' Alaric whispered. 'She's my *sister*. Bringing her here will protect you both. Please understand . . .' He embraced me then, and I realised that no matter what I said, there was no stopping him. For a brief, shameful moment, I considered asking Valaram to help me keep him in Truso, no matter the cost.

If I only had his geas . . .

The thought made me gasp. Had I gone that far? Was I really thinking of taking his free will to keep him here? Suddenly, all the rage was gone, replaced by resignation and a deep sadness.

I was losing him. If I let him go, I might never see him again. But if he were forced to stay, our bond would corrode into something abhorrent, and I couldn't do that to my beautiful fae. I was with Orm because he had chosen my freedom over his fears, and now it was my turn to trust Alaric, as my Ursus trusted me.

'Fuck, it hurts,' I whispered, thumping my chest as my tears blurred his face. Stroking the silken strands of his hair, I swallowed the sob threatening to escape. 'Fine. I won't stop you,' I said, my voice trembling. 'If you must go, then go with my blessing—and a promise.'

My fingers tightened in his hair as I leaned closer. 'If you're taken from me, I won't run. I won't hide in some backwater town. I will burn the Lich King's world to ash, and the gods have mercy on anyone who gets in my way,' I swore, swallowing my tears when he dropped to his knees. 'Go, knowing I love you. I hope the shard of my soul you carry will protect you wherever you are.'

'Annika . . .' he whispered, pressing his forehead to my midriff and inhaling deeply.

I tilted his head back until his gaze met mine, then bent to kiss his forehead. 'Go,' I whispered, barely audible, 'while I still have the strength to let you.'

Turning away so I wouldn't have to see him leave, I waited. I didn't hear him rise, but I felt the absence of his warmth. I knew he was gone.

Orm's voice broke the silence, low and close. 'That required a strength few possess. But it was the right choice. Let me hold you, love. We both need it.'

He stood so near that his warmth seeped into my skin, but I couldn't let it soothe me. 'Was it?' I asked bitterly, my voice raw. 'The right choice? Maybe it was the *strategic* choice—the one that might win us the war. Maybe he'll succeed and return to us, not too broken to mend. But what if he doesn't?'

I hadn't meant to lash out at Orm, but my irrational anger demanded an outlet. It felt like I had been dealt a curse I couldn't fight, and I didn't understand how it kept happening.

'Annika,' his voice softened, 'don't you think I *tried* to stop him? I used every argument I could think of, but he just stood there, covered in blood, telling me he had to go. I love him too, but Ari is right. He's found Cahyon's weakness, and we must take advantage of it. If you'd seen all those bodies at Roan Fortress . . . How could I stop him? Alaric's a powerful necromancer—'

'Stop,' I said sharply, raising a trembling hand to silence him.

His jaw tightened, but he fell silent, watching me with careful eyes.

'Please, don't. I know you're trying to help,' I said through gritted teeth. 'I know how important this is. But all I see is another sacrifice. How many times must I lose those I love? Gods, am I cursed?' My voice broke as I pressed shaking hands to my temples. 'I can't talk right now. I'm so angry I'll set the world on fire if you push me.'

The aether crackled around me, the need to lash out so strong that my elemental power responded. Crimson strands shimmered, blazing and pulsing to the rhythm of my heartbeat.

'Annika, please—' Orm began, his tone pleading.

'Orm, leave.' Vahin's calm voice echoed through the cavern, and I raised my head to look at my dragon. His eyes reflected a kaleidoscope of emotion. He understood. My beautiful beast, who'd loved and lost, knew that the last thing I needed were excuses for Alaric's choice. I felt his compassion flow through our bond. 'Come to me, Little Flame,' he purred softly, 'let us calm this raging inferno.'

I stepped away from Ormond's outstretched hand until I fell against the dragon's powerful body, feeling it coil around me.

'*Alaric will return,*' Vahin rumbled softly. '*And your magic cannot harm me. Orm still struggles to express his emotions, so give him some time to explore them. I can take your fury and your fire, but you need to let it out before it turns your heart to ash.*'

Orm's voice was strained, an unusual vulnerability evident on his face. 'Annika, please don't push me away. I know you're hurting.'

I gripped Vahin's neck tightly, burying my face against his scales. The words I wished I could offer Orm wouldn't come. I was too raw, too distressed to comfort anyone, including myself.

Vahin stirred, silent conversation passing between them before he spoke. 'Trust me, Ormond. Annika will join you when she is ready.'

There was a long moment of silence before I heard Orm's retreating footsteps.

I whispered my thanks to the dragon and let my rage burn.

CHAPTER 22

ORMOND

As soon as I reached the garrison yard, I swung down from my horse, my boots hitting the ground with a dull thud. The camp, set on the outskirts of the city, buzzed with activity, and I couldn't help but wonder why Reynard had summoned me here instead of to the palace—especially with a war council meeting to attend.

'Why are you so late?' Reynard asked, striding towards me.

I grunted, running a hand through my hair. 'My life suddenly turning to shit?'

'That bad?' He clasped my shoulder, his grip steady.

'You have no idea.'

'Come,' he said, his voice softening. 'We'll discuss it in private. There's still some time before the meeting, and I'll always have time to listen to my brother.'

We walked across the parade square, passing the lord marshal's office, the armory, and the quartermaster's building, where military bureaucrats meticulously tracked every coin spent on the army.

'How many men can you deploy into the city?' I asked. 'I have the names of several spies and allies of the chancellor. We need to move on them quickly.' I took a deep breath before continuing. 'Also, when was the last time you checked the chancellor's cell?'

'Why?'

Before I could answer, a sergeant marched past with his unit, shouting, 'Hail to the king!' The soldiers saluted crisply, and Reynard returned the gesture, though I didn't fail to notice his shudder.

'I haven't had time,' he admitted. 'Between the dark fae, an endless stream of whining nobles, and gathering the army, I haven't even thought about him. Last I checked, he's chained up, fed, and under guard while every spare man I have is searching for Ihrain.'

'Then you should check again,' I said. 'And don't bother looking for Ihrain. He's a bloodless corpse in our basement.'

Reynard's eyes widened for a split second before a frown replaced his stunned expression. 'Your report . . . Do I even want to know what happened?'

I waited until we were in his office with the doors locked behind us before relaying yesterday's attack, Ihrain's capture, and what Alaric had told me about the Lich King and his plans. Reynard sat through all of it with a stony expression, slowly sipping wine from a battered cup.

'These are the names of spies and conspirators,' I said, sliding a parchment across the desk.

Reynard nodded, then rang a small bell. When his adjutant entered, he handed over the list. 'Summon the Dark Brotherhood,' he instructed calmly. 'Send them to the people on this list. I want them dead before noon.'

I stiffened, frowning. The Reynard I knew was decisive but not ruthless. The man sitting in front of me was no longer the brother I had teased about his fleeting relationships with the ladies of the court. This was the King of Dagome, a leader capable of ordering the deaths of forty noblemen—some from the most powerful families in the realm.

The adjutant saluted without hesitation and left the room.

'Don't you want to spare any of them?' I asked. 'We don't know how deeply they were involved.'

Reynard shook his head. 'If the chancellor has escaped, any one of them could be aiding him. Dagome needs to be united. If it takes excising their cancerous presence to achieve that, then so be it.' A bitter grimace twisted his lips before he could control it. 'But that's not what's bothering you, is it? Tell me, Orm. Maybe I can help.'

'Nothing can help,' I muttered, slumping in my chair. 'Alaric's headed for Katrass. Annika thinks I should've stopped him but chose not to, and now won't even look at me . . .' My voice rose as I continued, desperation creeping in. 'Fuck! All it took was one night—one godsdamned night—for my life to turn upside down.'

Annika's tears and rejection were tearing me apart, and I needed someone to believe me. I wouldn't have sent Alaric to the Barren Lands if there were any other way.

Reynard studied me for a moment. 'Annika will come around,' he said finally. 'I'm sure she'll realise you're not to blame. If you didn't drive Alaric crazy with every little thing that could go wrong before he left, then I don't know you at all. She'll see that. I'm sorry, Orm. I'll keep my fingers crossed for you.'

His words eased some of the weight on my chest, and I rose from my chair. 'Thank you for letting me rant. Now, let's go. Your letter mentioned wanting to show me something, and if we dally, you'll be late for your own war council.'

Reynard hesitated as though wanting to say more, but I didn't need his pity. Besides, Vahin had sent a message through our link that Annika was getting ready to leave the manor, and I needed to see my woman.

We'd barely stepped out of the building when I caught sight of an archer aiming in our direction. 'Down!' I shouted, shoving Reynard to the ground and shielding him with my body just as an arrow thudded into the doorframe where we'd been standing.

'Someone's trying to kill you?' I asked, looking around for the culprit.

Reynard sighed, his expression unnervingly calm. 'No, Orm. Those are my fucking soldiers, or rather, the palace guard I inherited from the previous king.' A look of disgust twisted his features. 'That's what I wanted to talk about.'

After helping him up, we continued to the training area and he waved at the scene before us. Most of the men were playing cards, only a few bothering to train. It was painful to watch. Even those attempting to practise were tripping over their own weapons.

'Who put these idiots in the King's Guard?' I asked.

Reynard flinched, refusing to look me in the eye. 'It started slowly at first. Treasury cuts here and there, retiring veterans with no one to replace them, no new weapon or armoury orders. And the men recruited from the drafts . . . I did it, alright? I sent the decent soldiers to the border and replaced them with these nitwits. I didn't think it mattered. The old king just needed someone to stand around in a uniform.'

'So, this was your answer to the chancellor's manipulation?' I looked at him sharply.

Reynard nodded. 'Yes. That bastard managed to not only dismantle the court but also actively isolate the mages at the university. That's why they are so closed off now,' Reynard explained. He seemed so unconcerned that it gave me a pause.

'You're hiding something from me.'

He nodded, mischief flashing in his eyes. 'Remember when I asked your permission to use our funds to pay the veterans?'

'Yes? But I don't see any of them here.'

'That's because they're in Borovio, settled in the castle and around our ancestral estate. If you ever bothered to visit our territory, you'd barely recognise the old citadel.'

I was suspicious of the amusement in my brother's voice.

'Rey, what did you do?'

'What I had to, little brother,' he said, placing a hand on my shoulder. 'I used what wealth we had to gather the best soldiers in the country. You inspired me. Your fortress . . . the men working and training there. I built an army.'

'You created a *war camp* in Borovio?' I was surprised, but not entirely shocked.

'War camp, war town, what's the difference?' he said with a wide grin. 'I gathered the veterans and all who were suitable to be in the army and took them to Borovio. We have ten thousand infantrymen currently harvesting the fields by day and training in the camp by night. We also have five thousand archers stationed in the forests and my pride, a heavy cavalry brigade on the orcish borders, where it's easier to hide a herd of horses.' He gestured to the training grounds. 'And, of course, those shining examples of martial prowess.'

I gaped, staring at my brother for the second time that day, trying to comprehend what I'd just heard.

I laughed. I held the rails that divided the training grounds from the walking path and laughed so hard that tears flowed down my cheeks.

'Fucking hell, how . . . Rey, you could've taken over the country any time you wanted. We can fight off the Lich King! We might even be able to help Ari.' I smacked the wooden post so hard it broke in two.

All this time, I thought Annika was the only one with the power to stop the evil we were facing, but I held no illusions about our survival. All the while, my brother had an entire fucking army hidden right under Cahyon's nose.

'I never wanted to take over the country,' he said quietly. 'Just protect it.'

I turned, looking at him like I was seeing him for the first time before dropping to one knee.

'My king.'

Reynard flinched when I took his hand and pressed it to my forehead, acknowledging him, maybe for the first time since childhood. I knew he'd make an excellent king, but I didn't realise how much of himself he had sunk into the role. How much my burly, overly stern brother cared for a country that had pushed him aside.

'Not to you, Orm. Not to my family,' he said, pulling me up. 'Besides, you shouldn't be so happy. I cleaned out the coffers. Our wealth is long gone.'

'Rey, you're the bloody king now,' I said. 'And my life is tied to the fortress. What does it matter?' I could sense he still felt some guilt, but he nodded. 'Where are your men now?'

'They are marching to Truso as we speak,' he said, his grin returning. 'I sent the order as soon as the tussle in the throne room ended, but it will still be a couple of days before they arrive.'

His words triggered the strategist in me. Now that we had an actual army, we could do *more* than slow an invasion. We could take the fight to the Barren Lands, possibly even Katrass itself.

My mind began racing with calculations, starting with the number of forces involved and ending with the chain of supply and even latrines for such a large army. Absentmindedly, I turned and started walking towards the stables. I needed to work on the numbers.

'Ormond! I was talking to you.'

I turned around. Reynard was still by the rails, shaking his head and laughing. With an exaggerated eye roll, he joined me.

'We need to redirect them,' I said. 'Truso is too big a diversion from the border. We need them to head straight to Varta. They can rest there before marching to the Barren Lands.'

He nodded his agreement. 'That's a good idea. Were you planning the war just then? I remember that expression from when we were kids. That unfocused thousand-yard stare, as if you were weaving the fates in your head.'

'Yes,' I answered distractedly, 'and if the Lich King still can't leave Katrass, we should set up camp right on the other side of the bord—'

He raised a hand, stopping me. 'You'll have to find a way through the mountains first,' Rey said. 'Anyway, we have the war council to attend, remember? You can discuss it there with our allies.'

He continued as we made our way to the stables, 'Invading the Barren Lands is a sound idea. I'm assuming you want to avoid civilian casualties? Still, only the archers would be agile enough to cross the mountain using existing footpaths. Everyone else would have to go the long way around, and that will take time.'

'If we can enlist the mages' support, we can widen the mountain passes to go straight through to the Barren Lands,' I said. 'A few elemental mages can widen it enough for the small row of cavalry to pass. I can ask Annika to help. If she has her three Anchors present, she shouldn't have trouble . . .' I stopped, realising one of those Anchors was gone.

Reynard nodded, and I took the reins of my horse before it bit off the stable boy's hand.

'My king . . . a message.' A soldier ran towards us with an out-stretched hand, fighting for breath while holding a missive in his hand.

My stallion snorted, likely sensing my disquiet. The parchment was splattered with blood. Even if it had dried, the pattern of the rust-coloured spots was unmistakable.

Reynard took it from the messenger, ripping away the seal impatiently. His lips tightened, and I saw his hand shake slightly as he read the letter before passing it to me.

He stood there silently while I read. I could barely believe the words on the page. Zalesie had been attacked. *That doesn't make sense.* It was a small town of no strategic value. *But it's Annika's town . . .*

Rey clenched his jaw, and I knew what he was going to ask.

'I'll fly there after the meeting, Reynard. I'll have my soldiers and dragons hold the border as long as we can, but you'll need to send your men as soon as possible.'

'I will,' he said. 'Take Annika with you. Maybe it will help settle things between you.'

I nodded as we urged our mounts forward. The silence, disturbed only by the snorting of our horses, hung heavy between us. We could have planned and strategised, but we both knew the truth.

The Lich King's army was on the move. We were out of time.

ᛉᛏᚾᚨᛉ

Two hours later, I stood in the palace's war room, wondering if Annika had shown up. The room was large, yet with so many people crammed in there, I doubted it'd be possible to have a productive meeting.

A carved oak table with a large map dominated the space, its surface not just showing Dagome but all of the Lowland Kingdoms. Reynard sat at the head of the table, dressed in black leather armour, Talena seated next to him on what looked like a throne with a permanent scowl on her face.

On Reynard's other side sat the representative of the light fae court, Prince Iasno'ta. He needed no introduction as his long, golden hair and eyes—as blue as a cloudless sky—revealed his origins. And next to the prince was Iron Hammer, or Mlot, as his kin called him, king of the dwarves, whose prominent nose was the main feature on all dwarven coins.

'Let's get started,' Reynard said.

We were already late, and as much as I wanted to wait for Annika, we couldn't postpone the meeting any longer.

As if called by my thoughts, Ani walked in dressed in an outfit I knew all too well. Her practical, mossy-green velvet battle mage robe accentuated her feminine figure. My eyes were drawn to the slits that ran up to her hips to allow for freedom of movement and easy access to her daggers, but my attention soon focused on the tight breeches that fit her like a second skin.

A cough that sounded suspiciously like a laugh escaped my brother's lips, and I looked away from her thighs. I studied the rest of her uniform, convincing myself I was simply assessing the outfit's usefulness.

The silver embroidery on her collar guaranteed protection against bites from the undead, while the same pattern on her sleeves offered better protection than any leather vambraces. Annika had told me it was a practical outfit that had been improved over the ages and made conduit mages almost indistinguishable from other battle mages. The only difference was the small conduit pin on the corner of the collar. As she'd braided her hair into a peasant crown, the pin was exposed, reflecting soft rays of autumn light.

'Conduit mage Annika Diavellar,' a guard announced, and everybody in the room turned their attention to her.

'Better late than never. Is this the behaviour we can expect now that you are the Dark Mother's chosen?' Talena didn't bother hiding her distaste, and I felt myself bristle.

The dark fae empress seemed oblivious to the redness that rimmed Annika's eyes, but I could see it clearly, as well as her slightly swollen face and the tension in her shoulders. My Nivale looked miserable, but she had raised her mental wards, and I wasn't privy to her feelings.

'You can take your attitude and shove—' she started before taking a deep breath and composing herself. 'My apologies, everyone. Important family matters delayed my attendance.'

I watched as Valaram suddenly moved and approached Annika, bowing as he took her hand. I couldn't fault the courtesy, even as I wanted to roar in anger.

'My lady, please join me,' he said. She gave him a surprised look, but after the slightest pause, let him lead her to a seat occupied by another fae. After one look from Valaram, the terrified male promptly leapt up and left the room.

I couldn't take my eyes off her. The tension in the air made everyone unsettled, but just as I was about to get up, throw her over my shoulder, and leave, Annika's gaze met mine and she shook her head.

She still didn't want me around her, and the small gesture hurt more than a knife to the chest.

'Thank you so much for accepting my invitation,' Reynard started. 'For the first time since the Necromancer's War, all heads of the Lowland Kingdom coalition have gathered in one place. I am especially grateful to Empress Talena and her mage, Valaram. Your proficiency with portal spells is unmatched.' For the first time since I'd met her, I saw a genuine smile on Talena's face.

'So, you have us all,' the dwarven king said. 'What now?'

Reynard grimaced. 'Now we go to war.' A few people began talking about fortifying the border, but he silenced them with a raise of his hand. 'I'm afraid that will get us nowhere. The Lich King will only kill and raise the bodies of the fallen. Recently, my commander undertook a dangerous reconnaissance mission to discover what's happening on the border.'

He looked around the room to ensure he had everyone's attention. 'He found Roan Fortress annihilated. Apart from a single wounded dragon and his rider trapped in a warded alcove, everyone who lived there—humans and dragons alike—was slaughtered.' The silence in the room was deafening. 'Now ask yourself, if that can happen to a fortress full of dragons, what chances do we have?'

A buzzing hive of raised voices assaulted my ears. Discussions and arguments flew above my head, but all I could do was stare at Ani as she sat in her chair, her face drawn and worried.

'What killed them? What kind of monster is strong enough to kill so many dragons?' shouted Mlot, hammering his fist on the table to make himself heard over the bickering. 'Silence! Or I will split your japing heads. What killed the dragons, King Reynard?'

He was looking at the king, but I answered. 'Spectrae. Some perished from fighting other monsters, but most were drained of their life force by the soul-sucking wraiths.'

'We no longer have mages who can fight those phantoms. What do you expect us to do? No one can fight the spectrae,' cried a man at the end of the table, and I recognised Duke Tarvati, the fool who kept opposing Reynard during the rebellion and who now realised how defenceless his lands were.

'I can,' Annika said quietly, before raising her head. The room grew dark as the aether flowed out of Ani in a wave, silencing everyone while the empress and prince turned towards Annika with interest. My Nivale stood slowly, looking at the gathered group.

'I can fight the spectrae. But this meeting isn't about me or them. I will ride my dragon to clear the skies for you, but what will *you* do?'

'A challenge! What answer can we give our conduit mage?' Reynard leapt from his chair, his gaze sliding from one leader to another, but they only lowered their heads. 'I know what my response is. The entire army of Dagome, more than twenty thousand men and horses, is already marching towards the border.'

'Even if you've managed to conjure an army out of thin air, what makes you think you can succeed where others have failed?' Talena asked. 'You want my army, but who will lead the allied forces? You?'

Instead of responding in kind, Reynard only bowed his head slightly. 'I am happy for you or your brother to lead as Supreme Commander if you can kill the Lich King.'

She was unconvinced. 'If it's even possible to kill him.'

'Well, now's the time to find out,' he replied. 'Cahyon has found a way to exist without the magic of Katrass sustaining him. How long will we last when he brings the war to our doorsteps?'

'How do you know this?' the empress asked suspiciously.

'Alaric,' I said. 'He eviscerated Ihrain to get the information, and as we speak, he is heading to Katrass to prevent it from happening.'

'Is he planning to kill his father?' Talena asked sharply, interest flashing in her eyes.

'Yes,' I answered. We hadn't planned it, but something in her eyes convinced me the white lie might tip the scales in our favour.

Talena turned to the people observing our exchange with mixed expressions. 'Dark Mother chose her champion and maybe saved that wrenched fae for a reason,' she announced. 'I will honour her will. Care'etavos Empire will march with Dagome, and you, King Reynard, will lead us. As for the rest of you, I advise you to join. Those who stay behind will forever be alone in their time of need.'

After a moment, Reynard asked, 'Will everyone agree to renew the coalition?'

I watched as each leader nodded their head in agreement. The new king of Dagome had gotten his army. While I didn't feel the happiness the agreement should have brought, the weight on my shoulders eased slightly.

'Then it is settled,' Reynard said. 'Get your men ready. We march tomorrow. We may be too late to save Zalesie, but I won't let any other town share its fate.'

My head snapped to look at Annika and my blood ran cold at her suddenly pale face.

'Fuck,' I cursed, rushing towards her just as a massive wave of aether pushed me back. 'Annika, no. Look at me, Nivale.' I trudged towards her, but her gaze was locked on Reynard.

'Zalesie? What happened to Zalesie?'

Something in my brother's face must have given away the fate of her hometown because her power burst outwards, bending all to the table except the fae and mages quick enough to set up shields. Glass and debris rained down as Annika bolted.

I ran after her, hoping my Anchor would help contain her raging power. Ani was fast, and I didn't realise where we were headed until she suddenly burst into the open space of the gardens. She sank to her knees, raising her tear-streaked face to the sky, and wailed.

'Vahin!'

The sky roared, answering her call, and I once again watched helplessly as the woman I loved took comfort in my dragon's presence.

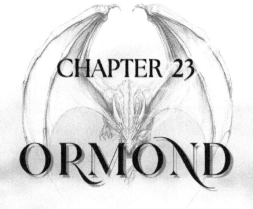

CHAPTER 23

ORMOND

T he following two days were the most torturous of my life.

After Annika had called Vahin to the palace, I thought she would disappear into his coils, warding herself from the world, as she did when Alaric left. Instead, she dragged me onto his back, insisting that we immediately fly to Zalesie.

I thanked the gods that she'd had enough patience to let me send a message to my brother before we set off. I asked him to bring Agnes with the army; Annika was distraught, and if she didn't want me near, she would need someone to look after her. Somehow, her maid had become the only person my Nivale listened to.

As we sat before our campfire, resting Vahin's overworked wings, I couldn't stop myself from covertly glancing at her. It pained me to see her so quiet and withdrawn, snuggled into the crook of Vahin's elbow. She looked so small as she gazed, unseeing, at the fire.

'We'll be at the fortress by the morning,' I said, hoping to ease her worry. 'I asked for Agnes to be sent with the army, and I don't want to get in trouble if she doesn't find her mistress there.' When I didn't get a response, I sent a silent message to Vahin, but his only reply was a feeling of disquiet.

'I told you, I'm going to Zalesie. If you want to go to the fortress first . . . fine. I know the way to town. I can walk if I have to,' Annika said as she flipped burning twigs with a stick.

'No one is walking anywhere as long as I can fly. Orm is just worried. As am I,' Vahin rumbled, curling protectively around her.

'Ani, we are too late to help. Why not go to the fortress, find out what happened, and go there prepared?' I asked, wincing as the stick snapped in her hand.

She shook her head, throwing the stick into the flames. 'I'm not stupid. I know it's too late, but what if someone survived? What if they are hiding, waiting for a miracle while we sit here, warmed by the fire? I should *be there*. It was my duty to protect them, and I failed. Gods, I left them because I thought I could help!'

She squeezed her eyes shut, taking a few deep breaths. Vahin reacted instantly, moving his head until she had no choice but to lean into him.

'I'm tired, Little Flame. I could not fly any farther tonight, but we can continue as soon as the sun rises,' he said, a rumbling purr rolling out, which seemed to calm her. Annika forced a smile, stroking his eyelid as I marvelled at hearing my dragon lie for the first time. Vahin could fly day and night, but he had lied to protect her.

'She feels guilty but she's exhausted. My Little Flame blames herself for Alaric's departure, and now she blames herself for Zalesie. She needs time to gather her strength. She can't face the destruction of her town like this,' he said, answering my unasked question.

'I'm sorry, Vahin. I didn't realise . . .' she murmured, and something inside me broke. I, too, wanted to give her time, but the beast inside me was restless, and before I knew it, I'd walked over. She raised her head as my shadow fell over her.

'Annika, please. You can't do everything, and you can't blame yourself for something beyond your control. Why do you take such a burden upon yourself?' I argued, again feeling utterly helpless.

'Because someone has to. You saw them during the war council meeting, heads up their arses and bickering like children. None of them cared about the borderlands . . . no one ever cared.' A tear slid slowly down her cheek. 'Do you remember telling me how you first saw me? You saw me as a weapon, as someone who could make a difference. What difference did I make to Zalesie?'

I was speechless, seeing the haunted look on her face as she looked up to the stars, gazing into the vast darkness while her tears fell silently to the ground. I would have given everything to take her hurt, but no one had taught me how to console a broken heart. Instead, I kneeled next to her and held her hand.

'How arrogant I was,' she said, finally looking at me. 'Thinking I was some great conduit mage just for killing some spectrae and an olgoi worm, for bartering with the Dark Mother.' She continued in a whisper as she swallowed her tears, 'How ridiculous. I thought . . . I truly thought I was strong enough to change the course of the war.'

I wanted to tell her, to remind her how brave and strong she *was*, that it was not her magic, but her compassion that changed so much for so many. That she wasn't just a warrior or a weapon, but someone who loved and lost and still stood firm against the worst of odds. That I would love her even if she hadn't Anchored my soul.

I cursed myself for being unable to find the words. Cursed that my mind was locked behind the stoic, emotionless soldier I'd been trained to be. Instead of talking, I moved closer, leaning my head against her shoulder, and joined her scrutiny of the stars.

I felt a warmth through my bond with Vahin, his silent approval.

'Just be there for her when she is ready,' he rumbled in my mind, his tail moving to envelope us. *'She loves you, and she will come around.'*

'How can you be sure?'

'Because I know her heart, and right now, she is afraid she will lose you, too. But my Little Flame's spirit blazes brighter than the darkness coiled around her, and she needs you maybe more than ever,' he responded with such certainty that I slowly relaxed.

I knew I wouldn't be able to rest. Not when, even in her sleep, quiet sobs escaped Ani's lips. I wiped away the salty tears with my thumb.

Despite Vahin's reassurance, my helplessness was killing me, until finally, I gave up, climbed to my feet, and covered Annika with my cloak.

My dragon gave me a questioning look, seeing I had drawn my sword, but he didn't comment when I marched into the woods to practise until I was covered in sweat, and exhaustion drove all thoughts from my mind.

ᛦᛖᚾᚨ�

After returning from my practise, I'd collapsed against Vahin's tail, desperate to be close to Annika, and slept until morning dew and bird song woke me from my sleep. Somehow, in the course of the night, I'd found my way to her side.

As I opened my eyes, the first thing I saw was her tired, pale face. She was in my arms, snuggled to my chest, awake yet unmoving, but I was grateful even for that small mercy.

'Good morning, Nivale,' I said, kissing her forehead. Her breath stuttered, and she opened her mouth as if to say something. I felt her nestle closer, but as soon as she'd started to, she was gone, pulling away with a tense smile.

'We need to go,' she said simply.

I stood, nodding as I began to pack up. 'Of course. As you wish, my sweetheart.'

We had one last flight to go, and I dreaded what would welcome us when we arrived. Annika sat stiffly on Vahin's back, lost in her thoughts, until, with a sharp curse, she pushed closer. I wrapped my arms around her trembling body and saw what had startled her.

Zalesie was a smoking ruin.

The cosy mountain town, with its picturesque houses and patchwork fields, was pockmarked with olgoi worm tunnels and jagged, smoking rubble. Bodies littered the streets, just like they had at Roan Fortress, and as much as I was prepared for the view, Annika was not.

'Land,' she ordered, and I winced as her magic bit at my skin. Her power danced over Vahin's scales, and I felt his concern about her loss of control.

Annika leapt off the dragon's back even before he fully touched down and stalked slowly towards the town centre. I drew my sword and followed her, vigilant to danger, eyeing the carrion birds that looked on as we neared the town square. There, we encountered the town's last stand. Peasant carts and tavern tables had been overturned to create a barricade. Around it, the ground was soaked with blood and covered in arrows, but it was the smoking ruin inside of the barricade that turned my stomach.

The stench of burned flesh still lingered in the air, even if the funeral pyre was already a pile of ash.

Annika wordlessly sank to her knees, picking up a small rag doll from the dirt. She looked at it for a long while, brushing the bloody mud from its painted face before she dropped it back on the ground.

I was ready to deal with her rage or her sorrow, but the woman who'd cried herself to sleep last night stood up without a word and silently walked away from the people who'd been her neighbours for years.

'We need to search the ruins,' she said detachedly. 'Someone may be trapped beneath the debris.'

Annika was open with her emotions, but the cold mage ordering this search wasn't the Ani I knew, and this quiet before the storm worried me to no end.

'*Vahin?*' I asked, hoping to gain insight into what was going on in her mind, but my dragon flooded me with his own worry.

'*She's cut me off, too,*' he said, his gliding shadow sweeping the ground. '*But the aether currents around her are too strong.*'

We searched one house after another, Annika using her power to remove fallen roofs and debris as if they were nothing, sending them flying with a simple sigil and a flicker of her wrist. Vahin was right. The aether built up around her until even I could feel it.

No one had survived. We only found more and more bodies as the debris from Ani's digging rained down on us. I ground my teeth as her elemental spells got worse, evidence that her power was becoming increasingly volatile.

'My love,' I said, grasping Annika's shoulder. 'Stop. Please stop. If anyone has survived, my men will have taken them to the fortress. There is nothing here but death and destruction.' The shuddering breath that escaped her was the first sign I'd seen that my Nivale was still there.

'No one buried them,' she whispered. 'All that remains of my friends are corpses left to rot.' She pulled away from me, kneeling on the ground. 'How is this right? How the fuck is this right!' she screamed as she drew her dagger, drawing a sigil in the dirt and muttering a cantrip until blood trickled from her nose.

'*Zareta erm, te erm o' praxis.*'[1]

I nearly fell as the ground shook violently. Instinct took over, and I covered Annika with my body as dirt and dross erupted from the earth. The soft caress of her power turned vicious, biting the skin the moment I touched her.

I loved when she cast her spells—the wave of warmth, like a summer breeze, that came with them filling me with energy. But today . . . Today, it felt like I had placed my hand on a sizzling skillet, and all I felt was pain. Worse, I wasn't sure if Ani even realised her spell was burning through too much power.

I pulled her closer, blood humming in my ears as my soul strained against the onslaught of aether she was channelling through the bond, Vahin's agonised roar mirroring my own struggle. I didn't dare move, however, as each body we'd found was carried on rolling waves of earth into the town centre to join those on the funeral pyre. Eventually, the debris hanging above us was slowly, reverently lowered, gently covering the bodies of Annika's friends and fellow townsfolk.

When it was all over, Ani dispersed her residual power, and I was overwhelmed by the backlash, suddenly filled with the energy of a thousand warriors. Meanwhile, the woman in my arms could barely stand, her nose bleeding and her breath coming in a rapid, broken rasp.

She'd just performed three separate spells with a single incantation. And with that level of control? Even though Ani thought herself powerless, I *knew* she could change the tide of this war.

---

1. *Bury them, give them peace.*

'Come, Nivale. There's nothing left to do here,' I said, silently asking Vahin to land. We climbed on the dragon's back and Annika swayed, shaking her head as she tried to keep her eyes open.

'Don't let me fall, Ursus.'

Her words were so quiet that I only just heard them as she placed her head on my breastplate. A few moments later, her tiredness caused her to sag into my arms and fall asleep. I needed this, her trust that I'd never let her fall and reassurance that she still welcomed my touch. The pet name she had for me had never sounded better, and the tight knot in my chest eased a notch.

'I'll always protect you,' I whispered, kissing her temple before bundling her up in my riding cloak. I knew I had to prepare myself for what was to come. Before Reynard's army arrived and we could push the battlefront to the Barren Lands, I would have to ensure every town and village was either guarded or evacuated.

That was a daunting task, even for me.

ᛉᛏᛘᚠᛉ

'My lord, you've returned,' exclaimed a young rider as Vahin landed. Several others saluted but kept their distance. I simply nodded an acknowledgement, noting the state of their gear and injuries, a silent testament to the efforts my men were making to hold off the Lich King's forces. I couldn't help feeling proud of each and every one of them.

As I carried my sleeping woman into the fortress, I noticed the increased number of civilians and just how many wore dark mourning clothes.

'Where is Tomma?' I asked a passing sergeant. My Nivale was dead to the world and didn't even stir as I spoke.

'With the herbalist, my lord,' he answered. 'They're tending to the wounded.'

'Good. Find him and tell him to meet me in my office with the report on Zalesie. And tell a maid to get Lady Annika's room ready.'

As the man bolted to fulfil my orders, I adjusted my arms to make Ani more comfortable, wishing I could ease the frown on her face and erase the dark circles under her eyes. When we eventually made it to her room, she murmured something in her sleep, grasping my riding cloak so hard that rather than prise it from her grasp, I simply slipped it off, using the fabric to cover her as I lay her on the bed.

She looked so peaceful, yet so fragile. I smiled sadly as I bent to remove her boots before I sat next to her, unbraiding her tight plait.

She was the miracle this world didn't deserve, a woman of immense power with a heart full of scars. I didn't know how she was still willing to fight for what she believed was right, but I would forever be grateful I could be there to help her.

'I love you, Nivale,' I whispered, brushing the chestnut hair from her forehead. 'Please don't push me away because you are hurting. I'm not a dragon, but a simple soldier who yearns to give solace to your soul.'

'My lord!' Tomma stormed in, and I had never been so close to killing a subordinate.

'*Shh* . . . sleep, sweetheart,' I cooed when Ani inhaled sharply, gesturing for my second-in-command to get out before I took the head off his shoulders. Unfortunately, the damn man just stood in the doorway, a relieved smile on his face, as if my presence was some divine intervention he had long prayed for.

I stalked toward him, grinding my teeth, but as soon as I reached him, my anger abated. Tomma was injured. His left hand hung limply at his side, and deep gashes ran down his neck, disappearing under a shirt that couldn't hide the thick bandages.

'Commander, is Master Alaric with you?' he asked, wincing as his lifeless arm swung against the door. 'We have many wounded, some gravely.'

'No, Alaric left for Katrass. Let's talk in my office. Annika has to rest, and we need to get ready to host an army. Did you know we lost Roan Fortress? Everyone was killed in a massacre a few days ago—'

He audibly gasped, and I paused, giving him a few moments to process the information.

'I've heard nothing, my lord,' he said. 'Though, a couple of days after you left, the attacks began. Initially, small groups of the usual monsters were targeting villages and forest settlements. It scarcely warranted any attention—a squad of soldiers or a dragon or two to deal with them—but last week was different. The monsters became more organised, and we noticed they were acting with purpose.'

I frowned. 'What do you mean?'

'Draugrs[2] were in command, sir. They still looked like the fae nobles they once were, dressed in gilded armour, even if their desiccated skin was more like tree bark. But when we approached, their eyes shone with otherworldly violet light, and wherever the draugrs pointed, the monsters attacked. One even got me with its sword and almost severed my arm.'

---

2. **Draugr /pron:drow-gar/** — a revenant awakened in his grave that retains some mental capabilities. Their primal reason for existence is to protect their treasures, but they can be tethered to the necromancer's will.

'Fuck, that must be how the Lich King controls them,' I said, opening the door to my office. My adjutant jumped to his feet, dropping a stack of papers on the floor, but I only nodded without paying too much attention. 'Tell me if we have any survivors from Zalesie. I saw the funeral pyre . . .'

'We evacuated most of the families when the attack started. It was Katja who convinced them to move to Varta Fortress, but some men were just too stubborn, convinced they could defend their homes.'

Steeling himself, Tomma continued, 'I was there for the last stand. We tried to take them, but there was just a few of us—a regular patrol group—when the attack started. The men who stayed behind were gathered in the middle, fighting with whatever weapons they could find. We were swarmed by spectrae and couldn't help much, but they fought with bravery rarely seen amongst the common folks. In the end, we could only burn some bodies from above before the spectrae chased us away.'

'Annika, she wanted to go . . . I couldn't refuse her.' I sighed. 'That town meant so much to her. She buried what was left of it. Someone will have to tell the survivors there is nothing to return to.'

'Do you want me to talk to them, sir?' Tomma's question dragged me out of my brooding.

'No, I'll do it tomorrow. Your task is to establish regular communication with Dagome's army,' I said, shaking my head as a delayed wave of tiredness blurred my vision. 'Use the junior riders. Send the first message at dawn. Reynard should be leading the troops along the river. That's what I'd do. Tell them to try to find him—he must be briefed on what's happening here. And call Katja. Ani will feel better having her around.'

'Katja is with the wounded,' he snapped before lowering his gaze under my scrutiny. 'I'm sure she can find a moment for our lady, but I can't force her to abandon her patients.'

The protectiveness in his tone made me smile. Before all this mess, I knew Tomma had hoped Katja would choose him. From the few interactions I'd observed between them, I'd guessed that if anyone had a chance with the no-nonsense herbalist, it was him.

'How did she take it?' The attack on Zalesie?' I asked.

'She is working herself to death,' he said. 'Katja eats and sleeps in the hospital. I'm worried, but she won't listen to me. Still, if not for her, I would have lost my arm.'

I nodded. 'Well, if she finds time, tell her to come to the castle. If not, just make sure she knows Annika is back, and tell that blacksmith, Bryna, too. Veles' pit, why do I feel the best way for them all to cope would be locking them in the tavern's basement with access to all of Ian's spirits? Fuck, at this point, I'd happily join them.'

'If you decide to do it, sir, count me in.' Tomma nodded, a half-smile momentarily tugging at his lips. With a quick military salute, he turned and left. I looked at my adjutant, who had been silently trying to pick up the scattered documents from the floor, as I contemplated what to do next.

Annika had started opening up to me, and I didn't want to jeopardise it by sleeping in her bed uninvited. That just meant I had to busy myself tonight, as I was sure I wouldn't be able to sleep.

'Bring the armoury register, contracted suppliers record, and the up-to-date storage reports to my room,' I finally said. After a moment of hesitation, I added, 'and ask Ian to send his strongest mead there.'

When he acknowledged my order, I turned and left for the bath chamber. I was filthy after the long flight, but my first glance at the billowing steam reminded me of the beautiful moment we'd had at the manor in Truso.

'I hope you are safe, Ari. I miss you . . . and I feel so lost without you,' I said, whispering a short prayer to the All-Father to protect him before entering the bath. I didn't have time to indulge myself, nor did I want to. So, I focused on washing quickly and planning what I should do next.

ᛉᛍᚾᛊᚼ

Something woke me.

I shook my head, trying to remember where I was and what I was doing. With an annoyed grumble, I removed the piece of paper that had gotten stuck to my cheek. It took me a moment to remember I was in my bedroom, and apparently, I'd fallen asleep at the desk. All that was left of the candles I'd used to read by were sputtering stubs, drowning in their own wax, the smell nearly obscuring the scent of Ian's apple cider.

I looked around, wondering what had pulled me out of my slumber, blinking at the sight of my visitor. Annika stood by the door in a white nightgown, hesitance written all over her face.

'Come, join me, sweet Nivale,' I murmured, welcoming her. She crossed the room and stood in front of my chair. Still half asleep, I reached out and pulled her onto my lap, inhaling the gentle scent of verbena lingering on her skin.

She didn't resist. Instead, she straddled my legs, wrapping her arms around my neck. Her loose chestnut hair fell against my cheek, melting away the tension I'd carried all day. I stroked her back, pressing my face into her bosom, allowing the newfound peace to seep in.

We were both people of few words, but she had come to me, and that was all that mattered. We could talk when she was ready. Right now, I just wanted to hold her, to feel her breath on my neck, to be with the woman whose presence made everything better.

She rocked her hips, kissing my neck, nipping the skin hard enough to leave a mark. 'Ani, what are you...?' I asked. For a moment, I thought I had misunderstood her intention, but then she repeated her movement, and I felt my trousers tighten against my rising erection.

'Make me forget,' she whispered, sliding her hands under the collar of my shirt. I pressed them to my chest, searching her face for answers. Ani opened her mouth as if to say something, only to shake her head.

I knew the feeling all too well, the struggle to find the words when you needed them most. But she found a way, the Anchor bond flaring to life, a maelstrom of emotion hitting me like a hammer, choking me with its intensity.

'Please, my Ursus. I'm drowning,' Ani whispered. 'The images . . . they keep coming. I can't—' She leaned in for a kiss, her heart racing under my hand.

'It's alright, sweetheart. Whatever you need, I'm here for you, but guide this clueless bear. Show me how to make it better for you.'

She came to me . . .

If my touch could help her survive the night, I wouldn't deny her. I let her pull at my shirt, lifting my arms so she could remove it, and when her soft lips trailed over my bare skin, I grasped her gown, pulling it up to reach between her legs.

Annika was soft, wet, and ready for me. Finally, I could do something to soothe my mate.

CHAPTER 24

ANNIKA

O rmond's hands on my hips felt right, mollifying the sense of dread that had been my constant companion since Alaric had told me his plans.

I craved more of his strength, his ferocity, of the love that knew no boundaries. He was the embodiment of all that was good and honourable in this world, and I *needed* to feel it. I needed my beast to tear me apart so I could put myself back together again.

'Harder,' I rasped as his grip tightened on my thighs, and he groaned in response.

'I will hurt you if I do as you ask,' he said. Despite the hesitation in his voice, his hands flexed, holding me just a little tighter while the yellow glow of his eyes grew brighter.

He needed this as much as I did.

My fear for Ari had blinded me, and I'd lashed out at Orm, pushing him away before the fates could take him, too. I'd seen the pain in his eyes, but I couldn't bring myself to reach out. It wasn't until Zalesie and the loss of everyone there that I saw the fragility of human life and realised the foolishness of my behaviour.

'I don't care if it hurts,' I groaned, sliding my hand down to grasp his member through the fabric. His hips jerked, and he threw his head back.

'Fuck, Nivale, you're strangling the life out of me . . .' he growled. 'Fine, whatever you wish, whatever makes you happy again.'

He grew harder, working against my hand, holding me possessively against his body.

My Ursus, my big protective bear, would stand by me through my rage and tears, bearing the brunt of the power that scared even me. He was my rock, sheltering me from the storm, the man whose strength lifted me when everything came crashing down. I loved my broken fae and cherished my bonded dragon, but it was Ormond's steadfast love that had healed me.

He took hold of his belt, undoing it, and I rose just enough for him to free himself. His cock sprang out, making me moan in delight as I rocked against it.

'I need the beast. Take me. If it hurts, so be it, but I need you, all of you,' I murmured before grasping his short beard and pulling him into a brutal kiss. 'Fuck me as hard as you love me . . .'

Orm liked to be gentle with me, acutely aware of his own strength, but I didn't need his gentleness tonight. When I bit his lip, he growled again, pulling away.

'You're playing a dangerous game, Nivale,' he said in a voice so low and deep it sent shivers down my spine. 'My control has its limits, and I will hurt you if I . . . Fuck, Annika . . . I can't. I will rip you apart,' he cursed, his hips bucking when I grabbed his cock, aiming it at my entrance.

It slipped from my grasp when Ormond roared, lifting me and slamming me back onto the desk. Papers scattered, falling to the floor, but I didn't care. My gaze was focused on him as he stood over me, panting harshly before he grasped my thighs and spread them open.

'Remember you asked for this.' His voice was a tense grunt as he slammed inside me in one harsh thrust. The move was so forceful that it pushed me back on the desk, but he locked his hand around my throat, drawing me back in and impaling me on his cock.

I groaned, half-throttled, as he slammed into me again. His harsh, punishing rhythm forced another cry from my lips. My control fractured, and strands of aether shimmered in the air, floating towards him. Orm snarled as our magic mixed, shredding the last of his control.

'*More*,' I groaned, wrapping my legs around his hips and pulling him farther into me.

His pleasure burned through the Anchor bond, fuelling my own; Orm was aroused by the searing heat of my primal power, so I let it flow. His eyes blazed brighter than any fire, wild magic roaring through the beast he'd unleashed.

I didn't care that the vortex of power roiling around us rattled the windows, shredding the scattered reports he'd been reading in the aethereal storm. Nothing mattered but him: my berserker, wrenching pleasure from my soul as he chased the darkness away.

'*Mine*,' Orm howled as the aether lit his skin from within with each punishing thrust.

Pleasure built in my core, washing away the stench of the funeral pyre and the feeling of failure, all eclipsed by his brutal touch. Suddenly, I was moving, held aloft by the sheer strength of his battle-hardened muscles.

'I love you,' I rasped, scratching his back. He roared, pressing my body into the mattress as he threw me on the bed, groping my breasts so hard I was sure I would have bruises tomorrow. My pleasure crested, and my world became overwhelmed by the absolute love radiating through our bond.

I felt him lose himself in the sensation, my body pulsing around him, gripping his shaft when he erupted deep inside me. I whimpered and held him close, stroking his back as his body shuddered, beautiful golden eyes dimming when the beast retreated, calmed by our joining.

When our breathing evened out, he rolled us to the side, wrapping his arms around me. 'I didn't hurt you, did I?'

Orm had just given me exactly what I needed, yet he worried it was too much. I felt the dam I'd built around my heart over the last few days burst. A short sob escaped me as I pulled away, panting to hold my tears at bay.

'I'm sorry, it's not your fault,' I said, feeling like I needed to run away, but Orm grabbed me around the waist and pulled me close.

'I know, and you are not leaving. You said you needed me, and now I need you to stay with me,' he murmured into my neck. I jerked my head back, shocked by the pain in his voice. 'I'm not forcing you. I will let you go if you truly desire it, but I need you. Please stay.'

'I can't, Orm. I'm afraid that if I crack, I'll break . . . Too many people are counting on me to be strong. I can't fall apart, so please, let me be. It hurts too fucking much.'

He caught my hand, pressing it to his chest before caging me in his embrace. Ormond was inhumanly strong, and without my magic, I couldn't break free, but nor did I actually want to.

'Will it hurt less if you let this guilt and doubt fester? Cry, my love,' he said. 'I know how much you love Ari. I know how angry you feel, how scared . . . I know because I feel it, too.'

Orm kissed the top of my head, stroking me gently. 'The night you slept in Vahin's lair, Ari gave himself to me. I've never felt that way before. It's different from what you and I share, but no less meaningful. When he told me he had interrogated Ihrain and needed to leave, I thought I'd done something wrong . . . but I didn't.'

He sighed, gently lifting my chin until I looked into his eyes. He brushed away the hair that was plastered to my forehead and smiled.

'Ari made a difficult choice, maybe the wrong one, but it was *his* choice, and we must respect it. No one's at fault, and only Cahyon's to blame for Zalesie.'

He looked down, tracing a finger over the Anchor mark on my chest. Within a dark, slowly swirling circle was a dragon, a sword, and a thorny vine, all entwined together in perfect harmony.

With a tender smile, Orm bent down and kissed each aspect of my mark. 'I never considered what it's like to be a conduit mage. How deeply you must feel the souls entwined with your own,' he whispered, his breath raising goosebumps on my skin. 'If I lost you, I would drown this world in blood and dragon fire, and yet you were able to let Alaric go. I could never be that strong.'

His calm words and soft caresses eased my trembling body, and I embraced him, pressing my face hard against his muscled chest. 'I shouldn't have come looking for you, but I'm glad I did. I don't deserve you.'

A low growl vibrated through Orm's chest. 'If you hadn't, I would have come to you. I need you, Annika,' he said, crushing me to his body. 'Promise me one thing, Nivale. Rage, scream, lash me with your words or your magic, but never turn away from our bond. If you love me, never let me feel so alone again.' His arms tightened around me with bruising force. 'Promise me, Annika.'

His last words were barely audible, but the love that surged through our bond was unmistakable.

'I promise,' I answered, returning his hug. As we drifted to sleep, I knew the darkness in my soul hadn't vanished, but the pain had lifted, just a little. Still, if I was going to get my fae back and ensure no one else shared the fate of Zalesie, I needed to be stronger, and the source of my strength was now snoring into my hair.

ᚱᚲᚾᚠᚼ

Angry voices and a loud banging dragged me from a deep slumber. I groaned, unable to remember the last time I got to sleep in. Muscular arms tightened around me, and my hairy, musk-scented pillow shifted, muttering curses. 'Spectrae'd better be attacking, or the gods have mercy on whoever is pounding on the door!' he shouted.

The door burst open to reveal Bryna leading the charge, followed by Tomma, who was trying to hold Katja back as my friend fought like a mountain lioness to get into the room. I could even spot Ian's scarred face peeking from around them in the corridor.

'What the—?' I muttered, pulling the covers over my naked body, but our friends seemed oblivious to our state of undress. Worse, Orm didn't seem to care either, and I had to grab his arm in hopes he wouldn't jump out of bed to chase our visitors away.

'You're back,' Bryna said as she sat down next to me. 'These fuckers wouldn't tell me anything, and you didn't come see me . . . I thought you were lost, especially when I had to chain your man to the forge. You should've come to see me as soon as you arrived.'

The next thing I knew, my face was crushed against her ample bosom while I frantically tried to protect my modesty.

'I was exhausted. I'm so sorry,' I said, my bones groaning from the friendly pats she delivered to my back.

'We know,' Katja said, 'and your two idiots didn't bother saying a word, either. The guards only said that the commander had landed. What if you'd needed help? And where's Alaric? I need him in the infirmary.' She was jabbing her finger into Tomma's chest, and the poor dragon rider withered under her accusing stare.

'You were tired from trying to help Zalesie's survivors—*oof*,' Tomma grunted as Katja stomped on his foot with such force that even I felt it. I realised that her attempt to silence him, coupled with Bryna's affectionate behaviour, were my friends' way of showing their worry about my reaction to the news.

'I know about Zalesie,' I said, untangling myself from Bryna's smothering embrace. 'We flew there as soon as I found out.'

My words silenced everyone.

Katja's shoulders sagged. 'Are you alright?' she asked quietly.

I shook my head. 'No. How can we be alright? They destroyed our home and all those people . . . I'm not alright, but I'll survive, and that undead bastard will pay for this.'

Orm shifted, pulling me back from Bryna to hug me. 'There will be time to reunite later, but as you can all see, Annika is uninjured. Unless you want to inspect my very naked body, I suggest you give us time to get dressed, and we can meet in my office in an hour,' he said, his grumpy tone leaving no doubt it was an order.

'Oh, I don't mind,' Bryna said. 'You're not the first man I've seen naked, Commander.'

Ormond's answering growl was enough for Katja to roll her eyes. 'Oh, shift your green arse off their bed, Bryna. No ogling that one—he's taken,' she said before looking Tomma up and down. 'This one's off limits, too.'

The smile that blossomed on the injured rider's face was worth a thousand words, and meek as a puppy, he let her lead him away. Bryna sighed deeply and followed, closing the door behind her.

Orm nuzzled my hair. 'They care about you, Nivale.'

Contrary to everything that had happened in the last few days, their affectionate chaos made me chuckle. 'I care for them too, but not enough to share. Get yourself dressed, *Commander*, and don't you dare offer yourself again.' Orm grinned as he leapt off the bed, presenting his perfectly chiselled body to the world. I slapped his thigh. 'No teasing. Get dressed, Ursus.'

'I'm not.' He winked. 'Well, maybe a little. I just wanted to keep seeing that beautiful smile,' he said, standing in front of me. 'I know difficult times are coming, but I will tease you, love you, and prove to you that life is worth living over and over again. As long as I can make you smile, whatever burden fate throws on my shoulders, I will bear it.'

I had no answer. I kissed Orm softly, marvelling at the gentle heart under those stern eyes and thick muscles.

'*A dragon would never choose someone unworthy to bond with,*' came Vahin's thought, '*although I was beginning to reconsider my choices after last night's inferno. Coaxing the berserker out of him . . . Really?*'

I blushed, scolding him playfully, '*Neither would I, so stop peeking into my thoughts.*'

�ᚾᛊᚨ

When we arrived at Ormond's office, everyone was already seated, except for his adjutant, who grumbled under his breath about missing documents while rifling through a chaotic stack of paperwork on Orm's desk.

The space was incredibly crowded, so as Orm dropped into his chair, I casually leaned against the back of it, content to remain standing. That is, until he let out an annoyed grunt and, without warning, yanked me onto his lap. The audacity earned him a sharp glare and a solid punch to the shoulder. Fully justified, in my opinion.

He was quiet for a moment, letting everybody settle down before he nodded to the adjutant. 'Please take notes. I want everything from this meeting's discussion to be written down and sent to my brother.' The old soldier inclined his head, fumbling with his inkwell and preparing a quill and paper.

'First things first,' Orm went on, 'we're expecting an army from Dagome and the allied forces of the dark and light fae, as well as the dwarven kingdom.'

The clattering of a goblet hitting the floor reverberated throughout the room. One of the younger officers quickly picked it up and bowed in apology. 'I'm sorry, my lord. But how? For years, we've known the senile old king has been dismantling Dagome's army, and now you're telling us it's headed here, and that the Lowland Kingdoms have honoured the alliance? How?'

The other riders nodded, wanting to hear the answer.

'Lady Annika,' Orm replied. 'She has managed to receive the endorsement of a goddess, so when my Nivale told them to honour their promises, they listened.' I noticed the mischief in his eyes just as I drew a breath to correct him. 'Right after she proclaimed my brother king, of course.'

The pure glee in his voice made me want to punch him again but the eyes of everyone in the room had turned to focus on me at his declaration.

'Fucking hell, I'm friends with a kingmaker,' Bryna roared, and not even an elbow in the ribs from Katja could shut her up. 'Ouch! Stop elbowing me, woman, or I will sew padded vambraces to your sharp bones.'

Katja ignored her, getting straight to the point. 'That's so Ani. I'm half expecting her to say it was just an accident, but as good as that news is for Dagome, we don't have enough space in Varta Fortress to accommodate three armies and their support. Especially not after relocating the survivors from Zalesie.'

'First, *I'm right here,*' I complained, 'and yes, it actually *was* an accident. We needed a king, so I named the best man for the job. Second, there is a good chance they'll be bringing their own supplies and . . . Well, if push comes to shove, I can ask Valaram to create a portal to the capital.'

Orm gave me a curious look, so I hastily explained. 'We can leave supplies behind that way. I don't think Talena will be happy to have her mages use their aether for such a mundane task, but we won't know until we ask.'

He nodded, and I felt the gentle play of his fingers as he absent-mindedly stroked my back. 'Good,' he said. 'Regarding the armies, we can make room in the castle for the leaders and fortify a field for the rest. I discussed strategy with my brother, and we'll be heading towards the Rift as soon as possible. Ensure all dragons are well-fed and ready. We need to clear the sky of spectrae so that the ground forces have a chance of facing the monsters.'

'Will Lady Annika be flying with us?' the man who'd dropped his goblet asked.

'I will,' I responded, aching to fly across the border. 'I have a score to settle with that immortal bastard and his minions.' Even surrounded by friends, I felt a crawling sense of doom.

At my words, the dragon riders visibly relaxed, and I could even see a few smiles, as if they were welcoming the upcoming battle.

'We'll join you,' Katja said, and I looked at her with a frown. 'You'll need healers and cooks. Someone has to mend soldiers' clothing, and many of the women here can fight and will protect the camp when you move farther into the enemy's lands.'

'There is no need for that,' I said.

She huffed, shaking her head. 'No need? Say that to the mothers, wives, and daughters of those who died in Zalesie, or to those from the mountain villages who lost everything in the attacks. They want revenge. Many couldn't even bury their families.'

I swallowed the bile that rose in my throat, wondering how many had perished.

'I appreciate the sentiment,' Orm cut in, 'but they will be a hindrance, and our soldiers will feel obliged to defend them. As much as I want to grant their wish, this is the wrong way to do it.'

Katja bristled. Before my friend could snap at him, arguing during what had turned out to be another war council meeting, I intervened.

'She's right, Orm. There is nothing more dangerous than a mother fighting for her child, nothing more vicious than a woman whose heart has been broken. You won't have a bunch of weak females to protect—you'll have a pack of wolves that will rip out the enemy's throats for the chance to spit in the Lich King's eye.'

Orm's eyes softened. He raised his hand, gently trailing his fingers over my cheek, uncaring of the looks we were getting. 'If you're sure they can fight,' he murmured, turning to Katja. 'Fine, get your pack of she-wolves ready. They'll train with the soldiers *and* behave like them.'

'Splendid, I'd better get to work. We need more chain-mail shirts and armour with tits,' Bryna said, rising from her chair, and her entirely inappropriate comment burst the bubble of tension in the room.

'Thank you, mistress blacksmith,' Orm said. 'I'm sure many will appreciate armour with . . . I mean, designed for females. Can I also ask you to work with the soldiers to fit a gate to the dragons' cave? Having a secure place like that saved a young rider at Roan Fortress, and I want our citizens to have a shelter, too.'

He looked around at the rest of those in the room. 'I'll have more details when Reynard arrives. Until then, please stay vigilant. Patrols must not engage in fighting unless a civilian's life is at stake. Miss Katja, as you run the town council, I'll need you to ensure the town has enough supplies for both our visitors and a potential siege. Tomma, you're in charge of the riders—I'll take the ground forces. Does anyone have any questions?'

'Since everyone's planning to march to war, who will be in charge here once you all go, sir?' asked Orm's adjutant, who sat quietly in the corner.

'We have a town council . . . and Ian will take over any military matters,' Orm replied.

The adjutant frowned. 'Ian? The barkeeper, Ian? But he is—'

'Disabled, yes, but not stupid. He was a dragon rider and a bloody good one. He'll know what to do. I don't need heroes to stand with naked swords. I need a leader who can keep his head when the worst happens. Ian is the perfect choice.'

If I thought I couldn't love him more, I was mistaken. Orm's logic saw past scars and physical constraints, finding qualities many over-looked, and as long as men like him were around, we had a fighting chance.

'You are right, my Ursus. Ian will be perfect.'

CHAPTER 25

ALARIC

A few days ago

I stood in front of the portal, contemplating my life choices. The weatherworn stone arch gleamed in the last rays of the setting sun. Now that they were activated, the carved runes shone with an inner light, seemingly mocking my indecision. I was alone on the island, with only the birds to witness me stepping into danger, the ruins of the fae palace I stood in a silent reminder of the threat the Lich King posed.

The portal lay hidden deep within the gardens, discreetly nestled into the partition wall. Over time, it had likely been overlooked, mistaken for a decorative arch entwined with climbing roses. Even the artisans who had worked here, chisels and hammers in hand, must have thought it nothing more than an ornamental relic, blending effortlessly into its surroundings.

And yet, this unassuming structure was my gateway to Katrass. I only had to take a step, and I'd be there. For so many years, that had been my only goal, but now, here I was, hesitating. Annika's tears burned a hole in my chest, more painful than the curse ever was, and knowing I was the reason for them shattered something deep within me.

I'd done my fair share of despicable acts in my life. However, not once had I ever felt this low, this guilty, this unworthy of the woman who'd sent me away with her blessing, stained with the taste of her sorrow.

You can still go back.

I shook my head to get rid of the temptation.

'If I can't even deal with her tears, how can I protect her?' I muttered, knowing that if my sister implanted Cahyon's soul into my father's body, the war would be much worse. Not even our combined forces would be able to defeat him if that happened.

Worse, as a living fae, he could Anchor Annika, and it was that thought that tipped the scales and pushed me towards the shimmering portal.

'Dark Mother, protect my light, and if I don't make it back, help her forget me,' I whispered, muttering the prayer as my foot disappeared into the dark void that swirled beneath the arch.

Nothingness enveloped me. It wasn't just the absence of light. It was the absence of everything. No touch, no smell, no sound permeated the space between realms.

For some reason, only fae were able to create portals, just as only humans gave birth to conduit mages and those able to bond with dragons. No one had ever discovered why, but many theories discussed our longevity and how our bodies wove and stored the aether.

It was interesting how academic research came to mind before I emerged into a twilight filled with gnarled branches, thorns, and the putrid scent of decay. The smell was so potent it made me gag, but I knew I couldn't make a noise. I had to find a hiding place—the sound of rustling and raised voices nearby alerting me that my arrival hadn't gone unnoticed.

As quietly as I could, I moved through the undergrowth, wincing each time my foot crunched through a dry twig or bone. But a quick

silencing spell did its job, and I crept past the guarding ghouls undetected.

I wasn't sure where I was. It appeared to be a nobleman's gardens, judging by the beautifully carved benches and cherry trees. From
experience, I knew that the Moroi, as any other fae, loved to build
lover's alcoves, hidden spots on their estates where one could hide from
prying eyes. So when I spotted a dark opening behind a rock, I didn't
hesitate.

I slipped into the darkness with a tracing spell and my dagger ready
to lash out, only to exhale slowly when I encountered an empty space.
Whispering a cantrip, I modified my spell to seal off the alcove's entrance then risked summoning a fae light.

The niche turned out to be a cave cut from living rock, with such
exquisite carvings that I could only marvel at the talent. The carvings
depicting life in Ozar before the fall, almost seemed to move, the story
they told flowing seamlessly from one image to the next. I felt an ache
for the loss of a race that loved art more than war.

I tore my gaze from the scene, sitting down and wrapping my cloak
tighter around me before closing my eyes. I couldn't afford to fall
asleep so close to roaming monsters, but I needed to wait until sunrise
before I tried to figure out where I was.

If my assumptions were correct, life in Katrass still followed the
nighttime routine that allowed the Moroi to thrive. Short, late autumn
days didn't give me much time to move, but with the first rays of the
sun, both the monsters and corrupted Moroi would become less active
and much less aware, giving me the best chance to travel unnoticed.

It would be a long night, but it gave me time to plan my next steps,
and how to deal with my family. An image of Orm and Ani flashed
before my eyes, bringing a smile to my face as I thought about how
both tried to follow dark fae customs for my sake. About how Orm

was dominant by nature, and how I never had a problem following his lead. About Ani . . . and how amazing she was, embracing her new role so well that even Valaram was tempted.

The thought of the dark fae ambassador anywhere near my domina sent a low snarl rumbling in my throat, one I struggled to suppress. I couldn't blame him, though—Ani's strength and magical prowess were irresistible traits among the dark fae, practically an aphrodisiac. That she was the Dark Mother's chosen only elevated her, placing her on par with the empress in the eyes of any dark fae male.

But Valaram's interest made me uneasy. Among our kin, there was a whispered affliction—*tal maladie*, madness of the heart. It was a shameful secret, rarely spoken of, where a man became so consumed by desire for a woman that nothing short of possessing her could satisfy him. History was littered with both noble sacrifices and unspeakable crimes born from this obsession.

I hoped Valaram was too wise to succumb, for I was more my father's son than I cared to admit. The thought of sharing Ani's attention with anyone besides Orm was unbearable.

It wasn't that I wanted him as an enemy—he was a valuable ally—but unless Ani herself desired it, I'd ensure he stayed far away from her. The mere idea of him sniffing around her made my blood boil.

Still, I couldn't afford to dwell on such thoughts, not here, stranded in enemy territory. So instead, I forced myself to focus, channelling the rising fury into planning my escape once I found Rowena.

ᛉᚲᚾᚠᛪ

The night passed by uneventfully, and I ventured outside once the sun was high enough to chase the shadows away. In the daylight, the former splendour of the gardens was even more apparent.

Annika would love seeing this when the flowers are blooming, I thought, looking at the tangled branches of oromea, a healing plant with bright yellow petals that gleamed like liquid gold.

I drew on my stores of aether, using a drop of my blood to craft a simple spell that could detect blood relations to locate my sister.

As I drew the sigil on my wrist, I felt a pull directing me to the north. The sensation was weak, which usually meant significant distance, but with my bag of supplies and a cloaking spell, I was ready. And unless I was very unlucky, whatever enemies I might encounter would be undead and, therefore, susceptible to my will.

I walked along the path, the wind blowing dry leaves into my face. Except for the overgrown gardens, nothing confronted me, and I slowly continued, trying to blend in whilst still following the magical tether.

Initially, everything went well, but my journey was not without obstacles. On the first day, I stumbled on a revenant sentinel. The creature was so still, its skin resembling dry tree bark, that I almost stepped on it.

It noticed me before I could change directions, and as the undead opened its mouth to raise the alert, I thrust my hand into its chest, absorbing the magic that gave it life. For a moment, I looked at the rapidly decomposing body before I resumed my journey, the pull growing stronger the farther I walked.

I was forced to make more frequent stops, spending nights in abandoned houses or other small alcoves. I had to strengthen my cloaking spell as more remnants appeared on my path, along with several corrupted Moroi, who, despite their sensitivity to light, still roamed the streets. What concerned me more was how many golems there were.

Those creatures were resistant to magic, and no illusion could deceive them. Sneaking by became painfully slow. I had to trust more in my own abilities than my cloaking spell to keep me undetected.

Finally, five days later, I arrived at the palace.

It was well past midday when I reached its white walls, stopping to catch my breath under a mass of climbing roses. I sent a silent prayer to the Dark Mother, blessing the evening fae for their love of flowers and beauty.

The roses, overgrown as they were, made the perfect climbing frame and hid me from prying eyes. I placed my dagger in my mouth and climbed the thorny branches as swiftly as I could until I found a darkened window and slid inside.

I'm in the Lich King's palace.

The thought shocked me, and I instinctively reached to my chest, patting the remains of my curse. But it was silent. I'd worried how the wretched thing would react in proximity to its master, but the Dark Mother's touch was truly a mercy.

I followed my magic, which now hummed like a tense rope attached to my wrist. I was close to Rowena, so I pushed forward, determined to find her and leave this place as soon as possible.

Those who stood in my way were dispatched quickly. I bound all the undead to my will, slaughtering those whose life force still burned under Cahyon's corruption. As I stuffed another body into a storage room, I couldn't suppress my dark humour. *Now, this palace has a skeleton in every closet.*

The farther I went, the more I mourned the lost Kingdom of Ozar. Despite centuries of neglect, the beauty of the palace was breathtaking. The faded, rich tapestries still gleaming with golden thread, exquisite paintings, candelabras shaped like roses, and polished marble floors impressed me so much that I scarcely noticed the layers of dust or occasional rodents in dark corners.

The sun set below the horizon, but in the meandering corridors, I was no closer to finding my sister than when I'd started. I was working through the last floor of living quarters, dreading the thought of going to the dungeons when distant footsteps diverted my attention. I was distracted for a moment, but then I felt it. A strong pull from one of the smaller rooms.

I entered it, and time froze.

'Don't touch me! Don't come closer, or I swear I'll gut you. If the master sent you here, tell him I'm working on it.'

The panicked female voice stunned me into silence, and I stood there, still in the shadows, staring at a petite, golden-haired woman wielding a dagger that looked more like a letter opener than a weapon.

She'd changed—matured—and the haunted look in her eyes reflected her suffering, but it was still the face of the little girl who'd smiled as I hugged her goodbye all those centuries ago.

'Ro . . . Oh gods, Rowena. I finally found you.'

The dagger clattered onto the desk, which was covered in half-opened books and drafted sigils. My sister backed away, pressing her back to the wall, looking at me in disbelief.

'No, you're another nightmare sent to torment me. You're not real. *You are not real*,' she hissed, staring at me with wild, bright blue eyes, and I felt the aether build around me as if she were trying to dispel an illusion.

'It's really me, Ro,' I said, stepping forward to stretch out my hand, then promptly ducking when she released a small fireball.

She truly believes I'm not here.

I knew only one way to convince her. In a blur, I lunged, and before Ro could draw another breath, I was beside her, crushing her to me in a fierce hug, whispering the lullaby I'd used to sing her to sleep with as a child.

'It's all right, little sister, I'm here,' I said once her thrashing slowed, little by little. 'I'm finally here.'

Rowena's shouting turned to sobs as she hammered her fists into my chest.

'Why now, why after all these years, did you come now?' she cried. The pain in her voice tore my heart to pieces.

'I couldn't come earlier,' I said. 'I'm so sorry, I tried. I even experimented with a conduit mage, but nothing got me past the Barrier. Only now was I able to find a way to come for you.'

Rowena inhaled sharply, placing her head on my chest. Years of torment melted away as I held her in my arms. I finally had my sister back and could get her home safely.

'Who is this conduit mage? Is it that Annika father's so intent on killing?'

I frowned, unsure why she'd asked. *Surely the Lich King has mentioned her?* The stray thought came and went as she stifled a sob.

'She is so much more than that, Ro,' I said. 'I found my domina. Annika is more than I could ever dream of—and yes, she is the conduit. You'll love her. She's suffered so much, but there is such kindness in her, and a fierceness that would humble any warrior.' I smiled involuntarily, almost as if invoking Ani's name made everything better.

'Your domina? Are you blood-bonded to her, brother?' Rowena wiped her tears, looking at me with a shy smile.

I nodded. 'Blood-bonded, Anchored . . . I belong to her in every possible way,' I said, releasing my hold since she seemed to have calmed. 'Come, we need to get back to the portal. Bring only the bare necessities, as it is a long trek. Everything else I can get for you in Dagome.'

'You truly came to take me away from him, away from these monsters?'

'Of course,' I said, 'but we need to hurry. Our luck can only hold for so long.' I pulled her towards the window, wishing I had a dragon of my own to climb onto and fly us away from this cursed place. Instead, I hoped the tangled roses could handle us both.

'We can't go, not during the night. His constructs . . . They all become active when the sun sets and they can sense me. We need to wait until sunrise,' she insisted, pulling me back into the shadows.

'It is better to risk a midnight hike than spend time here. The longer I'm present in his realm, the higher the risk the Lich King will detect me,' I said, noticing her eyes widen. 'Don't be afraid, I can protect you. Let's just say I left a trail of bodies in my wake getting here. And while this place is a beautiful maze, I don't think they'll remain hidden for long.'

'*No*, we need to wait until morning,' she repeated, pulling her hand from my grasp and backing away. Ro was panting hard, on the edge of panic. Whatever my sister was afraid of, I wouldn't be able to leave unless I threw her over my shoulder and carried her out.

'Alright, Ro. It's okay. You know this place best. We'll wait—but as soon as the sun rises, we're going. No fuss or fear. Don't be a songbird, afraid to leave the cage even when the door is open,' I said as I looked around. If we were to spend the night here, I needed to secure the room. Otherwise, I risked Cahyon, or even my father, recognising my magical signature.

Rowena watched me with interest as I walked from the door to the window, drawing sigils that would make the room invisible to any magical creature. She didn't help or offer other solutions, and I felt unease build deep in my core. I dismissed my suspicions. What did I expect from a sister kept captive all these years?

'There, all done. Now, come and sit with me,' I said, patting the bed once I'd finished warding the room.

Rowena perched on its edge, but when I pulled her to my side, she leaned her head on my shoulder, and although I didn't want to disturb the moment, I knew I had to ask some questions.

'Did you discover the spell to give Cahyon a new body?' I finally asked.

She stiffened in my arms. 'I did. I gave it to him. His monsters are now roaming the borderlands, capturing mages to use their blood for the ritual. I don't have enough aether to do it myself, and father . . . Well, he'll be the host, and he isn't likely to help,' she said.

I exhaled with relief. 'Good, then I've arrived in time,' I said, stroking her golden hair, considering the potential consequences. 'If only I could tell Ani to pull all mages from the borders, but it'll have to wait until we're back in Dagome.'

'Oh? I can help you talk to her,' Rowena said eagerly.

I studied her with a frown. 'How?'

'Through dreamwalking! With your blood bond, I can create a link for you to talk,' she said, but I wasn't convinced. 'That's how I reached you the first time.'

'Will she be in danger?' I asked. Years of psychological torment had made me very wary of any mental links.

'No, you mean no harm to her,' she said. 'You'll only be able to speak to her in her dreams, but you have to open yourself to me fully—no mental barriers. The spell is difficult enough alone. Of course, if you don't trust me, we can wait until we get to Dagome.' She shrugged, returning her head to my shoulder.

I weighed my options, but since Rowena had already given Cahyon the spell, every day brought him closer to freedom. Besides, I wanted to talk to my domina.

'It's been a few days, so they're probably worried,' I murmured to myself before exhaling slowly. 'Show me how to do it.' I said, and Rowena gifted me a beautiful smile, reminding me of the little girl who'd run to me to show off her latest achievement.

'Remove your shirt,' she commanded, pricking her finger with a metal quill from the desk, then mine.

'Why are you using your blood?' I asked.

She chuckled, shaking her head. 'Because I'll be the bridge between you, silly,' she said, drawing a sigil.

'Tell me about Cahyon's army and anything else that might help,' I requested, feeling the bite of her spell as it spread over my skin like frost. If I could send a message, I intended to give Orm as much information as possible before joining him in Varta Fortress.

'There's not much to tell. The one under the Barrier keystone is still slumbering. Cahyon is too weak to wake it from such a distance. Dagome is safe for now,' she said as she worked on the spell. 'There, I'm done. Focus on your domina, brother.'

I looked at the red marks gleaming on my chest. The symbols trailing over my skin were so similar to the curse that I had to fight the urge to scrub them off. Instead, I focused on Annika.

A feeling of weightlessness swept over me, and then I was moving through a cold barrier. It felt like my soul would freeze, until I sensed the familiar warmth of Ani's spirit wrapping around me.

'Domina? Annika, open your mind for me, love,' I whispered, repeating the call in my mind until I felt a prickle of uneasiness through the Anchor bond. It wasn't what I expected, but the more I called her name, the more I felt awareness flooding our link, and finally, I heard her voice in my mind.

'Ari? What in Veles' arse is going on? Is it really you?'

'Yes, I found Rowena. She's with me, and I will be back home soon. Tell Orm the Rift is safe for now,' I blurted, feeling the connection fade.

'Ari, something's wrong. What is tethering you? It feels wrong . . . Ari . . .?' Her voice was barely an echo, but the pulse of love and worry I felt through the connection felt so real that I clutched my chest.

I emerged from the psychic connection to see my sister standing in front of me. Her eyes narrowed as she weaved the sigil's runes like a yarn's thread while the symbol hung between her fingers, glowing crimson. I grunted when she finished the spell.

'It is done. We can rest now,' I said, trying to ignore the dull ache in my chest, but Rowena stepped back, a strange look of triumph twisting her features.

'Oh, no, brother,' she said. 'It is just beginning. Thank you, Alaric, but as our father said, you have always been a fool.' An oppressive wave of magic froze me on the spot, imposing her will on mine.

'What have you done?' I rasped, seeing her go to the door and open it to whoever stood there.

'You were right, my lord,' Rowena said, bowing her head. 'He walked right into the trap. I'm linked to the conduit now.'

Cahyon Abrasan, the infamous Lich King, snapped his fingers, and two golems lunged at me. At the same time, the bastard's illusion shimmered over his mummified husk as he turned to give me a benevolent smile.

'Alaric, my child. Welcome home. I have been eagerly awaiting your presence.'

CHAPTER 26

ALARIC

I cursed, struggling in the golems' grasps until, by sheer luck, I broke free. I drew on my magic to fight back, but the spells flickered and died, the aether drawn into the symbols scrawled on my chest. Rowena stood before me, holding her palm up, and I saw my power gathering there, pulsing obscenely while she smirked, draining my magic.

I wished I had more time to marvel at the phenomenon, but I had only one chance to escape before my sister's spell once again rendered me helpless. Years of resisting mental torment had strengthened my mind's defences, but I never had to fight both physically and within my mind, and I was struggling.

Rowena's smile grew wider with each passing moment. She knew exactly what was happening to me.

Corrupted Moroi crowded in behind the Lich King as he observed my attempts to fight with a bored expression and slightly raised brow.

'Are you sure you can contain him?' he asked Ro as more monsters entered the room to subdue me. I flipped up my daggers, cutting my way to freedom, but as soon as I despatched one, two more took its place, and without my magic, the outlook was grim. Still, I knew giving up meant a fate worse than death.

'Once I have him in chains, yes,' Rowena answered. 'He already can't cast. As for his fighting prowess, I'm sure you can take care of it, my lord.' Her voice was so indifferent that I couldn't help looking at her in horror. Triumph and cruelty warred for dominance on her face, transforming it into a mask of terrifying disdain.

A memory flashed before my mind's eye: the vjesci, moments before I dismantled his forced existence in the dungeons of Varta Fortress.

'*Trust nothing your sister says.*'

I should have listened. Instead, I'd walked into a trap, right into my own worst nightmare.

'Give up, Alaric,' she jeered as I sank a dagger into another attacker's heart. 'Didn't you want us to be one big, happy family again?'

'My only family now is safe in Varta Fortress,' I snarled through clenched teeth. I was fighting like a demon, my enemies piling up beneath my feet as I took one step after another, closer to the window, closer to freedom.

He'll eventually run out of monsters, I thought, hissing in pain when a Moroi's clawed hand ripped through the fabric of my shirt, gouging chunks from my skin. My sister frowned, watching my fight with disbelief as I gained another step closer to the window.

'My lord,' Rowena said, 'if you want me to fulfil my promise, we can't let him escape.'

Raw power hit me in the back, sending me to my knees. Thorny vines sprang from the walls, binding me. My daggers clattered to the stone floor as Cahyon placed his hand on my sister's shoulder before his stare bored into my mind, his power forcing my submission.

'Surrender, Alaric. You are strong, but I am immortal, and this land will do as I order,' he said when I continued to repel him.

It was a miracle that I could still think, and I saw the frown on Cahyon's face. He hadn't expected my resistance, but the shard of Annika's soul within me seemed to disrupt hostile magic, protecting me in a way I didn't realise was possible.

That tiny shard of the woman I loved fought against the combined force of a dreamwalker and the damn Lich King, protecting my mind even when my body had been defeated. I was losing the battle, and I knew it. Worse, as long as I was alive, my sister had a link to Annika.

It was my turn to protect my domina.

I let the thorns rip the flesh of my wrists as I scrambled for my daggers, thanking the Dark Mother when my fingers closed around the hilt of the closest one. I turned the blade inwards, twisting and straining to press it to my throat.

Forgive me, my love, I thought, throwing myself forward as the palace convulsed. The last thing I saw was a raw stream of aether streaking down to rip me apart.

***

'Don't move. You'll only make it worse,' said a soft voice, and I felt soothing cold moisture trail across my throat.

'Annika?'

That's all I managed to say, my voice dry and broken, but even as I asked it, I already knew the answer. The person near me was not my Ani, despite her gentle and caring touch. I forced myself to focus, meeting the gaze of my healer.

The woman was dressed in a loose garment tied at the waist with a hood that covered her head. A brass mask covered her face, and only her brilliant, bright green eyes were visible.

'Who are you?' I asked.

'She is Lara, an uncorrupted healer of this dead kingdom.'

My father's voice awakened memories I wanted to stay buried, and it took me a moment to compose myself.

'Cahyon needs a virgin healer?' I asked, Lara's hand still on my throat.

'I'm not a virgin, you moron, just a Moroi untouched by the blood craving. How else could I heal you after you attempted to slit your throat?' she snapped, and I belatedly realised that despite all odds, I was still alive.

I groaned. 'You should have let me die.'

'I would have, but just like you, I didn't have a choice,' she answered, picking up her tools as I struggled to sit up.

I was in the dungeons, chained to the wall with only enough freedom to shift my position. While it was dark and lit only by a single torch, I could see the steel bars of the cell and the mouldy straw on the floor. I yanked at my rusty chains, but they held. Desperate, I reached for the aether, and as the life-giving force flew through me, Lara's eyes widened, and she pulled away from me.

'Don't—' she warned, but it was too late. Power slid over my body in a chaotic wave of wild magic, and I started convulsing, thrashing like a fish on a hook.

My father's laugh echoed long after I regained the ability to breathe again.

'As long as you're wearing the manacles, you can't do anything,' Lara said, closing her bag. 'I'm sorry, Alaric'va Shen'ra, I would have let you die if I could. I hope you don't suffer too long.'

She walked away, leaving me alone with the monster I called father, and I finally turned to face him. I knew Cahyon had ordered his golems to seize him, but after my sister's deception, I thought that, too, could have been a ruse. Yet my father was in the cell next to me, chained to the walls with the same rune-engraved manacles as me.

'So, she dragged you here like she said she would. You always were a fool, Alaric,' he said with a shrug, ignoring my assessing stare.

'So I'm told, but at least I'm here for the right reasons. You served a monster and made Ro into one, too. Yet here you are, chained up like a rabid dog. Who's the bigger fool, father?'

Roan was quiet for a moment, but the tension in his body told me my words hit their mark. 'At least I chained him to this land, this palace! But you . . . you're going to set him free. The marks on your chest,' he gestured at me, 'you thought I did them, didn't you?'

'Oh, spare me your lies. What else will you claim? That you didn't sacrifice your wife?' I huffed with disdain, wishing my chains were long enough to reach across to his cell and choke the life out of him.

'Of course I sacrificed her. She was planning to leave me. Me! After I lowered myself to take her for a wife!' he shouted.

'I wish she had. I wish she didn't just leave you, but had gone to the empress to disclose the vile treatment you subjected her, and us, to . . . we were just children. Look at what you did to Rowena—' I cried, choking on my anger.

He burst into crazed laughter. 'What *I* did? You were always too blind to see the real Rowena, the one who watched your punishment with a smile,' he said. 'I suppose I can't blame you. She tricked me too, that beautiful, innocent child always defending you. Dark Mother, how she irked me with her mewling and begging, but now I know it was on purpose. How her pleas always revealed more details of your defiance, fanning the flames of my anger.'

I shook my head, unwilling to believe him. Still, the revelation reminded me of those moments when my little Ro had come to my rescue. Every time she wrapped her arms around me and begged father to stop, she would panic and apologise for some other rule I'd broken. Every time, our father's face would darken, and the beatings got so much worse.

'Ha! You see it now, don't you? All the tears, all the apologies. They had one purpose . . . I almost killed you once. Do you remember? Because I do, and gods, how I wish I hadn't stopped that day.'

'Why do you hate me so much?' I asked, almost whispering. Even now, he seemed to revel in the worst day of my youth.

'Because you are the mage your grandparents always wanted me to be. Because Talena saw in you a strength she never saw in me. She rejected *me* but waited for you to mature to . . . Her prime mate asked to be your mentor, for the gods' sakes, when I'd had to beg my way into the court,' he said.

'You were a rising dark star of the empire, the "saviour" of the Shen'ra family, while I was considered a failure,' he continued. 'No one even cared that you were whelped from the filth of a human, but gods, did they laugh at me. The dark fae touched by tal maladie, too pathetic to choose another domina.' Roan was raving by the end, straining against his bonds as he shouted his hatred through the bars.

'I didn't ask to be born!'

'No, I thought taking a human would cure me, but you were just another one of my mistakes. I hated you for that, but the irony is that you're the perfect heir. You've not only surpassed your father, but also all dark fae, the male blood-bonded to the goddess' chosen—'

He was blessedly interrupted by the creak of a door in the distance, and I sensed a familiar magical signature wash down the corridor.

'Aren't family reunions so much fun?' Rowena asked as she opened my cell. The sigil she'd drawn on my chest flared to life, and I felt as weak as a kitten.

'Why, Ro? I know I took far too long to get here, but why betray me? We had a chance to escape.' I needed an explanation that would disprove my father's words.

I was clutching at straws. After seeing Rowena's indifferent expression as I fought to escape, I knew the girl I remembered was gone, but I hoped there was a reason, an excuse, for her betrayal.

'You still want to believe I'm some poor defenceless victim?' she asked. 'Don't you remember me begging you not to fight our father's decision to come here? Did you not wonder why mother escaped alone? Why she left me here . . . or why was she captured?'

Rowena's laughter reverberated in the cell, and it finally sunk in that under her divine looks was a spirit so rotten it was worse than even the Lich King's or my monster of a father's.

'You had no ambition except becoming a scholar. I wanted power, and you and your conduit mage will give me more than I dreamed possible,' she said, brushing a strand of silver hair off my forehead. 'I'm so happy you found your domina, Alaric. I promise to take good care of her for the rest of her brief existence.'

'You're a monster,' I said as I pulled away from her touch, feeling the last ties binding me to my family snap, leaving me untethered and cut off from my roots.

'A monster? No, of course not. I'm the perfect, sweet, golden-haired, soon-to-be empress of the continent. I wish you'd consider serving me, brother. We could rule this world if we worked together. We still can. I came here to offer a trade—'

'No,' I sneered. 'You may be able to steal my magic, but you cannot force me to use it. You might as well let me die.'

She sighed, standing up as she gestured to someone in the shadows. 'Take my father. We have preparations to make.'

For the first time in my life, I heard the cruel, sadistic parent who'd abused me for years howl in fear.

'You can't do this, Rowena. Take Alaric. He's younger and more powerful. Take that fucking bastard! Rowena, I can give you power.

We can work together!' he kept screaming even as a corrupted Moroi dragged him from his cell.

'What is my role in this?' I asked calmly, even if everything inside me raged in silent fury. 'You can't be so delusional to think I'll help you channel Cahyon's spirit into our father's flesh.'

Rowena licked her lips, smiling as she listened to the fading screams before her gaze shifted towards me.

'You're a conduit to my conduit, the key to unlocking Annika's abilities,' she answered before tapping her finger to my chest. 'The spell I used to help you communicate with her will allow me to siphon her power. I only needed your cooperation to establish the link, hence our little play . . . *Oh brother, I'm so scared,*' she exclaimed with a suddenly fearful expression before bursting into laughter. 'We knew you were on our lands the moment you used the portal. Didn't you notice that your journey here was a little too easy?'

I'm sorry, my love. I shouldn't have left, I thought, half listening to my sister's bragging until she fell silent, realising she had lost my interest.

'Never mind,' she said. 'I will get what I want, even if your domina has to suffer a little discomfort.' With a snap of Rowena's finger, another two Moroi stepped forward. 'Take him to the Chamber of Rituals and chain him to the wall. Ensure he cannot hurt himself,' she instructed.

The evening fae approached me, and I saw the corruption only the blood hunger could cause up close. Elongated fangs distorted their mouths, their eyes permanently filled with crimson, and their bulging muscles had made their bodies monstrous and twisted.

My sister's spell had drained me so much that I could do nothing when they unchained me. I was dragged through winding stairs and corridors until we reached a candlelit grotto. There, they strung me from metal hoops bolted into the rock directly above a large, flat stone that appeared to be a sacrificial altar.

This must have been Ozar's Chamber of Rituals. The pathos and splendour were still there, visible in the thousands of half-melted candles decorating every nook and cranny. Deeper in the cave was an underground lake with a small island accessible by two bridges. And while the sound of splashing water was soothing, the view of the dark stone altar was decidedly not.

The hours passed as I hung there, trying to ignore the discomfort. I slowed my breathing, letting my body mend the cuts and bruises I'd received fighting Cahyon's monsters.

As soon as I felt able, I tested my restraints. I suspected the collar around my neck was made using augurec,[1] a metal known for its ability to disturb the aether. The chains, however, were pure iron. If my sister wanted to use me, she would have to remove the collar, and as soon as I had access to my magic again, I could try to escape.

So I waited. My limbs grew numb, extended above my head, and I had to squeeze my fists several times to restore circulation. Finally, the Moroi that had tied me to the wall returned.

'Are you ready, boy? The fun's about to begin,' one said, licking his lips, and I was sure he wanted to sink his fangs into my neck. The Moroi liked to taste blood—it prolonged their lives as well as gave them a boost of aether. Those corrupted by the Lich King, though, needed to drain their victims dry, and they liked them conscious, the kicking and screaming driving their bloodlust.

Moments later, they reappeared with my father, his naked body covered in runes. He cursed, thrashing in their grip, but he wore a

---

1. **Augurec** /pron:au-gur-retc/ — an alloy of silver, iron, and copper pro-duced by artificer mages with the ability to disrupt the natural patterns of all aether; magical shackles.

collar similar to mine, blocking his use of magic. I was so entranced by the sight of the Moroi tying him to the altar that I missed Cahyon's entrance.

'Ah, Alaric!' he said, approaching me. 'Once this is done, we will renew our bond. Something disturbed it, but no worries, there is nothing our skilful Ro can't fix.' The illusion he usually wore to hide his hideous body was absent, and I shuddered as he trailed his finger over the marks on my chest.

The Moroi came back to me and opened my collar. I couldn't move or fight, pinned by the immense power of the immortal lich, though his touch had revealed the source of his immortality. I could feel the magic of the land flowing into his body, fuelling his existence.

Unable to eat and drink, unable to store aether, he sustained his body by stealing the land's vitality, and Katrass was at the crossroads of three ley lines, the gateway to his power. It was why he was tied here, unable to leave it for long enough to control his monstrous army.

'The moon is in position. We need to start the ritual, my lord,' Rowena said, and the hand that touched my cheek slid to my neck, squeezing it like a vice. My world darkened, the air entering and leaving my lungs in short pants, as strands of aether encircled my arms and legs, replacing the iron chains.

My father's eyes filled with fear and fury, but he was as helpless as I was. Cahyon dragged me over to him, inspecting him with a knowing smirk.

'I have to thank you, Roan, for keeping yourself in such good shape. I'm sure your body will serve me as well as you did,' he said, laughing when my father tried to spit in his face.

'When you're ready, my lord, lay next to him,' Rowena instructed. 'You need to be touching him to allow your spirit to pass over.'

My father screamed in a mix of rage and despair, his eyes locking onto mine as though I could save him. For a fleeting moment, pity gnawed at me. Tal maladie wasn't his fault, but even madness of the heart could not excuse the way he had treated his children.

As the Lich King reclined his body, Rowena approached, standing at the head of the altar. Her hand pressed against the sigil carved into my chest, the other on my father's brow, and she began her incantation. I hoped her plan to siphon aether through my bond with Annika wouldn't work, but as it flowed through me, I was stripped of that illusion.

Fire erupted in my chest, tearing through me like molten blades. I screamed, writhing as raw, unrelenting aether coursed through me. Annika's shock rippled through our bond, swiftly replaced by her own pain, which fused with mine in an unbearable cacophony of torment. The spell worked.

The symbols etched into my father's body flared to life, their glow almost blinding. His hoarse, agonised screams echoed through the grotto, each cry reverberating with the excruciating process of having his soul flayed from his living flesh.

Rowena was meticulous, almost reverent, her lips curling into a serene smile as she wielded the aether with surgical precision, stripping away every fragment of his spirit.

A translucent form began to emerge above his prone body, its spectral fists pounding uselessly against Rowena as it wailed in silent fury. My father's body ceased thrashing, but I could barely register it through my own haze of pain.

Blood trickled from my nose, mouth, and eyes, falling onto his pallid face. The aether ripped through me mercilessly, tearing me apart from within. Yet Rowena didn't stop until she had turned him into an empty shell, ready for a new host.

Bit by bit, my father was unmade. His soul's final tether snapped, and the essence of the man who had sired me faded into nothingness.

Rowena continued, a malicious presence rising from the Lich King's corpse, and his spirit at last emerged, grotesque and serpentine, bloated with corrupted power. Roan's body jerked, spasming when Cahyon's soul forced its way inside—a parasite nestling inside its new, more comfortable disguise.

I hung limp in my dark bonds, knowing the powerful onslaught had caused a magical burnout, a most severe and likely irreparable damage.

'Lara, keep him alive.' My sister's commanding voice broke through my suffering, and a cold female hand landed on my forehead. I tried to pull away, but I was weak. Healing magic coursed through my veins, and my vision cleared enough to see Rowena reaching up to cut the ties that held my father's body in place.

The creature that rose from the altar looked straight into my eyes, and I gasped, sensing its power.

'You've done well, my necromancer. I even think I'll let you rest before we bond again,' Cahyon said, stretching his stolen limbs. 'Rowena, darling, bring me food and some unspoiled fae women.'

My sister nodded, and even if I knew it was a different person, it was still my father's body. At seeing the glee on my sister's face and her eagerness to please him, I drifted into the refuge of black oblivion.

CHAPTER 27

ANNIKA

I stood on top of Varta's high walls, watching the camp below as a sharp wind angrily whipped my dress against my legs. I could feel a hint of the first snow in its cold edge. The weather had changed drastically lately, cutting the days short and filling them with a gloomy greyness and wicked squalls that left one gasping.

Come to me before the first snow falls in Katrass.

The Lich King's words haunted me, and I wrapped my cloak tighter around my shoulders, forlornly looking at the sky.

We were intending to march to the Rift tomorrow. The combined forces of the Lowland Kingdoms were heading into the Second Necromancer's War, and I couldn't stop feeling guilty, knowing so many of our warriors would soon face death if I couldn't end this.

For the guests gathered in the castle and the soldiers in the camp, I presented a calm demeanour—a poised, confident battle mage, as if I knew exactly what I was doing. Here, alone, however, I could let the mask slip, and the wind steal away my woes. Here, and behind the closed doors of Orm's bedroom.

He knew I wasn't alright, that I hadn't slept properly since Alaric's departure. But Orm didn't ask for an explanation, letting me pretend everything was perfectly normal. I was grateful for that little mercy.

'I knew I'd find you here.'

I turned around, stretching my lips into a forced smile. Katja marched towards me, her gaze stern and locked onto my face with a harshness that only softened when she halted in front of me.

'It's just the wind,' I said defensively, acutely aware she had noticed my red-rimmed eyes.

'Yes, the wind is harsh this year . . . harsher for some than others,' she said and, much to my surprise, stepped forward to take my hand. 'Will you tell me what's going on, or should I drug you to get to the bottom of . . . this?' She waved her hands around me, sighing deeply. 'I don't want to see you broken again. I remember this haunted look from when you first came to Zalesie, it—' She paused. 'Please, talk to me.'

'You don't need to drug me,' I said, looking back out at the camp. '. . . I'm afraid.'

'I know. We all are. But you're the only one acting like we're going on a picnic. It's fine to be scared, Ani,' she said before asking, 'Is that lumbering oaf of yours forcing you to pretend like this? Or does he not know how you feel?'

'Orm? Oh, he knows, and he knows how to deal with it. A few rounds on his special rod, and all the nightmares go away' I said. 'Well, most of them. I can't sleep, and I think I'm going insane. Last night, I swear I heard Alaric—he said he'd found his sister and that they were coming home. But it had to be wishful thinking. Even dragon thoughtspeech doesn't work at such distances.'

'But he's your Anchor.'

'So is Orm, and even though I can sometimes pick up his feelings, we are not in each other's minds.'

Katja nodded, releasing me before turning to look at the army camp beside me.

'I guess we'll know if he suddenly appears,' she said, wrapping her arm around my shoulders. 'Have you seen the women who have volunteered to fight alongside the men?'

'Yes, they practise daily,' I said. 'But a couple of days of swinging a sword don't make you a warrior. We both know they are seeking revenge, yet most of them will only find death.'

She nodded. 'I know, but if revenge is all they have left, I won't deny them. I came to ask a favour. I want them to be your bodyguards,' she said with all seriousness.

I laughed. 'I don't need bodyguards.'

'I know, but they need *you*. Between the dragon, that oafish commander, and your magic, being near you will be the safest option on the battlefield. I don't want them dying, but if I give them any other job, they'll know I'm trying to protect them . . .' she said. 'But with you? They look up to you, especially the young ones, so please ask the king to make them your bodyguards?'

I took a breath to answer, and we both jumped as the harsh sound of trumpets suddenly blared.

'I'll see what I can do,' I responded, 'but I need to go. The dragons are flying first to clear the sky.'

Katja smiled. 'Then I'll see you tomorrow. Maybe we can steal some of Ian's apple cider to share between the three of us.'

'Ah, Bryna's coming too?' I asked.

'Yes, she'll be with the other artisans in the support train, *and*—brace yourself—she is training a special unit; a medley of females who already know how to fight: huntresses, town guards, veterans who've settled down. As she put it, Perun's[1] left nut will drop off before she allows us to have fun without her,' she answered.

I chuckled. 'Bryna and her definition of fun never ceases to amaze me. I have to go. Be careful, lady herbalist, and try not to knock anyone out with your tinctures.'

'See you later, dragon mage. Try not to burn any arses on your way.'

'Dragon mage?' I mused. 'I like the sound of that.' I gave her a quick peck on the cheek, grinning as she rolled her eyes. After our quick goodbye, I rushed towards the landing field, taking two steps at a time.

'*Vahin?*'

'*Waiting for you, Little Flame. Orm is still talking to Reynard, or I should say, arguing with him. He looks about two words away from punching our new king for putting you on the front line.*'

'*Fuck, can you calm him down? Is he losing control of his wild magic again?*'

'*Calm him? Why would I do that? I'd enjoy watching these two trying to knock some sense into each other. If anyone could give Orm a run for his money, it would be his brother.*'

I sped up, running to the landing field as fast as my legs would carry me. The moment I saw them standing so close their breath mingled, I opened myself to the aether and channelled it into the air, sending it forcefully between them.

Both men were knocked back but stayed on their feet, still glaring at each other. As soon as I was close enough, I punched each one in the shoulder to make them look at me, giving them a glare of my own.

'If you've both finished showing the world how mature you are, I'm ready to go,' I said, reaching out and grabbing Orm's breastplate to

---

1. **Perun**—god of sky and thunder.

drag him away. He resisted at first, but after a moment, he gave in and followed me to Vahin, lifting me up onto the dragon's back as though I were as light as a feather.

'I'll see you near the Rift, brother. The dragons will clear the area to make camp. I'm sure you'll be able to find the large, flat, charred space. We'll finish our conversation there,' Orm said before the wind from Vahin's powerful wings forced Reynard to shelter his eyes and turn away.

The swift, almost vertical rise left me gasping, and when I regained the ability to breathe, I looked down to see the massive army packing tents and loading wagons. I'd never seen so many people gathered in one place, and that wasn't even all of them, as the light fae army was coming directly to the Rift once we'd established a portal.

Cooperation on such a scale was unheard of in recent times. Thankfully, as Reynard explained, once Valaram took charge of the mages, he'd manipulated and convinced Talena and the light fae's prince, Iasno'ta, to work together.

'Do you think it will be enough?' I asked as Orm assumed his favourite position, his chin resting on my shoulder.

'It must be, Nivale. It's all we've got. Every soldier able to bear arms is down there. Even the dragon fortresses are being emptied to increase numbers. If we can destroy the sleeping army beneath the Barrier crystal, it should be enough.'

As long as we can *destroy the sleeping army.*

I knew Orm didn't want to add to the burden already threatening to crush me, but his words reminded me that my role was no longer just destroying the spectrae. The mountain passage I'd created all those years ago when I buried the wlok now had to be widened to allow our army to pass. Other passages and roads had been purposefully blocked during the First Necromancer's War, and none of them were wide enough for thousands of soldiers to march through, anyway.

Dagome's elemental mages could do it, but they needed an incredible amount of power to perform such a feat. Normally, they would have three or four conduit mages to share the burden, but thanks to Ihrain and the chancellor, I was the only one left. The prospect of dying from magical burnout was a possibility I didn't want to share with my Anchors.

'I can do it. I have to,' I said in such a quiet voice that I was sure Orm couldn't hear me, but his arms tightened around my waist.

'I've never felt so helpless, my love,' he said after a moment. 'I can fight, I can wage war and bear the pain of my wounds, but not knowing how to help you, how to ease the dark thoughts lurking inside your mind, is killing me.'

His words, raw and filled with concern, made me ache. We'd both held back, showing each other a brave face while knowing the situation was awful.

'I'm not . . .' I said. 'I'm sorry, Orm. I've been hiding from myself. So instead of the war, I think about the hot baths we've shared, and the field of nivale flowers. Or how the girls and I are going to get so drunk in Ian's tavern, you'll have to carry me home. It's the only way I can deal with this fear paralysing me.'

I turned my head to kiss Ormond's bearded cheek. In the last few weeks, he'd stopped shaving, and I found the new look very appealing.

He smiled, his eyes softening, and I felt a fraction of the tension leave his body.

'If that's what you need, I will make the baths big enough to fit a dragon and ask our farmers to plant nivale flowers throughout the entire fortress,' he said with such fire in his voice that I chuckled.

'Annika, if we survive this, I will throw the world at your feet. Nothing will be too much, too distant, or too extravagant.'

'I'm so going to throw those words back in your face one day, but for now we have company,' I said, seeing Tomma and his dragon drawing closer.

We were flying over the mountain, and it was enchanting to see the host of dragons gliding in formation between the clouds and snow-topped peaks. I had never seen so many, but with riders coming from every fortress, the sky was filled with colourful scales that gleamed in the early winter sun.

'Lord Commander, the scouts have returned from their reconnaissance. There's a small swarm of spectrae up ahead, nothing two units couldn't fight by themselves, even without Lady Annika's help. We can put practise to good use with our lady's backup. With your permission, of course.'

'Go ahead, but ensure the dragons contact Vahin if they need help. I don't want to lose any men for no reason.'

Tomma nodded, his dragon effortlessly drifting away, following an unspoken command.

'Since I have some free time now, what would you like to talk about?' I asked, watching twenty-four dragons form two units before wheeling away to create a perimeter around the two strongest dragons. It looked like a courtly dance, and I couldn't stop smiling. 'You trained them so well, Orm. I don't think they need me at all.'

'They don't need you now, but we must be ready. In the meantime, let's burn some ground. After all, we can't have the dark fae empress resting on gnarled tree roots.'

'Finally,' Vahin said, 'and don't even think about including me in those bath plans of yours. Some pleasures I vehemently refuse.' His protest made me laugh, and I observed the ground as he slowly descended over a desolate field near the border.

Without the shimmering barrier, the land felt oddly quiet. When we'd been here to check on the strange energy signatures, we'd discovered a sleeping army of monsters. Today, the terrain had changed, apparently settled and calm, as if nothing untoward had ever happened, and my anxiety grew. Without the Barrier crystal, the stasis spell should have worn off. I expected to see the area swarming with monsters, yet I couldn't sense any signs of life or life-giving spells.

'I don't like it. It feels as if the Lich King wants us here,' I said.

Orm nodded. 'I know, but this is the best spot to make camp this close to the border, and I'm hoping we won't be staying here for more than a night or two. As soon as the mages widen the passage, we'll be marching to the other side.'

I nodded, relaxing against Orm while Vahin and the other dragons seared the ground with short bursts of fire. Deadwood and debris burst into flames with a fountain of sparks, and the heat vaporised any moisture in the ground, solidifying the loose dirt.

When the Barrier still stood, we'd had time to discuss ways to protect our ground troops from the olgoi worms. Ormond told the story of how dragons helped build the fortresses, turning rock and sand into dragon glass so tough that only hitting it with large amounts of aether could break it. Now, I got to observe how they did that with my own eyes as the space slowly turned into an even, dry, comfortable plateau suitable for a camp.

Soon after we finished and settled onto the ground, the two dragon rider units returned, all slightly battered but without having lost anyone. The men clowned around while their dragons dropped carcasses of freshly hunted deer in front of those who'd served as bait.

At my request, we erected our tent next to a heather moor, far from the scorched ground. I walked through the sea of purple flowers that the magnificent beasts had also chosen for their beds.

I looked at Vahin when I noticed his kin looking at me with a strange kind of reverence before slowly inclining their heads.

'*Vahin . . .*' I asked. '*What are they doing?*'

'*They are recognising you as a last rider,*' he said. The warmth of his mind instinctively made me smile.

'*That sounds ominous. I'm not sure I like it?*' I teased, determined to understand.

'*I can't help that, Little Flame. Dragons know when one of our own has selected their last rider, the ones who they'll return to the aether with. You and Orm are mine, and my brethren are acknowledging your place in my life.*'

'*I don't know if I should be pleased or worried,*' I responded. '*I'm not rushing behind the Veil, but if it happens, I want you to continue living. Memories are beautiful things, but they can't replace a beating heart or warm dragon scales.*'

A loud thump shook the ground behind me, and I turned to look at my black beast, whose scales gleamed with blue lightning as he curled around me.

'Don't talk about the Veil, Little Flame. There is no happiness without you. Nothing will take you away from me. Not gods, not monsters, not even death . . . You are mine for as long as you wish to be mine,' he said, his hissing voice reverberating over the field. I stroked his eyelid, peppering it with little kisses until the coils of his body relaxed around me and the dark clouds lifted from his thoughts.

'Shift your scaly arse and share, you dolt.' The humour in Ormond's voice made Vahin grumble, but he moved just enough for Orm to slide in to stand behind me. 'May I ask what is going on here that you're challenging the gods for my woman?'

'*Our* woman,' Vahin rumbled, his tail smacking the ground, making him look like a pouty toddler. I inhaled his metallic scent, rubbing my hand down his sleek scales while pushing back against Orm to give me some breathing space. Neither budged and whatever silent conversation they were having, I could only roll my eyes and wait.

'Yes, *our* woman. Now let our woman go. Can't you hear the marching army? They will be here soon, and as annoying as I find it, we need to welcome Talena and Reynard and help them settle their troops,' Orm said finally, wrapping his arm around my waist and pulling me away from the dragon, who reluctantly uncoiled, releasing us.

'He's on edge like we are,' I said as we walked towards the old road. The stones were overgrown with moss and weed, but I could still see the outline of the old merchant path that the Lowland Kingdoms had used to trade with Ozar.

'I know, sweetheart,' Orm said. 'But he is also the leader of his kind, and I don't want his mood to affect the other dragons. The riders have reported that their beasts are already unsettled.'

We didn't have time to discuss it further as the first line of troops emerged from the forest, marching towards us. Soon after, Reynard and Talena came to a stop beside us. They both looked dusty and tired, while the empress also looked annoyed. She ignored us and gestured for her guards to set up camp.

'Any resistance?' Reynard asked as soon as he dismounted.

'No,' Orm responded. 'A small swarm of spectrae, though that doesn't count. It's worrying.'

He'd managed to verbalise exactly how I'd felt.

Reynard frowned. 'I know it's a bit late for this, but you know these mountains better than me. Is there any way the Lich King could flank us here?' he asked.

Orm shook his head. 'No. There are a few goat runs but nothing that would accommodate a larger force. That's the only reason I stayed even when we hadn't encountered any enemy forces.'

'Okay, double the patrols and guards. Ensure nothing can sneak up on us,' Reynard instructed before turning to me. 'Ani, as soon as Valaram and his mages finish making the portal, I want you to see what the elemental mages can do about the passage. Their leader mentioned creating a slow chain reaction instead of raw magic blasts, but his explanation was so convoluted I'm not sure what he meant.'

Reynard was still talking, the soldiers around us bustling with activity, but I couldn't pay attention as something suddenly reached into my chest and tried to tear the soul from my body.

'Annika?'

Orm must have noticed my reaction because he grasped my shoulders, turning me to face him. His eyes scanned my face, but I couldn't speak, trying to contain the vortex of energy growing inside me, all to no avail. Someone else was controlling my ability, and I felt helpless as the power ripped through me, stripping away the surrounding aether.

Orm gasped, catching me when my knees buckled. A metallic taste filled my mouth, and I coughed, splattering my Ursus with bright red blood.

'Rey, get the healer. Go!' he shouted, carrying me to the nearest tent. 'Annika, what's going on?'

I was panicking, unable to breathe, consumed by the maelstrom of magic tearing through me. *Why is this happening?* How was my magic raging out of control, and where was it going?

It took all my training to hold back the terror, to survive such immense energy. I felt Vahin's presence in my mind as he sacrificed his life force to sustain my burning body. I screamed, my mind finally latching onto the spell disrupting my ability, its intent so heinous it chilled the blood in my veins.

The darkest of all arts, it was a forbidden parasitic spell that siphoned a mage's power via their life force. The signature was so similar to Alaric's that I knew one of his kin was stealing my magic, and whoever it was had such malicious intent and gleeful hatred that it shocked me to the core. Worse, because I knew Cahyon had imprisoned Ari's father, I'm sure it had to be Rowena.

I was burning from the inside out, unable to resist. Suddenly, as if through a fog, I felt a cool hand touching my forehead and a stern voice commanding me as it chanted a healing spell.

'*La sutera at eatheream dolorum lara'mei.*'[2]

Valaram repeated the words again and again, infusing them with his power and constructing a shield around me. The torrent of magic slowed, allowing me to suck in a breath and utter a single sentence.

'Alaric. She's using Alaric's Anchor . . .'

'Breath, Nivale. Breath for me.' Orm's voice was filled with pent-up fear. 'Gods, why is there so much blood? Valaram, make it stop. *Why is she bleeding?*'

I wanted to reassure him, but all I could do was squeeze his hand.

'Annika, please. Whatever it is, you can fight it. Take what you need from me. Use our bond. I don't care how much it hurts, but please fight for me, Nivale,' Orm begged, pressing my hand to his lips. I wished I could tell him I was trying, but I wasn't strong enough.

---

2. *Share your pain and let me protect you, my chosen.*

The painful howl of a soul ripped apart echoed through my mind as something else took its place. Darkness stared at me and my body seized with recognition.

'My dear Annika. I told you we'd meet again. You had a chance to come to me. Now, I'll show you what my monsters can do to that rabble you call an army. My beautiful slave, I can't wait to feel your power licking over my skin as you squirm under my touch.'

His power slammed into me, and I heard a dragon roar in the distance as the blazing magic of Valaram's shields shut down the connection, but not before I felt my heart stutter and halt.

CHAPTER 28

ANNIKA

I thought I'd already crossed the Veil but came back to reality thanks to the cold hand pressed to my forehead. I'd suffered a magical burnout once or twice in my life—every mage did, especially early on in our training when we overestimated our abilities—but it had never been this bad.

'Get her in the water,' someone commanded, and soon, I was neck-deep in a horse trough, overwhelmed by the smell of Katja's herbal concoction.

'No . . . too cold,' I tried to protest, but calloused hands pushed me deeper while the water steamed and bubbled around me. A melodic voice chanted a cantrip, helping my body dissipate the magical energy.

'Will she survive? Can you use Vahin and me? We can take it.' Orm's voice was devoid of emotion, but his hands were shaking as he kept me submerged in the water.

'She will, but you can't help. She wasn't the one using her magic, and it caused an inversion of the flow, creating all these problems. In fact, you're making it worse, Commander. Take your dragon and find yourself something useful to do far away from her tent. Her magic is reaching for you, amplifying the problem.'

I tried to protest, but I could still feel the hostile mind attached to my core. As I gained some strength, I tried to rip it out, a jolt of power racing through me instead, sending me into convulsions.

'Fuck, fine, I'll go on patrol, but if she doesn't make it, I'll have your head.'

The sound of heavy stomping and a chill breeze told me Ormond had left. I called for him to come back, but what left my lips was a pained, keening screech.

'Don't give up, lara'mei,' Valaram whispered, gently stroking my hair as he sent another pulse of healing magic through my veins.

The magic prickled, but the sensation quickly subsided. I felt my power settle under the dark mage's touch. Tiredness replaced the intense burning, and I drifted into a shallow, exhausted slumber.

ᛉᛏᚾᚠᛒ

I didn't know how long I rested in the tepid water, but I was awoken by the rustle of a tent flap, the cold draft—and something else—making me shiver. An aura of power filled the tent as someone entered, and even with my eyes closed, I recognised Talena's signature.

'You can't spend the entire campaign in her tent, brother. Even her rider was present during the war council meeting.' Her tone was filled with disappointment.

'I will do what I consider necessary,' Valaram answered. 'And Ormond was only there because I sent him away. I will stay at least until I'm sure she's recovered. Play the war queen with my blessing. You don't need me for that.'

'What if I require your opinion?'

'Then you can always come here to ask, but we both know you don't listen to my advice, just as you didn't when I told you using icta poison on Alaric was a mistake.'

'He killed my blood-bonded mate and his mentor!'

'He was *fighting his curse*,' Valaram said. 'We've already had this argument, so tell me, what do you want? If there's nothing, let me return to my patient.'

I'd almost stopped breathing, hoping to not miss a word of the confidential conversation. Valaram might bow to the empress' will in public, but it was clear he was stronger in the privacy of some tent walls.

'Your fascination with this human is truly ridiculous. She's mated, for the gods' sakes! Stop fawning over her and leave her to that obnoxious herbalist.'

Talena's irritation made me snort with laughter. However, my throat was so dry that it sounded more like a choking cough. Valaram immediately lifted me from the trough, wrapping towels and furs around me until I was half-seated, leaning on his body.

'Take a drink, lara'mei,' he said. 'You've had a difficult night.' He pressed a cup to my lips, and I gulped its contents greedily.

'Ridiculous! Now you're acting like her bloody nursemaid?!' Talena rolled her eyes, storming out of the tent.

'Yes, fuck you, too,' I muttered.

The fae behind me shook with silent laughter before he bent to my ear, chastising me. 'She is still my empress. Don't make me punish you for insolence. Now, let's get you in bed.'

There was no real threat in Valaram's tone, and he carried me to bed, settling me against his body. I let him do it, still too weak to object, but it felt too intimate, and I was uncomfortable. As soon as I could, I gently pushed him away, determined to keep some distance between us.

'Thank you for your help, but your sister is right. It's no longer needed. I'm well enough for you to leave.'

'Are you in a rush to get rid of me, lara'mei?' he asked softly, and I saw the longing in his eyes.

'It's complicated. I am grateful, but . . . I feel you want more than I'm willing to give,' I started.

He smiled knowingly. 'You feel uncomfortable knowing that if you agreed, I would gladly abandon the dark fae court and join your household,' he said, taking me aback with such a straightforward answer.

'Yes,' I responded. 'I don't understand that. Why me? Whatever you want, courting me won't give you power. I'm not a dark fae female who enjoys adding men to my collection, if that's what you're after, either.'

'No, Annika. Power has never been my goal. But I envy Alaric,' he said, placing his hand on mine. 'I have lived for so long, but not once have I met a woman I wanted to submit to . . .'

I wished I could stop him, but he continued. 'When I saw you in the throne room, weak yet so powerful, defending your fae . . . I'm sorry lara'mei, I know you can't understand it. Some things even I can't explain,' he said with a tired smile before inching closer.

'I keep asking myself if there is anything I could do to sway you, to make you give me a chance to earn everything he has—a domina who would fight for me against the odds. You can't blame me for wanting to be a part of that.'

'I don't blame you,' I muttered, flinching away when Valaram reached out to stroke my hair. 'But you don't know me.'

'I want to know you,' he said softly.

I sighed. 'But you *don't* know me. You see me as I am because I'm healed, at the peak of my power, bound to a dragon and two exceptional men, but would you be interested in the drunkard who slept in the gutter and trusted no one?' I asked.

Valaram had helped me so many times, but what he wanted was impossible.

'You are a decent man, Val. I would like to be your friend, but my heart is taken, and nothing will sway me. That is my final answer.'

The tent flap opened to reveal Ormond's massive figure blocking the weak sunlight.

'Annika, I'm glad you're awake,' he said. 'Ambassador, your empress is requesting your presence.' The deep frown on his face left no doubts that he'd heard at least part of the conversation and expected Valaram to leave the tent immediately.

'You will always have a friend in me, lara'mei,' Valaram said, bending and kissing my knuckles before standing up and addressing Orm. 'Ensure Lady Annika drinks plenty of water, Lord Commander. I will check on her later.'

The moment my tent's rough fabric dropped behind Valaram, Orm was beside me, pressing my head to his chest.

'I know he saved you, but the audacity of that fae . . .' he said, shaking his head. 'What happened when you collapsed?'

Orm wasn't jealous, and although I was glad, I didn't know how to take it.

'That's all you have to say after a stranger declares his intentions?'

'And you declared yours. What else is there to say? I trust you, Annika. Yes, his actions angered me, but it is how *you* respond that matters, and you said all the right things.'

'I'm being childish, aren't I? Caring for such things when the world is burning around us,' I said with a sigh. Before I knew it, I was sitting on Ormond's lap while he towelled my wet hair.

'No, love. Sometimes, our minds wander to insignificant things when reality is too hard to bear. Will you tell me what happened?'

'The Lich King has his new body, and they used my Anchor bond with Alaric to achieve it,' I said, biting my lip while Orm cursed behind me.

'How is that even possible?'

'I think Rowena did it,' I said. 'The other day, I think Alaric connected with me. I didn't tell you because it didn't feel real. I remember Ari telling me his sister was a dreamwalker—that must be how he managed it. His message, I think he said they were coming home . . .'

I swallowed hard, my next words not wanting to pass through my parched throat. 'I'm betting she tricked him into connecting to me, that . . . Gods, what have they done to him?'

Orm gently sat me back on the cot before standing up. I watched his muscles bunch as he clenched his fists and took slow, measured breaths. I'd rarely seen him so unhinged, but the silent fury that radiated from his every movement was more worrying than if he'd trashed the tent in rage. When he finally turned to me, the golden rim of his irises had overtaken his eyes.

'Is he alive . . .?'

'I think so. I can still feel the shard of his soul.'

He was silent for a moment, his breath slowly calming down as he regained control.

'As long as he's alive, we can fix it. Stay here, Nivale. I will send someone to guard you. I need to tell Reynard. If the ritual is complete, an attack is imminent,' he said, taking my hand and placing a soft kiss on the palm. 'I'll be back shortly, so try not to die in the meantime. I don't think I'm strong enough to let Valaram touch you again.'

He left the tent, and I struggled over to the table where the pitcher of water promised to quench my thirst.

'There you are.' Katja's voice interrupted my chaotic thoughts, and I coughed, choking on the water. 'The commander said you were too weak to stand. What are you doing at the table?'

'Trying to drink, but clearly, I can't even manage that right,' I said when I could finally speak. 'Do you know where my dress is? I need to meet the mages.'

'Your dress is nothing but rags. It burned off of your smoking hot body—pun intended. If you pull such a trick again, I swear I'll keep you sedated until the end of this war. What the fuck happened, Annika? I've seen you in horrible shape, but that was a whole new level of awful.'

'Too much power—and no, it wasn't my fault this time,' I said, looking around in disbelief. 'I guess I'll have to wage war in a towel.'

'As if,' she said, passing me a vial. 'Your colleagues sent a battle mage uniform, but you only get it after you drink that.' I sniffed it suspiciously.

'I sedate you *one* time, and now you're going to sniff everything I give you?' she huffed, passing me a kirtle.

I chuckled, gulping the contents of the small bottle. 'But you *did* sedate me, so more fool me if I let you do it again, yes?' I said, waiting for the effects to hit me.

Katja smirked, unpacking the rest of the dress, and I felt warmth spread through my body, chasing away the weakness.

'This is good,' I said, noticing a faint blush tinting my friend's cheeks. 'Better than anything we used in university.' Katja was proud of her skills, and everybody who knew her said she was one mean herbalist.

'Good. Now, let's get you dressed. The riders are waiting to see their conduit.'

I was fastening the last button when a commotion outside caught my attention right before one of Orm's riders rushed inside.

'My lady, orders from the lord commander. The Lich King has made a move, and he said . . . he said . . .' the man stuttered under my inspective stare. 'He said, "tell my lady to stay sitting on her arse; I will handle this."'

The rider bowed, bristling as I glared at him. Before I could answer, the tent flap opened, and Bryna, dressed in full black armour, walked inside.

'Famous last words. What else did our illustrious commander say? "Hold my mead" maybe?' she said, and I gestured to the rider to go away before my friend made any more snippy comments.

'What's going on?' I asked when he disappeared.

Bryna shrugged. 'The ground shifted, and all three rulers are blowing their trumpets, gathering their men. Something is crawling up from the devil's bottom, and I'm sure we will soon see what,' she said before raising an eyebrow. 'I wasn't sure what I would find here, so I came to stand by you. I've brought your little army.'

She opened the tent entrance, revealing a group of women. Some of the faces were familiar, acquaintances from Zalesie, while others were new, but all had the same stern expression on their faces.

'Lady Annika, what can we do?' asked one of the oldest.

I stood up, straightening my shoulders as I walked out of the tent.

'I don't know yet but let me find out. Did the commander send you here?' I asked, suspecting Orm of trying to assign them to the rear, away from the fighting.

'No, they came here for you,' Katja answered, the rest of the women nodding their agreement. 'Your dragon is in the air, and someone has to ensure you don't do anything reckless . . . my lady.' She bowed, and I wanted to smack her upside the head for it.

'All right, let me ask—'

The sounds of battle erupted in the distance, and dragon fire set the sky ablaze. 'Fuck, he started without me,' I muttered, grinding my teeth.

When I'd discussed our strategy with Orm, we both agreed I should sit on Vahin's back, taking on the spectrae. I wasn't sure how I could manage it now, on the ground with my invisible leech still attached to the source of my power.

Suddenly, a familiar pain shot through my chest.

'Vahin, are you fighting the spectrae?' I asked when the ghastly echo of another spear made me wince.

'Yes, they are swarming, and we both know you can't help right now.'

'I bloody well can,' I said. *'Why didn't Orm bother to ask? Land and let me help.'*

'No, Little Flame, don't forget that I can sense how you feel. You're weak, and your magic is unstable. I can't fight if I'm worrying about you; neither can Orm.'

Vahin's thoughts were laced with pain, and I knew better than to argue with my dragon at a time like this. *'At least tell me what's happening on the ground?'*

'Reynard is leading the army. Dark fae mages, as well as your human kin, are preparing to open the passage through the mountains. Orm says that Talena's mages can sense a significant source of death magic there, as well as traces of the magic used to create a portal. It could be the Lich King. If we can get there and kill whoever's leading the monsters, we might have a chance.'

A roar shattered the sky, and the next time he spoke, he sounded utterly exhausted.

'There are so many of them, Little Flame, so much more than we expected. We are outnumbered on the ground and in the air . . . Take the

females and find a place to hide. I'll find you, but if I fall, don't mourn me. My time with you was worth a thousand lives.'

'*Vahin! No, take me across the mountain. Let me help!*' I shouted down our bond, but he didn't listen, focusing on staying airborne.

'Annika! Don't you dare faint on me.' Katja slapped me with a force that made my head bounce, and only then did I realise I was swaying.

Vahin was right. I was as weak as a kitten. My conduit abilities had been tampered with, but I knew what to expect. If I could ward myself against the attack and get to the sigil the mages had drawn to open the Rift, I still could create the passage and give Reynard and Talena a chance to kill the Lich King . . .

'Stay here. I need to go,' I said, explaining further when Katja gave me a sharp look, 'Vahin said Cahyon may be on the other side of the mountain. I have to open the pass and let Reynard's army through . . .'

My friend stood silent, so I continued, 'I can use primal fire to kill some fuckers on the way and use blood magic to access my conduit power. That should be enough to open the passage. The primal-order mages should have already drawn the sigil, so—'

'Annika Diavellar. You're standing there swaying like a newborn lamb and you're seriously telling me you're going to use blood magic?' Katja interrupted, shaking her head. 'You're asking me to escort you to your death.'

'I'm not asking you to do anything. I'm just explaining what's going to happen. I know I'm a mess, but you can sort that out, yes? Just give me something. I'll drink anything if it gets me over there,' I said, conveniently omitting she wouldn't need to worry about my return journey.

She placed her hands on her hips, rolling her eyes.

'Katja, please. Power me up, sister, because I need to *run* there, not waddle like a drunken duck. I can't sit on my arse while my Anchors are fighting, and I promise you this—I'm not going to outlive my Anchors again.'

At my pleading, one of the women stepped forward. 'I can help if she won't,' the grizzled matron said. I frowned as I studied her wrinkled face. I didn't recognise her, and a woman of her age shouldn't even be on a battlefield, but as hunched over as she was, the eyes staring at me in the challenge were clear.

'I'm a hedge witch from Vodianka. You mages look at us with disdain, but I can help you in a way they wouldn't dare. I'll give you my life, Lady Mage. My life, for revenge,' she said.

I blinked, shocked by her offer.

'Take mine too . . . For my child . . . Kill the bastard so my family can rest in peace . . .' A few other women stepped forward and volunteered, too.

'I can't . . . What the hell is wrong with you? You can't sacrifice your lives so I can walk into battle. That's insane!' I stepped back, sitting heavily on the ground, all of a sudden feeling like I was trapped in a maw of madness. But no, nineteen women stood before me with grim expressions, asking me to take their lives to strengthen my own.

'I know you think I'm old and crazy, but hear me out, Lady Mage,' said the old hedge witch. 'We came here with only one purpose, but we have no strength, no power. So here we are, following you around like stray dogs, hoping for a chance to sink a dagger in just one . . .'

She stopped, swallowing hard, while her eyes radiated such hatred I flinched. 'You said you could kill the Lich King. My life is a small price to pay to ensure that bastard dies.'

The others nodded their approval as she moved closer, placing her withered hand on my cheek. 'I'm already dead, child. My husband and son were killed in Vodianka. I have no one else left. My house collapsed during the attack. I live on the charity of the dragon riders, but I'm dead inside. I don't want to be here anymore, and I'm too old to start anew.'

I had to turn away, but I couldn't stop seeing the determination in her eyes.

'You can give me the chance to make my death to mean something,' she said. 'Please, take it, and use it well. When you sink your sword into that fucker's heart, look him in the eye and tell him old Martha says hello.'

A chorus of voices joined the old woman, each telling a similar story, stripping me of the chance to refuse because, in the end, if I didn't do something, we all would die anyway.

'I will carve your name on his withered heart,' I stuttered, barely comprehending what was happening. 'Thank you.'

She nodded before unsheathing a dagger and pricking her finger. I didn't recognise the symbol she drew on my forearm, but every time she copied it onto the skin of the others, I felt a rush of strength and a prickle of magic that raised goosebumps on my skin. My breathing became deeper, and my heart stopped beating erratically.

I watched in stunned silence as each elder slipped bonelessly to the floor, their expressions so peaceful and satisfied, as if I had devoured not just their lives but the pain and hatred they harboured inside. Tears filled my eyes, but I didn't allow myself the luxury of crying.

When the old hedge witch joined her compatriots in death, I felt stronger and more broken than I ever had before.

'Gather them, gently, and lay them in my tent, then go to the moors and try to hide until this is all over,' I said to the younger women left behind.

'Brace yourselves,' Bryna shouted. 'Conduit is ready, we're going in.'

She wielded her hammer, and the women I'd told to escape rallied around her, creating a shield wall between us and the battlefield.

I cursed the stubbornness of mountain women, nearly sobbing when several turned to me and winked. Bryna's special unit, her She-Wolves of Varta, were determined to stay by my side. That determination humbled me, and added one more brick to my heavy conscience with the need to prove worthy of such loyalty. As I dashed the tears from my eyes, I saw Katya grabbing several vials from her bag and pinning them onto her belt.

'Katja?' I asked, frowning as she drew a small paring knife from her pocket.

'Don't blame yourself, Ani. If anything, blame me. I knew they came here to die, and I let them because . . . Because sometimes, death is not the worst thing that can happen to someone,' she said, avoiding my eyes as she handed me a vial. 'One last thing, dragon mage. Drink this before we go. It will speed up your healing . . . and give you the mother of all hangovers, but you need all the help you can get—'

'Wait. You're not planning on coming, are you? No, I'm not fucking sacrificing you too, Katja. Gods be damned. *No.*'

'Really? Try and stop me,' she challenged. 'I know you, Annika Diavellar. You don't think you're coming back. You wouldn't accept those women's sacrifice if, for even a moment, you thought you'd live to see another day. I won't let you throw your life away. I will fucking revive your corpse if I have to, or keep you here long enough for that fae mage to do it. Where you go, *I* go, and the longer we argue, the more soldiers will die.'

I knew I had lost.

'Fine! But you'd better stay behind me,' I said.

As the sounds of fighting announced that the monsters had reached us, I exhaled slowly, feeling the aether build around me, and walked straight out into the carnage.

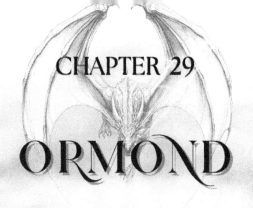

CHAPTER 29

ORMOND

The ground shook under my feet, and I struggled to keep my balance.

'Is this your woman's doing?' my brother asked. Everyone was acutely aware of Ani's past, especially as we were standing next to the rubble of its results.

'Did she *look* like she was in any state to cause an earthquake right now? Ani is . . . Fuck, she's so weak she can barely stand. I'm sure that stubborn woman will find a way to use her magic, but I wouldn't count on her in the upcoming battle.'

'Many battles are won by attacking at the right moment,' Reynard said. 'We are exactly where the Lich King wanted us, and the timing couldn't be better for him.' He sighed, rubbing the bridge of his nose. 'So you think it's the olgoi worms you told me about?'

'Probably. We used dragon fire to solidify the ground the camp is on, which will give us some time, but we should mobilise.'

Reynard nodded, turning towards a messenger, and I gently tapped my chest. Annika always filtered excess aether through our bond when casting her spells. I didn't know if she realised I could feel it even when she did something small and harmless, like creating fairy lights. But at that moment, I couldn't feel anything untoward.

Another tremor shook the ground. Reynard grabbed my arm to stabilise himself, and this time, it felt like the earth was determined to make us fall on our arses. I could hear the horses neighing and the shouting of the soldiers gathering together as they hastily donned their armour.

I turned to the east, half expecting to see the enemy's army gathering, and instead saw Valaram marching towards us in full armour.

'We detected the opening of a portal right before the earthquake,' he informed us. 'Talena is certain she can sense Roan'va Shen'ra's signature on the other side of the mountain.'

'No one's magic has such range,' Reynard contradicted swiftly, but I knew better than to argue with the ambassador.

'You forget, Your Majesty, that Empress Talena is not a forty-year-old novice sitting on a throne,' Valaram said coldly. 'She's honed her power over centuries, and one of her particular skills is the ability to locate her subject.'

'Assuming the Lich King is in Roan's body and personally leading his army, what now?' my brother asked with irritation, as if blaming the dark fae for bringing the bad news.

'Now we have to find a way to open the mountain pass and kill the bastard. The sigil is almost ready. We just need Annika's skills,' Valaram responded, though worry was painted across his features.

'The sigil may be ready, but Annika isn't,' I answered quickly. 'You know that better than anyone.'

Reynard grunted, a stormy expression on his face, cursing when another tremor sent us sprawling. 'Then we will fight using tried and true methods. Get your dragons ready, Orm,' he said. 'Valaram, I leave you in charge of the mages. You both need to get over that mountain and kill whoever's leading that army.'

'Have you considered withdrawing until she's ready?' Valaram asked. 'The outlook is bleak, especially with the terrain the way it is. The ground here may be firm enough for your heavy cavalry, but further down, the dirt is too soft for a full charge—'

'Withdraw to *where*? To the plains full of non-combative citizens? Don't worry about my cavalry. They will manage,' Rey responded.

I wondered what his plan could be.

My brother, in an impressively short period of time, had merged four nations into an imposing army. Dagome's foot soldiers were supported by dwarven infantry, well-armed with long pikes and heavy axes that gave them a decent advantage. The light cavalry for skirmishing was formed from both fae and human riders. And the main thrust of his attacking force consisted of his terrifying cataphracts, led by Reynard himself.

The cataphracts were, as Valaram so crudely referred to them, our heavy cavalry, with specially bred horses, larger by several hands than any other steeds, covered in overlapping plate mail. Their riders were encased in impenetrable steel and carried twelve-foot lances. When at full tilt, these warriors could smash through any infantry. As a unit, the devastation they could inflict was terrifying.

A unit that was exclusively human, only Dagome could breed horses able to carry such weight, but with the bulk came the caveat that warranted the cataphracts needing solid ground to gain their speed.

'Whatever you say, Your Majesty,' Valaram said, rubbing his temples. 'I'm assuming you gave command of the archers to the light fae prince?'

'Yes, I needed to keep him from leading the charge,' Reynard said. 'We both know that getting him to follow orders is like herding a bag of cats.'

We all knew how big an understatement that was.

Our archers were a mix of farmers, hunters, and scoundrels with a talent for the bow and a desire to bury the enemy beneath a volley of arrows. Mages, however, formed small, specialised forces that needed to be spread out. But where soldiers and riders followed orders, archers and mages listened to no one.

Battle mages stood at the forefront of the infantry and tore through their opposition with blades and elemental spells, while those with paladin traits protected the wounded and light fae healers under shield spells. Light fae healers refused to commit violence but wouldn't hesitate to dart into the thicket, fighting to pull out injured soldiers.

But what the dark fae did could turn even the strongest warriors' stomachs. Their necromancers went into battle alone, though it never took long for them to be surrounded by the enslaved undead, forming both shields and blades, while violet aether chained them to their masters.

'Just concentrate on your own orders,' Reynard said, heading for his horse. 'I have a bad feeling about this.'

I mentally called for Vahin. *'What can you see?'*

'Spectrae are coming,' he answered grimly as dragons rose into the air, one after the other. *'It's not just them. Every type of winged monster under the sun is heading in our direction. We need my Little Flame, but she is too weak . . . I won't take her on my back. This would kill her.'*

'I'm not asking you to,' I muttered, fighting that same fear.

The enemy had come.

I'd lost my necromancer, and my Nivale would be in danger if she joined the fight. I was ready to die in this battle but living without Annika and Alaric—if I lost them both . . . my brother would be digging three graves.

'You know Ani won't forgive us for leaving her on the ground,' I said, grasping the pommel of Vahin's war saddle.

'I can deal with her anger. This is the right decision, and if needs be, blame it on me,' Vahin answered, and for a moment, I could hear the spark of humour in his hissing voice. The damned lizard knew Ani would forgive him for anything.

Just as we were about to take off, a powerful spasm shook the ground. Vahin roared, snapping his wings open and raising them in challenge to the sky. In the distance, a fountain of dirt erupted high into the air, and three glistening olgoi worms screeched in reply to my dragon's defiance before burrowing back into the earth.

The Battle of the Rift had begun, and I prayed to the All-Father, once again, that we would emerge victorious.

CHAPTER 30

B ryna laughed as the first striga[1] breached the shield wall, swinging her hammer against the monster's skull. At the sickening crunch, she howled in triumph, turning to her female warriors to shout her encouragement. They roared in answer and braced their spears. Some of them were already wounded, but not a single one retreated from the overwhelming forces.

'C'mon you fuckers, who wants to live forever!' she shouted, and the women pushed forward, skewering the monsters attacking them. I didn't know who taught them to fight in a phalanx formation, an ancient military technique where warriors moved as one behind a wall of shields, but it was impressive to watch. However, it wasn't enough, and at the sight of so much death, I felt a dark fury rise inside me.

Fire, my natural element, came easily to me, and soon, not just my hands but the air around me burned with my rage.

'Annika, no! Your job is to get to the sigil!' Katja shouted when I pushed forward, but I felt like a woman possessed. Vahin's pain radiated through the bond, and the sounds of dying and the metallic

---

1. **Striga(s.)/strigae(pl.)** — a female demon born of a violent death who hunts those who have wronged them. Once their vengeance is complete, they will hunt any human, and appear as skinny females with two rows of teeth, large claws, and leather-like hair.

stench of blood permeated the air, releasing the hatred of the women who'd sacrificed themselves, a hatred that cared little for my safety.

I blasted aethereal fire into the horde of monsters, destroying those closest to my protectors. An echo of my power travelled to the leech attached to Alaric's Anchor, and I felt a flash of surprise followed by her pain.

Rowena had dared to use my Ari, the man who'd been foolishly caring enough to want to rescue her when he could have been here protecting his friends.

Eat that, bitch, I thought, laughing at the unexpected discovery. *Gods, we could have used Ari's help.*

A swarm of half-rotten remnants, ghouls, and other grave fodder covered the battlefield. They fought, uncaring of wounds or missing limbs, until their complete destruction. I saw fae necromancers freezing the undead in place so soldiers could crush the monsters' skulls, but there weren't enough of them. A thought came to me in a flash of inspiration.

Can I do it?

I wasn't just Anchored to Alaric, we were blood-bonded. I was sure that was how Rowena got to me, so if the link was still there . . .

Fire raged around me as I closed my eyes, trusting my companions to keep me safe. I dived into the Anchor bond, leaving a blazing trail of dragon fire, and reached for the corrupted connection. *Hello sister-in-law, you owe me one,* I jeered, tracing the connection with the little aether I had at my disposal.

Alaric's magic was there, a vast reservoir of spells and skills untouched by the Lich King. I called for it, not expecting it to work, but I was willing to try anything. Knowledge flooded my mind, his unique talent merging with mine, infusing my core with a surge of power.

Alaric had given himself to me with complete trust, as did his magic, recognising me.

I knew what I had to do.

When I opened my eyes to view the battlefield, I saw it bathed in the violet colour of necromancy. I recognised the patterns, and my new knowledge tripped off my tongue. I reached for the aether, drawing from the bond that burned in my soul.

'*Rashta!*'[2]

The surrounding undead immediately dropped to their knees, their heads bowing in submission as I held them.

'Kill them! Aim for the head!' I ordered, giving my she-wolf army their fill of blood.

I walked towards the Rift, letting the spell spread over the battlefield before me. Soldiers looked at me, stunned, but quickly shook off their initial shock and joined the attack. I could deal with the undead, but the Lich King had sent enough living monsters to prevent necromancers from turning the tide of battle.

'Annika, watch out!' Bryna shouted right before the ground erupted in front of us and countless creatures spewed forth. The undead dropped to their knees straight away, but the others charged at us, unaffected by my spell.

It wasn't just the sleeping army that had emerged to fight us. There were too many of them for that to be the case. It felt like Cahyon was throwing everything he had at us, convinced he could win in one fell swoop.

As Bryna ordered her women into defensive positions, I heard Reynard shout a command. I couldn't understand the words, but a

---

2. *Kneel!*

trumpet's clarion call sang out, and suddenly, the field around us was filled with soldiers.

'Where the fuck are you going? Orm said you couldn't cast,' Reynard shouted at me, his stallion dancing on hind legs, his hooves spraying dirt in my face.

'Men!' I muttered. 'I'm going to open that damn passage. Once I'm done, lead your riders there and kill the bastard. Now, get out of my way!' I shouted back.

The trumpets' call changed, and the army regrouped, targeting our major opponents after the olgoi worms, who were being tackled by the dwarven infantry. The king's cataphracts charged at the enemies surrounding us, aiming for the fiercest, like the biesy[3] and manticores, leaving the smaller monsters to our infantry, and my safety to Bryna and her soldiers.

It was a bloody and painstakingly slow march, but we pushed forward, supported by my spell. I looked up to the skies, biting my lip as I watched the battle above. Spectrae, harpies, and latawce[4] ripped into our dragons, and those who weren't dealing with the vampiric ghosts chased and burned the demons that tore chunks of flesh from the dragons' sides.

Vahin dominated the centre of the arial battlefield like a dark shadow blotting out the sun. He was the bait again, and he was fighting a losing battle. I felt his exhaustion through our link. I should have

---

3. **Bies(s.)/biesy (pl.)/pron:b-yes/** — a personification of all the undefined evil forces in nature. They were massive bison-like beasts with horns and hooves that were hostile and resistant to most types of weapons.

4. **Latawiec(s.)/pron:Lata-vi-etc/latawce(pl.)/latav-ce/**—shapeshifting demons. They flew in the currents of the wind. Their physical bodies were similar to large birds, with sharp claws and colourful feathers, but they had human heads

known it would end this way. The Lich King wouldn't have left anything to chance, and our dragons were our most potent weapon.

'Hold the perimeter!' Orm shouted at his men while Vahin endured the tortuous tendrils of the attacking spectrae.

'Ani, we need to move.'

Bryna grabbed my arm, pushing me through the temporary corridor the soldiers had created. My small unit naturally arranged itself into an arrow formation, my friend in the lead. That way, whoever didn't fall prey to the orc's hammer lost their lives on the swords of her unit.

A heavy thump and rumble against the trampled ground caught my attention. Reynard's cataphracts began withdrawing only to wheel around and ram into the beasts swarming on our flank, scattering them like chaff. The monsters regrouped quickly, and the heavily armoured horses and their lance-wielding riders clashed with them again. Biesy, trolls, and manticores rushed forth, smashing into the struggling army.

It was painfully obvious we were losing this battle, just like we were losing more women to our newest opponents. Corrupted Moroi, lithe and viciously quick, were slipping past the inexperienced warriors, but no one fell. The severely injured were pulled back from the front and immediately replaced by fresh fighters.

No one seemed to be free of injury now; even I had fresh blood dripping from my shoulder, and when I looked, I couldn't restrain my surprise at the long scrape from the arrow that had pierced my flesh.

I relentlessly pushed forward, casting one spell after another, subduing the undead as we slogged through the heavy mud.

We were almost there, so close to the shadow of my suffering dragon that I was buffeted by each beat of his wings.

He was dying.

I could feel it through our bond, and hatred curled my lips when I saw the damage caused by the spectrae. Vahin's thoughts were unfocused and unguarded as he faltered, his tired wings beating slower and more erratically. Vampiric ghosts trailed behind him, and his descent spread a bloody mist and the stench of death over the battlefield.

'*Goodbye, my light . . .*'

The weakening echo of his thought flooded my mind with memories that weren't mine, just like the whispers from the Dark Mother's maze.

The memories burned with the stench of a funeral pyre, each scene steeped in despair. A ravaged village. A helpless mother cradling the lifeless body of her toddler. Each vision was a shard of anguish, the memories of the nineteen lives I'd taken, their hatred for the enemy making me a vessel for their revenge.

All rational thought disappeared, consumed by their collective pain. I stared at my arms, etched with the symbols of their sacrifice. Ablaze, they seared my flesh with an excruciating, soul-deep chill that demanded justice.

'Be kind to them, Arachne, and help me put their spirits to rest,' I whispered the name I hadn't said since I left her realm, unsure what else to do.

'*Always, my child,*' whispered a voice in the wind, and I reeled, shocked that the unfeeling goddess had heard me.

Within my mind, a spell shone with unearthly coruscating light, marked by the touch of a goddess. The magic, as ancient as time itself, could bind the dead, feed on their destruction, and rain chaos on an unexpecting world.

'*Death is never the end, but those ensnared in my web must be purged to move on. Take their deaths—feed on them and end their torment,*' the Dark Mother whispered in my mind, her spell revealing itself with all the power of the forbidden arcana. Death magic wasn't meant for living, and I knew the price was inevitable. The price for death was always life.

My power was already tied to the goddess, the lives of nineteen brave women sacrificed to pave the way. I let the primal force lead me as I closed my eyes, weaving necromancy with the dragon fire burning in my soul. The aether built inside me, amplified by each fallen soldier, a raging torrent I held back by sheer force of will.

I felt my body unravelling under the strain, knowing this was my one and only chance to annihilate the enemy before I was destroyed.

Deep inside, I knew I should open the Rift. That was the reason I'd fought, but I wasn't strong enough to watch my dragon die.

Suddenly, a dark presence rose inside me, and I felt them all. The twisted spectrae, caught between life and death, forever denied respite in the arms of the Dark Mother. The stumbling remnants, whose last hours were warped by Cahyon's touch. The fallen soldiers, desperately reaching for the Veil, hoping the afterlife would grant them peace.

It was time to right the wrong, to cleanse the taint of our undead foe. To bring justice to the fallen and to purge the tormented souls from the world of the living. That was what Arachne wanted. It was what I wanted. But the choice was mine and mine alone.

'*Yes, my child, I chose you for a purpose. Now burn them all.*'

The echo of the Dark Mother's laugh resonated in my mind as I gathered all the threads in my hand, screaming my hatred into a simple command.

OLENA NIKITIN

'*Išātum!*'[5]

---

5. *Burn!*

360

CHAPTER 31

ORMOND

We fought for what felt like hours, but no matter how many of the enemy we destroyed, there were always more to take their place. We were losing. Worse still, Vahin was in trouble, and even though he refused to admit it, his thoughts were sluggish, and his wings were struggling to keep us in the air.

'*Orm!*' he roared in warning before dropping several metres. I knew we were nearing the end, despite my sharing every ounce of strength I had. My dragon was dying—he'd sacrificed his life essence for too long.

'*I know. Hold on as long as you can, but land when it gets to be too much. If you can't fight, head for the camp so I can protect Ani,*' I said, pointing towards her tent.

From the corner of my eye, a violet light caught my attention. At first, I thought it was a necromancer using their magic, but as I focused, I saw it twist and turn, reaching ahead like a forest fire. That was when I felt it: a wave of power that tugged in my chest moments before the conflagration washed over us like a tidal wave.

The spectrae flickered, freezing in place, but what I saw on the ground left me speechless.

The undead attacking the camp were on their knees, soldiers cutting through them as if harvesting wheat.

Not only were the spectrae paralysed, but every monster on the battlefield had stopped. The pause was brief, but when they moved again, they had reverted to their primal state. They no longer followed orders, instead running amok in every direction, attacking friend and foe indiscriminately.

Undead draugrs were on their knees, and every wraith unmoving, leaving the Moroi frantic and confused. At the very centre of the commotion, wielding the uncanny magic, was Annika. She walked through the battlefield surrounded by a cohort of women, and everywhere she went, the undead fell to the ground.

As I looked down at my stubborn woman, I realised her magic felt different; it didn't give me that soft thrill in my chest it usually did. Instead, there was a dark, ominous aura surrounding her. It was the death of light, the end of hope—and it frightened me.

It wasn't Annika. It wasn't even Alaric. It was something so primal that I felt claws tighten around my throat.

'*Vahin?*' I asked, but he couldn't answer as he tried and failed to keep us airborne. The spectrae followed us as we hurtled towards the ground, their bodies almost tangible, bloated with the life they'd siphoned from my dragon. Annika must have sensed us because she raised her head, tilting it slightly, and I flinched from the emotionless, icy gaze.

Despite my reaction, I couldn't look away, falling into the depths of her black eyes, feeling death itself weighing on my soul.

The woman I loved with every fibre of my being terrified me and even the beast hidden inside me recognised that what looked back at me was no longer my Ani, but a being that had existed before time—as if Nyja,[1] the goddess of death, herself had come down to even the scales.

I didn't hear what she said as she cast a spell, but the world around me exploded, consumed by fire. The spectrae screeched as they were incinerated, their tethers instantly vanishing from Vahin's core.

The wind roared in my ears as my dragon beat his wings, the flames filling his body with vitality. We ascended at such speed that my breath was ripped from my lungs, and my ears deafened when he roared his defiance.

Vahin was unstoppable, black scales glowing blue as purple lightning streaked down his wings and heavy storm clouds rushed down from the mountains.

He circled, creating a ring of fire, but it was the lightning that scorched the ground that stunned me. My prime dragon, the Aether of Storms, showered the ground with thunderbolts and only then did I see the biesy descending upon Annika's group.

I could barely hold myself in the saddle as the immense power of Annika's spell reverberated through my very core, the excess of its power straining our Anchor bond. I knew Vahin's flames—we'd been through this many times fighting spectrae—but the searing cold was new, freezing the remaining breath in my lungs.

Annika's spell didn't stop, branching out like lightning and saturating the clouds until ash poured from the sky. The soft powder fell on my face as the spell spread, incinerating the spectrae and decimating everything dead and undead. It even burned the corpses untouched by the Lich King's magic. Everywhere I looked, dragons were free to

---

1. **Nyja** — goddess of war and death and guardian of souls that have died a violent death.

fight the living monsters, and they roared in challenge, chasing after their winged foe.

The ash turned into a bloody haze filled with the screams of dying harpies and the maddening song of latawce. They all died, ripped to shreds by our raging dragons. Thunder shook the sky, and the heavy clouds thickened. Bloody ashen mist became blackened rain, clinging to clothes and dragon scales alike.

I'm riding the storm, I thought, taken aback by the display of power.

Vahin seemed to grow stronger, as if the clouds were replenishing whatever the spectrae took of him. But he didn't engage in the fight. He flew above Ani, his worry growing with each passing moment.

'*I cannot reach her, Orm. Our bond is there, but her thoughts are obscure, and I can't read them. I thought I was doing us both a favour when I blocked her, allowing myself only one last goodbye. Now she doesn't want me back.*'

'*She may be angry that we left her on the ground, but she will always want you back,*' I said. '*It must be something else. Stop fretting and land. We can't help her from up here.*'

He folded his wings, plummeting to the earth, but before we touched down, he snapped his wings open once more, pulling us back into the sky.

'*What are you doing?*' I barked, feeling the uncertainty in his mind.

'*Tomma's dragon requests our presence. Rarógs² are heading for the centre of the battle and my Little Flame's circle.*'

I cursed. The last thing we needed were those damn fire demons. They were massive raptors with burning feathers, wickedly sharp

---

2. **Raróg (s.)/rarógs (pl.) /Pron: ra-roog/** — a fire demon that appears as a horse-sized falcon with a beak and claws made of burning embers, and wings that start fires while in flight.

claws, and deadly beaks that could even tear through a dragon's scales. They were so agile that it would take a concerted effort to defeat them.

'*How many?*' I asked sharply, remembering how many men and dragons they'd wounded during our last skirmish.

'*An entire flock. They are coming from behind the mountain ridge,*' Vahin answered, '*We need to help the others, but my Little Flame . . .*'

'*I know, but we need to keep them away from the battlefield. It's our best chance at keeping Ani and the army safe.*'

I could sense the conflict in his thoughts—the same conflict I was fighting within my own heart—but he couldn't dispute the logic in my words.

We looked down one last time. Carnage reigned over the battlefield, but the space around Ani was eerily quiet, as if the monsters feared approaching her. Annika's valkyries took full advantage, slaughtering their way across the battlefield.

My thoughts of protecting the woman who was single-handedly dealing with most of the enemy's forces felt so ridiculous now that I laughed. I didn't know what her plans were, but I knew she'd cleared the sky for the dragons, and whatever else she was planning, my presence didn't seem essential or required.

'*Look down,*' I said. '*All we have to do is ensure nothing attacks her from above. She is perfectly fine there with her women.*'

I felt Vahin's intense focus before his thoughts filled with contentment. '*Yes, my beautiful destruction; sometimes she terrifies me,*' he rumbled with such pride that I smiled, grasping my sword.

'*That makes two of us.*'

I remembered how I'd dismissed Ani's circle of homegrown warriors, suddenly ashamed. Those women, barely trained and unused to battle, truly resembled the All-Father's mythical warriors as they protected not just Ani but each other. If we survived this, I'd make sure to raise a monument to those brave souls. I raised my sword in salute as Vahin changed directions.

'*Homegrown warriors? She will rip out your tongue if she hears you calling them that,*' Vahin rumbled in my thoughts.

It was nice to feel his strength returning. Dragons recuperated fast, and Annika's strange magic and rumbling storm clouds had bolstered his recovery. I couldn't be happier, even if it raised the hair on my body, which was not a pleasant experience.

'*They are valkyrie warriors, and I shall deny calling them anything else from now until my dying day,*' I said. '*Now, are you ready to rip out some feathers?*'

'*I thought you'd never ask. Come, Ormond, let's prove our worthiness to her.*'

The pride in Vahin's voice made me smile, and I held onto the pommel as he made a sharp left. Flying towards our next battle, Annika cast a spell that silenced the battleground like the tolling of funeral bells.

'*Asaro!*'[3]

My sweet, loving Nivale was death incarnate.

---

3. *Die!*

CHAPTER 32

ANNIKA

The agonised roar of a bies shocked me into awareness, and I looked around, confused.

I'm alive. How the fuck am I still alive?

I frowned as I inspected my arms. Flakes of dried blood fell from their unblemished surface, the strange symbols drawn there by the old hedge witch now nothing more than a faint memory.

'*Arachne?*' I called out to the goddess, but her presence was gone from my mind. Only silence answered my call. *What did she do?* I wondered, knowing the Dark Mother had done more than show me an ancient spell.

It was then that the surrounding devastation registered in my dazed mind. Where countless undead had scrambled forward, piles of smouldering ash now lay. I whispered my gratitude to Martha and the matrons that made it possible; I had made some progress in repaying their sacrifice, but until I watched the light in the Lich King's eyes die, I would hold this life debt close to my heart.

'Annika, watch out! One survived the lightning,' Bryna shouted, and I instinctively ducked, narrowly avoiding the claws of a striga that had somehow fought past my guards.

'*Asaro!*'

The word came to my lips without conscious thought, and I felt my magic stop the monster's double heart.

'Fuck,' I muttered, unsure what had just happened, only now noticing the dendritic marks only a thunderstrike could have left on the ground. *Did Vahin . . . and how the hell did I miss it?* I shook my head, but the memories of the last few moments were hazy at best.

'One thing at a time, Ani,' I mumbled, deciding to deal with it later. I may have obliterated the undead, but this battle was far from over, and I still had more work to do.

As we moved forward, it became more of a trek as monsters threw themselves in our way, abandoning their previous targets. Every time I'd glimpsed the enemy leaders, the Moroi generals pointed towards me, and a horde of monsters descended upon us.

'Brace!' Bryna barked out the command as we neared the sigil. Several women rammed their spears into the ground while others locked shields, creating a thorny wall in front of three charging biesy.

Before the beasts could reach us, the ground shook as the cataphracts rammed into them. The sound was deafening, a thunderous collision, followed by the screaming of monsters, animals, and men. I watched as the enormous bison-like creatures were flung metres away—yet even as they hit the ground, the biesy were back on their feet, claws swiping at their attackers.

I saw a flash of gold as I glanced at the lead rider and realised that King Reynard was commanding the unit. I couldn't help but be impressed as his sword crashed down to parry a monster's deadly onslaught. Our gazes met briefly, and he nodded before the swipe of a clawed paw almost injured his horse.

'Hold your ground, protect the mage!' he roared.

I cursed at my distraction, remembering why I was there. Runes covered the ground in front of me, gleaming with potential, ready to explode into action the moment I completed the spell. As Bryna and her warriors dealt with any attackers that made it past the cataphracts,

I slogged across the muddy ground to reach its centre, tracing the soft hum of stored power emanating from its lines.

Deep groves were burnt into the ground so thoroughly that not even a vicious battle had erased them. The complexity of the spell was a genuine marvel, designed for it to withstand appalling damage.

The rest of the spell was a master class in controlled destruction, far beyond anything I could create. Its focus concentrated on shaping hundreds of explosions in one direction whilst also supporting the soon-to-be walls of the new pass.

'I'd hate to be on the other side of this pass,' I muttered, unable to hold back a grin.

'You can do it, yes? I mean, do you have any power left?'

I wiped the sweat from my forehead, startled when I saw Katja's frown inches from my face. I had completely forgotten she was with us, but somehow, she'd managed to get here safely.

'Yes, I can do it . . . That is, I *think* I can do it,' I said when she leaned back. 'But you can't help me here, so go to Bryna. You'll be safer there, and you could help the injured.'

'Do you really see me leaving? We have three healers in that wall of steel and stubbornness, so don't even bother trying to send me away.' She rolled her eyes. 'You're queen of the fucking dead. I thought you'd burn us all and that your dragon would finish the rest, but your fire only engulfed the monsters.'

Katja laughed before continuing. 'I don't know how you did it, but if the dark fae aren't on their knees worshipping your arse after this, I'll bang their heads together.' She passed me one of her potions. 'Drink this. Someone has to be here to catch you when you finally crash and fall, and I bet it's going to be spectacular.'

The stench of death hung around me, but Katja was smiling. It caught me off guard—her expression. My down-to-earth friend radiated something I'd never thought to see from her during this war: hope. Maybe for the first time since meeting her all those years ago, she wasn't expecting everything to go to shit.

'Look, you're right, but there will be an earthquake, and gods know what else.' I hesitated before revealing what was gnawing at me, 'Katja, I used death magic. The spell was supposed to claim my life, but it didn't, and I don't know . . . I don't know what price I'll have to pay for that.'

She paled but grasped my hand, locking it around the vial. 'I don't care. It'll be alright . . . but if it isn't, I still don't care. I choose you. You may have scared the shit out of me when your eyes turned black, and you may have pulled necromancy out of your arse, but it doesn't matter because you are my friend. So drink the damn potion, and let's rock this world!'

Her touch, caring and without a hint of hesitation, soothed my fears. I tipped back the bottle and let the burning liquid flow down my throat, gasping as it took my breath away.

'What'd you give me, bloody moonshine?' I coughed out when I could speak again.

She shrugged. 'Damn right, I did. You needed some liquid courage. And for the record? I can defend myself.'

'Katja Laster, since *when* have you had such a potty mouth?' I asked.

She shrugged before casually throwing a vial at a rampaging manticore. Yellow smoke covered the creature's face when the vial broke, and in moments, it began clawing its face until it fell, twitching, to the ground.

'We're in a bloody battle. So what if I curse?' she asked, shouting to Bryna, 'Get the unit away from here. Ani wants to cast without an audience.' The half-orc grunted in response, calling the remaining

females away. 'There, happy now? And hurry up. There's a swarm of
. . . whatever those are heading our way.'

I watched Katja take a few steps back, smirking as if she were challenging me. I didn't have time to argue further as the epicentre of
the fight was heading our way, the thunder of heavy cavalry and the
grunting of monsters growing louder as they neared.

It was now or never.

*You wanted me in Katrass before the first snow? Then I'll be there. I'm
going to enjoy seeing your face when I burn it to the ground*, I thought.

I knelt in the centre of the sigil, and with a few quick gestures, wove
a spell to connect its power to my elemental magic. I was focused on
stabilising the connection when a vast shadow swept across the ground
before it turned, heading in our direction.

A piercing screech disturbed my concentration, and my eyes
snapped up to the skies. I watched as flames burst from the beak of
a raróg, melting the soil into glass and erasing the runes of the sigil.

I screamed, still linked to the construct, as the explosion of aether
engulfed me. Instinctively, I transformed it into a bolt of condensed
energy, aiming it back at the beast as it obliterated the world around
me.

My connection with Vahin protected me to a certain degree, but I
could feel my skin blistering in the heat. The formless energy I'd flung
up missed its target, and the raróg twisted around to attack again.

The fire demon screeched as it dove, and I tried blasting it with pure
aether once again. I needed to stop the tenacious beast; I might be fire
resistant, but the people surrounding me weren't. As it spouted flames
once more, I turned to protect my friends.

'Katja, *run!*' I screamed as I spun around, but instead of doing so,
Katja leapt forward, pushing me out of the way of the raróg's flames.

I watched, helpless and disbelieving, as the fire engulfed her.

She was gone.

Katja, my friend, my family, was gone.

I couldn't breathe, the weight of what just happened crushing my chest.

It was my fault. The price for death magic was always life, and it seemed when Arachne, goddess of fate, saved mine, she'd doomed my friend to lose hers. Katja had died because of *me*, because I couldn't protect her. Bile rose in my throat, the bitter taste of my failure choking my screams.

It should've been me. Not her. Never my Katja.

Bryna bellowed, her large body tearing through the enemies that swarmed us. The pain in her voice matched mine, but all I could see were the horrifying remains of the sister of my heart.

She was actually *gone.*

The woman who had welcomed me when I first arrived in Zalesie, the one who had treated me while I mourned my Anchors and tried to drink myself to death, the one who always had my back . . . was gone.

I dropped to my knees, digging my fingers into the scorched ground, and keened in pain. Primal magic erupted from my core, flooding the world with its destructive power. It had no direction or control, but the half-ruined sigil beneath my knees flared to life, warping the ground around me.

A trumpet sounded the retreat, and everyone scrambled away from the crumbling rock as it rose and fell in devastating waves.

It wasn't enough, wouldn't *be* enough, until this place drowned in destruction. So I raised a hand and dragged the aether of the storm down and twisted it into something dark. Countless monsters were caught in the chaos, but my wrath was entirely focused on one: the raróg.

Pulverised rock scored its wings as a vortex of death held it in place. The overwhelming wind extinguished the flames covering its body, but I wanted more. I wanted to see it suffer.

I clenched my fist around the aether, watching as its wings disintegrated, and laughed. I caught sight of more of its flock and expanded my reach, quickly destroying one after another. My laughter increased in volume, and as the last one died, I turned to the mountain.

The Lost Ridge had taken everything from me, and now it protected my enemy. Somewhere in this mountain, Aro and Tal's bones were buried beneath tonnes of rock, and now Katja's ashes were mixed with its cursed soil. This graveyard of my heart held no markers, no memorial, but I would make sure no one forgot this place ever again.

Darkness arose inside me, numbing my senses. I was going to find the heart of the mountain and rip it apart just as it had mine.

The ground cracked beneath my feet, the fissure spreading outwards and heading straight for the Rift. I was rooted to the spot where my magic had become the nexus of power. The elemental aether became a part of me, even as it shredded my insides while my consciousness escaped the torment, travelling through the rock, seeking its heart.

Finally, deep beneath the earth, beneath the Barrier stone chamber, deeper even than the sleeping army's cave, I found it. In a grotto of molten magma, held aloft by a lonely spire, I found the immense, jagged boulder—the Heart of the Lost Ridge.

'*Little Flame, stop. We've won. You can let the magic go. Annika, please! Stop!*'

Vahin's roar thrummed through my mind, but I refused to listen. I embraced the aether, twisting it, revelling in the pain. My power burned, building, spiralling, until agony became my existence. I laughed like a maniac, reaching for more even after blood gushed from my nose and the air burned in my throat.

I raised my hand, squeezing it into a fist with a command that fractured the world around me.

'*Karvet*.'[1]

Cracks formed on the cavern's roof, spreading outwards, and vast chunks of the ceiling fell into the molten rock below. I withdrew my consciousness as the earth shook, the mountainside crumpling in on itself. Time seemed to slow as an explosion of dust and debris obscured the world while I watched numbly the destruction around me.

The dust settled and everything was silent. The Lost Ridge was no more, but I'd found no peace in the act of destruction and felt only the grief that tore my heart asunder. A gust of wind tugged on the loose strands of my hair, but I didn't raise my head even after I saw a massive black paw settle before me.

'Little Flame, let me in.'

Vahin nudged me gently, hot air from his nostrils prickling my skin. When I didn't react, he lay on the ground, his massive head pressed against my body, just like a cat trying to get its human's attention. The storm of aether slowed inside me.

'Ormond, I don't know what to do.' The uncertainty in Vahin's voice made me gasp for breath.

I'd killed a flock of rarógs and destroyed the mountain, but it changed nothing. I buried my face in my hands as a sob burst from my lips.

'I do.'

---

1. *Shatter.*

Strong masculine arms encircled me as my Ursus knelt before me. He pressed me to his chest, rocking my body as it shook in the aftermath of grief and excessive magic.

'If it helps with the pain, then let the world burn, Ani. Just do it; it's not worthy of your tears. My love, my beautiful Nivale, I'm so sorry for your loss,' he whispered as I buried my face in his chest, sobbing uncontrollably.

'Little Flame, let me help soothe your pain. Share it with me as you did before. You don't have to face this alone,' Vahin's voice rumbled in my mind as he coiled around us, creating a wall to protect me from the external world.

It was just the three of us, both of my Anchors' skin glowing softly from grounding my power, and as time slowly passed, I let their love ease my heart so I could control my magic.

With tears rolling down my face, I finally let them in, the stream of aether thinning and fading away. I slowly stood up, my body protesting every movement, only to find Tomma's condemnation. The betrayal in his eyes stabbed me in the heart as he turned away and headed towards his dragon.

'Where are you going?' Orm called after him. Tomma didn't turn around, didn't even slow down as he mounted Rashul, but before they shot into the sky, he finally spoke.

'I'm going to Katrass. Your woman cleared the skies, so I'm going after the bastard who released the firebirds. I will return with their head . . . or not at all,' he said, and his dragon snapped his wings open, lifting them both into the air.

Orm sighed heavily before turning to his men.

'I want two volunteers to follow him. The rest of you help with the aftermath. Take special care to search for any wounded. Annika's spell may have won us the battle, but it wasn't selective.'

That was when I saw the scorched earth, rough ground, and carcasses of monsters. Between them were also soldiers caught in the destruction I'd caused. But I felt nothing. No pain or remorse, only an overwhelming tiredness that numbed my senses.

'Well said, brother. Annika, please join us at the camp. We need to plan our next steps. I didn't expect you to be so . . . effective,' Reynard said with a twitch of his jaw.

'That's what you wanted from me . . . to kill and destroy everything around me,' I said to the king, ignoring his frown. 'Enjoy your victory, Your Majesty, and leave me the fuck alone.'

'Annika!'

'Leave her alone, Rey!'

I heard the clashing of steel as I walked away but didn't slow down, blinded by the tears I finally realised were falling from my eyes.

CHAPTER 33

ALARIC

A portal shimmered gently before me, captivating my attention. It had been several hours since the Lich King and his military leaders left. They'd dragged me here to witness their victory, the grand glory of the Second Necromancer's War. As golems secured me to the wall, locking my wrists into the same iron manacles they'd used on me before, Cahyon promised to return victorious, with Talena's head in one fist and Annika's chain in another.

My surroundings were strangely calming. We were in a beautiful room with a glass ceiling supported by exquisitely carved columns. As I waited, the sky darkened, stars shining down and flooding the space with muted, cold light. Candles and torches were lit to brighten the room while human and Moroi servants prepared a feast, and next to me, on an ornate chair, sat a woman as beautiful as only a fae could be—a queen waiting for her king.

Only, she was far from calm, and I couldn't stop laughing.

The portal's surface flickered, distorting as it spit out an unidentified form onto the floor. The chancellor and several Moroi generals followed before the Lich King emerged, and only Cahyon remained standing as the black surface collapsed behind him. The blast of his power swept through the room, sending everyone to the ground and scattering the tables and food that had been prepared for his celebration.

My unrestrained laughter caught Cahyon's attention, a rage that promised suffering burning in his eyes. But the longer he stared at me, the calmer he became—as if having a witness to his failure was offensive enough without him showing how it affected him.

After a moment, he grunted some orders, and his court scattered to fulfil them.

'Care to explain yourself?' he snapped at Rowena. 'You said she was incapacitated. That you controlled her power. Or was it another conduit mage that just decimated my army? Oh, and care to explain how the *fuck* she used necromancy?'

My laughter grew louder when he grabbed a filigree cup from a nearby table and hurled it in Rowena's direction. My sister ducked, the missile smashing against the wall.

'I don't know. There was something . . .' she stuttered. 'She was protected. She burned me, and I had to withdraw—'

'You stupid bitch! And you wanted to rule by my side? *You?* A little pain and you tucked your tail and ran like a rat.'

Cahyon was seething, and even knowing it would hurt, I just couldn't help myself.

'You thought you had a chance against my domina? The woman who made a bargain with a goddess. How does it feel to taste defeat, to see your precious army scattered by her spells?'

Rowena hissed, rushing towards me and backhanding me so hard my head smacked the wall painfully.

'Silence!' she snapped as I glared at her, spitting blood onto her boots. 'No one asked your opinion.'

Cahyon's gaze bore into me, wearing my father's face like a grotesque mask. I despised the sight of it. Yet despite the loathing that burned in my chest, I could read his expressions clearly—anger and disdain, emotions I knew well. But beneath them lingered something foreign: fear. I knew Ani had used necromancy; I felt it in the gentle tug on our Anchor bond as I willingly opened my mind and soul to her. It seemed my domina had used it well.

The Lich King approached, calculation replacing the uncertainty before the corner of his mouth lifted into a smile. I cursed silently. We both knew I was the only thing that could force Annika's compliance. Escape was impossible, so I had to force him to kill me before he could use me as a bargaining chip.

'You've experienced a taste of her power now. Are you ready to face Annika face-to-face? As long as I live, her necromancy will outstrip yours. I will sacrifice every ounce of strength, of power, to see her rip that army from your control and destroy you with it,' I sneered, my manic grin expressing the truth in my words. 'When she'll come Katrass, you will kneel at her feet like the beaten cur you are.'

'You think I've lost, foolish boy? I still have you, don't I? I wanted a thriving kingdom, and I *will* have it. She won't stop me.'

'How naïve of you to believe you still have a chance' I said. 'She whipped your arse, didn't she?'

He raised his fist, struggling to control himself, and I wondered if he was going to end me now, but I wasn't so lucky.

'Collar him and drop him in the oubliette,' Cahyon commanded before he grasped my chin, forcing me to look at him. 'She won the battle, but I will win the war. She levelled the mountain, mourning some woman; for you, she will offer me her magic and Dagome on a silver platter.'

'What did you do?' I hissed, shocked by the revelation. I gaped at him, not reacting when his golems grabbed me from behind and snapped a cold metal collar around my neck. It burned, extinguishing my magic, and I clawed at my throat as the constructs dragged me to the dungeons.

When they pushed me through a small hatch in the floor, I fell, landing on a pile of bones that scraped my skin. It reminded me so much of the Dark Mother's Grotto of Dreamers that I was almost grateful that the collar throttled my magic, preventing me from drowning in the whispers of the forgotten dead.

I stared at the ceiling, studying the hatch far beyond my reach, the glow at its edges my only light in the overwhelming darkness.

I needed a plan. Sooner or later, Cahyon's golems would come for me, and if I was still here when Reynard's forces reached Katrass, I needed a way to die to stop the bastard from using me against Annika.

'Hrae, what did they do that hurt you so, love?' I murmured.

Ani was a caring woman, but she hadn't made many friends at Varta. There was her maid, Agnes, who had made a strong impression in a short time. Bryna, who, despite her gruff and coarse nature, loved fiercely. And Katja, the herbalist whose quiet strength kept those around her calm even when the world went to shit.

'He said Ani levelled a mountain. If he hurt one of her family, they're lucky she didn't burn the world to ash,' I said into the darkness.

I knew Cahyon had wanted to win the war in one fell sweep, one grand battle that would break his enemies. My sister had explained it in great detail as we waited. What I didn't know was what he planned to do now.

I whispered a quick prayer to the Dark Mother. All I needed was a little luck, a hint of a miracle, a crack in my collar, an unexpected guest ... just *something* I could twist in my favour.

ᛈᛏᛘᚠᚼ

I lost track of time, but it felt like days had passed. As weariness burned my eyes, something caught my attention: a noise, a quiet but unmistakable shuffling of feet, before a light blinded me and something fell onto my stomach, winding me.

'Eat, fae. I will return, but you must build up your strength. Your domina will be here soon.' I wasn't sure, but it sounded like the reluctant healer who'd saved me after my capture.

'Wait! Tell me what's going on,' I shouted, but she was already walking away. I scratched around for the package, trying to grasp it before the light disappeared completely.

It smelled of dry meat and bread, and despite the grim situation, I chuckled after ripping it open. It was a sandwich and a canteen of water. My miracle had come in the form of a healer and a sandwich, and although the bread was stale and the meat tasteless, I devoured it with gusto, washing the mush down with fortified water.

In this pit of hell, I had an ally who'd hated Cahyon enough to help me, and that was more than I'd ever hoped for.

The healer's intervention also provided something else: information. Annika was close, likely with Ormond and Reynard leading the army.

I had to leave. I inspected the walls, running my fingers across their surface. I had done it before but had given up after finding nothing but rough stone. This time, I would continue until I found a way out.

I moved along the wall, poking and prodding every nook and cranny for some way to climb out. Finally, I found a crevice wide enough to force my fingers into. It wasn't much, but I had to try.

I fell countless times, the many skeletons in the pit crumbling from the impact, but each time, I discovered something new—a crack or an uneven stone that allowed me to climb higher. I was exhausted. The small amount of energy I'd gathered from that dry meal didn't last long, but I was determined to continue until I was free or dead.

After several hours, I was panting hard, my clothes in tatters from all the falls, my body covered with a thick sheen of sweat.

I finally grabbed hold of the trapdoor that barred me from freedom. But as I hung there, trying to catch my breath, I heard the heavy stomp of two golems marching in my direction.

'Hrae,' I muttered, shifting until I was near the edge of the hatch, trying to position my body to the side.

I knew there was no point in trying to negotiate, but with their strength and lack of awareness, I could likely just hang onto the hatch as they lifted it. This was my chance.

I controlled my breathing, my muscles tensing when the constructs grasped the trapdoor. As the first golem lifted it, pulling me upwards, the second twisted around when it saw me. I jerked to the side, propelling myself between them. It was a clumsy and painful move, but it got me where I wanted, and I sprawled on my back just under their feet.

They turned in unison, hands outstretched, and reached for me, crashing into each other and allowing me to scramble away.

My luck ran out as I discovered the corridor I ran down was a dead end and I was stuck with nowhere to go.

I attempted the same tactic, hoping they weren't clever enough to learn from past mistakes, but as I flew past, a massive clay hand caught my collar. I coughed, clawing at the iron band and the golem's hand. When it didn't work, I reached up to gouge out its eyes, the only thing I knew that could incapacitate it other than crushing it to dust.

I missed.

Instead, my hand smashed into the golem's forehead, and thin lines appeared on the smooth surface. The creature froze, the cracks spreading. In the desperate attempt to free myself, I must have struck the sigil written in the clay that powered the golem.

'What are you doing?' The healer's voice hissed down the corridor as I punched the same spot again. This time, it didn't merely crack a little—the whole form crumbled into a pile of dust.

'Starting a pottery class?' I snapped, rushing at the remaining golem, who seemed determined to smear me all over the walls for destroying its brethren.

'Then do it *faster*,' she said, keeping her distance. 'The chancellor wants you on display to welcome your invading army. Your position has improved from prisoner in a shithole to caged bird over the city gates.'

I wasn't paying attention, entirely focused on the clay moloch that reached for me. Its massive fist whistled past my face as I jumped back. I prayed to the Dark Mother for Cahyon to have been too arrogant to place his spell elsewhere as I leapt between its arms and hammered my fist into its forehead.

Time stood still as I watched the cracks appear again, and the golem's movements turned sluggish until they stopped altogether. I exhaled in relief, punching its chest, and the clay broke, falling apart like an old flowerpot.

'Are you done now?' the healer asked, just as I recalled her name. Lara.

'Yes, come, Lara,' I said, reaching for her hand. 'We need to get out of this city.' I didn't know her, except for a few unpleasant encounters, but she had helped me, and I would not leave her to that bastard's punishment.

'I can't, but here. I brought you this,' she said, passing me a key.

I looked at her, dumbstruck. The unassuming healer had somehow retrieved the key to my collar.

'Thank you. Now, please come with me,' I insisted, unlocking the device that crippled my magic.

'I can't, there's . . . just go. The gardens are swarming with the undead, but the kitchens are almost empty, and the drains lead to a working canal that connects to the port. No one works there now, and as long as you reach the sea, you'll be safe.'

The collar clicked and fell, and I took a deep, relieved breath, feeling the aether inside me. Lara was suddenly by my side, her hands cupping my face. I frowned before I realised what she was doing.

'Thank you, my lady,' I said, letting her magic finish its job. The goddess knew I needed her healing touch.

'I couldn't help my family, but you . . .' she trailed off before gathering her courage. 'If your people defeat that bastard, please speak up for us. Tell them the Moroi didn't stand a chance and ask your king to show mercy for my remaining brethren. I can cure the blood fever, and there are still a few of us left . . . Please. That's all I ask for.'

'You have my word, and if my domina were here, she would give you hers, too. Annika is . . . she would understand. Look after yourself, gentle healer,' I said as I darted towards the exit. Lara might not have heard it yet, but there were footsteps approaching, and I didn't want to fight another monster.

I was a safe distance away when I heard her scream, 'My lord, the prisoner, he escaped!' I couldn't help but smile. *Wise woman.* I hoped we would meet again.

I was soon lost in the winding corridors, but sneaking through castles was all too familiar to me, and I drew on my old skills to remain undetected. Glimpsing through the windows, I knew Lara hadn't exaggerated the dangers outside. The gardens were overflowing with monsters, and I wondered if Cahyon expected me to head for the portal if I escaped.

Lara was right, the port was the safest option. I smirked when I finally reached the kitchens and found the waste chute that led straight to a narrow canal.

There were several boats there—or rather their remains, most rotten and broken, but I found a small one stored on the pathway that must have been used to transport messengers. It was still sturdy enough to use, and I prayed to Jurata, goddess of the sea, to grant me safe passage.

I was returning to my domina, and there was nothing that could stop me now.

CHAPTER 34

ANNIKA

A fter leaving Reynard and Orm, I'd spent some time trying to piece together my broken heart. But it didn't work, not even a little. Wherever I turned, soldiers bowed or thanked me, and their whispers followed me everywhere. None of it seemed real. How were they celebrating when so many had died?

It was at that moment I realised something. These men hadn't expected to survive, let alone win. As I walked through the camp, I started noticing the haunted looks, the false bravado, and the looks they gave me as if I could somehow change their fate. So, even as each forced smile, each gentle pat to a bowed back, felt like a betrayal, I stopped and offered them the comfort and reassurance they needed.

At some point, Valaram, for whatever reason, decided to block my way with a concerned look on his face.

'Annika, please let me help. Talk to me, lara'mei. Don't let this grief fester when I can—' he said, stepping closer, but I cut him off before he finished his sentence.

'That is none of your concern, Ambassador. So please move.' The harshness of my tone made him wince.

'Perhaps not, but that ironclad rider of yours should be here for you. I ought to hammer that into his head.'

I looked at the dark fae mage. He had shadows under his eyes and he'd overused his power, and when I saw where we were, I knew he'd spent it healing everyone he could. He stepped closer, reaching for my hand, but I backed up, ignoring the forlorn look in his eyes. The expression disappeared before anyone else noticed, and his fingers curled into a fist as he dropped his hand to his side.

'Leave Orm out of this,' I said. 'He has duties to attend to and can respect my wishes to be left alone. Can you do the same, or should I shatter another mountain to prove that to you?'

I was holding on by a thread. My mind was still refusing to acknowledge that Katja was gone, pretending she was safe in Varta, waiting for me there, snarky and unharmed. The last thing I needed was anyone's compassion and the reminder that the sister of my heart was gone. Valaram had good intentions, but he didn't understand I couldn't talk about it right now.

'Annika, that's not what I was trying to say.' He frowned, taken aback by my words.

I exhaled slowly, trying to centre myself. *He just cares for you,* I thought, but he was the wrong fae, it was the wrong time, and dealing with my own feelings was hard enough.

I forced a tight smile before turning away. 'And that's why you get to keep your pointy ears. Leave me alone, Val. *I wish everyone would just leave me alone.*' The last words I'd added quietly, but I heard his deep sigh behind me.

I continued around the camp, smiling and nodding, answering polite greetings and observing as the soldiers packed to march onwards. We were heading to Katrass, and I wondered if I would lose another piece of my heart there.

Whatever physical injuries I'd received were cured by the gentle hands of our healers, but some wounds cut deeper than magic could reach. Katja's death and the hedge witches' sacrifice crushed not just the mountain but my spirit, leaving me numb to the world.

'Give me that, soldier.' I reached out to a warrior taking a deep draught from a flask. The man's initial protest died on his lips when he saw my outstretched hand.

'Yes, my lady . . . but 'tis not a drink for woman,' he said, passing me the foul-smelling canteen.

'Are you saying I can't handle it?' I challenged. 'Here, take this as payment.' I weaved the aether to fix a dent in his metal breastplate. As he examined his newly repaired armour, I took a sip, and the world blurred with tears as the alcohol burned its way down my throat.

To you, Katja. Maybe if I drink myself stupid, I won't remember the raróg's screech and the stench of your death.

ᛢᛂᚾᛂᛝ

I wandered some more, drinking from the borrowed flask. I shivered, tiredness catching up, but sleep eluded me. Every time I closed my eyes, my thoughts spiralled into a vortex of shame, guilt, and anger.

The night was buzzing with activity, and I sat on a large granite outcropping in the heather field, observing as the wounded were helped and the dead were cremated. Orm and Reynard were pulled in so many directions I doubted they noticed the time passing, but I was still out there, rocking back and forth, chilled to the bone, when the sun rose over a bloody horizon.

I was drunk, but not drunk enough. With each sip of the flask, the noises from the camp deadened. When the last drop fell onto my lips, I stood and walked undisturbed over the rough terrain. The gnarled trees were gone, burned or broken during the battle, and the hooves of heavy cavalry had ripped up chunks of the already sparse grass. My grief-fuelled magic had not only levelled the mountain but also created a small spring. Its bubbling water was still full of mud, but I could see the sediment already settling as I passed.

I ended up near the sleeping dragons, who were resting there until noon when the army would set off over the plateau that had once been the Lost Ridge Mountain.

A monument to my power . . . and my failure.

I swallowed hard, shaking my head to clear the images flashing through my mind, the faces of the dead that came back to haunt me.

I know what you'd be saying to me now, Kat. That it was worth it, that we finally have a chance. It was true, and I would've happily sacrificed myself for it, but why did she have to pay the price instead?

My thoughts were a jumbled mess, not helped by exhaustion and alcohol, but in my mind's eye, I saw Katja wearing the scowl she reserved for whenever she thought I was being too hard on myself.

Yeah, I know. I should get my arse in gear and see it through until the end . . . I just need time, just a little more time.

The alcohol burned in my stomach, but it couldn't fill the emptiness I felt inside. 'Fuck! I'm not made of stone, alright? I just need time!' I shouted, throwing the empty flask into the distance. The riders tending to their dragons turned to look at me but no one said a word.

'Vahin,' I cried out to my dragon, staggering across the field. A black shadow immediately descended from the sky, landing gracefully in front of me.

'Little Flame?' he answered, his body encircling me until I faced a wall of black scales glimmering with a faint blue glow.

'I need you!'

A shuddered breath escaped my lips as I pressed my forehead to his neck. I could pretend for Orm's sake, to lift morale, but my dragon knew my heart.

'*Whatever you need, I'll give it to you. The sadness in your heart is killing me. What can I do, Little Flame?*'

Vahin sounded so sincere. I was hurting him, and I considered closing our connection, but I was too selfish to go through with it.

'*I want Katja back. I want her to be alive, Vahin.*'

I clenched my fists, digging my nails deep into the flesh, wishing the simple gesture could wake me from this nightmare. As his pupils narrowed to a slit, I couldn't take it anymore, and my grief spilled out.

'*Tell me there's something—anything—I can do to bring her back. I'll do it. I will crawl on my knees to the Dark Mother or Veles. I will fulfil any challenge. But, please, help me bring her back.*'

He was silent, just gazing at me with a singular focus, and I dropped to the ground, clutching my knees and sobbing uncontrollably. I needed more alcohol to numb the pain, or at least the blissful ignorance of unconsciousness.

'*There is no spell that can bring someone back once their body is destroyed. Even if there was, do you think Katja would want to live as a wraith . . . or even worse, a spectre?*' he asked.

'*I just want her back. She didn't deserve to die. She wasn't even a soldier.*'

The tip of a forked tongue slid over my cheek, wiping my tears away.

'*Nobody deserves to die, Little Flame, but we all do eventually. Even dragons can be killed. Katja lived by her own rules and died saving her friend. She lived a good life, and her death had meaning. She wouldn't want you to mourn her like this.*'

There was truth in his words, but it was a truth I didn't want to hear.

'*Meaning? Being burned to a crisp by a fucking raróg? There's no meaning in that. She's fucking fertiliser for the damn grass. There wasn't even enough left to bury.*'

An angry sob escaped me as I jumped up, pushing at Vahin's neck to escape his embrace..

'You have your memories—the love and legacy she left behind, Little Flame,' he said with a rumbling purr. 'For as long as you keep her memory alive, she will never be gone.'

'Right, do you truly believe that? Just . . . never mind. Can you do your mind trick? I need this pain to go away so I can survive long enough to *rip* that bastard's heart out with my bare hands.'

Vahin hissed, jerking his massive head away. I'd felt his concern all this time, but it was nothing compared to the blast of raw emotion that hit me now.

'Tampering with your emotions didn't end well last time. Please don't ask this of me, Little Flame.'

'You asked me what you could do. I told you. So please, help me,' I insisted, clenching my jaw as Vahin's body unfolded, releasing me. I could sense his disapproval, but moments later, a wave of calm indifference washed over me.

'*It is temporary. That's all I'm willing to do. I'm no mage to take your feelings away, nor would I, even if you asked for it. I know it hurts. I know how much you loved her. But numbing yourself to the world is not the way.*'

'*So says the dragon who hid inside his mind when the pain of losing his riders became too much to bear.*'

I regretted the thought as soon as it flashed through my mind, but I couldn't take it back.

'*You're right. Humans aren't the only cowards.*'

Vahin spread his wings and leapt into the sky. I'd hurt him. He didn't block our bond despite my harsh words, but more than those, it had hurt him that I pushed him away.

My eyes followed his silhouette until only a shadow was visible, gliding between the clouds.

'*I'm sorry, I didn't mean . . .*'

Was I really trying to excuse myself? The painful void in my heart was no excuse for lashing out with such cruelty.

'*I know, Little Flame. Take your time and let me know when you need me to land,*' he said, leaving me alone in the field.

I stood there, staring into the distance, but I couldn't escape my guilt. As I turned and walked back to my tent, I decided to use the short respite Vahin had given me to push forward. I helped pack my tent and belongings away before hiding in one of the supply wagons, nursing all the moonshine I could buy from the soldiers.

For all I cared, the world could freeze, burn, or carry on regardless, but I was done for the day. I emptied the first bottle before we even set off, and when the wagon wobbled, finally moving, I was already drifting off into welcome oblivion.

ᛉᛈᚾᛃᛣ

'You're telling me she's been here the whole time? I searched high and low, sending dragons to scout the area, thinking she'd run away. Or, the gods forbid, kidnapped, and she was here, drunk in the blacksmith's wagon?' Orm's raised voice broke through my stupor, and I stretched, feeling every bone in my body creak in protest.

The wagon no longer rocked on the uneven road, and I realised we must have stopped somewhere. The bustling voices around us meant camp was setting up for the night. My stomach rumbled, and I stumbled in the darkness, kicking the empty bottles as I tried to stand up. The world was still spinning on its axis when I pulled back the heavily waxed linen curtains.

'Yes, I'm here. Marching with the army like a good soldier should, just in a more prone position. I didn't feel like riding a horse . . . or a dragon,' I said, finding Orm's stunned expression. He rushed forward as I took a step to exit my transport, catching me before I landed face-first in the mud.

'Annika Diavellar, I am endlessly happy that you are safe, but didn't it cross your mind to let me know? We are in enemy territory, and you didn't mention your choice of transportation—' He sighed, pressing me to his chest. 'Let's put that aside for now, Nivale. You look like something the dragon chewed up and spat out. I won't mention what you smell like,' he said before scooping me up and marching away.

'Well, thank you, gentle lord. It's not like you smell like roses, either,' I grumbled. I wouldn't admit it even if the enemy broke my bones, but a part of me craved this love and attention. Craved the knowledge that, despite my actions, he still loved me.

I didn't know where he was carrying me to, but as my mind slowly cleared, I took in the world around me.

The stench of stale water was overpowering. We were in a swamp, or some kind of marshland, where the ground undulated beneath Orm's feet, and all the jolting made me nauseous.

'Put me down,' I groaned, desperately trying to keep my mouth closed.

'No, we are going to the healers,' he answered with a stony expression.

'Put . . . me . . . down,' I snapped, hitting his shoulder, the moonshine threatening to decorate his armour. Understanding dawned in his eyes, and he hastily set me on my feet, catching my braid moments before I expelled whatever was sloshing around in my stomach.

'I should have known better,' he murmured, wiping the sweat off my forehead and pressing me to his chest the moment I was done.

'Yes, you should have. It's just a hangover. Not my first, and unlikely to be my last. I'll live, just . . . I need some water,' I groaned, the burning in my throat subsiding.

'Did you find her, Commander?' Valaram's voice from behind Orm made me roll my eyes. Of course, it had to be him.

'Yes, he did, and now you have, too, so you can shake hands and point me to the nearest tent. I need water and a place to sleep. Where is Vahin?' I asked before I remembered how poorly I had treated him. 'You know what, never mind.'

I couldn't stomach Valaram's pity. He wasn't Ari, and the more he cared, the more I felt as if he was trying to step into my fae's shoes. I wiggled in Orm's arms, trying to force him to release me, but he tightened his grip.

'Let me make one thing clear, Nivale. I'm not a man you can just send away. I'm also not a man that would let you drink yourself sick in a fucking wagon. I will take care of you whether you want it or not,' he stated, before turning to Valaram. 'As you can see, Ani is safe. I appreciate your help, but I need to be alone with my woman.'

Valaram nodded stiffly, his gaze lingering on my face, waiting for my confirmation. At my nod, he walked away, frowning. Once he'd gone, Ormond's attention returned to me.

'I can't believe you tried to send me away, or that you lied to me when I asked how you felt,' he said, carrying me to a small tent at the edge of the camp.

'You have soldiers and riders who depend on you,' I said. 'I can manage.'

He shook his head. 'Ani, we have an empress, two kings, and a prince. Any one of them can replace me. Why wouldn't I want to help you? I can see how much you're hurting. Did you know that Vahin was blaming himself for your disappearance? He thought you'd locked him out because of your argument. No one thought you'd be passed out in a wagon.'

Orm paused, taking a deep, calming breath. 'I'm not mad at you, my love . . . well, only a little. I know Katja was special to you, and I should have known this calm was just a façade. I'm sorry I didn't push to stay by your side. I should have known better.'

He sat on the bed, settling me onto his lap, and grabbed a canteen. 'Here, drink this, then we'll talk.'

'I don't want to talk. I just got drunk and didn't realise I'd be out for so long,' I said, pulling away. 'I didn't leave or expose myself to danger; you're making a mountain out of a molehill.'

'I wish you could "just get drunk," but you no longer have the luxury of hiding away. You are loved and respected by so many, and they will notice if you disappear—not just your friends or the dragons. The entire fucking army looks up to you as their personal saviour. They revel in your strength. Do you know what they're calling you? The Harbinger of Light. Light, Annika. Brutal men who embrace death for breakfast are calling you their light, and their light can't disappear without leaving the world in darkness.'

'And if I want to? What will you do—chain me to a post, use my geas? I never asked for this. All those people you mentioned, do they know what I am? What I have become? I'm not their fucking light. I'm their death!'

My outburst left me exhausted, and my head hung limply as I let the tears fall to the floor.

'Death? Sweetheart, are you blaming yourself for Katja's death?'

'Katja's, the hedge witches', it's all on me,' I answered. He sighed gently, taking a strand of my hair and wrapping it around his fingers.

'I should have known when I saw that haunted look in your eyes. Katja's death was tragic and cruel, but it could have been anyone standing there when the raróg attacked. And what hedge witches are you talking about?'

'The peasant women from the borderlands. They sacrificed their lives so I could fight . . . Weren't you surprised I suddenly appeared on the battlefield? I was a broken mess the last time you saw me.'

He was confused and I could tell he didn't understand. I explained how old Martha had used her magic so I could absorb the women's life force to restore my power. The more I talked, the more he frowned. When I mentioned using the death spell, he stopped me.

'Necromancers do that all the time' he said. 'I don't see how your actions were any different.'

I huffed a brief laugh. 'Necromancers work with death. The Dark Mother granted me a spell that fed on life. Death magic is forbidden for a reason. Only a madman feeds the spell with the lives of others because, in the end, the spell would consume them, too. I knew how it should've end when I accepted the sacrifice, but I needed my power back and the women . . . they wanted revenge.'

'You shouldn't blame yourself, Ani. It was their choice. You gave them what they wanted and more.' Orm grasped my hands and placed them on his chest. 'If I had to sacrifice nineteen riders to save the army, I wouldn't hesitate. War leaves scars, and no one walks away from the battlefield intact. There are always choices to be made and blood to be spilt. I wish I could spare you from it, but I can't. Life isn't fair, but instead of taking the blame, think of how many lives you saved.'

'Maybe, but Katja didn't volunteer to die in my stead.' I ground my teeth as I hammered his chest with my fists. 'She was there because of *me*, and she died because the Dark Mother spared my thread.'

'You can't know that,' Orm argued, but I turned my gaze away because having said it out loud made it even more real. He wrapped his arms around me. 'Oh, love, you carry a burden that would crush the strongest heart. It's not your fault. Katja's death is not your fault; the hedge witches' were not your fault. Even if you took their lives and the goddess spared your thread, it was *their* choice, not yours.'

Orm cupped my face, urging me to look him in the eyes, his golden rims shining brightly. He knew now what I hid inside, yet he still held me close to his heart. He pulled me off his lap and gently sat me on the bed before kneeling at my feet.

'I failed you. I'm your Anchor, but I let you down, let you suffer alone and seek solace in a bottle. I'll do better, but you have to promise me—no more hiding. I'll break any wall, any shell you build around yourself. You are mine, Nivale, and even if your heart bleeds smoke and pain, I will be there to chase the shadows away. All you have to do is let me in.'

I nodded, unable to speak. Orm's love unlocked the layers of grief, and even long after we went to bed, my gentle bear of a man held me close, stroking my back as I cried myself to sleep.

CHAPTER 35

ORMOND

I'd hoped that Annika's mood would have improved after our conversation, but I couldn't have been more wrong. The woman whose mischievous smile could light up a room became withdrawn, and nothing I did changed it. She was calmer, though it felt like the calm before a storm.

The situation was made worse by the constant attacks during our journey to Katrass. Cahyon had learned from the previous battle, and in order to prevent Annika from taking control of his forces, he used guerrilla tactics.

The persistent hit-and-run attacks kept our soldiers from resting peacefully, and Ani was becoming frustrated at not being able to stop them. I made sure to reassure her that the attacks were being handled; we either destroyed the enemy or chased them away.

Reynard was gaining confidence the farther we travelled, especially after encountering settlements of humans and fae, descendants of the survivors of the Lich King's purge during the First Necromancer's War. He even confided in me that he hoped to rebuild Ozar after we freed the kingdom. I didn't want to dampen his mood, but I was worried about our supplies, which were dwindling too quickly for comfort.

A soldier saluted me, stiff as a rod. 'Commander, another group is headed towards the camp. Any orders?'

'Reinforce the sentries and prepare for an attack, but don't fire on them until you know if they're hostile. And send the dwarven infantry and light cavalry commanders to my tent.' I returned the man's hasty salute and wondered how long we'd be delayed this time. 'Wait, send the quartermaster, too.'

The soldier acknowledged the order and disappeared quickly, leaving me with a pile of reports, which did nothing to improve my mood.

They can wait, I thought, dropping onto the most uncomfortable foldable chair ever created. It creaked ominously under my weight as I considered Annika's words.

To my satisfaction, she had joined our war council meetings. During the last one, while everyone enthusiastically discussed attack strategies, she had used a moment of silence to ask a question: '*Where are the golems?*'

The question had stunned the entire assembly. Within minutes, everyone made their excuses and left, not one of them addressing it.

Now, I found myself mulling over the issue. Where *were* they? We hadn't encounter any in the battle at Lost Ridge, and they were never a part of the guerrilla attacks. The Lich King's most famous creations—resistant to magic and difficult to destroy—were singularly responsible for the destruction of Ozar. And we had yet to encounter the frighteningly effective fighting force.

We had thought that Cahyon had used all of his army during the Battle of the Rift, but I finally realised he'd been expecting an easy victory, so he hadn't bothered committing his best forces.

I was starting to worry, and not just about the golems. As we advanced, the land changed. After the barren soil of the border, we'd passed through salty marshes where seasonal tides seemed to want to reclaim the land, our men, and supplies.

We'd emerged with minimal losses and were now travelling along an old road surrounded by roughly cultivated fields that proved people still lived here. But we were sadly lacking when it came to information. Who, or what, would we face when we arrived at Katrass?

'I heard another group's been spotted heading towards us,' Annika said, slipping into the tent. I was on my feet and embracing her before the flap fell closed, breathing in her scent and calming my worries.

She sighed, but her small smile eased the knot in my chest. She gently tapped her finger on my leather armour. 'Are you guarding yourself against me, Commander?' she asked.

I groaned, bending down to capture her lips. 'Never, but my soldiers might not appreciate their leader parading around naked for his lady's pleasure,' I said when we parted. Ani chuckled, and the melody of her laugh almost brought me to my knees.

'You know what? Fuck it. They can endure my hairy arse if it makes you smile. I missed the sound of your laugh, Nivale.'

I reached for the clasp of my breastplate, but Annika promptly covered my hand with hers. 'No, some things are only for me. I just came to ask what you plan to do about the upcoming attack.'

Another thing I had noticed was that Annika didn't speak of Alaric at all. Since the battle, she hadn't once spoken his name, and each time I brought it up, she promptly changed the subject.

'Ani, we'll get him back,' I said.

She placed her hand on my lips. 'You don't know that . . . and I can't . . .' I saw tears well in her eyes before she turned her head, blinking them away. 'Tell me what you're going to do and if you need me.'

'*Orm?*' Vahin's voice in my mind made me sigh. He must have picked up on Ani's feelings again.

'*Everything's alright, but she still refuses to talk about Alaric,*' I answered.

I kissed Annika's palm. 'I was going to go and welcome our visitors. I don't think you'll need to fight, but I'd enjoy your company. Would you like to join me?'

The hope I had felt at seeing her in my tent was promptly extinguished when Annika shook her head.

'Not this time. Bryna and I are going through Katja's wagon. Her potions could help our healers, and if any women need clothes . . . they can . . . they can pick some,' she finished, swallowing hard.

'You don't have to do that, love. I'll ask the mages to send some healers. They will be better versed in deciding what tinctures could be used, and as they sort that out, they can help with the rest.'

'No, Katja was a private person. She wouldn't want strangers rummaging through her belongings. I will find what can be used and burn the rest. That's what she'd want.'

She forced a smile for my benefit, wiping tears away. 'I'll get to it. That way, I might be able to avoid coming to the evening meeting,' she said with one last pat on my armour, leaving the tent.

'*Will she get better?*' I asked Vahin, feeling his presence in my mind as he listened in on the conversation.

'*With time, yes, but I don't think she'll ever be the same. Some wounds never heal, and while everyone's idolising her, she can't see her own path clearly.*'

'*What can I do?*'

'*Give her time, give her love . . . and pray for your mate's return.*'

'Commander, you wanted to see us?' Three men walked into the tent, cutting my conversation with Vahin short.

I nodded, pointing to the chairs.

'Yes, there is another group heading our way, and if the information from the humans we captured is right, we are two days away from

Katrass. I want to send a reconnaissance unit to scout their defences,' I said, pointing to the crudely drawn map on my table.

'We have three potential routes to reach the capital, and I want them all checked before deciding on the best approach. And, for goodness' sake, ensure the soldiers are ready. The way they're behaving makes me think they believe the war's already won.'

'Well said, Lord Commander.' Reynard entered my tent, nodding to the men. 'I came here to ask you for exactly that. The sooner we get to Katrass, the better for us all, and once we take the capital, subduing the rest of the Lich King's forces will be much easier.'

'My lord, may I request Lady Annika's presence on the reconnaissance mission? In case we encounter unexpected resistance?' The infantry captain asked with hopeful expectation, but his smile died when I shook my head.

'You are all trained to deal with the unexpected. Are you suggesting your men can't deal with the threat? If so, I can reassign your unit to the vanguard.'

I let my words hang in the air, the reddened cheeks of the dwarf letting me know that the insult hit the mark.

'No, Lord Commander. We are perfectly capable of dealing with any threat. I was merely thinking of reducing possible casualties.'

Oh, he was good. My jaw tightened at the suggestion that I didn't care about my men.

'Lady Annika will be attending tonight's war council meeting,' Reynard said, unexpectedly coming to my rescue. 'We need to plan the attack on Katrass, and I can't lose her expertise for a walk down the road.'

'Of course, Your Majesty.'

After that, we discussed several more minor matters before I finally sent them away. Alone with my brother, I leaned back in my chair, gesturing for him to take a seat.

'How bad is it? With Ani? Can she fight?' he asked.

I rubbed my tense neck. 'Is that why you're really here? To ask if she can kill more monsters for you?'

'Cut the bullshit, Orm. I care for Annika, but I'm responsible for eighty thousand men and have almost no supplies left. We need to finish this or set up a permanent base here so I can send back the injured and resupply. Can you blame me for asking if we can resolve this in one fell swoop?' Reynard asked, pulling a flask from his pocket. 'Here, maybe this will mellow you out.'

I drank heavily from the flask. The burning in my throat and taste an unmistakable sign that Reynard had gotten hold of some soldier's moonshine, distilled from the gods know what.

'I'm not . . . Fuck! Annika is . . . She will fight if you ask her to, but unless the situation is dire, I won't ask. Katja's death hit her hard. Don't force her hand. Please. I'm asking as your brother.'

'I don't want to, but I may have no choice. After Annika mentioned the golems, no one's been able to think of anything else. For fuck's sake, even Valaram voiced his concerns.'

Reynard watched me, waiting for my reaction, so I finished his thought for him.

'And you think the reason our progress has been so easy is that Cahyon has pulled everything back behind the city walls, and that we should get ready for a nasty surprise or a long siege?'

'Yes. The question is, what are we going to do about it?'

'Catch a few who come our way, interrogate their scrawny arses—or ask politely if they're friendly—and then decide. Why?' I asked.

He looked like he had something to say.

'I guess I could ask someone else to do that and send you to Katrass with Vahin instead,' he suggested. 'Have you see for yourself if the walls are still standing and whether there are any visible defences.'

'Guess? Just tell me what you want me to do.'

'Fine.' He sighed. 'Go to Katrass. And if there is anything I can do for Annika, let me know—maybe the light fae healers could help?'

Reynard had good intentions, but I burst out laughing.

'If you could get them close enough to even touch her,' I said with a sigh of my own. 'Ani has refused even Valaram, and he's someone she tolerates. No, we just have to wait.'

I pulled back the flap of my tent and walked outside. We were camped in a meadow and looking at the almost flat field of autumn grass and purple heather, I felt strangely at peace.

'You're leaving?' Reynard asked.

I nodded without taking my eyes off the fleeting beauty of autumn. 'Yes. I'll see you this evening. Keep an eye on Ani. I entrust her well-being to you while I'm gone.'

It was his turn to laugh then.

'You mean you entrust her to look after mine? Brother, your woman is a military marvel; if only she learned how to follow orders.'

I knew Reynard meant it as a joke, but I didn't laugh. He didn't really know her, and because of that, for him, Annika would always be a weapon of war, while all I could see were the tears in the eyes of my heartbroken Nivale.

'Vahin.'

I said it aloud for Reynard's benefit, and when my dragon descended from the sky, I turned, placing my hand on my brother's shoulder.

'Just look after her for me.'

CHAPTER 36

ANNIKA

I stood, my feet rooted to the spot, looking at the brown wagon parked alone on a carpet of wildflowers next to the small sandy bank of the nearby river.

It looked so . . . ordinary, and yet, I knew it was perfect.

'Are you sure you want to do this?'

Bryna stood next to me, her face uncharacteristically solemn. I reached out and squeezed her hand. We'd spent all day going through Katja's belongings. I'd lost count of the times we'd fallen into each other's arms and cried, saving the useful items to be given away and carefully putting her personal possessions aside. My always pragmatic Katja would have wanted this.

'Ani?'

'Yes, I want to do this. Let it be her resting place, here by the river. Do you think she'd like it?' I asked, sniffing back the tears.

'Oh, knowing her, she would complain that it's too wet or the frogs make too much noise,' Bryna answered, pulling me close. 'She would love it, Ani.' She sighed. 'You know, I always thought Katja would be the last of us to go. She was always so careful about everything.'

'Not about choosing friends,' I mumbled, but Bryna heard and grasped my shoulders, turning me to face her.

'She had the *best* friends she could ever wish for. Katja loved us, loved you. It was her choice to fight, and she'd be so pissed if she could hear you now. She saved you, Ani. So pull your head out of your arse. Katja wouldn't blame you. I don't blame you. The only person who blames you is *you*.'

The half-orc pushed me towards the wagon. 'Now, light the fucking fire, and give Katja's spirit the send-off she deserves! Let your guilt burn with it.'

'You don't understand,' I said.

'Oh yes, I fucking do! You don't think I feel guilty, too? If I'd been faster, stronger, more observant . . . I could have kept you both safe. But ask yourself this: "What would Katja say?"'

Bryna put her hands on her hips and stared at me with a challenging look in her large brown eyes. 'What would Katja say, Annika?'

I looked up. The sun had already set, but a pink hue still lit the horizon, and the soft lights of the stars were emerging in the evening sky.

Are you there, my friend, exploring the stars and rolling your eyes at me now?

The sky was silent, as always, and only the shadows of soaring dragons disturbed its peace. I would have to find my own answers.

'To stop with this nonsense and kick the Lich King where the sun doesn't shine,' I said, giving Bryna an apologetic smile. 'I'm so selfish, Bry. You also lost a friend, and I didn't even ask how you feel . . . I'm so sorry, I haven't been myself lately.'

'Oh, no. I know you, I know how much you care, so don't you fucking dare apologise to me. I'll be alright. Now, burn something. Maybe it'll help.' Bryna nodded at the wagon. 'It's time, Annika. Let's say goodbye to our friend.'

I called out to the stars, not for an answer this time, but for their power.

It may have been soft and gentle, but their answer sheathed my arms in flames. They felt so pure, familiar, untainted by the death trapped in my heart. The fire warmed my hands, and I rolled it between my fingers. Soft, crackling flames—smokeless, yet somehow, I caught the scent of the healing balm that always trailed after Katja infused within its heart.

'Goodbye, my pragmatic herbalist. In every colour of our time, here and beyond the Veil, you were my friend, my sister . . . I feel so lost without you,' I offered to the flames before releasing them, watching as they enveloped the wagon, burning brightly.

The scent intensified, and I inhaled sharply, choking back the sob that threatened to escape my constricted throat. Bryna frowned, but I had already turned towards the fire. We stood there silently, watching until the flames finally died and all that remained was a mound of cinders.

Bryna eventually spoke. 'I need to get back. But I'm glad we did this. She would have liked it.'

I embraced the half-orc. 'I'll stay a bit longer.'

Bryna nodded, giving the pyre one last look as she squeezed me goodbye before walking back to camp, leaving me alone with my thoughts.

The night's chill ran down my spine as I approached the smouldering remains, mesmerised by the soft, glowing light. I should have gone back to the tent before Orm called for another search mission, but for the first time since the battle, I felt at peace.

'I know I stayed late and missed the meeting,' I said as I heard footsteps behind me. 'I'll do better tomorrow and even listen as you brief me on what was said when we return.'

'I don't know about the meeting, but I'm glad I didn't miss you, Domina.'

The melodic voice had a distinct rasp, and I shook, frozen in place. I was afraid that if I turned, if I faced the man who spoke, he would disappear, and all my hope with him.

He came closer, and I swallowed hard, my throat so dry I couldn't speak a word. 'Ani, I know I made the wrong decision, and it cost you dearly, but can't you even look at me?'

I dragged in a strained breath that was half sob and turned rapidly to face the man looking at me with utter devotion.

'Annika . . .' he whispered, a soft smile lighting up his tired face.

My fingers curled into fists, my nails cutting deep into my palms. *If this is a trick . . . another latawiec sent to torment me.*

'You . . .' I finally managed. 'You . . . Who the fuck are you? Are you even *him?*'

I lunged at Alaric, hitting him in the chest. My attack must have startled him because I got a few hits in, and when he leaned in to grasp my hands, my poorly-aimed punch got him in the face. I gasped, pulling away as I realised two things: one, that he was physically *real*, and two, that it *was* my Ari—the first thing he'd done as he grasped my wrists was mutter a healing cantrip.

'Alaric! Oh gods, but how?' I asked, looking up at him. 'I thought he was going to kill you, that I'd have to live without you . . .' My words were punctuated by my fists against his chest. 'How did you escape?'

'I came to you as soon as I could . . . Annika, please, stop,' he pleaded. 'Are you hurt?'

I struggled to break free and he raised my hand to inspect it in an all-too-familiar gesture.

'Stop it. Stop acting like nothing happened, like you haven't been through hell.' I pulled my hand back and shook it. 'This doesn't hurt. You can't hurt what's broken. They killed Katja . . . and I mourned you. Do you think any physical pain can match that?'

I cried, relief mixing with anger when I noticed his sorry state. Alaric looked like he had crawled through bloody sewers, and all he cared about was my aching hand. I wanted to wrap my arms around him and kiss every single bruise on his body—right before giving him a few new ones for endangering his life.

But I must have spoken the wrong words because shock widened his pupils, and Alaric released me, dropping to his knees. He pulled a crude-looking dagger from his belt and pressed its tip to his heart.

'What the fuck are you doing?' I asked, clasping the blade as a wave of fear washed over me.

'The honourable thing,' he answered with a sad smile, reaching for my hand. I watched in disbelief as he wrapped my fingers around the hilt.

'I made a mistake, ignoring the vjesci's warning and falling for my sister's ploy, even feeling something was wrong,' he said. 'I endangered your life and almost caused us to lose the battle. If you can't forgive me, then take my life. It is better I die by your hand than live without you.'

I shook my head, pulling back, but he stopped me. His hand tightened over mine, and our struggle pushed the knife into his flesh.

'Alaric'va Shen'ra, let go of my hand!' At the command in my voice, he instantly released me, and I threw the dagger as far away as I could. 'Stand up!'

'Annika?'

My name on his lips carried so many unspoken questions. Hope flashed in his eyes, but I shook my head again as I glared at him.

'How dare you? How could you think I would ever . . .?' My voice wobbled, and I had to stop to calm myself. 'I was just scared and angry. I thought I would have to beg that bastard for your corpse, and you just jumped out of the bushes like you had just been taking an evening stroll. I overreacted. But thinking I want you dead . . . Ari, just stand up and hold me, you idiot.'

He gaped at me. 'What?'

'Did the Lich King pour lead into your pointy ears? Stand up, embrace me, and start behaving like my fae before I start to wonder if Cahyon jumped into another body,' I said.

Ari's heart hammered against his ribs as he swept me up into his arms. Pressing his cheek to my hair, he breathed in my scent while stroking my back and playing with my braid. I felt his hands shake, his breath hitch, as if he were overwhelmed by a maelstrom of emotion, so I gave him a moment.

Closing my eyes, I listened to the night, the soft hooting of the owls and the rustling of dry autumn leaves. We were so close to Katrass that the air had a distinct salty scent despite the lingering smoke from the wagon's remains.

'Hrae, I'm so dirty but . . . can I kiss you, Domina?' Alaric's lips brushed my ear, causing goosebumps.

'Do you have to ask?' I answered, raising my gaze to his.

My heart ached at seeing how tired he was. The dark shadows under his eyes were matched only by the stubble obscuring his sharp jawline. His new look was so unexpected that I held my hand up as he leaned in to kiss me.

'Wait. You can grow a beard?' I asked as his lips pressed into my palm.

Alaric chuckled. 'If I try really hard. Fae kind were not overly blessed with facial hair. Now, can I kiss you, or do you wish to explore what else hides under the layers of dirt?'

I pulled myself higher, standing on my toes. Ari's lips met mine with a sweet tenderness, and I sighed, melting into his arms. He didn't rush, perfectly sensing my mood. Finally, he broke the kiss, brushing away strands of my hair from my face.

'I'm sorry for leaving. I'm sorry I wasn't there to support you during the battle. I'm sorry for Katja,' he said, peppering my face with little kisses. 'Will you forgive me?'

'It wasn't your fault . . . I scorned you, but if she was my sister, I would probably have done the same . . .' I said, my thoughts drifting to Katja, but my dangerous fae looked so remorseful that I couldn't help but smile. 'But I need your promise. Swear you'll never leave me again.'

'On my honour!' Alaric said it so vehemently, and when he sealed the words with a hard and possessive kiss, I felt them imprinted on my soul.

I chuckled, my cheeks red as we parted. 'We need to get back to the tent. Orm most likely thinks I'm lying drunk in a ditch,' I said. He gave me a sharp look and I shrugged, explaining, 'I didn't know how to handle everything that happened, so I coped the best I could . . .'

Ari only sighed, pulling his hood over his head, hiding both his white hair and aristocratic facial features. 'Let's go. Things will improve now that I'm here to look after you.'

'Good,' I said. 'I've run out of excuses to keep Valaram away.'

Alaric's hands tightened on my body. 'That wretched fae . . . Did he try to entrap you?'

'No, he was helpful. Maybe just a little *too* helpful,' I answered, resisting the urge to chuckle at Alaric's unhappy expression.

'I shouldn't care, Domina, but I think I will break his fucking legs if I catch him chasing after you.'

His words were harsh, but Alaric's presence soothed a deep ache in my soul, and even though I still felt guilty, holding his hand allowed me to smile again.

'I'm so glad you're back. No one can replace you, Ari, no matter how hard they try,' I said, stroking his face and pulling him towards the camp. 'Come, I want to see Orm's face when he sees you.'

As we strolled back to camp, I cast one last look at the ash by the riverbank.

Thank you, Katja. Thank you so much. Take good care of her, Arachne.

Alaric's appearance right after I had said my goodbye felt like her blessing, and if I knew my Katja, she would already be pulling Arachne's strings to help us.

ᛉᚲᚾᚠᛟ

The camp was quiet as we walked through the sea of tents. A few curious glances turned our way, their frowns deepening when they saw me walking arm in arm with a strange man. Their disapproval only stoked my rebellious streak, so I leaned closer to Alaric, a playful smirk tugging at my lips. For a moment, I wondered if anyone would be bold enough to defend my virtue, but it seemed the soldiers knew when to keep their heads low and their mouths shut.

As we neared Ormond's tent, I stopped and turned to Alaric. 'Let me go in first. I'll soften him up for this sweet little surprise,' I said with a wink.

Alaric nodded, positioning himself near the entrance.

I stepped inside and sauntered over to the cushions where my warrior sat sharpening his blade. His expression didn't change, nor did his tone when he spoke.

'I'm glad you're back. Do you need anything?'

The flatness of his voice caught me off guard, pulling a frown to my face.

'No. How was the patrol? Did something happen? I'm not drunk—I was just busy,' I blurted out, wondering what had prompted his strange mood.

Orm set his sword aside, standing up with a deliberate calmness that sent a shiver down my spine.

'I know you were busy. The soldiers saw you kissing a fae next to a burning wagon. Why, Annika? You promised there would be no one else besides Ari and me. Who is it? Valaram?'

The golden ring of fire flared in his eyes, betraying his jealousy, and I suddenly realised how far his thoughts had spiralled. The absurdity of it struck me, and I struggled to suppress a laugh, which only deepened his scowl.

'Does my pain amuse you?' he asked. 'Who is it, Ani?'

I simply raised an eyebrow. 'And if I told you? Would you kill him? Is that why you've been sharpening your sword?'

'No, Annika. If any man forced or coerced you, that would be different. His life wouldn't be worth the mud under my boot. But we both know you are too strong to be forced and too smart to be coerced, so it was your choice, and I have to accept it. So, who is the lucky bastard I'll have to call brother from now on? Tell me—before I go sleep with my dragon.'

Ormond was furious, and as much as his jealousy pleased the vixen in me, I couldn't continue with him hurting like this.

'Come in, my mysterious fae. The commander wishes to see you,' I called, my voice loud enough to carry beyond the tent.

'You brought him to *my* tent?' Orm growled, rearing back like an enraged bear as the entrance flap opened. His eyes narrowed when Alaric, still hooded, stepped inside with unhurried grace.

417

'I hope you are satisfied with our lady's choice,' Ari said smoothly, pulling back his hood to reveal his face. 'Because I intend to stay.'

Ormond stepped back, grasping the edge of the table.

'Fuck me.'

'If you wish,' Alaric replied with a wry grin. 'But maybe tomorrow. I'm exhausted, and Annika looks like she could use some sleep.'

Orm crossed the space in three long strides, pulling him into a rough embrace before kissing him with a passion that made me wonder whether it was me that should sleep with Vahin tonight.

As I was pondering my sleeping arrangements, Ormond took Alaric's chin, tilting his face to the light before he growled, 'How did you manage to escape? Fuck! I'll kill the bastard that did this to you.'

My moan of embarrassment made him look over as I sank heavily onto the pillows, horrified by Alaric's black eye.

'I don't think you will, although I admit our wicked woman has good aim,' Ari said with a grin. 'As for the rest, I climbed my way out of an oubliette and escaped via a very unpleasant sewer. That's why it took me so long.'

Orm looked between Alaric and me, shaking his head as I tried to disappear within the cushions. 'Let me sum this up. You, by some miracle, escaped the Lich King's prison almost without a scratch only to . . .' He closed his eyes and inhaled slowly. 'Annika, is this some strange foreplay between the two of you? Also . . . why his face?'

'I can try to heal it,' I said, offended by his tone.

Alaric laughed, extracting himself from Orm's arms to untie his cloak.

'Leave healing to me, Domina,' he said, looking around the tent. 'But right now, more than healing, I need rest. I haven't slept much since escaping Katrass. It was an arduous journey, and fighting golems was not fun. Still, here I am, smelling like rotten fish but safe, so if I could . . .?'

Ormond nodded, pointing to a bucket of water in the corner. 'Wash off the worst of it. The smell is pretty awful. We'll get you a bath tomorrow after training.'

I wrapped my arms around my knees, curling up in the nest I'd created, observing their interaction. While I'd lashed out like a madwoman at seeing Ari, Orm took it in stride and immediately started organising things.

I couldn't help but smile sheepishly as they both approached me. Orm carried a few blankets, effortlessly transforming the simple space into a cozy bed. He settled in first, leaning back against the pillows and patting his chest in invitation.

Without hesitation, I lay my head against him, feeling the steady rhythm of his heartbeat. Then he reached for Alaric, who was still damp from his ablutions, pulling him close until Ari nestled against his other side, his grin mischievous as his eyes met mine.

I chuckled, reaching across Orm until my fingers entwined with Alaric's. My Ursus let out a deep breath, his chest rising and falling beneath my cheek before he exhaled slowly. His arms tightened around us both, and I felt a gentle tremor run through his body—a release of tension he'd been holding too long, and I heard him whisper.

'Fucking *finally*.'

CHAPTER 37

ANNIKA

K atrass was exquisite. The winter chill had stolen the last leaves from the trees, and the ground glittered with frost. The white walls of the Moroi city sparkled as the light of the rising sun illuminated the artistic beauty of the buildings. The scene would've been idyllic if not for the undead swaying on the city walls. I was stunned, wishing I could have seen the city when it was a bustling trading port, thriving from its inhabitants' magic and finesse.

'Nothing inspires a woman more than the stench of rotten flesh,' I commented when a gust of wind gifted us the unmistakably sweet odour of decay.

'Those are sentinels. A set of eyes in every corner. What truly worries me is that I can't see any golems or corrupted Moroi,' Valaram said, approaching me.

He looked good in his armour and rode his horse with the confidence of an experienced rider. Noticing my inspection, he inclined his head. 'Good to see you smiling again, lara'mei. After the battle, I was afraid we had lost your radiance forever.'

I nodded, acknowledging his words, more concerned with what Alaric was doing.

My fae manoeuvred his horse to block Valaram, glaring at the dark fae ambassador.

'The Moroi won't attack during the day, and the golems were gathered around the palace. What can we do for you, my lord?' he asked, and I felt we were heading into an all-too-familiar confrontation.

I suspected that if not for me, those two could be friends, but Valaram's persistence in courting me upset Alaric, who considered it a personal offence.

I enjoyed the older fae's company when he wasn't flirting. During our campaign, he had frequently found the time to see me, always under the pretence of some military matter, but different topics of discussion would soon emerge. He was charming, and I enjoyed our conversations, but I would happily distance myself from him for Alaric's peace of mind. However, that had proven to be impossible.

Talena had entrusted her army to her brother, heading back to Care'etavos herself. As much as I welcomed her departure, Valaram was now in charge of our dark fae members and even more inclined to seek my company.

'Prickly as ever, Master Shen'ra. I came to enjoy Annika's company and offer to guard her during the upcoming offensive.'

'Guard her? Did you sleep through the Rift battle?' Alaric asked incredulously. 'Besides, Annika already has plans for the siege of Katrass, and she has three Anchors to guard her.'

'At least I was there,' Valaram answered, circling Ari until he was beside me, so close that his leg brushed against mine. 'Tell me your plans, my lady. What kind of earth-shattering experience should we prepare ourselves for?'

'I'll do what I'm told. Reynard is the strategist. I'll just destroy whatever he tells me to,' I said dismissively, annoyed by his attitude. 'Shouldn't you be with your men, my lord? Or at least discussing their positions with the king?'

'Oh, you do much more than that,' Valaram said with a smirk. 'Will you do me a favour? You called me Val once. I liked it. We are already allies. Maybe it is time to drop the formalities for good?'

Alaric's horse danced as my lover tightened the reins, once again getting between us. 'Valaram, your presence here is not welcome.'

The menace in his voice and the hand that reached for a dagger made me snap.

'Will you both stop? Save these games for after the war,' I scolded, and both fae instantly drifted apart.

'My apologies, sweet lady,' Valaram said. 'It is a shame your mate's insecurities prevent me from helping.'

'My insecurities? You're crossing the line, Ambassador. Someone might even speculate that you're affected by tal maladie,' Alaric quipped in response.

Valaram snarled, showing the tips of his sharp fangs.

'Oh, for fuck's sake,' I muttered, urging my horse to move away.

Reynard had positioned himself on top of a small hill, and as I approached, I could see the entire city sprawled out in front of us. Our army was arranged and ready to attack.

Orm issued his last few orders to Tomma while Reynard sketched out a crude map, marking the position of his units next to the gates. Both men looked at me when I halted my horse so abruptly that the stallion reared back on his hind legs.

'What's happened, Nivale?' Orm asked, eyeing me with a frown.

'Ari and Valaram are bickering again,' I said with a deep sigh.

Reynard's mouth twitched. 'If not for my brother, I would try to persuade you to give our lovestruck ambassador a chance. It would be a perfect alliance for Dagome.'

'Any more suggestions like that, and I'll start considering regicide,' Orm said casually before taking my hand. 'If you want to fly with me, you are always welcome. Vahin would be happy even if we simply patrol the area.'

In yesterday's meeting, we'd agreed that the dragons should patrol the sky, as their effectiveness on the ground would be seriously reduced, possibly even causing problems for our own army.

'No, I need to join the mages,' I said. 'They may need a boost to break through those walls. I'm trying to keep myself from summoning total destruction, and I thought seeing you would help.'

Movement in the city's heart caught my attention. The undead had stopped swaying, as if listening to a command, before every last one turned their heads and looked directly at us. A wave of power passed through me, and I heard the uproar from the mages as it hit them, too.

The brilliant blue sky darkened. Clouds, barely visible on the horizon, rushed towards the city as if pulled in by a powerful spell. Soon, they obscured the sun, shrouding the world in darkness. Ormond looked at me as if hoping for an explanation, but I shook my head.

'I don't know. He may be making it dark to be able to use the Moroi?' I offered, unsure what Cahyon was doing but knowing it took an immense amount of aether to influence the weather. If he *was* the one doing it, then we'd be facing a terrifying ordeal.

Valaram and Alaric appeared by my side, weaving complex shielding spells together as if they hadn't just been at each other's throats. Both men stared expectantly at the city gates. My thoughts were racing, and as if in answer, a dark shape rose from inside the city.

Massive, leathery wings stretched out, overshadowing half of our army as the monstrous beast ascended. Its twisted, reptilian body glistened with an oily glow, turning the darkening sky a sickening, bruised violet. As I stared, eyes riveted to its horrifying form, the monster's three heads turned in our direction.

The Żmij.[1] An eldritch beast, a devourer. They could be bribed to guard a city, but if their price wasn't met, the Żmij would turn on its master and consume everything it was contracted to protect. I didn't want to think what, or rather, who, the Lich King had sacrificed to call it into service.

'That arrogant fool opened a portal to the Void,' Valaram gasped, exchanging horrified looks with Alaric. My breath hitched.

Could he really be that stupid?

But the proof of Cahyon's arrogance was circling above us. Żmij consumed magic, and his skin was so thick that most weapons couldn't harm him. At least, that's what the legends said, but those stories were so old they had long ago been dismissed as myths.

As I looked up at the sky, a small figure stumbled from the gates, heading in our direction. At Reynard's gesture, a rider rushed forward, throwing them over their horse before returning to us.

'Lara?'

I heard the shock in Alaric's voice as I surveyed the dirty, bloody heap that fell onto the grass before us. The poor woman's eyes were full of tears when she spoke.

'That monster sent me here with a message. The portal is open and will stay open until the conduit mage comes—*alone*—to close it. If she refuses, he will unleash the old gods on the world,' she sobbed before collapsing to the ground. 'He killed them, my people. He cut their

---

1. **Żmij** /pron: **z-** as in English:vi*si*on -**me-j**/ — a powerful demigod associated with water and marshlands. Manifesting as a three-headed viper with immense wings, a żmij can be summoned from the Void between worlds through the offering of a woman as tribute. Once bound by a pact, a żmij will defend a city until its own demise, after which it is reborn in the void, awaiting the next call.

throats and bled them all to open the Void. It's not only the Żmij . . . more are coming.'

'Fuck.' Reynard's menacing snarl cut through the sounds of despair before he looked at Ormond. 'What now, how do we fight . . . this?'

'With dragons . . . Dragon fire cannot penetrate a żmij's skin, but if they can rip through that protection with teeth and claw, then we can burn that monster from the sky,' Valaram replied, swallowing hard before turning to me. 'But as dangerous as it is, the Żmij is nothing compared to other horrors from the Void. Annika . . . You have to go.'

'No!' Ormond and Alaric said in unison, but I didn't look at them.

'I'm human. I can't manipulate portal magic,' I said, but my mind was already working on an idea.

'No,' Valaram said, 'but I can. You can insist on bringing a guardian. I'm not your Anchor, so he may not object. As long as I'm near the portal, I can close it.'

'Hrae! That's ridiculous,' Alaric said. 'Stay here, Ani. I'll return through the tunnel I escaped through and close the damn portal.'

'Even if you manage to get back into the palace, do you really think Cahyon would let you go anywhere near his grand spell?' I asked, shaking my head. 'No, first we need to know where the portal is. I'll take Valaram. If we go openly, trumpets blaring, we can create a big enough distraction for you to sneak in. Use the tracking spell and I will be where the portal is. That way, one of you will be able to close the it, and I'll do my best to keep that bastard occupied without getting myself killed.'

I moved my horse closer to Orm and placed a hand on his cheek. 'Please be careful dealing with the żmij, my love. Focus only on that while Ari and I ensure nothing else crawls out from this arsehole's spell.'

Orm grasped my hand, kissed it, and then pressed it to his chest right above his heart. 'I will see you before nightfall. Just promise me you won't take any risks that aren't absolutely necessary.'

'I'll try,' I answered with a smile, hearing a deafening roar as Vahin plummeted to the earth. I looked at my dragon, knowing he would be fighting the eldritch beast, and my heart tightened.

'Come, Ambassador. I hope you haven't forgotten how to charm self-absorbed tyrants,' I said to Valaram before smiling at Alaric. 'See you inside, my love.'

I pressed my heels against my horse's sides, and the chestnut stallion shot forward. There was no time to waste. The longer a gate to the Void stood open, the more horrors could pass through, and I really wanted to survive this battle.

'*I will come for you, Little Flame. Even if I have to tear down the sun, I will come for you.*'

Vahin's dark promise echoed in my mind long after my dragon roared his challenge and shot into the sky.

I felt the stares of every undead creature as we approached the gates. Valaram lowered his head, hiding his identity in the shadow of his hood, but I sat proudly on my horse.

'I'm waiting!' I shouted as we stood before the ornate iron gates, and a moment later, a postern opened, seemingly by itself. No one questioned Valaram's presence as we entered, though several Moroi fixed their bloodshot eyes on him, their tongues sliding across their lips in a gesture both feral and unnerving.

'Bloodthirsty bastards,' I mumbled under my breath. Realising my slip, I quickly covered it with an arrogant sneer.

One Moroi stepped forward with a menacing growl, his movements tense as he gestured for us to follow. I nudged my horse forward, feigning indifference, while carefully observing his companions from the corner of my eye.

I couldn't afford to show weakness. Whatever control Cahyon had over them seemed tenuous, and the slightest sign of fear could snap it. Drawing inspiration from Empress Talena herself, I tilted my chin up and regarded every monstrous being we passed with cold disdain, my eyes sweeping over horrors I couldn't even name.

There were some I recognised from my university studies, like the lamias, with their snake-like bodies and venomous bites, and the monstrous psoglav,[2] a dog-like creature whose iron jaw was able to bite through granite.

My heart sank. The lack of resistance and the ease of our journey to Katrass finally made sense. The Lich King hadn't bothered creating more undead monsters—he'd just invited these creatures instead, leashing them like dogs, ready to hunt.

'Val, whatever happens, you must close the portal,' I whispered, touching his shoulder. I exhaled slowly, desperate to hide the tremor that shook my body. I was grateful he'd come with me. Facing the Lich King alone would have been much more daunting.

'I'll do my best, lara'mei,' he said, covering my hand with his own. We passed under a decorated portcullis only to enter a courtyard full of golems—silent sentinels—guarding the palace. I wondered if Cahyon was worried his fearsome guests would turn against him.

---

2. **Psoglav (s.)/psoglavs (pl.)** — a grotesque demon with a human torso, the legs of a horse, and the head of a dog adorned with iron teeth and a single glaring eye in the centre of its forehead. Dwelling in shadowy caves or a perpetually dark land brimming with gemstones but devoid of sunlight, psoglavs are infamous for their insatiable hunger for human flesh, favouring the taste of fresh corpses.

We passed the army of constructs, arriving at another closed door. I felt something wet on my cheek and raised my face to the sky. A heavy dark cloud loomed overhead, but the cold moisture on my cheek wasn't rain.

It was snowing.

I had arrived at Katrass as the first snow dusted the palace's courtyard, just as the Lich King had requested.

'Bloody fate,' I muttered, annoyed.

'Welcome to my home, Nivale. Though if I recall correctly, I *explicitly* told you to come alone.'

The voice drew my attention sharply, my head snapping as I turned to see a middle-aged man standing in the doorway. He looked so much like Alaric that I nearly scolded him for greeting me in the open. Thankfully, I noticed how much older he was before the words left my mouth.

'Must've misheard that part,' I said lightly, dismounting my horse with deliberate grace. 'After all, what lady wouldn't bring her servant along?'

A second voice, more feminine and wickedly sharp, rang out from the dark interior. 'Watch your tone, mage.'

I peered into the darkness and noticed the female hiding in the shadows. 'Or what, Rowena?'

I'd guessed right, judging by her annoyed sniff.

The impossibly beautiful woman walked into the light, tossing back her hair. I could see the family resemblance, but the differences were also glaringly obvious. Alaric, with his cupid bow lips and sarcastic smile, looked like sin personified; Rowena looked like sweet innocence whose touch could ease any sorrow.

'Or I will skin you alive and throw you to the Void,' she responded. 'You have your uses, mage, but don't overestimate your value.'

The cruel glint in her eye told me she would thoroughly enjoy the experience, but I wasn't here to talk to Cahyon's minions.

'You and your threats. Pathetic, just like your father was.' I waved my hand dismissively at Rowena and rolled my eyes at the Lich King. 'How do you tolerate her? Well, I suppose you were made for each other. Anyway, I've arrived—so call off the żmij.'

Cahyon tilted his head, his expression unreadable as his piercing stare pinned me in place. Despite myself, I flinched under his assessing gaze. Then, with a sharp snap of his fingers, he broke the silence.

'Seize them.'

Valaram reacted instantly, unsheathing a long dagger while murmuring the incantation for a shield spell. Before the spell fully took form, the heavy thud of approaching golems filled the air. I didn't fight. I let one of the constructs grab me and didn't resist when he pulled me towards his master.

'Annika! What are you doing?' Valaram shouted as he fought, and I wished I could tell him to cease fighting and follow my example.

'Take me to the portal,' I said calmly. 'If you don't want me to fight, take me there, or I will ensure your pretty palace becomes ash, and you along with it.'

'Try it, and I'll kill your fae,' Cahyon answered with a cruel smile.

I shrugged. 'He's not my fae. Alaric died trying to rescue this bitch,' I lied, pointing at Rowena. 'Do you think I'd be here otherwise?'

A cloud of dust blasted past, making me stumble. Valaram was demolishing golems with the skill of a seasoned battle mage. I admired his choice of spells. He didn't attack directly with magic, instead using elemental spells to smash physical objects over the golems' heads.

'Fine, Nivale. I'll take you to the portal,' the Lich King said, gesturing to Rowena. 'Deal with this but keep him alive for now.'

She huffed angrily in response, but I noticed darkness seeping from her fingers, its tendrils reaching for Valaram. The last thing I saw before my captor carried me away was the fae ambassador on his knees, blood flowing from his nose and ears as he stared at Rowena with glassy, unfocused eyes.

I'll come back for you, Val. I just need to know where the portal is.

I hung limply over the golem's shoulder as we entered a large chamber. Far away, the distant sound of clashing swords, human screams, and monsters' roars rose and fell like a wave.

'*Vahin?*' I asked, but didn't get a reply. All I could sense was an echo of pain through our bond. The sky was ablaze, large, winged shadows illuminating the clouds with devastating bursts of fire high above the palace.

We stopped, and I was dumped unceremoniously in front of a frame constructed from bone and twisted rose vines. Elaborate runes glistened red over each bone.

As I watched, darkness formed within the structure, and a clawed foot passed through it, testing the ground. I gasped in shock when the rest of the psoglav proceeded. The monster fully emerged only to whine, clawing at its throat, and I noticed a red cord wrapped around its neck, digging into its fur.

'Join the others,' Cahyon ordered. The monster submitted, stalking into a dark corridor. The Lich King turned towards me in anticipation, as if he was expecting me to be impressed.

When I said nothing, his expression became one of annoyance before he said, 'You see, Annika? It takes little effort to call the monsters but much more to control them. But as with my golems, I found a way.'

'Good for you. Do you expect me to clap and cheer? Now, close it before you destroy the rest of the continent. Or maybe that was your plan from the start?' I replied with a sneer.

Cahyon grasped my throat, squeezing hard, but I stood firm, smirking at his attempt to intimidate me.

'I planned to take Dagome without needing a war,' he said. 'To finally rule a living kingdom. I asked you to come. All you had to do was join me in Katrass and let me Anchor you, and this war would have never happened.'

He brushed my unruly hair from my face with his free hand as he continued, 'I admit I underestimated you, but I'm older and much more cunning than you could ever hope to be. I can feel your pulse flutter under my touch. I can see the way your eyes dart away to see if Valaram has freed himself from Rowenna's snare.' He laughed, squeezing my throat harder. 'Yes, I know who he is. You are afraid, little mage, and I admit, I like it.'

The portal shimmered, a wave of unstable magic flooding the courtyard. I felt its wrongness, but Cahyon didn't seem to notice. It appeared he didn't know how dangerous his construct had become—or maybe he just didn't care.

'You're so proud of being older. I guess it was fun living as a bag of bones?' I asked, feeling the closeness of my Anchor in my soul. Alaric had made it here safely.

The slap that followed my words snapped my head backwards, the hot pain overwhelming my senses. 'You will love this "bag of bones" when I Anchor you,' he smirked.

I rolled my eyes. 'As if . . . You will never get anything from me by choice. I will never accept you.'

'You will, darling. You will,' he said confidently. 'My dear Rowena will take care of your resistance. She's become quite skilful in manipulating minds after practising for so long on Alaric.'

Just fucking perfect. I thought I'd planned this encounter from every angle, but as ready as I was to face the Lich King, I didn't realise he had a psychotic dreamwalker with the ability to control minds on such a scale.

As if summoned by my thinking of her, Rowena appeared, dragging Valaram by the scruff of the neck.

Valaram's eyes were still glassy, but I caught the quirk of his lips when he saw me looking, and my jaw tightened. The proud fae mage—reduced to a slave by a cheap mind trick. Or maybe not so cheap.

Sweat beaded Rowena's forehead, and even if I knew little of psychic spells, it was clear she was struggling to maintain control.

I felt a pull in my core. A crisp, refreshing caress as sharp as my fae. My time playing the docile, powerless mage was ending. I reached for the aether just as Valaram jerked in Rowenna's grasp, and I froze when I saw her knife against his neck.

'Continue fighting me, and you will die. Submit, and I may let you live,' she said, drawing a thin line that barely cut the skin, but the pain brought more clarity to Valaram's gaze.

'The only woman I would submit to will make a whistle of your bones,' he rasped, looking at me.

A roar shattered the sky, and both Vahin and the Żmij clashed above our heads, their bodies contorting in savage battle. Suddenly, something fell from the dragon's back, plummeting towards a tower's high roof and my heart sank. If Ormond had jumped off the saddle, the situation must have been dire. Was that why Vahin had blocked his feelings?

The portal shimmered again, and a basilisk[3] rolled out. The lizard's body thrashed on cobblestones, the creature spraying a liquid that burned through the stone floor, and I instantly dropped my gaze.

The former chancellor rushed in, skidding to a halt in front of the beast. 'My lord, the Dagome army is in the city. We weren't able to hold them back.' The basilisk hissed, and the entire power of its stare fell on the chancellor's face.

'Kill it!' Cahyon ordered a golem as he pointed to the beast, but it was too late for Dagome's former advisor. His face paled, mouth opening in one final cry as he clutched his chest and dropped like a felled tree.

Alaric took advantage of the moment to step from the shadows and cast a spell aimed at the portal, rattling the bones.

'What? She said you'd died!' Cahyon screamed, oily death magic forming in his palm.

Alaric didn't budge. The bones rattled louder as he chanted, the arch slowly crumbling. With each loose bone and vanishing sigil, uncontrolled aether lashed out, turning the air into a blizzard of ash and debris.

'Why can't you just die?!' Rowena's scream fused with the sound of the splitting portal. She had her eyes on Alaric while the blade in her hand glided effortlessly across Valaram's throat.

'No!' I shouted, slamming my hand on Cahyon's chest and pushing him away from me, but I wasn't close enough to Rowena to stop her. Red blood sprayed across the floor as pulsing black energy spread from the Lich King's hands, shooting towards Alaric. My fae's eyes widened, and he looked at me with bitter regret but didn't stop his spell.

---

3. **Basilisk** — a beast with a serpent-like body, fatal venom, and a deadly stare.

As I created an impromptu shield to counteract Cahyon's spell, the portal crumbled and fell. Its magic smashed into me, a perfect maelstrom of destruction. Time stopped, wreckage and blood suspended in the air as crimson aether surrounded me.

'Old Martha says hello.' I sneered, staring at Cahyon's shocked expression as I let portal's power flew through me and unleashed the inferno.

CHAPTER 38

ORMOND

*F*uck, *that hurts.*

I bounced off the roof like a rag doll, feeling the impact in every inch of my body. My ribs cracked as I hit something else, trying to slow my descent, but I used it to twist around and grab whatever I'd collided with.

'Shit!'

My legs whipped around while I clamped my hands onto the cold object. It took a moment to focus, my arms straining, until I realised what I was holding onto. I was face-to-face with a grinning gargoyle, my life depending on the strength of its stone fangs.

Jumping off Vahin's back mid-flight was one of the stupidest things I'd ever done, but it was necessary. My dragon was fighting the Żmij with unyielding ferocity, and I realised I was more of a burden than a help. He'd received too many injuries protecting me from his enemy's venom-laden fangs, so I had to give him the chance to fly freely without worrying for my safety.

This entire battle had been a clusterfuck of epic proportions from the very start. Whatever plans we'd made were scrapped the moment Annika entered the city. I was riding Vahin, watching as she disappeared behind the gates, when the Żmij attacked, the rest of the monsters following suit. Reynard had organised the ground forces, but all

I could do was draw a sword and direct my riders to where I saw an opportunity.

My fight never came, and now I was dangling from the roof, watching as Cahyon led Annika towards the strange-looking portal.

After several attempts, I contorted my battered body enough to catch the edge of the highest window with one boot, and then, praying to All-Father, I threw myself forward, barrelling into the light frame and crystalline glass with all my strength.

After yet another round of cursing that would make a pirate wince, I opened my eyes to look around. I was in a dusty attic room full of bird nests that stank of mould bad enough to make me gag.

'Kill it!' The voice from below sent my heart into a painful stutter, and for a split second, I considered jumping down to shield Annika. Then I realised the man said *it*, not *her*, and that even with my heavy build, I wouldn't survive falling from such a height.

Instead, I ran.

Despite the intricate carvings that adorned its surface, the tower's design was simple and utilitarian. Narrow at the summit, it widened as I descended the spiralling staircase, leading to rooms on the lower levels. I'd been lucky with my landing because the moment I opened the door, I found myself face-to-face with a monster.

The wild magic in my blood hummed with approval as I gave it free rein. I didn't even need my sword, jamming my fingers into the monster's eyes before smashing its head against the wall until it collapsed to the floor, dead.

'Is that all you've got?' I roared, charging down the staircase.

The beast within me revelled in the carnage. Each step I took left a trail of blood. Monsters, corrupted Moroi—it didn't matter. They all fell under my fury, every one of them a barrier between me and the woman I loved. The woman I needed to reach before that undead bastard could harm her.

By the time I reached the tower's base, my armour dripped with ichor and gore. I barely paused to wipe the mess from my face before bursting into the chamber. The sudden brightness blinded me, but I pressed forward.

And I still arrived too late.

The air thrummed with magic, heavy and volatile. It stung my skin like icy needles, as though I'd plunged into a freezing mountain stream. Annika's power roared around the room, so potent it locked me in place. I fought against its snares, my skin cracking with frost the harder I struggled.

Then Ani said something to the Lich King, her voice sharp and defiant, just before blue fire shot from her hands, engulfing him in a raging inferno. My breath hitched as Cahyon, his eyes filled with darkness, stepped forward.

The flames recoiled from his body, leaving him untouched. He laughed—a deep, mocking sound—and with a flick of his wrist, his magic surged towards Annika. Oily black tendrils wrapped around her, searing her skin and leaving red, angry welts wherever they touched.

My woman screamed in rage, her magic answering her fury. The torrent of blue fire intensified, punching through Cahyon's dark shield. The ground trembled beneath me, the clash of their immense power shaking the very foundation of the world.

The Lich King, with the strength of the land at his command, met Annika's unyielding might—she, a conduit capable of limitless spells, wielding raw elemental force. Black flames writhed against blue fire, and for a moment, time itself seemed to hold its breath.

But Annika wasn't alone.

A faint, otherworldly presence emerged behind her. The air shimmered as though the Veil had thinned, revealing nineteen spectral women. Their forms were indistinct, but their power was undeniable, a force that bolstered Annika's own. Her blue flames burned brighter, their light searing through the choking black tendrils.

I didn't fully understand what was happening, but when Cahyon staggered back, his face twisted in disbelief, I roared in triumph. He stared at Annika as if seeing her for the first time, his expression contorting with fear. Her icy fury burned through his defences, and for the first time, the Lich King hesitated.

'Impossible . . .' he mouthed as he was forced another step back, wailing as his gaze fixed on something behind Annika. '*Rowena!*'

Following his line of sight, I surged forward, desperate to intervene, but ice and ash clung to me, slowing my movements. I watched in horror as Rowena raised a beautifully ornate dagger and sank it into Ani's back.

My Nivale responded instantly, whipping her arm towards Alaric's sister. A blast of magic flung Rowena against the wall with a sickening thud. It was an effective counterstrike, but it cost Annika dearly. The interruption broke her focus, and Cahyon seized the opportunity.

His black magic surged forward, engulfing her.

'*No!*' My scream mixed with a dragon's roar and Ari's anguished cry.

Annika choked, blood pouring from her lips as she fell to her knees. One of the ghostly figures standing behind her moved suddenly, its ephemeral form darting between Annika and the oncoming attack.

The spirit took the brunt of the death magic, its shape solidifying momentarily. A familiar scent of herbal remedies filled the air as I saw Katja protect my treasure one last time. Annika's shock reverberated through our bond, but with a guttural cry, she pushed herself to her feet.

Time stood still. My breath hung in the air, frozen mist suspended mid-motion as Annika drew on the aether with an intensity that was both terrifying and awe-inspiring.

It felt as though the Void had opened beneath our feet, draining the life from everything around it. I was sure we were dying. Darkness crept at the edges of my vision before, just as suddenly, it all stopped.

The world shifted, and Ani's voice, low and cold, whispered a spell that resonated with finality.

'*Tae niti tue etera mago.*[1] The thread of your existence will end here.'

Pain shot through me when a bolt of aether shot from her hand, brilliant as the sun and icy as a winter storm. It struck Cahyon square in the chest, and he screamed, thrashing in agony, but Annika was relentless. The black tendrils of his magic shrunk and vanished under her assault while the Lich King howled in fury, clawing his chest.

'You can't do it. My magic . . . you fucking witch!' he screamed before his voice pitched when crimson dragon fire replaced blue flames.

His body burned like a torch, but Ani didn't stop. The more blood she lost, the more the fire intensified, and I stared in utter shock at how she destroyed Cahyon's magic, leaving nothing but a burning effigy of the immortal lich.

The ash thinned, and the storm subsided, ice and snow falling lifelessly to the ground. Freed from the magic that had held us all in place, I moved with desperate speed, but once again, I was too late.

My Nivale crumpled to the floor, gasping for breath.

---

1. *I unbound the essence of your power.*

I reached her just as she looked up at me, her tear-streaked face illuminated by the dying embers of her power. Blood foamed at her lips as she mouthed, '*I love you.*'

'Annika! No . . . gods, no! Dark Mother, save her!' Alaric's voice broke as he rushed to her side.

Cahyon's burning husk writhed in Ani's flames as I kicked him far away. 'I bet you regret your immortality now,' I growled before turning back to Alaric, who was cradling my Nivale against his chest. His hands trembled as he pulled the dagger from her back. I dropped to my knees beside her, laying my hand on his as his green, healing magic enveloped them both.

'Orm, I need to focus . . . I need to . . . Hrae! She's gone so far . . .' he whispered frantically, and I pulled away, barely breathing, desperate not to disturb the spell he was casting.

Fight my love, fight for me, fight for us.

I repeated it like a mantra, my world narrowing to those three words and her face where the ash mixed with the tears flowing down her cheeks.

Movement behind me caught me off guard and I twisted just in time to intercept Rowena, her dagger aimed for my throat. The blade grazed my shoulder, but I caught her wrist and twisted it until it snapped. I'd forgotten about Ari's sister, but there she stood, all sanity gone from her pale blue eyes. With a snarling curse, I squeezed harder. I wanted to punish her, to crush the hand that wielded the knife, but Annika came first.

As I prepared to send Rowena after her burning master, she screamed, and my vision blurred. Thoughts not my own invaded my mind, insidious whispers telling me that my mate was dead and urging me to join her beyond the Veil.

My consciousness was thrust from my body, and I watched in disbelief as my hand grabbed her dagger, turning the blade towards my heart. I knew it was wrong, but the compulsion was too hard to resist.

The tip of the blade passed through my armour like butter, scoring my flesh and drawing blood. With a snap, everything stopped, and Rowena sank to her knees, whimpering in pain. A net, woven from smoke, had wrapped around her body, its coils tightening with each breath she took, slowly suffocating her.

Valaram's rattling laugh echoed in the courtyard. I glanced at the fae, shocked at his appearance. He held his bloody throat, the same green healing energy pulsing around his hand, while the other grasped the smoky tendril wrapped around Rowena. I was in awe; I had never heard of a mage who could wield two different kinds of magic simultaneously.

'Lara'mei, I loved you last, but I'll follow you first,' he wheezed, more blood seeping between his fingers.

I frowned, my gaze locking on Alaric, whose eyes swirled with crimson. He whispered an invocation, his hands pressing against Ani's chest, but the desperation in his voice revealed his thoughts.

'I can't . . . I can't heal her,' he muttered, his voice thick with grief. 'The death spell that bastard used—it's unlike anything I've seen before. It's limitless. The wound . . . Her spirit isn't drifting behind the Veil, it's hurtling through the Void like a fallen star. I can't stop her or even call her back . . . I tried to close the Veil, but . . . The one time I truly need my necromancy, and I'm failing.'

With a quick, urgent motion, I pulled Ani from his embrace. The gaping wound in her chest had vanished under Alaric's healing touch, but her chest remained still, an ominous silence hanging in the air. I pressed my lips to hers, forcing air into her lungs in the hope that she would respond, that maybe, just maybe, she needed a breath of life to bring her back.

'Breath for me, Nivale. Please, my beloved. I'm lost without you,' I whispered desperately, trying to breathe for her, but my efforts were in vain.

Above us, the two titans collided, their roars shaking the heavens. Vahin's cry split the sky, and lightning rained down, striking the palace walls with enough force to turn rock to ash.

The world trembled as the storm tore the air apart, lightning and thunder clashing in a vicious dance. The dying convulsions of the Żmij sent shockwaves through the earth, and fire and molten rock surrounded us. The very skies seemed to scream in agony.

I cradled Annika's lifeless form, wrapping my cloak around her, as if the simple act of protecting her could somehow tether her to this world.

'I will never let you go,' I told her. 'How could I? You have my heart, my soul. I would give you my life if I could ... Annika, you are the strongest of us all. You can't just fucking die!' I shook her body, praying she would just open her eyes and scold me for waking her too abruptly. I would happily endure her harsh words if I could only hear her voice again.

Ari rose to his feet, his gaze locked on Cahyon, whose soul clung desperately to his charred body—an impotent spirit in a broken vessel, suspended between life and death.

'You took her from me.'

Alaric's voice was a low growl, thick with anger. 'I wanted to kill you ... just kill you. But now, I'll make you suffer for eternity.' His eyes burned with an intensity that sent a ripple of dread through the air.

'You will never die, Cahyon Abrasan,' he said. 'The gods themselves will pity your fate. The mountains will turn to dust, the oceans will dry up, but you—*you*—will remain here. Powerless, locked in unending torment, knowing that one woman was your downfall. And even that won't be enough for what you took from me!'

Alaric's skin glowed, his power surging outward. Cahyon's lifeless body was lifted off the ground, crashing violently into the walls of the palace. On impact, his chest split open as flames erupted from his still-beating heart.

But as the Lich King's heart began to fade, Alaric's power held it in place, encasing the organ in a shimmering, purple glass shield—preventing death from taking its due. Cahyon's decaying form twisted in anguish, his silent scream a grotesque mockery of life, but this time, it was not his body that burned—it was his very spirit.

Molten stone flowed like thick syrup, controlled by Alaric's will, until it encased Cahyon in a crystalline prison. Only then did my fae turn his attention to his sister.

Terror flashed across Rowena's face as Alaric approached, death dancing gleefully in his eyes. He leaned over her, trailing a finger over her cheek with chilling tenderness before shaking his head in disbelief.

'What are you?' he asked softly, his voice a rasp of disgust. 'What pit of nightmare spawned your hateful soul?'

He seized her throat with brutal force, the smoke net around her vanishing under his touch. From the corner of my eye, I saw Valaram slump to the floor, hand holding his bleeding throat, reaching towards Ani.

'I . . . He forced me. Ari, I didn't want this, but the Lich King . . . He made me suffer until I complied . . .' She shrieked when Alaric squeezed her throat tighter.

'Your lies won't work anymore,' he hissed, his voice empty. 'I'm dead inside, sister. You took everything from me and turned it to dust. My last wish is to see you dead before I follow my domina behind the Veil.'

Alaric pressed the dagger he'd pulled from Ani's back to Rowena's chest. Slowly, with deliberate precision, he drove the blade deeper, the sound of the metal scraping through her ribs a sickening melody. Rowena's screams were raw and agonizing, but I didn't look away. I drank in every moment of her pain as she thrashed until, with one last gasping sob, her body hung lifelessly in Alaric's grasp.

The courtyard was eerily quiet. The man I loved approached me, pain and loss finally cracking his emotionless façade. I glanced down at the dagger in his hand, his sister's blood still dripping from its blade.

'Help me, my love. I can't let her walk alone,' he said, his voice cracking as he passed the knife to me hilt first. I pulled away from him as if he'd offered me a poisonous snake.

'No!' I shouted. 'There must be another way.'

He shook his head. 'If there is, I don't know it. Such power is beyond me.'

The earth trembled with the heavy thump of Vahin's landing and I shielded my eyes from the blinding blue light that coated him. My dragon was a broken sight—bloodied and battered, with scales missing and one wing hanging flaccidly, bone jutting from his flesh. But despite the carnage, he was alive.

Vahin's eyes widened as they fell on Ani's lifeless form, and a sharp pain twisted in my chest. He took a tentative step towards her, but his legs buckled beneath him. 'Bring her to me! Now!'

Without hesitation, I did as he commanded, placing Ani's body into his gentle embrace. She looked almost as if she was sleeping, cradled by the dragon.

'What are you going to do?' I asked when he lowered his head, his muzzle touching her chest.

'A miracle.'

I stumbled back, nearly tripping over Alaric, who was kneeling beside us, whispering prayers in his native tongue. I mimicked his posture, drawing a sword and resting it across my thighs as I prayed to the All-Father, pleading for the life of the woman whose bravery put the heroes of old to shame.

'My troublemaker, this time I'm locking you in my lair,' Vahin murmured, his voice tender as his breath stirred Ani's hair. The blue glow of his scales deepened, radiating with intensity, while lines of lightning flickered across his wings. A tremor ran through his body, and from deep within his chest, a low rumble echoed, accompanied by a strange melody that seemed to resonate through my very soul.

Then, Vahin spoke. I didn't recognise the words, but there was a decisiveness to them. A chill ran down my spine as his head dipped lower, his breath hovering over Annika's lips. I blinked, stunned by the golden mist that swept across her heart-shaped face, a faint ethereal glow that twinkled in the stillness of the moment.

Annika no longer appeared as if death's embrace held her so tightly. My muscles were painfully tense, but I was afraid to move, afraid to lose this sliver of hope and disturb a ritual I didn't understand.

'Dark Mother, she gave you everything you asked for and more. Please do not cut the thread of her fate. It is not her time,' Alaric whispered in prayer.

'Come back, Little Flame,' Vahin's weary voice spoke again. His scales, just now vibrant with power, had dulled, the fire within him dimming with every agonised word. 'I know it hurts. I know it is easier to shy away, but we cannot lose you. Not yet.'

He continued, his voice growing softer, 'Come back to me, my light. My beautiful soul . . . Take my gift and live for me. I offer my immortality. For you, I give Veles everything. I'll stray from the endless path and no longer soar the edge of eternity.'

Though Ani remained still, a faint blush of life seemed to paint her cheeks. I wasn't sure if it was wishful thinking or Vahin's power, but something shifted in the air, and my heart dared to hope.

Alaric broke first. With a sudden, determined movement, he threw himself towards them, his hands drawing healing sigils in the air that burned with the force of his power before sinking into her body.

'I'll seal the Veil for you—consequences be damned,' he cried, his voice cracking with anguish. 'Hear these words, Domina. Hear the one who commands the dead. You'll not join their ranks. I forbid it!' He turned to me, desperation etched into every line of his face. 'Do something! She loves you the most.'

His words cut through me like a whip, urging me to act, but I had no magic like Vahin or mastery over the dead like Alaric. All I had was the heart of the beast she'd tamed and the words I swore never to say again.

I stripped off my armour and tore my shirt off, ignoring the raw pain of my injuries and the crackling magic coursing through my veins. Kneeling beside her, I cradled Ani's head to my chest, pressing my heartbeat against her ear.

'My beautiful Nivale,' I whispered, my voice trembling. 'Can you hear my heartbeat? I still remember that first night, when you were so delirious you ripped my shirt off just to feel it.' The memory burned in my mind, a blissful sweetness I could never forget. 'I remember everything—the confusion, the bliss, the certainty that my life would never be the same.'

I willed my heart to beat faster, pushing the blood through my veins with all my will until the roar of it drowned everything else. I lifted her gently, cradling her head in my hand as I pressed my lips to her ear to speak the words of her geas.

'*Iruḷai efsun khavarin*.² Come back, Nivale. I command it.'

A sharp gasp was the only warning I received before Annika's eyes snapped open, the golden ring around her irises identical to mine. She screamed, wrapping her arms around me as she buried her face in the crook of my neck.

'I don't want to die . . . I don't want to . . . I'm not ready. Please, let me go . . . Please, I can't leave them . . .' she cried out, frantically clawing at my chest. I was sure Ani didn't realise she was back with us.

'You're safe,' I whispered, stroking her hair gently as I tried to calm the tremors that wracked her body. 'Listen to me, my love. You're safe. No one will take you away.'

After several gasping sobs, she finally spoke again, her voice clearer this time. 'How?'

'It was a joint effort, but . . . Annika, I used your geas. Forgive me, please, but—'

'You used my geas?' she croaked.

I crushed her to my chest. 'You were dead. You were fucking dead. I want you to know the truth, but I would use it again and again if it brings you back to me. You can be mad, but I have no regrets,' I said vehemently, waiting for her punishing response.

She cupped my face in her hands, her gaze steady. 'Orm, fuck the geas. I'm back.' She threw her head back and laughed.

The gentleness of her touch and the unbridled joy in her laughter shattered my control. I buried my face in her hair, and sobs shook my body, releasing all the pent-up fear and despair.

'Yes, fuck the geas, Nivale. Fuck everything except us,' I replied, knowing I should release her and let Alaric and Vahin reunite with the

---

2. *Rule by your heart.*

451

divine creature we'd saved, but I couldn't make my arms loosen their grip.

'*Take your time, Orm. I can feel her deep in my soul. I can see her joy. That is enough for me. But your fae . . . he needs her, too.*'

Before Vahin had finished the thought, I reached out, grabbing Alaric's jacket and yanking him over. I couldn't let Ani go, not yet, but it didn't mean I would make him wait.

'If you ever dare to die on me again, I swear I will revive your corpse and turn you into a fucking lich,' he muttered, kissing her neck.

I rolled my eyes. 'Mind your manners, fae. We're surrounded by dead people,' I joked, the relief flooding me making my voice lighter than usual.

'So?' Alaric shrugged, grinning. 'I'm a necromancer. Dead people are the spice of my life.'

Annika slapped him playfully before turning towards Vahin, her gaze softening as she took in the sorry state of our dragon. She was still for a moment before she lunged at him, and I had no choice but to let her go.

She slammed into Vahin, wrapping her arms around his neck. 'I heard you. Your voice was calling to me in the darkness. The golden thread that tethered me . . . It was you, wasn't it? How did you do it?' she asked, placing a hand on her chest.

'I gave you a dragon's final gift,' he answered softly. 'Your life is now tied to mine. We will live, and live well, for a very long time. And when the time comes to cross the Veil, we will go together. I am no longer immortal, Little Flame. I have chosen my last rider.' He glanced at me with a wry smile. 'I'm afraid you were also caught in the spell, as it extends to anyone bound to the dragon who grants it.'

If I thought I couldn't have been happier, Vahin had proved me wrong. Now I knew I wouldn't be the first to say my goodbyes to those

I loved. Looking between Vahin and me, Annika must have sensed the dragon's contentment, for she didn't question him further. Instead, her gaze drifted to where Valaram sat, slumped against a wall, a faint smile still on his lips.

'He fought for you,' Alaric said quietly. 'He could have healed himself, but with his last breath, he thwarted my sister. I was wrong, Domina. He was worthy of you.'

Bowing his head, Ari's remorse was evident as he approached the fallen fae. 'Thank you for your help, my lord. May the Dark Mother be merciful to you, too.'

Annika joined him, but instead of kneeling, she moved to Valaram's side, her hand stroking his face, avoiding the half-healed cut on his throat.

'I'm sorry, Val,' she whispered, tears glistening in her eyes. 'You were my best friend during the most difficult time. I wish I could have loved you like you wanted me to, but my heart was already taken.' She kissed his forehead, her tears falling quietly as she whispered her goodbyes.

When the sounds of the fight disturbed the silence, Alaric helped Annika to her feet, and they joined me.

'We won,' Annika murmured, almost to herself. 'But at what cost?'

'I know, sweetheart, but maybe now we won't need to fight again,' I said, stepping in front of her just before Reynard and his men charged inside and skidded to a halt.

CHAPTER 39

ANNIKA

A month after the final battle

My mind wandered as I sat on the windowsill, watching the dragons soar and dip in a beautiful dance of joyous celebration. Agnes was plaiting my hair, but I hardly registered her brushing and gentle handling, sitting as still as a doll.

The day of the winter solstice dawned beautiful, with the sun shining brightly over a cloudless blue sky. After the snowfall last night, the skies had cleared to reveal a fresh layer of shimmering white covering the world, hiding the battle's aftermath that we had to finish clearing.

'Vahin, will you take me to the sea?' I asked, focusing on his black silhouette as it swooped down to the ground.

'Right now, Little Flame?' he asked. *'I thought you had to get ready for the Solstice Ball.'*

'Not now. But maybe later? Before we leave for home? I want to fly so close to the sea that I can touch the waves.'

'I think I can manage that after my wing has fully recovered. I wouldn't want to risk giving you an icy bath . . .' Amusement flashed in his thoughts. *'On second thought, that would be quite entertaining.'*

I rolled my eyes at the mental image he sent of us plunging into the freezing sea as I screamed, clinging to his neck.

Not funny, I thought back, observing him as he flew up before performing a challenging spiral ascent. *'Should you be trying that manoeuvre already? What if your wing gives out?'*

I hadn't realised how badly injured he was when I had woken up in the courtyard. I'd learned my dragon had given up his future to save my life, but the shock of returning from beyond the Veil meant I had missed seeing the full extent of his injuries.

His wing had been broken whilst fighting the Żmij, and after binding his life force to my mortal life, his ability to create a storm and heal using the primal power of nature was severely limited.

'I am well, Little Flame. This doesn't even tire me,' he said, and I watched in awe as he twisted in mid-air and swooped down towards the palace. *'I like it here. This land calls to me. When I soar between the land and the sea, with nothing but the horizon before me, it feels like home.'*

Our bond filled with a feeling of freedom and happiness, making me smile.

'Orm likes it here, too. He likes to . . . sort things out.'

I couldn't help but chuckle. My Ursus had a meticulous, methodical nature that made him perfect for managing the chaos that followed a battle. Barely had he sheathed his sword than he was already issuing orders—organising supplies, overseeing repairs, and ensuring the injured were cared for. That whirlwind of activity, though necessary, often had me volunteering to hunt down any surviving monsters. It was far more appealing than putting up tents or clearing the wreckage of war.

And there was certainly no shortage of monsters to kill. Cahyon and Rowena's demise had freed the creatures summoned from the Void.

We couldn't send them back, for no one truly understood what the Void was—only that it was a realm entirely separate from ours, and that the tear they had created in reality had let loose beings no one wished to meet. Some even theorised that the monsters in our world had once came here from the Void and evolved, influenced by the aether in our realm.

Still, we had to deal with the horde of intruders. Their freedom may have shortened the battle when they had taken the opportunity to run away, but now they'd spread over Katrass like a plague.

As soon as we were able, Alaric and I had organised hundreds of soldiers into hunting parties. They went out every single day, and apart from when Talena arrived to collect her brother's body, I made sure to join and do my part.

A shudder ran through me as my thoughts returned to the day Talena had stormed into the throne room where I kept vigil. I wasn't able to do it for Katja, but Valaram had loved me in his own peculiar way, and even though I didn't reciprocate his feelings, he had become my friend.

Talena, of course, saw things differently. I couldn't blame her. The slap she'd delivered had sent me flying across the room, but I didn't raise a hand in retaliation.

'At least you could've loved him,' she said with tears in her eyes.

I dropped to my knees. 'If I could have, I would. I'm sorry. I'm so, so sorry. I didn't want any of this to happen,' I said, humbling myself to the woman who hated me with every fibre of her being. I knew that in her eyes, I was guilty of his death, and maybe she was right.

Vahin's anger broke through my reminiscence.

'*You weren't,*' he said firmly. '*The fae mage chose his path. He knew you couldn't love him, but he followed you anyway. He chased a dream and stood by his choices to the very end.*'

I thought of Valaram, remembering the many times his subtle interventions had helped me out of trouble. '*He was a good man,*' I responded, a pang of regret twisting in my chest.

Vahin's tone softened. '*No, he wasn't. He was a cunning, ruthless fae lord, known for centuries to be the power behind Talena's throne. But for you, he was a good man. And for that, I will always hold him in my memories.*'

'You seem deep in thought, Domina,' Alaric said, kissing the top of my head. 'Let me guess, a certain dragon is entertaining you while he soars the skies?' He chuckled, kissing his way down to the shell of my ear, making me squirm. 'Are you ready? People are waiting.'

I hadn't heard him coming, but I wasn't surprised.

Free from the curse and burden of his family, Alaric was a new man. Today, he looked every bit the dark fae lord—dashing in a black kaftan embroidered with silver runes, his necromantic power subtly woven into the fabric. His hair, braided back from his temples, left his upswept ears exposed. As I turned to scold the mischievous fae, my eyes caught the many earrings decorating his ears and the silver beads nestled in his braids. He had the polished look of a noble, but beneath that, he was a predator—one who had spent the last month either decimating the rest of an undead army or bending them to his will.

The success of the cleanup was largely due to his power to control the remaining undead, using them for the heavy lifting that needed to be done.

They worked day and night to clear the palace and city from corpses and rubble, which were later incinerated by our dragons in massive pits away from the city walls.

The stench lingered for days, but as the work neared its end, Alaric had gathered the remaining undead outside and granted them their eternal rest.

'Is my presence really necessary?' I asked, sliding off my perch, careful not to hook my gossamer-thin spider-silk dress on any malicious protrusions.

Winning the war had uncovered the hidden face of Ozar, initiating a change we weren't ready for. As news of the battle's result and the demise of the Lich King spread over the Barren Lands, its remaining citizens flocked to Katrass in surprisingly large numbers.

Perhaps they sought refuge under the safety our army provided, or maybe it was the mountain of gold and treasures we'd discovered in the palace vaults. The undead had no use for wealth, and Cahyon had been ostracized even before he became the Lich King. Now, we had inherited the spoils of his pillaging—the riches of the former Ozar Kingdom at our disposal. Even the dress I wore came from those newly discovered vaults.

'Yes, you are needed,' Alaric replied, his voice low with admiration, 'and Annika, you are a vision in liquid fire.'

He slid his hand along my back, the touch sending a shiver down my spine. I had to admit, the old Moroi dress looked good on me, and the sensation of his fingers on my bare skin made my heart race.

'How about we stay here, and you can play with that fire?' I teased, noticing with pleasure the swirling crimson that crept into his eyes.

'If you genuinely don't want to go, I won't make you,' he murmured, his fingers tightening on my hips, his breath warm against my neck. 'But Orm is waiting with Reynard, along with a hall full of Ozar citizens.'

I shuddered as Ari's breath caressed the sensitive skin of my neck.

'I can't refuse you anything, but we should at least tell them not to wait for us.' Ari's voice sounded like a purr, but we both knew we wouldn't give in to temptation.

'Let's go. The sooner we deal with this, the sooner it's over,' I said. 'Though I'm not naming any kings this time,' I added. The throne of Ozar had been the subject of constant discussion, and I didn't care to indulge further. Alaric looked at me, and we both sighed in unison before bursting into laughter.

As we walked down the long hall, the throne room doors swung open. Inside, the space was majestic—galleries of carved columns lining either side, polished white stone floors leading to floral tiles with a golden rose at the centre. Fae lights and candelabras illuminated the room, reflecting off crystal flowers etched into the walls. Semiopaque curtains covered the windows, allowing the Moroi to join in the gathering without discomfort.

A wide array of people filled the room—humans, dark and light fae, uncorrupted Moroi, survivors from the Barren Lands, and even orcs and dwarves who had once lived or intended to settle here. The diversity of the crowd made the chamber feel like the beating heart of a reborn kingdom.

'All hail Annika, Harbinger of Light, the last conduit mage of Dagome, and her consort,' the herald's voice rang out. My steps faltered at the announcement, and I immediately felt the urge to choke the life out of the man as every eye in the room turned towards me.

'Are they fucking serious? *Harbinger of Light?*' I muttered under my breath to Alaric.

His lips twitched, struggling to suppress a laugh. 'You're talking to *her consort*. At least you were mentioned by name,' he teased.

We continued walking, and I nodded my head, occasionally greeting those who called my name as I passed. I knew Reynard was about to name the new king, but this all felt like too much, even for such an occasion, and the uncertain expression on Orm's face made me feel uneasy about the entire situation.

He stood in the centre of the royal dais, Reynard by his side, as well as representatives from the dark and light fae courts. A sense of grandeur hung in the air, and my frown deepened as Ari and I drew closer.

Reynard stepped forward as we neared, gesturing for us to take our places on either side of Ormond. Only then did I notice the large throne behind my rider and, on either side of it, two equally impressive seats. As soon as I was close enough, I tilted my head to my Ursus.

'Please tell me this is not what it looks like,' I hissed, anger simmering in my veins.

'I'm sorry, Ani, I'll explain later.'

'The hell you will,' I said, turning to look at Ari. 'Did you know?'

To my horror, he looked at me sheepishly and said, 'I may have heard a thing or two.'

'You are both in *so* much trouble,' I muttered, forcing a smile when Reynard began his speech.

He talked a lot about the trials the once-prosperous Kingdom of Ozar had endured under the Lich King's rule before speaking about the events of the last few months. I fought to stifle a yawn as he eventually moved on to speak of Orm's unyielding bravery and leadership, and of my power that had helped free the country from Cahyon's tyranny.

'This land has suffered enough, but after losing so much whilst fighting for its freedom, we can't allow it to fall into the hands of another madman. This kingdom needs a king who respects the people and will return Ozar to its former glory,' Reynard said.

'Therefore,' he continued, 'after consulting with our allies and representatives of the fae and humans that still live in this kingdom, I name this man as the first of his name, King Ormond Erenhart of Ozar. Those who wish to object may step forward now.'

He fucking did it, I thought, though the tiny voice in my head whispered that Orm was the only logical choice. Regardless, the question remained: was I ready to live here?

The answer came with surprising clarity. Alaric may be free to return to the Care'etavos Empire, but his family estate was lost, Zalesie was ash, and Varta Fortress would forever hold memories of Katja and all those we lost in the war.

Maybe Ozar is the perfect place to start anew, I thought. *Vahin does like the sea . . .*

My anger slowly subsided, but it didn't mean I was going to let them off the hook for blindsiding me like this.

'Annika, will you care to answer our new king?' Ari's amused voice broke through my stream of thoughts. I look down to see Orm on one knee, holding up a beautiful ring with a red gem the exact colour of my soul's aether.

'This land needs more than a king,' Orm said, his voice steady but filled with emotion. 'It needs hope. From the moment I saw you fighting at the lake in Grey Stone Valley, alone and determined, you became my ray of hope that brightened my darkest days. I can't do this without you.' He looked up at me, a shy, boyish smile tugging at his lips. 'My tenacious Nivale, will you be my Queen?'

The bear of a man had knelt in front of all those people, leaving Ozar's future in my hands. He would make an excellent king, that I was sure of, but I certainly wouldn't make a good queen.

'Oh, for fuck's sake, say yes. I want my new forge!' Bryna's voice broke the tension, and the gathered nobles started laughing.

'Yes!' I said, letting Ormond slide the ring onto my finger. 'You'll all end up regretting it. I'm not the best choice for the queen, but yes!'

Orm stood and turned to face the crowd, his voice carrying authority as he spoke.

'According to the old laws of Ozar, there can be only one king. But while I have chosen my queen, there is also a man who holds my heart, without whom this country wouldn't be free. Alaric'va Shen'ra will stand by our side. This will not be a monarchy, but a triumvirate. I will dedicate my life to restoring Ozar to its former glory, but Alaric will stand with us as our equal. That is my only condition, and it is one I won't forfeit.'

Reynard looked at us, clearly surprised by the turn of events. He studied the three of us for a long moment before he smirked, raising a fist to his heart in salute.

'You make your own rules, King Ormond. As long as they benefit your people, I doubt anyone will question them,' he said, backing away to leave the three of us on the dais.

Orm addressed the crowd again. 'The day my heart chose my queen, there was a big celebration in her town. Today, we will celebrate again. A winter solstice and a new beginning. Eat, drink and be merry. The time of grief is over.'

Ormond's words were met with cheers, and I chuckled quietly as I nudged Alaric. 'Our illustrious king forgot to mention that on the day he so-called chose me, I wanted nothing to do with him and got so drunk I could barely stand,' I whispered.

Ari only smiled softly, his gaze filled with devotion as he looked at Orm.

'I didn't expect that,' he murmured.

'What? To become a king, or the celebration?'

'Acknowledgement. I would be happy living in his shadow as long as we were together, but this . . .' Alaric said, a slight hitch in his voice. 'Even in my empire, the second male is but a silhouette, rarely seen and almost never heard.'

I reached for his hand. 'You are a warrior and a mage. I wouldn't let you hide in the shadows. Orm did the right thing, and if this is to be our home now, we can rebuild it as we see fit.'

I stepped closer to Ormond, and he wrapped his arm around my waist, pulling me into his conversation with an elderly Moroi nobleman and the young woman beside him with a vaguely familiar face.

'My lady. Err . . . I mean, Your Majesty. I was just—' the Moroi man stammered, his alabaster face flushed with panic.

'Call me Annika,' I said with a smile. 'I've lived long enough as a peasant mage to feel uncomfortable with titles.' I raised an eyebrow. 'So, what you were discussing?'

'Lady Annika, I was asking the king to grant mercy for the corrupted Moroi. There are ways to reverse the bloodlust, or at least control it for those too far gone,' the woman said, looking between Orm and me, the spark of hope dimming the longer we remained quiet. 'So many of us were lost. If there is any chance . . .'

'If there is a chance, then we'll take it. I will honour my promise to you, Lara,' Alaric finished for her as he turned his attention to us.

The woman beamed at him with such a beautiful smile that I felt a pinch of jealousy and reached for his hand, instinctively staking my claim. She bit her lip as I raised my chin, knowing nothing would hide the blush that crawled up my cheeks.

'Very well, we won't hunt your corrupted brethren, but I won't make exceptions for those who kill to feed,' Orm said, unknowingly saving me from further embarrassment. 'Until you deal with the problem, find them a willing donor and ensure they can restrain themselves.'

Lara nodded, pulling the older man into a bow. 'We will, Your Majesties. Thank you for your time.'

As soon as they left, Bryna took their place.

'What about the soldiers? Those from Varta want to stay here, or at least a large portion of them do. They've asked for land to settle, and this kingdom needs farmers and workmen . . . fuck it needs everything,' she said, placing hands on her hips as if daring Orm to argue with her.

'As long as Reynard grants them leave, they are welcome to stay and claim any land they feel they can manage—as long as it doesn't belong to any human or fae already living here. They'll also be obligated to return to service if the need arises—either they, or their children or grandchildren,' Orm said.

Bryna frowned. 'Only one per household,' she insisted, her tone sharp. 'You can't strip farms and shops of every pair of working hands.'

'Fine, you got them a deal,' Ormond agreed, then smirked. 'What would you like for yourself, Mistress Blacksmith?'

I held my breath as I listened to the exchange.

'An artisan quarter, with low taxes and freedom to trade with whomever we chose. I want to bring dwarven smiths and my kin here. You need a skilled workforce to rebuild this city,' Bryna replied, then paused. 'Plus, if Annika is staying here, I may as well,' she added.

I couldn't help but leap forward, wrapping my arms around her sturdy frame.

'Thank the gods! I didn't want to ask, to pressure you, but you promise you're staying, yes? Gods, I wish Katja were here. She would whip this place into shape without breaking a sweat,' I said, tears slipping down my cheeks as Bryna patted my back.

'Katja would be so proud of you,' she said softly. 'She always believed you were made for greater things than hunting monsters in a backwater village.' She squeezed my hand then, pulling me towards the exit. 'Come, O mighty Harbinger of Light. I've got *the* finest moonshine stashed in my tent.'

Before I could follow her, Orm's hand shot out, pulling me back.

'Oh no, you can have your artisan quarter and low taxes, but Annika stays here . . . at least for today,' he insisted, and despite my weak protests, I knew I had to stay until the celebration ended later that evening.

ᛉᛐᚾᚨᛯ

'My back is aching, and my legs . . . Why did we have to listen to everyone's petitions? What kind of celebration is it when you have to work all evening?' I grumbled, leaning against Orm for support. 'And these bloody heels. . .' I hissed, finally pulling off the torture devices.

Ormond laughed, embracing me as he pointed towards a small door at the back of the throne room.

'I think our subjects will relax more if we leave. It is time for this repentant king to kneel before his fiery goddess and grovel for forgiveness while massaging her aching toes,' he said, his mischievous grin making me forget about my exhaustion.

'A few hours of being king, and you're already trying to steal my job,' Alaric teased, approaching us. 'If my lady needs a healing touch, I'm clearly the obvious choice.'

'You know I have two legs, right? And you're supposed to share,' I said, smiling as I watched their baffled expressions.

I burst into laughter, realising with surprising clarity that if this was my new life, I bloody loved Ozar.

CHAPTER 40

ANNIKA

My bare feet hit the cold stone floor of the corridor. I was too tired to pretend to be some dainty lady, and all I wanted was to curl up in bed with my men. Before we'd left, Orm and Alaric had bickered over who would carry me, so I'd taken the decision out of their hands and set off alone. The chill of the stone was a welcome relief to the ache in my feet, and soon enough, the two men stopped their arguing to catch up with me.

We soon found ourselves in one of the many small interior courtyards, and I stopped, looking up to gaze at the night sky. *This*, I realised, *is home*. This beautiful palace, with its gardens full of stars, was a place I could finally call my own.

A smile tugged at my lips. The old Moroi king's palace was nothing like I'd imagined. Built atop a small hill, it wasn't a single building but a collection of them, each a masterpiece in its own right. Galleries and pathways connected the structures, and walled gardens hid hot springs that kept the air warm even in the dead of winter.

The changes in the palace were nothing short of miraculous, and I knew it was all thanks to Alaric. While Orm had focused on rebuilding the town and caring for the citizens, Alaric and his undead army had taken on the monumental task of clearing the palace ruins.

The work wasn't finished, but the living and administrative quarters were cleared, and aside from the epicentre of my fight with Cahyon,

469

most of the palace had remained untouched. Ari had even retrieved furniture, décor, and fabrics stored in the vaults. As much as Ormond insisted on using all the money to support the rebuilding of the country, Alaric had advocated for keeping the old masterpieces in the palace to preserve the heritage of the old kingdom.

I had taken a step back from those responsibilities, spending most of my free time with Vahin. The wounds of war had left scars that didn't want to heal, and even if the reasonable part of me was at peace with what I'd done, my heart couldn't accept it. I missed Katja, thinking of the moment her spirit had come back from behind the Veil to help me during my last stand. She was as much a part of me as one of my Anchors, and my dragon was the only one who truly understood.

'What are you doing?' I asked, breaking my thoughts when Orm pulled me to his side.

'That's a surprise,' he said with a grin. He brushed my braid aside and bent to place a kiss on my neck, his teeth playfully nipping at my skin. Before I could react, he swept me off the ground, and I squealed, instinctively wrapping my hands around his neck.

'Hmm, that's much better,' he murmured, pressing his nose to my collarbone. 'I should punish you for denying your Anchor the simplest of pleasures.'

'And what would that be?' I asked, my feet dangling in mid-air.

'Caring for my woman, touching her, making her sigh with pleasure after she's hissed in pain with each step.' His eyes sparkled with a familiar glint. 'What do you think, Alaric? Should we take this hardened warrior to her quarters instead of showing her the surprise we worked so hard on?'

'I'm not sure,' Alaric replied with a sly smile, his hand sliding along Orm's spine. 'If we did that, then we'd have to find something else to do for the rest of the night.'

I felt a shiver run through Orm, and my grip on his neck tightened in response.

'Alright, you win,' I said, throwing my head back and placing one hand on my forehead in a dramatic gesture. 'Oh, please, good warrior, take me, take me to . . . ehh . . . where exactly are we going?'

Orm roared with laughter, shaking his head as he began walking again. 'I told you, it's a surprise,' he said, exchanging glances with Alaric.

A few minutes later, we stood in front of a pair of double doors. They were made of dark oak, intricately carved with ornate floral decorations that glimmered with the faint glow of magic, the soft light brightening the corridor.

Orm pressed his lips to my ear as Alaric gripped the brass handles, saying, 'Welcome to our new refuge, Nivale. Our very private quarters, where only a trusted few can enter.'

Ari pulled the doors wide open, and I couldn't suppress my gasp. The room was beautiful.

An enormous window, glazed with mountain crystal, framed the sprawling city below. Its lights, many and bright, twinkled like stars, reflecting the sky above. Beyond the city, the sea stretched out, waves crashing against the shore. Even from here, the soft hum of wind and water seemed to pulse with the world's heartbeat.

Orm stepped across the threshold with a proud smile, almost as if carrying his new bride, but I immediately gestured for him to set me down. The floor, made of polished granite with veins of gold and quartz, was warm beneath my feet, and soft plush rugs cushioned the rest of the space. Along one wall stood a massive bed, large enough for three—if not more.

'Agnes moved your belongings over while we were at the Solstice Ball. Mine and Alaric's were already here,' Orm explained, shifting on his feet, his coy smile at odds with his burly frame. 'I hope you like it. But you can change anything you don't.'

I stood speechless, my gaze flickering over the room. Dragon-rider armour and weapons, along with a desk covered in reports, took up the entire south corner. Alaric's daggers hung neatly on a rack, and several shelves of books caught my eye, my fingers itching to explore them. My own belongings and weapons were neatly displayed in an open wardrobe that looked to be worth ten times the entirety of its contents.

The room was perfect, but it felt too grand for me, especially since some people were still camping in tents next to ruined houses.

'It's so beautiful,' I said, my voice barely above a whisper. 'Where did this all come from though?'

'The vault,' Ormond replied. 'We kept everything we couldn't sell, or what Ari insisted was part of Ozar's heritage. And before you ask, yes, I've seen to the people. Riders went out with sacks of gold to buy food and supplies, and the Dagome army is already rebuilding houses. But this,' his hand swept around the room, 'this is for us. The upcoming months will be difficult, and I wanted to create a space where we can leave the world behind and just rest. No titles, no duties, just peace. Just us.'

I opened my mouth to protest, but the sincerity in his eyes silenced me. 'You're impossible,' I muttered, before breaking into a grin. 'Utterly impossible. It's the best bedroom I've ever had.'

Orm laughed as I leapt forward, stealing a quick kiss before running to the bed and throwing myself onto it with a delighted squeal. As I buried my face in the plush pillows, I heard Alaric's low voice behind me.

'She seems pleased,' he said before turning to whisper something into Ormond's ear.

'Good,' Orm said, his tone carrying a hint of mischief.

I propped myself up on an elbow, narrowing my eyes at the two of them. 'What are you two whispering about?'

Orm turned to me with a playful smirk. 'Your feet don't seem to hurt anymore.'

'They don't,' I admitted, watching as Alaric stepped closer, his hands moving to the buttons of Orm's shirt. My breath hitched at the sight of his deliberate, graceful movements.

'What are you doing?' I asked, my voice faltering.

'Getting ready for bed, of course,' Alaric replied smoothly, his bright hair catching the light as he slid the shirt from Orm's shoulders. His eyes locked with mine, a teasing smile playing on his lips. 'Unless you'd rather I stop?'

I swallowed hard, heat rising to my cheeks. 'That's not what it looks like.'

'Oh?' Orm said, his tone heavy with amusement. 'And what does it look like?'

Before I could answer, Alaric turned his attention back to Orm, his hands trailing down the muscular planes of his chest. 'What do you think, Domina?' he asked, his voice low and intimate. 'Do you like what you see?'

'Yes,' I breathed, the word slipping out before I could stop it.

Orm's gaze darkened, a command lingering in his expression. 'Then tell him what to do.'

The air between us thickened as I sat up, my heart pounding. 'Kneel, Alaric,' I said, my voice trembling with both nerves and anticipation. 'And touch him.'

'Yes, Domina,' Ari murmured, sinking gracefully to the floor. His nails traced a deliberate path along the seam of Orm's trousers, pausing just before he reached the laces.

'I'm too overdressed,' I muttered, tugging at the collar of my gown, the growing heat inside me threatening to consume me. Orm's hand rose in a silent command, halting me. His other hand gently brushed through Alaric's white hair, his touch reverent yet possessive.

'Patience, my love,' Orm said with a knowing smirk, his gaze locked on mine. I knelt on the bed, my hands curling into fists as I watched them. The moment Alaric loosened the laces, Orm's shaft sprang free, and with a steady hand, Ari took hold of him. His first stroke was slow and exploratory, bringing the thick, hardening flesh to his lips.

'Taste it, Keresik,'[1] Orm growled, his fingers tangling in Alaric's hair, tilting his head at just the right angle.

The sight stole my breath.

Orm's back arched in pleasure as Ari took him deep, his skilled tongue and lips drawing a guttural sound from the commander. Orm's thumb brushed Ari's cheek in a fleeting, tender motion, even as his hips began to move in deliberate rhythm. A quiet moan escaped my lips, and my hands instinctively moved, seeking relief from the growing ache between my legs.

'Oh gods,' I whispered, my body thrumming with need as an undeniable wave of desire coursed through me.

'Patience, Annika,' Orm said again, his voice firm and commanding. His gaze didn't waver from mine, even as his thrusts grew more hypnotic. 'You will touch yourself when I allow it.'

'Shove your patience where the sun doesn't shine,' I stammered, fighting with the delicate fabric of my dress as the hunger in me burned hotter. 'I need you. Both of you. Please.'

---

1. **Keresik** — a term from the fae language. An endearment for the secondary male in a dark fae household. Direct meaning: beloved.

Somehow, amid war and grief and the aftermath of battle, we'd been abstinent. I hadn't been ready, the pain too raw, and they'd both respected that, sharing nothing but comforting cuddles. But seeing my men touching each other, my body awakened with a craving that set me on fire.

Orm's low laugh sent shivers through me. He grasped Alaric's chin, tilting it upward so Ari met my gaze. My cheeks burned, my body aflame under their shared intensity. I became wetter, a flood coating my thighs as I saw their devotion—unyielding and all-consuming.

'You feel it, don't you?' Orm murmured. 'You know you're ours as much as we're yours. Take what you need, Annika. Ask for it.'

'Gods, *yes*, I need you,' I begged, unashamed. There was no room for modesty, not with the love and trust that bound us.

Orm chuckled, his voice laced with desire. 'Perhaps our demonstration can wait,' he said, pulling Alaric to his feet as they stripped with practiced efficiency.

My breath hitched when Ari stood bare before me, his silvery skin glowing in the candlelight, but it was Orm's fierce, predatory gaze that rooted me in place.

The two of them advanced, their movements fluid, their hunger evident. My heartbeat fluttered wildly as Orm captured my foot, his lips pressing against my ankle before he began a slow, sensual ascent.

'What does my lady command?' he asked, his teeth grazing my calf as he tugged me closer.

'I want you both,' I breathed, arching into Alaric's touch as his nimble fingers began unfastening the intricate buttons of my gown. 'I need to touch you, to feel you.'

'Then show me,' Orm said, his voice a low rumble. 'Take what you need, Nivale, and I'll let Alaric pleasure you after he finishes undressing you.'

I wanted to taste him, to feel my lips where Alaric's had been, but words escaped me, my desire too raw to articulate. Instead, a moan slipped past my lips as I slid lower, peppering Orm's chest and abdomen with heated kisses. When I reached his cock, I took the head into my mouth, swirling my tongue around its ridge. His growl, low and primal, reverberated through me, sending a shiver down my spine.

I sucked him harder, drawing him deeper as I savoured the heat of him, moaning at how delicious he tasted as I gagged on his length.

'Fuck, you're perfect,' Orm groaned, his voice a husky caress. 'My Nivale, my queen . . . Fuck, *yes* . . . just like that. Such a good girl.'

His praise unravelled me, and when his hand tangled in my hair, the slight twitch of his fingers betrayed his struggle to hold back. I adored those growly moans of his, the subtle tilt of his hips signalling his need for more. My nails raked across his abdomen, and an influx of strange power coursed through me, threading with my magic to flow through the bonds with my men.

A sharp jolt of pleasure hit me as Alaric's tongue found its way between my folds, his touch expert and maddening. He teased me, the tip of his tongue circling my clit with torturous precision before sliding a finger inside, twisting it slowly, deliberately.

I was lost, a frenzy overtaking me as I bobbed my head, Orm's groans of desperation spurring me on. Every stroke of my tongue along the thick vein of his shaft pulled more need from him, his body trembling under my touch. Behind me, Alaric's ministrations grew bolder, his mouth and fingers driving me to the brink as he sucked in my clit and inserted a second digit.

I pushed my backside into Alaric's face, riding him as Orm ruthlessly fucked my mouth, and a wave of bliss overtook me. As my body started to spasm, Orm pulled me up by my braid, his cock slick from my attentions.

'My turn,' he growled, the words barely registering before he lifted me, seating me on his hips.

The head of his cock slid along my slickness as I rocked against him, desperate for relief, but his steel grip stilled my movements.

'Look at me, Annika,' Orm commanded when I whimpered in protest. As my eyes met his, a satisfied smile spread across his face. 'You are not in control now. I am. Surrender to your Anchor. Release your magic—I want you raw and needy, and I want to feel *all* of you.'

When he slid into me, the fullness was exquisite, and I tightened around him instinctively. The aether surged through me like a tidal wave, vast and consuming. A stormy, raging sea that carried me into sweet oblivion.

'Sweetheart, relax. Arch your back for Alaric. Our fae wants his fill, too,' Orm murmured, his voice softening as he leaned back, and I felt Alaric behind me. His cock pressed against my rear, his movements slow and steady, urging me to yield. The intimate pressure built, and I trembled.

A sob escaped my lips, and Alaric stilled immediately, his concern evident.

'Annika?' he asked, uncertainty filling his voice.

'Don't stop,' I whispered, pushing back against him. 'Please, it feels so good, don't stop.'

When they both moved within me, the strange magic returned, dancing with my pleasure. It called for me, and I groaned, no longer taking what was given but taking what I needed. My body and soul ignited with power, pleasure cresting into an intensity that felt infinite. This was mine—this love, this freedom. It was the life I had fought for, earned through blood and suffering.

The magic flared within me, spilling out in a radiant surge, a new strand of aether wrapping around me and reaching for my lovers. It was alive, sentient, and it responded to my call with a gentle, yearning touch. My conduit power flared to life, enhancing the sensation and turning our surroundings into a shimmering vista. I rocked, riding my Anchors' cocks harder and faster. The ley lines of Ozar awakened, glowing with a vibrant life as they entwined with my essence and those of my Anchors.

'Annika, what is—? Hrae . . .! So much power,' Ari moaned as he grasped my breast, pumping into me like a man possessed.

Orm grunted, his eyes filling with golden fire, and my pleasure crested as he roared, erupting inside me. His beast, the berserker, stared out from his golden eyes, but all I could see in his gaze was his love and promise to guard me until the end of time. '*Mine*,' he growled, his voice softening into a purr, the beast within him subdued by love.

Alaric's movements became frantic, his hands grasping at my body as he, too, surrendered and his cock swelled inside me. Together, we all fell into the storm, our bond solidified by strange force, and the promise of forever.

Then I felt it—a piece of something, the spirit of the shattered kingdom embedding itself in my soul. It was mine to love, mine to protect, a kingdom as broken as I once was. Now, it was mine to mend.

When the last waves of pleasure ebbed, I collapsed onto Orm's chest, sobs wracking my body as emotion overwhelmed me. They both withdrew and I saw the concern on Ormond's face when he brushed the strands of my hair stuck to my forehead.

'Annika, what happened? Are you hurt?'

I laughed through my tears, shaking my head. 'No, I'm fine, but I think I just Anchored the kingdom.'

Alaric fell onto his back, arms outstretched, as he laughed. 'Only you, Domina. Only you could casually Anchor a kingdom.'

'Do you think it's real?' I asked.

Ari nodded solemnly. 'I felt it. A power like no other, the aether of the land and sea. I don't know how you did it, but whatever happened, its power merged with our bond.'

A shiver coursed through me, and I clutched the blanket tighter, wrapping it around my suddenly chilled body. 'I didn't know that could happen, but . . . I felt its need.' My voice softened, my words more a confession. 'It called to me.'

'And you answered,' Orm said gently, his gaze steady and warm. 'You opened your heart to another. If this land—however impossible it sounds—chose you, it knows what's best for its future. We'll deal with it if any problems arise.'

His smile, soft and reassuring, eased the tightness in my chest. He tugged the edge of the blanket, pulling me closer. 'I, for one, am not worried about it. But for now, we're exhausted. Rest is the only thing we need tonight.'

His gentle scolding prompted Alaric to close the gap between us, his arms wrapping around me like a protective barrier. 'Yes, sleep, my heart,' he murmured. 'I'll seek answers in the morning.'

Sandwiched between their warmth, the steady rhythm of Orm's heartbeat in my ear, I had no choice but to succumb. Soon, my worries faded into nothingness.

ᛉᚲᚾᚠᛉ

'My lady, it's time to wake up. It's almost noon, my lady. . . Annika, don't make me splash water on you!' Agnes' voice broke through the haze as she removed the warm blanket that covered me.

'Don't you dare, or I'll hex you,' I grumbled, grasping the edge of the blanket and pulling it over my head. Then her words registered. 'Noon?'

'Yes, *noon*. You slept through breakfast, and Master Alaric told me to check on you when you didn't show up to the morning meeting,' she responded as she grasped the blanket and yanked it from my naked body with one smooth pull.

'Agnes!' I shrieked, clutching at the now-empty air.

'Perfect. The bath is ready,' she announced triumphantly, ignoring my protests as she ushered me to the adjacent room.

The steaming water enveloped me, but Agnes didn't stop there, scrubbing my skin until it was raw. Her sharp tongue accompanied every stroke. 'Tell Master Alaric to bite below the neckline next time. What will people think when they see those marks?'

I glanced down at the faint crescent impressions left by Alaric's fangs, memories of last night flooding back. Lust, magic, and love—everything blurred together. And then the realisation hit me.

I had Anchored the kingdom.

'Oh shit!' I said, bolting upright in the water.

'What? Did I say something wrong? What is it, my lady?' Agnes asked, startled by my outburst.

'No, but I need to see Vahin. I'll finish up here. Please get my riding leathers ready,' I said, desperate to see my dragon.

When Agnes left, I closed my eyes, submerging myself fully under the water. I focused on my core and the thin barrier that divided me from the vast, wild power that filled this world. I felt the three soul shards within me, guarding the essence of my being and tethering me to this world. But I could sense something else threading its way through us all, too.

We were all connected to the Chaos of Life.

It pulsed in rhythm with the sea, the soil, and every soul tied to the land. The awakened aether of Ozar resonated with me, its energy vast and patient.

Gasping for air, I surfaced, wrapping a towel around myself as Agnes returned to help me dress.

'*Can we fly somewhere?*' I asked Vahin.

'*Of course, wherever and whenever you want, Little Flame.*'

'*Now, please. I want it now,*' I said, desperation colouring my tone.

His surprise rippled through our bond, but he agreed. Moments later, his massive shadow passed over the palace. I ran to the gardens, where the riders had cleared a space for landing, shouting for Agnes to tell my men I would be with Vahin.

'*What's bothering you, Little Flame?*' he asked as we flew towards the port.

'*I think I did something stupid, and I don't know how, or even if, I should fix it,*' I answered, before recounting the events of the previous night.

He listened silently, his wings carrying us high above the sea as we left land behind. Flying lower, he let the tip of his wing brush the water, scattering salty droplets, the air saturated with the scent of the sea, seaweed, and something else—a primordial power that called to me.

When I finished, his low laugh vibrated through me. '*Why do you think you have to fix it?*' he asked.

'*Because it's the land?*' I replied, exasperated. '*You can't just Anchor land. I must have done something, and now I can feel something sentient observing me with quiet patience.*'

'*You awakened the spirit of Ozar just as you roused me from my slumber,*' Vahin said, his tone filled with pride. '*Little Flame, you are a miracle this world scarcely deserves. Of all who came to free this king-*'

dom, it chose you. The humans crowned Ormond their king, but Ozar made you its queen—its guardian, its heart.'

His words settled over me like a revelation, their weight both humbling and empowering. With a powerful twist of his massive body, Vahin surged upward, soaring high above the world.

Below, Katrass and the land surrounding it glimmered in the sunlight, blanketed in fresh snow. Ozar had awakened, ready to live again. The kingdom spoke to me with the voices of those who, for too long, were afraid of the darkness.

As I explored my connection to the Chaos of Life, I raised my hands. The sea responded, its waves growing higher as the aether flowed through me. I built it up, shaping the power with a singular focus before releasing it, whispering a word of power to the wind that rushed through the land.

I was the Queen of Ozar, the Heart of the Kingdom, and I had commanded it to *live*.

ᛟᚲᚾᚠᚼ

Dear Reader

Thank you for reading the Cursed Bonds duology.
If you would like to support me in my writing journey, please consider leaving short review or rating. I would be extremely grateful for this.
And if you want to stay with Annika a little longer I've got you, here is a novelette
Royal Wedding

A wholesome ending to Annika's and her men's adventures.

GLOSSARY

Augurec /pron:au-gur-etc/ — an alloy of silver, iron, and copper produced by artificer mages with the ability to disrupt the natural patterns of all aether; magical shackles.

Basilisk — a beast with a serpent-like body and fatal venom and death stare.

Bies(s.)/biesy (pl.) /pron:b-yes/ — a personification of all the undefined evil forces in nature. Once, they were placed amongst the most dangerous and oldest demons in Central and Eastern Europe. They were massive bison-like beasts with horns and hooves that were hostile and resistant to most types of weapons.

Borovio — one of the seven dukedoms of the Dagome kingdom, governed by the Erenhart family.

Domine — the official title of the primary (alpha) male in a dark fae household responsible for protection and external affairs. His authority is almost equal to a Domina's.

Domina(s.)/dominae(pl.) — a lady of her own domain; dark fae

Draugr /pron:drow-gar/ — a revenant awakened in his grave that retains some mental capabilities. Their primal reason for existence is to protect their treasures, but they can be tethered to the necromancer's will.

Falchion /pron:falkion/ — a broad, slightly curved sword with a cutting edge on the convex side

Geas (s.)/geasa (pl.) — a form of magical compulsion, curse, or obligation. Those under a geas are required to follow certain conditions or orders, risking death for disobedience.

Ghoul — minor Vel demon

Harpy/Harpies — a rapacious monster described as having a woman's head and body and a bird's wings and claws or depicted as a bird of prey with a woman's face

Jarylo — God of Fertility and Spring

Kirbai — a hybrid of a horse and a snow leopard. Created by Cahyon Abyasa before he was corrupted by foul magic. The animal is known for its intelligence, fierce nature, and loyalty. It can survive in the harshest environments and climb almost vertical walls.

Kirtle — a dress similar to men's tunics. They were loose and reached to below the knees or lower. Slits on the sides were pulled tight to fit the figure. Kirtles were typically worn over a chemise or smock and under formal outer garments or surcoats.

Keresik — a term from the fae language. An endearment for the secondary male in a dark fae household. Direct meaning: beloved. (actually, it is a Cornish word for beloved, which we really like)

Lanara poison — a potent poison explicitly invented for mages. It suppresses the ability to connect with the aether and, therefore, cast any spells.

Lara'mei /pron:Lara-may/ — My chosen. Endearment used by dark fae males for the women they consider suitable mates—a signal of intention used in courting rituals.

Latawiec(s.)/pron:Lata-vi-etc/latawce(pl.) /latav-ce/—shapeshifting demons. They flew in the currents of the wind. Their physical bodies were similar to large birds, with sharp claws and colourful feathers, but they had human heads. They could temporarily shift into human shape to tempt the victim with their song, and when they sang, those who heard it clawed their bodies, ripping the flesh as an offering for the ravenous demons.

Mamuna — a female swamp demon in Slavic mythology known for being malicious and dangerous.

Manticore — a beast with a lion's body, human head and scorpion tail that loves to eat its victim whole after paralysing them with its scorpion's venom.

Morgenstern — a handle attached to a chain with a metal spiked ball on the end. Otherwise known as a Morning Star flail.

Morana — goddess of death and winter.

Nyja /pron:Ni-ya/ — goddess of War and Death, guardian of the souls that died a violent death.

Olgoi worm /pron:ol-g{oi}/ — giant blind earthworm with rows of serrated teeth, famous for drilling tunnels in the dirt and rocks. They rarely hunt sentient beings, but during starvation periods, they can move to the surface and hunt for warm-blooded prey.

Peasant's crown — a traditional crown-like braid for women

Psoglav /pron:p-so-gwav/ — a demon with a human body with horse's legs, a dog's head with iron teeth, and a single eye on the forehead. They live in caves or in a dark land that has plenty of gemstones but no sun, and they love to eat people, especially fresh corpses.

Raróg /Pron: ra-roog/ — fire demons coming in the shape of horse-size falcons with beaks and claws made of burning embers and wings that start fires while they fly

Skein — a length of thread or yarn, loosely coiled and knotted.

Spectra (s.)/spectrae (pl.) — major Vel demon

Striga(s.)/strigae(pl.) — Minor Wel demon, A female demon born from violent death. They hunted those who wronged them, and once their vengeance was completed, they hunted for any human. They looked like skinny females with two rows of teeth, large claws, and leather, whip-like hair.

Utopiec(s.) /pron:uto-pi- etcs/— spirits of human souls that died by drowning, residing in the element of their own demise. They are responsible for dragging people into swamps and lakes as well as killing animals standing near still water.

Upiór (s.)/upiory (pl.) /pron:u-pi-oor/ — an undead being that arises from one cursed upon their death, appearing as a freshly deceased corpse. An upiór drives their strength from drinking and bathing in the blood of the living and can kill with their shrieks.

Vambrace — forearm guards are tubular or semi-tubular defences for the forearm worn as part of a suit of plate armour that was often connected to gauntlets.

Vjesci /pron:vi-yes-chi/ (s./pl.) — (originally from Polish folklore adjusted to the lore) An undead demon that retained the thoughts, personality, and body of the person. As their body slowly cooled down, the cheeks and lips would have a bright red colour, and blood could be found underneath the nails and on the face, while their limbs remained supple.

Vyraj /pron:vi-ray/ — an afterlife paradise for those who deserve it and warriors who have fallen in battle.

Wlok (s./pl.) /pron:w-wok/ — a major vel demon that looks like tumbleweed made of bones. It rolled over the roads and fields, killing any living creature that had bones inside, adding them to its "body" in its constant need to grow.

Żmij (z- as in English:vi_si_on **-me-j)** — a powerful demi-god associated with water and marshlands, a giant, three-headed viper with large wings. He can be called from the void between the worlds, and his favour can be obtained by offering him a sacrificial woman. Once the żmij makes a deal, he will protect the city to its death, only to be reborn in the void.

CLASSES OF MAGIC USERS:

HIGH MAGIC ORDER
Healer
A mage that uses the aether to alter the natural processes in the body. This is usually applied to healing but can also cause alterations and mutations in natural beings.
Enhancer
A mage able to take the power in objects and other mages and weave it into patterns that enhance the effectiveness of what spell is being used.
Illusion mage
A mage who manipulates light to create realistic images but can also sense the surface thoughts of a person to trick them into focusing on it and not their surroundings
Psychic/Psionic mage
A mage able to discern the aether within a person's soul and who can interact with it on a base level, influencing emotion and thought to various degrees depending on their ability to relate and empathise.
Artificer
A mage able to create artefacts that perform magical spells by altering the flow of aether through an object. It often requires various stages to construct, with many glyph diagrams infused, melded, or etched into the artefact.
PRIMAL MAGIC ORDER
Paladin
A mage of the warrior class well versed in classic fighting techniques who applies magic in conjunction with his fighting style.
Elemental

A mage who uses primarily elemental force in his spells or is able to direct elements. Mages can be specialised or versatile in their use of elements.

Animage

A mage able to both communicate with animals and shapeshift into animal form. Minor talents include often being able to communicate with animals marked by aether, such as dragons, gryphons, and manticores.

Seer

A mage able to foresee future events as well as recall the past from a person or object. This class is often used as advisors or investigators pending individual affiliation.

FOUL MAGIC ORDER

Necromancer

A mage tainted by foul magic who is able to manipulate the flesh of the dead, extract the spirit of a living being, and manipulate the life essence through nefarious means. As a subclass, the blood mages use blood rituals to bind the aether and transform both living and dead flesh into undead creatures.

Summoner

Often outcasts in the mage community, a mage able to use foul and wild magic to break through the Veil and draw Vel demons from their plane of existence, often cooperating with necromancers to corrupt the aether of the dead bodies and create Vel demons.

Cursegiver

Cursegiver mages are weak in aether manipulation but have a talent for disrupting the aether of objects and people, causing what seems like bad luck but is, in fact, their inherent magic running wild. Often known for creating objects that cause similar effects (fetishes).

Dreamwalker

In order to be a dreamwalker, a mage needs to have foul magic in their blood. However, dreamwalking itself—a controversial branch of magic—is looked upon as a subset of psychic magic, as the mage influences the unconscious person's emotions and thoughts while in a dream state. Powerful dreamwalkers can also possess a person's mind and put them in a living nightmare.

ABOUT AUTHOR

Olena Nikitin is the pen name of a writing power couple who share a love of fantasy; paranormal romance; rich, vivid worlds; and exciting storylines. In their books and out, they love down-to-earth humour, a visceral approach to life, striving to write realistic romances filled with the passion and steam people always dream of experiencing.

Meet the two halves of this Truro, UK-based dynamic duo!

Olga, a Polish woman, has a wicked sense of humour with a dash of Slavic pessimism. She's been writing since she was a small child, but life led her to work as an emergency physician. While this work means she always has stories to share, it often means she's too busy to actually write. She's proud to be a crazy cat lady, and together with Mark, they have five cats.

Mark, a typical English gentleman, radiates charm, sophistication, and undeniable sex appeal. At least, he's reasonably certain that's what convinced Olga to fly across the sea and into his arms. He's an incredibly intelligent man with a knack for fixing things, including Polish syntax in English writing. If you give him good whiskey, he might even regale you with his Gulf War story of how he got shot.

Olena Nikitin loves hearing from their fans and critics alike and welcomes communication via any platform!

For more information or to follow them on social media, check their website: www.olenanikitin.uk

For updates and to sign up for their newsletter, please scan the code

ALSO BY

**Epic Fantasy Romance
(completed series)**

In a land where the Old Gods still walk on earth, the antihero, the harbinger of Chaos, and the daughter of Autumn, Lady Inanuan of Thorn has to face her magic and choose between power and the life she has always wanted.

While for many, she is known as Striga for her explosive temper or Royal Witch for her role in the kingdom, she is just Ina, a woman of many colours who wishes to live her life free without too many expectations.

Unfortunately, because of her rare Chaos magic, she becomes the centre of a power struggle between those who desire to rule the world with her hands. And when her life gets tangled with Marcach of Liath, and Sa'Ren Gerel, her heart has to choose between them . . . even if her magic has already claimed them both.

Amber Legends

Do you know the place where your nightmares exist, the Nether? A realm shifted in time, a shelter for those hunted to almost extinction by iron and silver, a place where the gods rule and monsters thrive? The place where magic flows freely?

No? I thought so. It was separated from the mortal plane for a reason, but it is still there. This hidden world that lurks in the shadows, caught in the periphery of your vision when you speed your steps, afraid of the darkness.

What you saw in your dreams is real. What you see in your nightmares is even more because now the Gates are open, and danger no longer hides but barges into your life, demanding nothing less than your soul.

Walk the cobbled streets of Gdansk, where the living stone, amber, measures the magic of time and the guardians of the Nether ensure that unsuspected humans don't discover the existence of those for ages considered a myth . . . unless they are tonight's prey.

Amber Legends is a series of standalone books inspired by Slavic mythology and the legends of Pomerania. They are dark paranormal fantasies for audiences 18+ years of age.

Printed in Great Britain
by Amazon

62105032R00292